I, NEPHI…

by
k m mittan

CRK BOOKS
Salt Lake City, Utah

This book is dedicated to the man who inspired it:
Nephi Moulton, homesteader, rancher and prankster
extraordinaire.

ACKNOWLEDGMENTS

To Chris, Pam, Mary Ann, Mike, Sue and Steve for your patience in reading and critiquing this book.

To Micky, Leelee, Spence, Rich, and Everett for your unfailing support and encouragement.

To Russ and David for your conviction that my story merited printing.

To Christopher, for your invaluable technical support. Without you, this book would have never happened. And my eternal gratitude to you and Micky, both, for a beautiful cover.

Most of all, to the pioneers and old-timers of Jackson Hole, Wyoming, whose stories nagged at me until I had to write them down: Nephi, Alma, John, T.A., Wally, Mose, Jim McInelly— thank you for the memories. You are gone but not forgotten. May you rest in peace.

Polygamist Joseph Moulton's Families

Joseph (1845 - 1935) with Lizzie, his first wife

(1) Mary Elizabeth Giles (Lizzie)
(1852 – 1932)
Married Dec. 15, 1868

Lizzie's Children
Sarah	-	1869-1942
Joseph	-	1871-1968
Thomas	-	1872-1944
George	-	1874-1882
Charles	-	1876-1967
John	-	1878-1973
Alma	-	1880-1911
Nephi	-	1883-1966
(pronounced Knee-fie)		
Malinda	-	1885-1946

(2) Annie Katrina Jensen
(1857 – 1950)
md. Feb. 28, 1876

(3) Jensine Marie Jensen (Mary)
(1859 – 1932)
md. Feb. 28, 1876
(div. before 1900)

Annie's children

Elizabeth	1877-1883
Joseph	1880-1881
Lyman	1881-1959
Lillian	1884-1975
Violet	1888-1978
Heber	1889-1891

Mary's children

Josie	1877-1964
Joseph	1878-1879
William	1880-1956
Sarah Amelia	1882-1912
Chase	1884-1958
Franz	1887-1979
Lyle	1889-1978
Thomas	1892-1979

I, NEPHI...

CHAPTER ONE
1901
HEBER CITY, UTAH

I don't know where my father wandered off to that bright October morning but he sure wasn't where he belonged at the head of our dining room table. All that even brought him to mind was the ancient tintype hanging on the plaster wall behind his empty chair. The photo showed him, a teenaged militia scout during the Blackhawk Indian war, standing guard outside the Heber City fort, musket in his hands, his body at stiff attention, his face fearless. I had no idea as I glanced at the likeness on Mother's wall how the memory of that photograph would later change the direction of my life.

"Glad he isn't here," I muttered but I said it quiet enough my mother couldn't hear me. The way she sat at our breakfast table, ramrod rigid, told me he was probably over at her nemesis' house on second west—the home of his plural wife, Annie.

Mother didn't say anything about his absence, though. My brothers and sister were carefully avoiding the topic and I, for darned sure, wasn't going to poke my mother's sore spot. Nineteen years of being Nephi Moulton, the youngest son in Joseph and Lizzie Moulton's family, said there were enough things that could come along and ruin a perfectly good day, I didn't need to help them any.

I never guessed, as we sat around the breakfast table that my next-older brother, Alma, was fixing to turn the day upside down anyway. So I was busy entertaining myself.

My younger sister, Malinda, had braided a ribbon in her dark, hip-length hair, finishing it off with a bow at the end of her braid. And that end was laying on the seat of her wooden chair.

Now what self-respecting young American male would just leave it laying there? Not me. While my brother, John, droned out his typically endless blessing on the food, I slowly slid my right hand off my lap and over behind her braid. It wasn't hard to untie the bow. I didn't even have to open my eyes and look. I just had to make sure she didn't notice any tugging on her hair.

Of course re-tying the ribbon around the chair's hip rest was a tad more of a challenge but I'd done it to her so many times I was pretty good at one-handedly making hair ribbons secure around things they weren't designed to be secure around.

That left Mother to be reckoned with. I opened one eye just wide enough to peek. She was reverently deep in prayer so I was safe. I bowed my head, the picture of virtuous piety. By the time Mother said "Amen" and looked around the table, she probably saw a halo around my head.

I was innocently waiting for Lindy to lean forward and find herself tethered when Mother spoke.

"Boys," she said, "your father wants you to take the team and wagon to the aspen patch and get a load of wood for Annie. Your dinner is in a flour sack out in the kitchen," Mother's tone was even as she passed a plate of pancakes to Charlie.

I glanced at my mother. Her oval face, framed by graying, light brown hair secured neatly in a bun at the nape of her neck, appeared calm. The dark blue fabric of her high-necked dress brought out the vivid blue of her eyes. Everything about her seemed normal except that her left eye was twitching—a sure sign she was tense about something.

It wasn't the most thoughtful Order of the Day for Father to expect Mother to pass along, but then 'thoughtful' wasn't among the adjectives that normally came to mind when I thought of my father, either. I think everyone stiffened, involuntarily, when Mother had to forward his orders. I know I did. And it was clear, just by the words she used, who the order was meant for.

Only five of Mother's children still lived at home—spastic Charlie with his perpetually tousled hair and rumpled clothing; dapper John who always did everything right; Alma, who was my best friend; then me, Nephi—with our sister, Malinda, at tag end.

Except for Charlie, her sons were all tall, sturdy men accustomed to hard work, but when Mother said, 'Boys, your father wants...', she meant Alma and me. John owned his own farm and Charlie . . . well, he was just Charlie.

This time he grunted deep in his throat, grimacing as he struggled to get enough air through his vocal chords to make a sound. It finally came out in a barely-discernable, raspy whisper. "mmme, too?" His face looked hopeful and his right arm jerked, nearly knocking the syrup pitcher off the table. At the same time his left foot landed a sharp blow to my shin. I knew he really wanted to go with us because he jerked and twitched like that any time he felt intense about something.

"Charlie, I was counting on your help today." John said, as he caught the syrup pitcher before it spilled on Mother's bleached-white tablecloth. Making it look like something he'd planned to do all along, he poured a little puddle on his already sodden pancake before explaining, "I have a stretch of fence to fix between Father's farm and mine."

Charlie looked crestfallen, but he nodded. *Bless John for his tact. The last thing Alma and I need today, or any other day, is our spastic brother turned loose with an axe.* It was at that moment, when my attention was focused elsewhere, that Alma dropped the bomb that totally changed my life.

"Mother," he said as he slid a fried egg and several pieces of thick bacon off a platter and onto his plate before passing the platter to me, "I'll get this winter's firewood for Annie but it's the last time. It's her own son's job. Lyman should be taking care of his mother and I'm tired of doing his work for him. Come spring I'm going out homesteading."

I dropped my fork, Malinda gasped, and John and Charlie reared up, paying attention. Only Mother seemed unaffected, acting as if her sons announced their independence every day of the year. I saw something flicker across her face but it was too quickly gone to figure out. Then, after a couple of eye twitches, her normal composure returned.

"Where do you plan to go?" Her soft alto voice was calm.

"Probably up north somewhere." Alma cut a piece of his bacon with the side of his fork, rocking the tines up and down, making enough of a business of it that he didn't have to look anyone in the eye. His wavy deep brown hair, cleanly parted down the center of his head but, as usual, flipping up in wayward wings at his temples; his clean-shaven, pleasant face with its startlingly blue eyes, straight nose and wide, rounded chin; and his dark grey pants and shirt were all spotlessly clean. Except for his rough work clothes and heavily callused hands, he could have passed as a banker or a shopkeeper instead of a farmer.

"I want to be far enough away that no one can expect me to come running when Lyman's too lazy to get his work done," he continued. 'No one' meant Father, of course, only he wasn't saying so.

I held my breath, waiting for Mother to speak but she just gave him a long, thoughtful, wordless stare.

What was she thinking? What would she say?

From the corner of my eye, I could see Malinda's slender hands reach under the table to play with the end of her braid, anxiety stamped on her normally-pretty face. What a time for me to have played my favorite trick on her! But I don't think she even thought about it as she untied the ribbon and started twirling the end of her hair. She was too upset. Across the table Charlie gaped and even John, for once in his life, was speechless.

The longer the silence lasted, the more stifling it became until I could feel it, like a vise, squeezing my chest so tight I could scarcely breathe.

She can't just let him go.... Can she?

4

It wasn't the extra work that bothered me. I could do Alma's chores as well as my own and barely break a sweat. *If he leaves, who will talk for me?* All my life if I wanted to know something he didn't have the answer to, Alma'd waltz up to the closest adult and start asking questions. His tongue wasn't an ice block around outsiders.

And that wasn't my only problem. I was old enough that pretty soon my parents would start dropping hints. "Those Morgan girls sure are growing up to be a good-looking bunch," my father might say or, "When I was visiting Sally Jones today, her Becky served a cherry pie she'd just taken from the oven. My land but that girl can bake!" from Mother.

I'd watched them maneuver my older siblings toward marriage and snickered when my sister Sarah tied the knot. I was still a kid, then, and the way she suckered to their manipulations was funny. But by the time Joe and Tom fell into the chains of matrimony, I was older, wiser, and the process was starting to make me nervous. Now John had a cabin half built on his farm with Suzie McDonald's heart chained to it and Alma was making an idiot out of himself, trying to convince Maude Johnson he was the brightest star in her night sky. John wasn't married yet and Maude hadn't committed to anything so I'd felt marginally safe.

Marginally.

…But if Alma left town….

The minute he was gone my parents would be all over me like tom cats on a fence rail at midnight. Next thing I knew, Mother'd have me all gussied up like little Lord Fauntleroy. Then she'd drag me along while she paid social calls on the mothers of every eligible girl in the entire county. A trickle of cold sweat formed at the base of my neck and rolled slowly, relentlessly, down my back. *What can I do? How can I get out of this?*

"Nephi," Mother said, abruptly shifting her gaze to me, "If you stay here, you'll be doing the chores for everybody, all by yourself. Lyman's an adult. It's time he took responsibility for his mother and little sisters. You need to go with Alma."

I was so stunned all I could do was gape. John, Charlie and Malinda looked just as shocked. Me go with Alma? Was she serious?

"I hoped you'd let him come," Alma leaned back in his chair, smiling his satisfaction.

"Actually," Mother said, "it's not his choice. I'm sending him—and I'll expect you two to get along. Not that I'd worry about that, anyway, but just so you know—."

"Mother, you can't mean it!" Malinda cried, twirling the end of her braid in even tighter circles. "How could we manage without Nephi? It's impossible!"

"Yes, I *do* mean it, Lindy," Mother's tone plainly said, 'No arguments allowed'. "It's high time your father took care of us. And Charlie will help him. Besides, Nephi's nineteen now and he's old enough he should be out on his own. He's been Annie's little slave long enough."

So there it was.

Because Mother didn't like me helping Annie, she was handing me a future beyond my wildest dreams—homesteading with Alma somewhere off by ourselves! If I hadn't known my mother as well as I did, I wouldn't have believed it. But I did know Mother and once she made up her mind about something, she wasn't much for changing it. Alma and I were as good as gone, already.

I was grinning like a fool and I wanted to jump, yell, dance a jig.

"Alma, we'd better get out to the aspen patch," I said, pushing my chair back from the table. "The day isn't getting any younger."

But Mother was too quick.

"Not so fast, young man," she ordered. "You just sit right back down there and finish your breakfast. A venture like this takes a lot of serious consideration and planning. You're not going off half-cocked, now *or* next spring, and you're not moving out of my home until I know you have all your ducks lined up."

I groaned. Having your 'ducks lined up' was one of Mother's favorite sayings when she meant something had to be thoroughly Planned-And-Pre-Pared-For. Besides that, when she called me 'young man' I knew better than to cross her. Quiet and mild as she normally was, my mother could be a wildcat when she thought it was warranted. I wasn't anxious to create a warrant.

...But planning and lining ducks up? That meant handwriting. Lists . . . detailed lists. . . .And plans. She'd see to it that we didn't step a foot out of her door next spring until we were Pre-Pared.

"You aren't stepping a foot out of my door next spring unless you're prepared," she added, looking straight at me.

I knew it—and I knew she meant every word of it, too. Before we left, she'd tear every plan we made apart just to make sure we'd dotted every i and crossed every t. I sighed as I sat back down.

I hated planning—what's the purpose, anyway? If there's a job to do, just go do it!—And anything involving handwriting was even worse. John, whose penmanship always flowed perfectly in even, straight lines across his paper, delighted in looking at my attempts and saying, "Hmmm. Looks like a chicken stuck its foot in the ink bottle and wandered around this page." Other than marriage, there weren't too many fates worse than death but this planning/preparation business had to come close. I groaned, again.

But I couldn't stay dejected for very long because I knew our future was set. The grin relit my face. Even Father didn't oppose Mother once she made up her mind about something. He couldn't because she, as first wife, held the purse strings and had all the family property in her name.

All we have to do is keep her happy between now and the time we leave—and Alma will do the writing anyway.

Youth can be so blissfully optimistic.

CHAPTER TWO

All that autumn Alma and I poured over Mother's Sears and Sawbucks catalog until it nearly fell apart. Every time we thought we had everything all worked out—what equipment we had to buy and what supplies we needed to take—Mother got a pencil and start adding up and crossing off.

"Did you boys even think about the kitchen utensils you'll need?" she might say. "Go look through my cupboards. Better, still, take turns helping me fix meals—starting with you, Alma. Tomorrow morning. Five-thirty a.m. Nephi can milk the cows and feed the stock alone."

"Aw, Mother, I hate to cook. Teach Nephi. He likes poking around in the kitchen."

"You can't always rely on someone else, Alma. You need to be able to take care of yourself. Starting tomorrow."

Or, "Did you boys even think about fencing? I don't see any wire, staples or fencing equipment on this list. Nephi, you sit down and figure out what you'll need to fence 160 acres."

She *would* make me write. And it didn't matter how hard I tried, I never got it right, either.

"Nephi, did you think about the animals you'll be fencing in? Can you hold a sheep with barbed wire? No. You know that. You two need to decide how many sheep you're taking and how much pasture you'll need for them, then refigure this."

More writing!

She could just as easily have done it all for us—saved us a whole passel of work and mental agony trying to figure out what she'd expect—but I guess she wanted her two youngest sons to be able to Stand On Their Own, Amount To Something, and Be Successful. Or something of that ilk.

And then the sheep issue led to the question of exactly where we were going. Alma wanted to homestead and I was eager to start yesterday but we didn't know how to tell Mother "up north" meant deep into Idaho, not closer to home in Utah. How much sheep pasture we'd need depended on where we went—whether we found a place with native grasses or scrub and sage.

Two of our uncles lived in Teton Basin, near the Wyoming border. I voted to settle near them but Alma leaned in another direction. Maude had an aunt whose husband had dragged his family to some remote spot called Rexburg, some fifty miles west of the Basin. And of course Alma wanted Maude to have family nearby when he married her. I didn't see it at the time, though. I guess I was pretty dense because, for the life of me, I couldn't understand what beckoned him in the Rexburg direction. We bantered back and forth about it all fall.

"I think we'll find what we want near Rexburg...." Alma might start out and I'd be up and running.

"If Rexburg is so wonderful, why didn't the uncles settle there?" Then we'd argue about that long enough for me to steer the discussion down another avenue.

Or he might try to sneak it in with some casual comment about, "When we get to Rexburg . . ." and I'd come right back with a laughing, "Got a rock in your pocket?" or an innocent, "It sure will be good to live near our cousins again."

I think Alma was so worried over how to tell Mother about Idaho in the first place that it never connected just how serious I was. On the other hand, I didn't understand why he thought telling Mother was such a problem, either.

"Why are you fretting so much?" I asked him one night after we'd crawled into bed.

"You really don't know?"

"If I knew, I wouldn't be asking, now would I?" I said as I blew out the candle on our bedside table and settled down under Mother's quilts.

He patiently spelled it out for me. "The major to-do will be about us settling so far away. I don't want her to decide you can't come after all. I'd rather homestead with you than anyone else I know, Nephi."

I think I must have glowed enough to light up our little attic bedroom. Still, Alma's concern made me a tad edgy, too. "Do you really think she'd make me stay here? What d'you think she'll say?"

"Oh, you know. The usual. Why are we going so far away when we could find something around the Ogden area or maybe up in Cache Valley?"

"Cache Valley! That's nothing but a breeding ground for mosquito bugs! And Ogden smells like dead brine shrimp whenever the wind blows. Yech!"

"Yes, but you can get good crops at either place and they're a lot closer to home than Rexburg is. She may be willing to get us out from underfoot but she isn't going to want us forever out of her hair. You know how Mother is with her grandchildren. She's crazy about them. She'll want us close enough she can get to know our little ones once we marry."

"Speak for yourself. I'm not tying any knots!"

"I am speaking for myself. By the way, how shall we handle things after Maude and I get hitched? Will you want your own cabin?"

"Just how soon is this hitching supposed to come off?" I asked, every muscle in my body taut as a newly-stretched fence wire. "I thought our homesteading was just the two of us." I didn't like the sound of that 'hitch' word one bit.

"Oh, not for a few years, at least, so you can relax." Alma chuckled. "Our place will have to produce well before I bring her up."

Good thing we were homesteading instead of buying a farm. If Alma was determined to marry, I supposed Maude was as good a choice as any and a darned sight easier on the eyes than most. But the idea of sharing my brother with a meddlesome, talkative female was unsettling. And outside of my own immediate relatives, 'meddlesome' and 'talkative' fit every woman I knew.

Personally, I preferred silence. Which was probably why I got along so well with Alma in the first place. With him around I could hear meadowlarks of a morning because once we'd discussed what needed to be done, we shut up and got busy. And stayed that way. Stick a yapping female in the middle of our twosome and I could see the leaves on the shade trees of heaven wither and fall. It could end up hotter'n hades on our little spread. I wanted to tell him so but I knew he wasn't in the mood to listen.

"You can have your own cabin to honeymoon in," I said, shortly. "I don't want the patter of little feet waking me when I want to sleep in, mornings."

I could hear a grin in Alma's voice. "Well, that's settled," he said with obvious satisfaction, "although I happen to know you never sleep in and little feet aren't likely to wake you, either. You sleep like the dead. There wouldn't be any little feet for a while, anyway. But that's ok with me. Newlyweds need their privacy."

10

So would I. Away from females. Thoughts of how to keep our homestead productive enough for two but not for three, teased the edges of my thoughts until settling the issue of exactly where we were going to homestead took precedence.

I still wanted to be near our uncles in Teton Basin. I preferred Uncle Charles over Uncle George because Uncle Charles had sons about my age but it really didn't matter to me where we settled as long as we were close to them.

CHAPTER THREE

"Mother's hounding me for our plans," Alma told me one evening while we milked Father's cows. "Look, Nephi. I know you don't like social affairs but we really don't know that much about the Rexburg area and...."

"We know where our uncles are. That's good enough for me."

"If you're going to make an intelligent decision you need to look at all the facts."

"Want me to take a trip? Don't have the money. Besides, it's winter. You can't see anything when it's under six feet of snow. What's the decision, anyhow? We know enough about the Basin. Seems pretty straightforward to me."

"Yes, the uncles have talked about the Basin every time they've been down to visit but we haven't talked to anyone who knows the Rexburg area. Do me a favor, Nephi. At least take the time to listen to someone who's lived there."

"Don't know anybody that fits that description."

"Maude's uncle will be here Christmas eve. Her mother's invited us over for dinner and some entertainment afterwards. We can talk to him then."

What choice did I have? I didn't plan to change my mind but I agreed to go, hoping it would get Alma off my back. With luck Maude's uncle would tell us enough that Alma'd decide against Rexburg. Then we could get busy with our plans for the Basin. I was counting on it.

In fact, I was so confident about the outcome of our meeting that it was nearly Christmas before I realized what I'd gotten myself into.

Meeting the uncle meant being in a social setting—meeting people I didn't know; eating in front of people I didn't know; *sitting beside people I didn't know*. How in the world did I manage to get dragged into such a predicament? The number two fate worse than death was staring me in the face, looming closer every day—waiting to pounce on me and devour me in its gaping maw. I nearly broke out in hives every time I thought about it.

The night we met Maude's uncle was a clear, cold, moon-flooded December evening. Alma and Mother made sure I was presentable, my hair combed to perfection - "What're you doing that for? I'm wearing a cap, aren't I?" - and my shirt pristinely pressed - "You're wasting your time, Mother. I'm putting on a coat so it'll be wrinkled before I'm even out our door." - and my tie tied correctly - "Get that thing off, Alma, it's choking me. I am *not* wearing it!" By the time we started across town, I was so nervous I was almost ill.

"The minute supper's over I'm out of there." I said as we walked up Maude's street.

"You can't leave. Remember the entertainment?"

"I absolutely will not stay for it."

"You may have to, so be prepared," was all Alma would say. Great!

What if I spilled soup down the front of my shirt or made embarrassing noises? What would I do? Supper was agony enough without adding Entertainment to it. I hoped, in desperation, that we'd be through talking before the production started so I could make my escape. Maybe I could suffer through the stares of Maude's younger siblings at the table but to endure some screeching female's version of *'Silent Night'* afterwards would curdle everything I'd eaten. It was positively beyond the call of duty. I held my fingers crossed all the way to Maude's door.

I may as well have not bothered. Uncle Jake was a talker. In fact he never even paused for breath as near as I could tell. He was talking when Maude showed us into her mother's dining room ("And when the First Presidency come out and asked...."), he talked while he shoveled elk roast, gravy-smeared mashed potatoes, pickled beets and mincemeat pie into his mouth (". . . and them Elders up in Rexburg done got together and...."), he talked in between the very infrequent chews he gave his food (". . . if it hadn't been fer the quilts them gals pieced together....") and if his windpipe hadn't been closed off when he swallowed his un-chewed food, he probably would have talked as the stuff went down. Nobody got a word in edgewise and after a couple of half-hearted attempts, nobody even tried.

By the end of the meal when Maude's mother shepherded us into her parlor, I was near despair. I hadn't noticed the fellow had said one single thing all night that would be of any use to Alma or me. Oh, he could spin a yarn all right, but yarns are yarns. We needed some hard facts about the Rexburg area—something that would cool Alma's desire to settle there. ...And I didn't see how we were going to get any from him when we couldn't get him to pause long enough for a body to even ask a question.

It wasn't until after the Entertainment was over (Maude pounded out various Christmas pieces on their harpsichord—my head throbbed in time to the 'music' while Alma looked like she'd just won a prize—and her mother shrilled through 'O Holy Night'—I thought my spine would fracture into a thousand pieces when she flatted those high notes) before Maude's father finally got Uncle Jake to slow down enough for my brother to speak.

Alma told him we were thinking of homesteading up his way—I wondered just who was doing the thinking because I hadn't changed *my* mind any—and what was his opin.... And that was all it took.

He started in on everything he knew about Rexburg, Salem, Teton, Parker, St. Anthony, Ashton, and every dot on the map in between and ended up trying to sell us a little farm on the Egin Bench near Salem. He must have had a hundred reasons why we needed to buy that particular farm instead of homesteading, and wouldn't you know my brother suckered for every one of them?

There I was, looking around the parlor with all its garlands, Christmas bows, and candles tucked wherever there was a space between the Johnson's gewgaws, doilies, and overstuffed furniture, pretending to ignore Uncle Jake's youngest three brats who were trying to outdo each other in sticking their tongues out at me, and not really paying that much attention to Uncle Jake when suddenly I heard Alma exclaim, "That's exactly what Nephi and I are looking for!"

Since we hadn't come to an agreement of what we wanted I started paying attention. Fast!

"Sure would help the owner out," Uncle Jake was saying. "The wife died in childbirth and he done took the baby back east to his family. Pulled out in late summer or thereabouts so nothing's been done to the place this fall. Find yourself with a choice piece of property on your hands, though, that place. Rich, fertile soil, that Egin Bench. Crops just jump out of the earth to reach the sky and there's a snug little cabin and a barn and corrals and the place is already fenced and ditched, and the water rights're good—canal runs right by the front door."

14

I had to admit it sounded good but I'd listened to Uncle Jake at the table and while farmers want to believe the most productive land still exists, just waiting to be snapped up, I figured this was nothing more than another one of his tales.

Besides, I was holding out for the Basin. And homesteading. How many times had we counted our hoard, anyway? There was barely enough to buy the tools and animals we needed and here Alma was talking about buying a farm?

I wanted to say what I thought. But not in Maude's parlor. Not in front of all her family. Time to get Alma off by himself and talk some hard sense into that soft head of his.

Amazing how daft Alma's become.

...Wait a minute!

I'm the one who's daft. Snug cabin, barn and fences, indeed! That means less time before he'll get himself hitched to that fresh-faced young woman sitting beside him on her mother's settee. If I'm not careful, the next thing I know we'll be living on the Egin bench; me in a "snug cabin" and him in a house filled to overflowing with unnecessary junk cram-jammed into every nook and cranny along with a whole passel of dirty-faced, crying urchins with extra-long tongues—and the icing on the cake will be Uncle Jake and those little brats of his coming out to Sunday dinner.

If Alma wants to homestead with me, why is he so set on bringing a woman into the mix? Women are just a pack of trouble and inconvenience.

I stewed about it until I finally got my brother pried off the settee and prodded out of Maude's door some two hours later.

CHAPTER FOUR

"Wasn't Maude's home decorated nice? I really liked how her mother had the mantle covered with cedar and bows and candles." Alma gushed like a grammar school girl as soon as we were decently out of earshot. "Did you like the candies Maude served? I thought her divinity was especially good. And that fudge—."

"Didn't notice!"

"Hey, what's wrong with you?" He playfully poked me in the ribs. "Here we've had a wonderful evening, learned a lot about the area where we want to go, and you're grousing?"

"Area where you want to go, you mean. I never said I wanted to go to Rexburg."

"Wait a minute." Alma stopped in mid-stride and turned to face me in the cold, white moonlight. "You never really came out and said you didn't, either. What's gotten into you, Nephi?"

That's when I knew he hadn't heard a word I'd said all fall.

"Where did you get the idea we could afford to buy a farm?" I said with fury. "You helped count our money. You helped price our supplies. You know good and well we don't have enough for a farm and supplies, too. We don't have any choice but to homestead."

"You ever heard the word 'borrow'? Maude's uncle said we can count on at least two good hay crops a year—maybe three—and the farm's going for real cheap. We can pay it off in no time and we won't have all the work we'd have to do if we homesteaded. It'll be more than worth it."

"Borrow money!" I stiffened, horrified, my hands clenching involuntarily. "You're crazy!"

"No, practical." Alma stood firm. "Just think of the work it will save. The cabin's built. The barn's built. The ditches are dug and the fences are up." He ticked them off on his gloved fingers. "Those are all absolutely necessary things that we won't have to do ourselves. It will be worth it, Nephi. You'll see."

"No, I won't. I'm not going into debt just so you can bring your sweetie pie up sooner."

"So that's what's eating you. What difference does it make when I marry Maude? What do you have against her, anyhow?"

"She's a woman and women are trouble."

16

"That's an excuse. I happen to know you don't feel that way about Mother or our sisters, so what's your real complaint?"

"Why are you so set on changing what we planned?" Suddenly I just had to do something. I pried my fists open wide enough to scoop up a handful of snow and crush it together into a ball, packing and repacking it as I spoke. "We had everything almost worked out but then you listen to someone who sells you a bill of goods any fool could tell is too good to be true and you don't even think before you let him talk you into dropping everything we planned to do."

I looked for a target. Across the street was someone's tree, standing naked and skeletal in the thin winter moonlight. The next moment my snowball splatted against it's dark trunk—a white blemish on inky blackness. I scooped up another handful of snow.

"You wanted me to homestead with you. You said you'd prefer me over anyone else. Now you want to go into debt and buy an already-proved farm just so you can bring a woman along?" I threw the new ball viciously. "It's a ridiculous, spendthrift idea!"

Splat!

"Trouble with you is your nose is out of joint." For once Alma wasn't being the sympathetic brother I'd always known. In fact, his jaw was clenched and his normally pleasant blue eyes were steely. "There's nothing wrong with wanting a wife and family and just because I'm thinking about the future doesn't mean there's no place for you in my plans. It's time you grew up a little."

"Grew up!" My hands shot into the air. "Well, that beats everything. We plan. We price. We compare. We spend weeks working everything out and then you have to ruin it all, wanting to go into debt just so you can drag some skirt along."

"She's not 'some skirt', Nephi. Her name is Maude and I'd thank you to be a little more respectful when you speak of her!" The thrust of his words was so unaccustomed it was almost a physical force. Involuntarily, I took a step backward. I didn't remember ever hearing my placid brother speak like that. I was so shocked that if I hadn't been so worked up, myself, I would have shut my trap right then and there. But I was too angry to stop.

"Pardon me." I could almost taste the vinegar dripping from my tongue. "You've gone plumb off your rocker and changed everything we've planned just so you can carry your love-life, Miss

Maude Johnson," I made an elaborate bow, one arm across my stomach, the other flung out behind me, "over the threshold. Is that better?"

Alma ignored my sarcasm. "And what if I do want to bring her sooner? Why are you so against it?"

"You mean to tell me you can look at all the problems our family has had because our father wanted wives - notice the S there, that stands for plural, in more ways than one - and families - observe another S - that he never could afford *or* satisfy, and you can't see the sense of staying single? Are you blind?"

"Plural is not my game, Nephi." Although I knew he, too, was angry, his tone was even. I never could figure out how he managed to keep so calm in times of stress.

"You should know that," he continued. "And even if it was my inclination, it's illegal now. Besides, Father and Mother were happy before Father brought Aunt Annie and Aunt Mary home...."

"Without Mother's permission, you'll recall."

"I know what he did but I'd never do that to my wife. I agree with everyone else in the family that it was a pretty underhanded thing to do to Mother, to say nothing of being against Church rules. That's beside the point, though.

"And your point is?"

"One man and one woman can make a good, happy home if they want to try."

"I hadn't noticed."

"Then start noticing. Tom and Joe and Sarah are all perfectly content with their little families. Uncle Heber has always been what I'd consider the happiest of married men. John's looking forward to marrying his Susan. There is such a thing as wedded bliss and I want my share of it. One day you'll be mature enough to understand and when you are, you'll want the same thing, so give it up, Nephi."

I could ignore the gibe about my maturity but 'give it up'?

"I'm not going to give it up, I'm not going to get married– ever—and I'm *not* going into debt just so you can!" With that I stomped off, leaving Alma standing alone in the frigid winter moonlight.

CHAPTER FIVE

"When are we going to talk this out?" Alma asked one night a couple of weeks later as he shivered his way between the cold flannel sheets of the double bed we shared.

"Nothing to discuss," I said, jerking my share of Mother's hand-stitched quilts up to my chin. "You're not homesteading and I'm not buying a farm."

"Well, I'd think we could compromise if we tried."

"I'm not compromising," I said as I turned to the wall. Alma sighed.

Being on the outs with him cut me to the quick but I wasn't changing my mind, ever, so I said nothing. Eventually his breathing deepened as he drifted off to sleep. I laid awake, fretting.

We had everything worked out. Now nothing's right and it's all because of Mistress Maude. She's created an un-crossable gulf between us.

Trust a woman! God sure messed up when he made their ilk . . . except for Mother and Sarah and Lindy, of course. And I guess my sisters-in-law aren't so bad. Tom and Joe seem happy enough. But Maude? She's even worse than Annie and Mary.

It didn't bother me to resent Mary, Father's third wife. After all, she'd divorced him. But thinking ill of his second wife, Annie, sent a twinge of guilt through me. Annie was a good woman—a lover of all children—and I was actually quite fond of her. If she'd been a true widow instead of separated from Father because of the law, I wouldn't have minded all the chores I did for her even though they were lazy Lyman's responsibility. Mother wouldn't have minded either. Of that I was certain.

I thought about when Father married the two Danish sisters. He and Mother were still living in their cramped, one-roomed cabin with four small children clinging to Mother's skirts and Charlie on the way. I could imagine my Mother, desperate for a larger home, urging Father to collect the money the Danish sisters' step-father owed him. So off went Father.

I pictured Mother's anticipation when my father left. She wasn't demonstrative but I knew she loved my father. At least she did then. She probably waited at the cabin window, watching for his return, while the tantalizing smells of his favorite stew, cooking on the hearth, filled the cabin.

But he didn't come.

Not that day. Not the next. And when he did show up, he brought a surprise that wasn't money.

How like my father! Send him off to collect a debt so he can build something better for his wife and children to live in and does he come back with money? Not Joseph Moulton! Instead, he brings home two teenaged brides. Two more mouths to feed and no place to even house them. No wonder Charlie was born defective, Mother was that upset.

Resentment against my father boiled over—just as it always did whenever I thought of him—and I raised up, punching my pillow in irritation. I would have hit that pillow until there was nothing left but feathers flying around the room except for the sudden draft of frigid air that shot down the front of me clear to my toes. It sent me, shivering, back under our quilts.

Father. And Annie. And Mary. Homewreckers!

Again a twinge of guilt, but it only lasted an instant. I might be partial to Annie—who remained married to Father even though he no longer co-habited with her—but, still, I knew she and Mary had caused intense heartache for my mother ever since Father brought them home.

Mother never dreamed she'd have to share Father with another woman, let alone two of them. I could almost feel her despair as, struggling to care for her rapidly growing family, her hopes were dashed and without warning her meager resources and Father's time and attention were spread between two more, very prolific, women . . . women who couldn't even peaceably share him with each other, let alone her....

I wondered why Mother stayed married to him. *She could have divorced him. He certainly deserved it.* Her reasoning escaped me. *It can't be because she still loves him.* I tried to think of any indication that she did love him but I saw them together so seldom—he was always off doing something for the community or the church or who knew what. About the only time I saw them together was at church on Sunday where she sat at one end of the pew and he at the other with my brothers, Lindy, and me in between.

Then I had a new thought. *I wonder if the reason they sit that way is because of her resentment? After all, who could actually love a man who pulled such a dirty trick? I wouldn't want to sit by him. I always thought they sat that way to keep us in line but maybe it's because she refuses to be beside him any longer. It would serve him right. Is that why he's always gone? He knows he's not wanted?*

Probably the only reason Mother stayed with him was because of the fine woman she was. *She's not a vow breaker like Mary. She doesn't fight with Father and she won't fight Annie—or Mary either.*

But those two. Talk about typical women. Troublemakers just like all the rest. Why can't Alma see that a woman will mess up our lives to the point we'll be eternally miserable?

Well, if he's determined to ruin his own life, so be it, but he'll have to do it without me. I'm not as blind as he is. There will never be a woman—any woman—making my life miserable. With firm resolve, I finally drifted, emotionally and physically exhausted, off to sleep.

Malinda Moulton (Lindy)

CHAPTER SIX

"We're taking out a homestead in Teton Basin, Mother." You know how a person's voice sometimes hangs on the air after they've spoken? It's as if the words and the tones stay there, not dying away like they normally do. The sound of Alma's deep voice and the words he said hung over our supper table just like that.

Only Mother, Alma, Lindy and I were home that night. I was so astonished at what Alma said, I nearly choked. I glanced around the table. Lindy had a decidedly smug look on her face, Mother

22

looked so calm she could have been expecting this all along, and Alma was totally composed.

A hundred thoughts chased each other through my mind before the sound of his words died away. He hadn't mentioned homesteading or farming for weeks—not since the night he'd suggested a compromise—and I'd buried all thoughts of leaving Heber City with him. Now, suddenly, I couldn't keep a triumphant grin off my face. *He wants me with him enough to do it my way.* I should have felt guilty but I didn't. We didn't need Maude.

"I was expecting you to go to Idaho." Mother dabbed at her mouth with a napkin that matched her bleached-white tablecloth, then cocked her head as she looked from Alma to me and back again. "Actually, I thought you and Nephi decided to buy out near Rexburg instead of homesteading in the Basin."

I felt like someone punched me in the gut. "How did you know about Rexburg?"

"I have my sources," Mother said.

Malinda giggled. "Yes, she does." Then she laughed, "You should see the look on your face, Nephi. I can't wait to tell the girls at school."

"Lindy, when you get your first beau I'm going to tell him a story or two on you if you ever breathe a word of this." Lindy was usually a jewel, but occasionally she could really annoy me. "You're three beaus too late," Lindy informed me, her nose in the air. I wanted to shake that smug smile right off her face. "Anyway, how do you think Mother found out about all your plans? *I* told her."

"And just where did you get your information, little missy?" Alma's eyes were wide but was it show or real? Suddenly, I wasn't sure about anything or anybody.

"I got it from my third beau. You've been so busy with Maude, and Nephi's been so moody blue lately you haven't noticed Maude's little brother walking me home after school." Her Lindy-giggle bubbled up; joyous, contagious and excessively irritating. This was no time for laughter; I was trying to maintain a frown. But no matter how hard I tried, when Lindy giggled, a smile persisted in tugging at the corners of my mouth. It irritated me no end.

"I heard all about your Christmas visit with his uncle," she continued. "You were all ears, Alma, and Nephi scowled and spent

23

his time looking around like he wished he was a hundred miles away."

"I sure did," I agreed, slipping back into the mood I wanted. "What a total waste...."

"That's not important now," Mother interrupted in her, 'There'll be no more nonsense, boys', voice. "What's important is those finalized plans I've been waiting to see. ...Alma?"

"Don't have any, Mother. We'll homestead but we haven't worked on plans for weeks."

"Then have you talked to anyone about the Basin? Is there land still available?"

"Mother, you aren't serious about letting them go to Idaho! How will we manage if they're so far away? Who will take care of us?" Large tears welled up in Lindy's eyes. "I thought if I told on them you'd scotch the whole idea."

Without even thinking, I slipped her my handkerchief under the table. Lindy never carried one of her own. Sharing mine was a ritual from as far back as either of us could remember.

"Well, I guess you thought wrong, young lady. Your father *can* take care of us, he *will* take care of us, and it's high time he *starts*. He has Charlie for help, and Alma and Nephi need to go out on their own. Now you get busy with the dishes and then go to bed. I want to hear what your brothers agreed on before their falling out."

She turned her attention from Malinda. "And don't get into any silly arguments. Nephi, you get that last list you boys drew up and let's look it over. It's mid-February already and you don't have your ducks lined up. If you're to get a decent crop this summer, you need to order your supplies now so you can leave here before May."

"Nephi's got the list?" Alma reared back in his chair, his eyes wide.

I'd squirreled it away in the hidey-hole in our bedroom where I hid things I wanted to keep all to myself. It was the only thing I'd never shared with my brother—or anyone else, for that matter.

"He put it in his hidey-hole up in your bedroom," Mother told him.

"What hidey-hole?" Alma asked. He looked like he'd just missed a train or something. Her words shocked me so much I was sure *I* had. That hidey-hole was my private place . . . or so I'd always thought. Was she bluffing?

24

"It's in the corner under the eaves," she said. She wasn't bluffing. "He pries a board up and hides things between your floor and the ceiling in the parlor. Sometimes he even uses it when he wants to listen to company conversations but doesn't want to be seen."

She smiled at the look on my face. "Don't look so dumbfounded, Nephi. I wasn't born yesterday. I've known what you were doing for years. I guess, now that you're leaving, it's all right for me to tell."

This time the breath *was* knocked clean out of me. "Since when did you know about that?" I squeaked. I was suddenly seeing a mother I knew nothing about. Sure, I'd always known she was intelligent and unusually capable, but this savvy? How had she found out when even Alma, who knew almost everything there was to know about me, hadn't known?

The more I thought about it, the more it puzzled me. How did she find that one loose little board under the eaves in the corner of our room? How could she know I listened through it? Besides, the Johnson boy couldn't have told Lindy everything because he wouldn't have known about Alma's and my disagreement. And Alma was too closemouthed to have told Maude. For a moment there was a buzzing in my ears and the room seemed to swirl around me. It only lasted for a moment, though, before Mother spoke.

"It doesn't matter how long I've known. That's not important. Now pay attention, Nephi. Go get that list and, Alma, you round up some paper and a pencil and let's finalize those plans. I want a dollar amount on what you two have available to spend, and we're filling out an order form from the catalog tonight." I was so shocked by her personal knowledge of me and my habits that I obeyed her without questioning.

Which was probably what she intended all along.

CHAPTER SEVEN

It was long past midnight before my mother was satisfied with what she referred to as 'you boys' plans'. She probed and prodded, making us look at every aspect of homesteading and farming all over again, from every possible angle, until we were both so exhausted everything was hazy. Give me two hundred acres of rocky, hard-baked clay soil to plow behind a stubborn mule, *any day*, over ever having to do that again.

But finally we were finished. She had carefully tallied lists of what we needed to purchase, including household items and farming supplies she said we'd need that we hadn't even thought about buying . . . a thirty-yard coil of hemp rope, for instance:

"What for? We have our lariats."

"You never know, Nephi, when it'll come in handy. You'll need more than your lariats." And bread pans:

"I can't cook bread and neither can Nephi. But he makes biscuits. We'll live on that." "It's *bake* bread, Alma, and you *will learn* before you leave my home."

Then she made me, of all people, fill out the order forms. She knew I hated writing. What was the point of making me fill out the forms when someone needed to read them at the catalog house? I pointed out to her that my handwriting was always jerky, not smooth and flourishing like hers or Alma's:

"Mother, if I write it nobody will be able to read it and we won't get the things we ordered. You or Alma had better do it. Yours is easy to read."

But it didn't do any good. She insisted I fill out the forms and she would check them over to make sure I'd done them right.

"Nephi, if you're thinking of going out in a man's world you have to learn to do these things. Get busy, now. I'll check it when you're finished and if I can't read it, you'll just have to do it again."

I guess this Preparation for the Future was supposed to be Good for my Soul or something.

While Alma looked up the items we needed and I wrote them down on the order form, she took the notes she'd been making and asked even more questions. There was a knot at the base of my skull and a chord running down my neck that were throbbing unmercifully by the time she gathered her papers and my completed order form together and laid the pencil neatly on top. Finally, I could go to bed. Even freezing-cold sheets in our icy little attic seemed welcoming after that ordeal.

But no. Mother wasn't finished with us, yet. "I've been piecing quilt tops for you boys since about October," she said as Alma and I started out of the dining room. "I'll get some of my friends together and we'll have them quilted in time for you to leave in late April." Then, as she stood up from her chair, she made one final decree.

"All in all, it makes more sense to me for you boys to buy that farm Maude's uncle told you about up on the Egin bench. Now, Nephi," she turned her head away and raised her hand, palm out, as if pushing the words I was starting to say back into my mouth, "I'll not hear a word from you about it. I have enough money that you can borrow from me instead of a bank. I'll expect timely payments, of course, and I'll expect you to work hard and make this venture pay but I won't charge interest so long as you keep current. I'll tell your father about it when he comes back from his trip to Salt Lake City but, since I handle the family purse anyhow, we can draw up an agreement tomorrow—just you two and me—so you can get on with your purchases.

"You'll be leaving in two months and there's a lot to be done between now and then. You both best get to bed and get some sleep. Tomorrow's coming all too soon."

With that, and a slight, secretive smile in Alma's direction, she swept out of the room, her long dark skirt swishing, leaving me to stumble, numbly, up the stairs to bed. I didn't quite know how she'd managed it but somehow I had the distinct impression I'd just been neatly outmaneuvered.

27

CHAPTER EIGHT

"Your father needs to be more involved. Please take him with you today," Mother requested the morning we bought our team of work horses. It was our final purchase and, although I had argued for a cheaper pair of mules, Alma favored a pair of Percherons.

"Father hasn't shown any interest in our plans what—so—ever," I protested, voicing the first excuse I could think of as I shrugged into my coat in the front hall. "He won't want to go."

"Have you tried to involve him?" Mother reached up to turn down my collar as if I were a little boy once more. I ducked away, annoyed—as much by her demand as by her hovering.

"Nooo," Alma draped his coat over his arm, then opened the outside door to stand, tall and strong, in the early April sunlight. It glinted off his hair, slanting across his broad shoulders. "He doesn't care what we do," he continued. "You told him, months ago, that we're leaving but he's never even mentioned it—and here it is, April already. We'll be gone in a couple-three weeks. I'd ask him along if I thought it would matter to him."

"You've been with us every step of the way, Mother, but Father never says anything except to tell us what chores he wants done for the day," I agreed. "And that's only when he's home—which is rare."

"I know," Mother sighed, unconsciously pushing a wisp of hair back over her ear. "But, still, he needs to do something with you before you go; he needs to be involved. I want you to ask him."

"We will ask him if you really want us to," I said as I walked out of the door, "but he won't have time. He never does." I counted on his refusal.

To my astonishment, however, when we finally found our father wandering up the path toward the big Heber City Tabernacle a few blocks down the street, he turned as we hailed him and almost eagerly approached the wagon. That was unexpected. Unwelcomed too. Sharing my morning with my father had never been a top priority.

As I stepped down to let him climb into the wagon I wondered, for a minute, when we'd last ridden somewhere together. I actually couldn't remember, I'd avoided him for so long. Then it came back to me . . . I'd started dodging him when Charlie lost his voice.

Charlie used to shout—a lot—particularly when he was excited. Piercing yells and frequent obscenities—with no warning and for no apparent reason. I almost chuckled as I remembered how upset Father got whenever Charlie cussed. It would have been funny except for the way Father chose to take care of the problem. That still horrified me.

I wasn't at home when he invited Charlie on that infamous 'father-son excursion' to Salt Lake City—I was probably out playing marbles or cutting a willow whistle or something—but I never forgot their return. While in the city, my father had a surgeon cut Charlie's vocal chords.

I was just a little child at the time but Mother's devastation when Father brought my silently sobbing, nearly mute brother back home was forever etched in my memory. You can bet I made sure *I* never went on any excursions with him after that. As I thought about it, I realized today was the first time since then that I'd gone anywhere with my Father without Mother along. A shiver of apprehension ran up my spine.

Guess he can't do much to hurt me with Alma holding the reins and him sitting in the middle. Alma and I are as big as he is, now. As I climbed back onto the wagon seat I made sure I sat as far from him as I could.

I half expected him to say something on the trip across the valley to the breeder's farm—ask about the team we were considering, or something about our plans, or maybe just comment on the weather to get a conversation started. I wondered what I would answer.

But he was silent.

Typical of Joseph Moulton. Sits between Alma and me without saying a single word. Could be deaf, dumb and blind—or dead.

In the meantime I'm ready to jump out of my skin. He's ruined this whole morning. I should be enjoying the breeze on my face. And the 'spring's here' of the chickadees. And the pungent smell of spring-sloppy farmyards. I planned to enjoy this trip but I'm miserable and it's all his fault.

This is awful. I can't breathe. I edged so far away I was half off the wagon seat, hoping some space would ease my chest. It didn't.

29

If we don't get there soon I'm going to jump off this wagon and walk—or run. Anything to get away from him. I think I died a thousand deaths before Alma turned the team off the main road and I had the breed farm to occupy my attention.

On either side of the lane leading to the breeder's Swiss-style farmhouse were pastures and cultivated fields slashed with long, wide drifts of still-unmelted snow. At the end I could see the lane curve beside a large pole corral with a tall, steep-roofed barn on one side, a turn-around in front. On the other side was the farmhouse.

Everything about the place was neat and tidy despite the spring mud. I liked that. It reminded me of the precise, sparse order of Mother's home. Even the huge draft horses in the pastures were clean—sleek and healthy looking, their coats glistening in the April sun. Maybe Percherons weren't such a bad idea after all. These horses were built to work. I wanted to comment on them but not with Father sitting beside me. I'd probably say something that would show my ignorance. That was usually the way things went around him.

"Who ever heard of chestnut-colored Percherons?" Father spoke for the first time, shaking his head, when the breeder led Alma's choice of teams out of the barn. "I've never seen any but black or gray." It was the first time he'd spoken all morning.

"They're Percherons, all right," Alma assured him as we climbed down from the wagon seat. "I've seen the papers. Same sire; different dams. What do you think of them?"

Suddenly I wanted my father to approve. It didn't matter that it was Alma who'd argued for the team; Father didn't know that. Somehow his approval meant validation of Alma's and my status as independent men. I sensed Alma felt the same way as he looked at our father, an anxious expression on his normally good-natured face.

This team couldn't look better to me—but Father knows exactly what to look for when he studies a horse's conformation. And he's so critical. I held my breath.

Without answering Alma's question, Father stepped back, then walked around the horses, quietly studying each from a distance of some twenty-five or thirty feet. Speaking almost to himself, he began a running commentary on what he saw as he went.

Not wanting to be obvious, I kept behind him, trying to see what he was seeing. It was difficult since he was as tall as either Alma or I and definitely as well built. We were all rugged men cut from tough cloth—not heavy but muscled with broad shoulders, long legs, strong hands. I ducked and peered as he started to catalog the gelding's qualities.

"Good head—no roman arch in the nose." That wasn't hard to figure out.

"Eyes set well—bright and intelligent looking. No ewe neck." I had no idea what he meant by that but the horse's neck was straight and looked strong. What did a ewe neck look like, anyway? I looked at the other horse but it mirrored the one Father was studying. I'd have to ask Uncle Heber next time I saw him. I knew Father's younger brother would tell me.

"Good shoulder attachment, here." Father had gone on. I hurried to catch up. "Wide between the front legs, deep chest there . . . a lot of muscle in the forearm, that's good." It didn't occur to me until much later that our Father was giving us a lesson on horse anatomy that morning.

After a thorough visual exam, Father went over the animal with his fingers, feeling for abnormalities under its skin. He didn't find any. When he was satisfied with his probing, he eased his hand down to the fetlock of the nearest leg and pressed, gently. Unruffled, the horse lifted its great hoof for inspection.

"Good obedience, there." Father approved. "Not fractious. You sure don't want a fractious animal."

Fractious had to be his favorite word. On the rare occasions when he did speak, it was usually to tell one of his wives or children to not be 'fractious'. He hated contention although, in my opinion, he was frequently the cause of the fractiousness in the family.

When he'd inspected each horse in turn, he motioned Alma and me to lead the pair around him in a wide circle while he studied their action.

"Hitch them up to the wagon, boys," he finally ordered.

After they were harnessed and hitched to our wagon, he climbed up onto the wagon seat and Alma handed him the reins. Slapping them gently on the horses' rumps, he clicked his tongue. The Percherons stepped out smoothly, as if one horse. The only difference I could see between them was that the mare, anxious to work, tossed her head as she waited for him to give command.

We'll call her Sassy. I mentally named her on the spot. *And the gelding 'Sleek' because of his shiny coat.* I didn't consider Alma's wishes when I named them. He wouldn't care.

Across the barnyard, around in a circle, then through a figure eight, Father walked the horses before turning them down the lane and quickening the pace. They trotted in unison. He pulled on the reins and called a quiet, "Whoa". They stopped. He backed them back up the lane to the barnyard then turned them to bring the wagon to a stop where it had first been. Finally, satisfied with what he saw, he offered his approval.

"Look pretty good to me."

Although we both would have liked more from him, it was as much as either Alma or I could hope for.

CHAPTER NINE
LATE APRIL 1902

The mournful wail of a distant steam engine whistle sent a quiver through my stomach where a hard lump was solidly in place before I even woke up that morning. I hadn't been able to tell Mother I didn't feel like eating the huge breakfast she'd prepared—I didn't want to hurt her feelings on my last day at home—so I'd struggled to do the meal justice. But now, with departure looming, I wasn't sure all the ham-and-eggs-and-pancakes-and-syrup-and-jam-and-stewed fruit-and-milk-and-everything-else Mother had set before me were going to stay down.

One of the clichés Mother brought us up on, 'Work'll get you through the tough times,' sounded in my mind. *Right now, I need to work!* I searched the crowd for Alma. *Drat the man, where is he, anyway?*

Crates with our equipment were stacked on the railroad platform beside me. Trunks of clothing, household supplies and bedding—including a quilt Maude pieced and quilted, herself, for Alma—were still on the thick bed of straw lining Father's wagon, along with various smaller items including a crate carrying a brooding hen and a young cockerel from Annie.

"You need every chicken you have," I'd protested as she'd trudged up the path to Mother's door earlier in the day, pulling the chicken crate in the small cart she normally used to transport the laundry she took in. Her still-blond hair and blue eyes masked her years but her work-worn, chapped hands told of her endless hours of toil to provide for her little family.

"You boys have always been good to me, Nephi," she'd said. "I can give you these chickens to get you started. Next year you'll have more. She's a good brood hen and he's a healthy young rooster—one I've been saving since I heard you were leaving."

Hers weren't the only chickens we were taking with us, of course—Uncle Heber and Aunt Euphemia had already brought a half-dozen laying hens—but Annie's gift represented true sacrifice. A cockerel she'd 'saved' meant a meal she hadn't eaten. That fact wasn't lost on me but all I did was thank her. Anything more would have embarrassed us both, to say nothing about upsetting Mother.

33

I looked past the chickens and the wagon to the milling throng waiting to see us off. Half of Heber City seemed to be there; Uncle Heber and Aunt Euphemia with their cheerful smiles; my oldest siblings, Tom, Joe and Sarah, with their little families; always-natty John and perpetually-rumpled Charlie; little Aunt Annie with her two girls, our half-sisters, Lillie and Violet—Lyman conspicuously missing; Father, Mother and Malinda, who was furiously twirling the end of her braid; Maude's entire family; and a gaggle of other adults—friends of our parents—some with their families in tow. Half of the elementary school pupils seemed to have played hooky just to get in on the excitement, as well. But where was Alma?

... *For that matter, where's Maude? Dumb question.* I swung off the platform and strode around the two emigrant boxcars car we'd hired to transport our animals and equipment to Idaho. There on the back side, hidden behind the wheels of the second car, were Alma and Maude locked in—I ducked back around the corner of the car.

"Mother, I found Alma!" I hollered as if calling to Mother, then walked around the corner once more, grinning as I watched Alma and Maude jump apart, their faces scarlet.

"All we need is a photographer," I said. "Bet I could sell enough copies of that pose to pay for our entire trip. Now, how was it, exactly? Alma, I think you had your right hand in the small of her back and Maude must have found the blackberry jam you stored on your upper lip at breakfast. Pretty tasty, huh, Maude?"

"Get lost." Alma tried to be angry, not quite succeeding as his lopsided grin reluctantly emerged.

"You going to Idaho or staying here? Didn't you hear the whistle? We need to get our equipment loaded."

"I'm coming," Alma pulled Maude close, again, for another quick embrace then followed me around the car. We skirted a noisy group of small lads playing a fast-paced game of marbles, then dodged a serious contest of mumbledy-peg involving some of the older school boys.

"Watch that knife!" Alma ordered one of them. "You just missed my foot. There's too many people here for you to be throwing knives. Come make yourselves useful!" I was already up on the platform when Alma caught up with me, boys in tow.

Suddenly there it all was—a reality. Bleating sheep, a recently-freshened milk cow with her bawling heifer calf, a half-dozen yearling heifers, a blustering bull calf and our Percheron team, Sleek and Sassy, as well as Alma's and my two saddle horses, Darky and Star, being herded up a makeshift ramp and into simple, hastily constructed pens in the first car. A mound of loose hay stood between the pens and the door.

What needs to be done? Load the equipment . . . second car. 'Work'll get you through....' I started for the car door.

"Help me open this door, Alma," I called, "and we'll get the heavy equipment in first." As I spoke milling townspeople churned into action.

"Are the sheep secured?"

"Let's put this straw from Joseph's wagon in here to pad the jolts better. You boys don't want to be delivering fourteen lambs out in the middle of Nowhere, Idaho."

I'd wondered why Father'd brought the straw but it hadn't occurred to me what two days in a railroad car might do to a pregnant ewe. I grabbed a pitchfork, eager to help.

"Where d'yu want the chicken crates?" The conversation continued to swirl around me. "Will someone help me with this cussed bull calf? He's trying to break out of this here pen."

"Yeah, selling *him* was the smartest thing Bill Thacker ever did—too bad for the boys," (General laughter met with an offended, "That was m'best bull calf," from Father's neighbor, Bill).

"Those boys could pull the plow up now."

"Better tell Nephi and Alma to make a place for the boys, too. They'd make as good draft animals as any and they don't eat hay." (Again, general laughter)

"I'd give my eyeteeth to go with them!"(From Maude's little brother)

"Bet you're not the only one in your family who'd like to be going." (More laughter as Maude's face turned a bright pink)

"Here's a chest of bedding. You want it on the harness box?"

"No the chicken crates are going there."

"Well, you could put the crates on top."

"Don't you dare set chicken crates on that quilt chest!" (From Maude)

I couldn't resist a chance to tease. Before I even thought, the words tumbled out.

"The scent of chickens'll make it sweeter,
When I'm wrapped tight in your quilt, dear.
I'll smell their gentle, sweet aroma
And I'll feel that you are near."

"Nephi!" Alma's roar filled the boxcar as loud guffaws swept through the crowd. I found urgent business elsewhere.

Suddenly the steam whistle sounded again; this time in my very ear. *The engine's here! Is everything loaded?* With so many people crowding around, I couldn't see. *Won't they just get out of the way?*

I ducked and wove between groups of people, looking for anything that might have been left behind. There was nothing by the rails or on the platform and the wagon was empty. I looked around the boxcar.

"Make sure those ropes are tight," I heard Father direct Alma as my brother checked the ropes holding the heavier equipment. I didn't want my father telling me what to do so I walked to the first car for one last inspection of our animals.

Just inside the door was a basket I'd seen Lindy weaving from green willows just last week, its mounded contents covered with one of Mothers dishtowels. I paused a moment to look. *Baking powder biscuits—my favorite; cheese—yum; jerked venison—Mother's best.* I poked a little farther and on the bottom found a tin of dried fruits—apples, apricots and raisins—mixed with nuts. *Does Mother know Lindy raided her fruit supply? Beside the basket a covered crock, brimming with water freshly drawn from Mother's well, was snuggled down into the hay where it couldn't tip over. Malinda wouldn't have thought to put it there. Mother must have helped with this.*

I looked over the hay mound. On the other side were the old, worn quilts from our attic bed, spread where Alma and I could ride, cushioned from the jolts of the uneven rail line and insulated from April's chill. Malinda wouldn't have dared send those quilts without Mother's approval.

Dear Mother . . . she knows me so well. These old quilts mean home. As I walked to the horse pen at the front of the car, I knew I'd continue to sleep under them, badly-worn as they were, and leave the new ones in the chest when we reached our Idaho farm.

CHAPTER TEN

"I guess you're ready." Iron suddenly screeched behind me as Father slid the boxcar door partway shut. "Better come say your goodbyes, Nephi." Those were probably the first words he'd said directly to me all day.

There he stood, as quiet, straight and slender as he'd always been. Only the grey hair at each temple and some threads of grey in his carefully clipped mustache and goatee suggested his advancing years. Beyond him was Alma, seriously deep in discussion with Maude—again. At least they were talking, not smooching.

My oldest brothers, Tom and Joe, stood on the platform with their wives and children while John was by the wagon, one arm around Mother and the other around Malinda, whose eyes were red, swollen and streaming. I saw John slip her a handkerchief and guilt swept over me. *It was always me to give her one but I forgot today . . . the very last thing I could have done for Lindy and I forgot.* The knot in my stomach returned, double-sized.

How can I say good-by to all this? Will Father take care of Mother and Lindy? I looked at my mother, again. *Who knows when I'll have enough money to visit her? Will she still be here when I can afford to come?*

And what of Lindy? She'd been red-eyed for the past month. *When will I see her again?* I knew she was wondering the same. *Will she be married and gone before I come back to visit?* I looked past her tear-stained face, unable to think of it.

Standing behind her was Annie. Again, guilt. *Will Annie end up doing the chores Alma and I have done for her all these years?* I knew she was fond of us both—not because we'd taken care of her needs but because she had a gentle, loving heart. And yet, as I looked into her eyes, I suddenly realized I'd never really known her very well. *I never took the time to talk to her or to listen to her; I just split and stacked her wood, filled her water buckets, and hurried off to my chores at home. Did she ever wish I'd stop a while? Did she need a listening ear?* Too late to find out now. I was leaving.

The whistle sounded once more, startlingly close. Then the boxcar jerked as it was coupled with the rest of the train.

"I'd better check the animals!" I disappeared into the car once more, making a hasty business of checking the stalls as a tear slipped down my cheek. *Tears! I'm supposed to be a man, going off to a man's future but here I am, scared and I haven't even left Heber City yet.*

Impatiently dashing the tear away with the back of my hand, I gritted my teeth, willed myself to smile, and walked to the boxcar door. Swinging to the ground, I marched toward my mother to begin my good-byes. There was so much I wanted to say but, as I stood before her, nothing would come out. Slipping up behind me, Alma spoke for us both while I awkwardly shook hands all around.

"Good-by, Mother. We'll be down to visit when we bring our first cattle sales to Ogden. Good-by, Malinda, here's my handkerchief so you'll always have one. Keep it, now! G'dby John...Joe...Tom...Sarah. Keep an eye on Lindy for us, now. Don't let her take any wooden nickels off the young men around here." Alma was almost too breezy with his farewells. "Good-by, Aunt Annie. We'll send you the first eggshell we get from one of those chicks your hen'll hatch. Good-by, Uncle Heber, Aunt Euphemia. Your laying hens are much appreciated. Maude...."

The whistle sounded, a final mournful wail, as the conductor called us to board the car and fasten the door. "Good-by," Alma called, vaulting into the boxcar where I'd already escaped the pressing throng. "Good-by, Father." We both leaned down to shake the hand our father proffered.

"Here are some raspberry and strawberry starts." Father lifted a shallow wooden crate from the ground beneath the boxcar. "And a little apple tree. Your mother and I wanted you to have some fruit of your own. They won't produce this year, of course, but you should have something next year." He offered his hand again, to each of us in turn, then together—Alma and me on the inside, Father on the outside—we pushed the heavy iron door shut.

To me, the deep metallic clang of the latch clamping into place was like a death knell.

CHAPTER ELEVEN

A chorus of goodbyes came through the slits in the boxcar walls as the train lurched forward, chugging to gain speed. Bracing ourselves, Alma and I inspected the livestock, once more. Ropes tight, panels in place, nothing shifted. Satisfied, we made a comfortable bed for ourselves on the hay, and settled in for the long journey ahead. I had found it easier to let work mask the feelings I neither wanted nor knew how to express but now, with nothing to do, they rose up like ghosts in a graveyard.

Freedom. No more doing Lyman's share of the work while the big L. lazes the day away, target practicing or fishing. No more being used as everybody's gofer. No more having Father tell me what to do. In a way I felt almost triumphant. But not quite. Something pulled me back to the home I was leaving behind.

"We'll visit when we bring our cattle to Ogden." Brave words but the truth was it would be several years, at least, before our herd was large enough to pay for such a trip. *What will happen before we get back? Mother's no longer young. Will she still be there? And what about Lindy? She'll be married and gone. Nothing will be the same.* The knot in my stomach tightened until the ache was almost unbearable.

Suddenly I felt a warm hand on my shoulder. "It's difficult to leave," Alma's deep bass voice sounded in my ear. "Things will be different when we come back. Malinda will grow up on us, of course, but our parents will always be the same.

"It was a good place to grow up in," he continued after a pause, although I hadn't responded. ". . . Heber City. It's good when you're a child, but I'm glad I'm starting out somewhere new. I never could understand how Tom, Joe and John could stand to live forever in a town. I've always been happiest out in the fields or forests where there weren't a lot of people, haven't you?"

"I guess so." I wasn't sure I even wanted to think about it.

"The fields or the hills," Alma repeated. I looked at him but his blue eyes were seeing something miles away. "That cabin we found up in the hills was a lot of fun. Good shade from the sun, although it wasn't much shelter from the rain. I don't think either of us minded, though."

I smiled. It was a place of our own; a place to go when we were lads and had to herd everybody's milk cows or when we went hunting as we got older. In my mind I saw it, again, as it was on the first day we found it.

Alma and I, along with our two half brothers, Lyman and Bill, were herding milk cows for our ward in the city. As the day wore on, we trailed them across the sage flats to the edge of the foothills several miles out of town, letting them graze as they pleased.

Late afternoon shadows were lengthening into jagged lines stretched across the uneven sage before anyone noticed that Mother's contrary old cow, Mahitabel, was missing. Leaving Bill and Lyman to trail the herd back for evening milking, Alma and I struck out into the forestlands of the foothills, listening for Mahitabel's bell.

It was nearly dark before we found her happily grazing on tall grass in a little alpine meadow way up the mountainside. At the far edge of the meadow, nearly obscured by pines and shadows, was a ramshackle cabin. Its roof sagged, there was no chinking between the logs, and the only window opening was empty of its glass–if it ever had any.

We thought it was a mansion.

It was probably just an old abandoned trapper's cabin but neither Alma nor I ever asked. We didn't want anyone else to know about our find, especially our brothers. From then on we begged to herd the cows alone. The only other human being we ever saw at the cabin was the hobo.

Alma was teaching me to use a slingshot the morning the hobo showed up. My brother had killed a rabbit, skinned it and was cooking it on a green-willow spit over a small campfire when an erratic pebble slung from my slingshot accidentally laid a squirrel low. Not to be outdone, I'd skinned my kill and begged Alma to cook it, too.

"You never know until you've tried something, whether it'll be good or not," I argued.

Alma wasn't easily convinced. "I'm not so sure I want to find out about squirrel," he said.

"Awww, come on. It can't be all that bad, and if we cook it thoroughly it won't hurt us."

"Maybe—if it's burned—but by then you'd have to throw it out to the dog."

Alma finally gave in and added the tiny body to his green-willow spit. It was thoroughly cooked by the time the hobo came along. He'd smelled something and was very hungry. Was there enough to share?

"Sure thing," I motioned towards the squirrel, still on the spit. "Fresh ground-squirrel, there. Ready to eat."

Under his dirt and whiskers, the man's skin paled as a look of horror spread over his face. Then he turned and literally ran off through the woods.

I never could remember what the squirrel tasted like—I was too busy laughing when I ate it—but it couldn't have been as foul as the hobo thought since neither Alma nor I noticed the flavor. Had it been skunk or bear, that might have been a different story.

"Hey, Nephi," Alma's voice yanked me out of my pleasant memory. "Remember the hobo? I wonder what he'd have done if we'd told him your squirrel was skunk?" I pulled a face and Alma immediately went defensive. "I've heard the Indians eat skunk. He might have been willing to try it."

"How can you skin and cook a skunk without smelling like one? Phew! Those Indians probably don't notice the flavor."

"Tell you what doesn't smell like skunk . . . that basket Malinda packed. I'm getting hungry. How about you?" Alma crawled out from under the quilts to bring Malinda's basket around the pile of hay.

"Don't want anything." I looked away, then realized, suddenly, the knot I'd been nursing in my stomach all morning wasn't as strong as it had been. In fact, it wasn't even there. Maybe I *was* interested in what Malinda sent. "On second thought...." I turned back towards Alma, reaching for a biscuit.

As we settled into serious food, Alma steered the conversation to what lay ahead and I found my enthusiasm rising once more. By nightfall, homesickness had permanently faded into the background. The clicking of the emigrant car's wheels against the uneven tracks, and the rhythm of its constant swaying, were as hypnotic as the monotone lullabies I'd often heard Mother sing to her grandchildren. Sleep came easily as I snuggled down into the pile of hay and pulled

Mother's quilts tight under my chin, a sweet sleep laced with dreams of a thriving farm on the Egin Bench somewhere near a spot in southeast Idaho known as Salem.

CHAPTER TWELVE

We were in trouble as soon as we turned our little livestock herd down the lane toward our new home. There wasn't an upright fence post on either side of the dirt track and what wire the previous owner had actually managed to string, sagged clear to the ground. Cross one item off the list of things we "wouldn't have to do". I looked for the barn and cabin, dreading what I would see.

Cross another one off. The barn wasn't much bigger than Mother's chicken coop at home. Only difference I could see was Mother's coop had four walls. Our wonderful barn only boasted three. Who, in their right mind, wanted to milk a cow in the open? I glanced at Alma.

He was carefully gazing at the distant horizon.

And you called that a corral? The gate hung at a crazy angle and the only thing holding the posts up was an occasional cross bar. Those rail ends needed a post on either side the way Father built his corral at home.

I didn't inspect the cabin. Why bother? I'd noticed the door was open as we turned into the barnyard. That meant our wonderful "snug little cabin" would be full of birds and mice and poop. Maybe even a skunk—I'd smelled one when we started down the lane. Good thing Uncle Jake hadn't showed his face today. I probably would have rearranged his profile.

With no fences that would hold a cow or sheep, we tried penning them in the corral.

"Remind me why we bought sheep," I groused after one old ewe nearly hung herself trying, for the sixth time, to squeeze through the corral fence rails. By then twilight was descending as Alma and I feverishly worked to make the corral secure. I was tired, my hands were cramped, my back was sore and the occasional growl in my stomach had long since voted to become a constant rumble. I was ready to slaughter the old girl then and there and put both of us out of our misery.

It didn't get any better.

"Those cussed sheep have *got* to be about the dumbest animals God ever created." I grumbled several days later as I pumped the fence stretcher to pull the last stretch of fencing taut. "I've spent more time chasing them than I have stretching wire.

"There." I gave an experimental shove against the sturdily-set fence post after Alma stapled the wire. It held steady and the wires leading from it were tight. I smiled. At least something was tidy.

"That should about do it," I said. "You want to start plowing or shall I?"

"Go ahead." Alma picked up the bag of staples and his hammer. "I'm going to clean the cabin. I'm tired of spending my nights sleeping around sheep."

As I'd suspected, the house was too filthy to move into so we'd parked the wagon beside the corral and spread our quilts on the ground beneath. It was just as well. Every one of those blasted ewes had lambed in the past ten days and every one of them had dropped her lamb during the night.

Not in the daytime. Oh no. A sheep couldn't be that accommodating. But at least the fencing and lambing were over. I was itching for a little release and Alma was the only game available.

"Here I thought you were getting in practice for sleeping with Maude." I grinned. "I wonder if she'd be as fluffy an armful as one of those ewes? You've sure spent a lot of time with them lately."

"Watch your tongue, now." Alma's growl might have warned me if he hadn't had that quirky, lopsided smile. "At least she'd hold still once in a while and her voice is a darned sight easier on the ear."

"Yeah, I'll bet she'd hold still. Real still. In fact, I never noticed any sign of her running—unless it was *after* you."

Alma flushed. "You've got too much time on your hands," he said. "You're brain's getting mushy."

"*My* brain's mushy. There isn't any photograph lighting *my* life as I shave." I was referring to his photograph of a smiling Maude peeping mischievously over her shoulder, her long dark hair cascading down in ringlets and her grey eyes wide.

Alma had carried it to Idaho in his breast pocket and on the trip I'd caught him slipping it out, occasionally, when he thought I wasn't looking. After our arrival, he put it in the quilt chest on top of the quilt she made him. He reverently brought it out each morning when he got ready to shave. I'd see it propped up on the corral fence

44

beside our small mirror as he lathered his face and scraped away with his straight razor. I wondered, sometimes, how he managed to keep from slitting his throat, he was so busy mooning over that darned photograph. As far as I was concerned it was fuel for a good ribbing but I knew when I teased him I'd better not plan on hanging around. My brother may be good natured but he was ridiculously overprotective of Maude or anything to do with her.

True to form he growled, "Don't get started on Maude, now," but I was already beating a hasty retreat.

CHAPTER THIRTEEN

"Looking mighty good," our nearest neighbor, Bob Daniels, a widower from a mile down the road, approved one day as he looked around our farmyard. He'd stopped to chat while driving his small herd of sheep out to the open wastelands beyond our farm where his teenaged daughter, Emma-Jane, and his younger son herded them in the daytime. "You boys sure do know how to work."

I watched, fascinated, as he scratched a portion of the flabby pink belly showing between the buttons of his ragged, tightly stretched shirt front.

". . . But you know? Your horses and cows would do better if you weren't pasturing them sheep along-side of 'em. Sheep eat the feed clean into the ground."

"Yes, they do," Alma agreed, "but we can't turn them loose. We'd never see them again and we don't have time to herd sheep."

"It's a fact." Bob rubbed the rolls of his stubbly chin. "Tell you what. If you'll lemme put my sheep up in your corral, nights, my boy an girl can herd your sheep along-side ours during the day. That'll give you an extry field too harvest an it'll be much easier for my boy an girl to only drive my sheep to here, nights."

Alma and I looked at each other and I smiled broadly. "Fair enough trade," I said. Life was getting easier. The corral was big enough we could keep our sheep there at night, too. The cussed things would be someone else's worry during the day and I wouldn't have to continually check our wire fences for breakthroughs. The longer I owned sheep the stronger my dislike was becoming.

I didn't know what I was getting myself into.

"Think of it." Alma exclaimed after Bob was gone, our sheep following along with his small herd. "The more feed for the cattle, the sooner we can pay Mother and Father off. I'll build a little home for Maude and myself. You can continue living in the cabin, of course, but you'll be welcome to take your meals with us."

Why was Alma so intent on bringing Maude to Idaho? The solitary farmer's life was just to my liking. As long as I had Alma to talk to when I wanted company, I was content. He should have been

46

content, too. Why ask for trouble when there was enough to keep a man busy as it was?

But the problem of Alma pining for Maude was nothing compared to what developed with Bob's daughter, Emma-Jane. To Alma's delight and my total dismay she decided I was *the* glowing star in the night sky surrounding her narrow little world.

It was first noticeable in her attempts to wash her face and do something with the wild mop of frizzy, dirty-blond curls that stuck straight out all over her head. Not knowing, at first, why she was making the effort, Alma complimented her one morning.

"You're looking nice, today, Emma-Jane."

I didn't agree but she glowed, visibly, looking at me to see if I did—worship stamped so clearly across her face that even I couldn't miss it.

Alma's eyebrows raised, ever-so-slightly, and a sly smile curved his lips. As soon as Emma-Jane started the sheep down the lane to the wasteland range, I knew I was in for a good ribbing. I found something to do elsewhere.

Too soon, if she didn't see me around when she came to get the sheep, she'd start looking.

"Will you please not tell her where I am?" I begged my brother but Alma, out of pure revenge, joined in her searches with a poker face until I was near to distraction. The Egin bench-land was so flat there was no place to hide. Between Emma-Jane hanging around hoping to see me or, worse yet, wandering around the farmyard *looking* for me, and Alma's tongue-in-cheek comments about the beauty and temptation of the horse-faced, overweight girl with the wild hair, blemishes and dirty, broken fingernails, I thought I would go mad. The only place I could escape to was up the lone cottonwood tree on the west side of our cabin.

She always seemed to know when I was home for breakfast so I began keeping the back window open, mornings. The minute I heard a footstep on the porch I shoved myself through that little window at top speed. By the time she knocked on the door I was already around the corner, up on the first limb and climbing fast. I didn't like cold breakfasts but I sure got used to eating them that summer.

"Hey, Nephi," Alma said one day. "Looks like we'll be needing another cabin this fall. You'll want your own after you marry Emma-Jane."

"Not going to happen." I snorted. "That girl of Bob's is the peskiest critter I've ever seen. I have to put a stop to her eternal hanging around. She can think up the dumbest questions and she's always babbling to the point I doubt she even shuts up when she's asleep. Good match for her sheep. She's as dumb as they are and she bleats like one, too!"

"Is she as fluffy an armful as our ewes?" Alma was the picture of innocence. The only answer I gave him was another snort as I stomped away.

Emma-Jane's bids for my attention were taking up valuable time that I wanted to spend on farm work. I didn't have time for a woman. Or the inclination. Alma didn't have time for women either. I wished my brother would forget the breed, altogether, and get on with the business of making this place produce like we both knew it could. I conveniently overlooked the fact it was *me* wasting time, sitting in the tree, instead of him.

"All a woman does is come between a man and what he ought to be doing," I'd mutter as I huddled on the highest limb I thought would hold me, stomach crying for food, waiting for that dad-blasted girl to give up and wander her sheep down the lane. Emma-Jane wasn't doing a thing to improve my estimation of the female species, which was on a sharp, downward plunge.

Of course Alma, bless his ornery hide, took delight in ribbing me about my escapes up the tree.

"You building your honeymoon nest up in that cottonwood, Nephi?"

"Hush! You're talking too loud. Actually, I'm checking the garden. You didn't do a very good job of weeding those tomatoes yesterday. There's a big weed smack dab in the middle."

"You're complaining about one lousy weed? Get down here and pull it, yourself, if it bothers you so much. You're wasting your morning watching Emma-Jane herd sheep."

"Never look at her," I said as I climbed down.

"Sure you don't."

The next day wasn't any different. As soon as she wandered off down the lane, my brother came looking for me.

"You know, Nephi," he said, "you're spending so much time in that tree, trying to catch a glimpse of Emma Jane, that we're getting nothing done around here."

"Oh, tell me about it! Our garden and fields look better than anyone else's on the bench and you know it."

"If they do, it's because I work so hard while you're roosting."

I ignored the virtue plastered across his face. I knew it was there just to irritate me.

"Not roosting. I'm making sure you're doing a good job with the irrigating."

I had to admit the view of our farm from high up in the tree was almost worth the hassle. The glow of pride I felt when I looked out over our little spread each morning carried me through the aches and fatigue of the day. How could any man enslave himself in an office when he could have the freedom and satisfaction of a farmer?

"You ought to climb up here and take a look at the fields, yourself," I told Alma as he was teasing me one day. "You might decide to join me instead of playing nursemaid to Emma-Jane."

"Don't see why I'd want to bother," he said. "There's enough to keep me busy down below, doing my work and yours, too." I ignored his good-natured jibe.

"If you ever change your mind, the view's worth the climb," I assured him.

Rimming the western horizon was the remote Sawtooth mountain range while on the east, past ever-rising swells of sage land, I could see the faraway tips of the Tetons. The Sawtooths were about as wild and lonely appearing as anything I'd ever seen, particularly in the evening with the flaming desert sunset behind them. As for the Tetons, Bob snickered when he told Alma and me about their name.

"You know what Teton means, don't you?" I guess we both looked blank because he didn't wait for us to tell him we had no idea.

"Breast!" He laughed at the looks on our faces. "In French."

"Whaaaat?" Alma looked sidewise at him.

"Why?" I demanded. "And who would name it that?" The word embarrassed me but I had to know.

"Some French trapper, pining for his woman," Bob snickered again. "He decided the three most prominent peaks looked like women's breasts."

I thought that trapper must have been pretty desperate because *I* couldn't see the comparison even if I stretched my imagination to the limit. Still, the mountains were alluring enough that I wanted to explore them. It was more than a want, actually. They possessed a magnetism that tugged at me every time I looked at them. I had to force my eyes away to views that were closer to home, views like our garden with it's rapidly growing potatoes, tomatoes, carrots and beets. I was particularly interested in the tomatoes—a vegetable I'd never tasted before.

"If you don't like 'em, you can always use the juice to get rid of skunk smell if you're unlucky enough to get downwind of one," Bob told us the day we found our first little fruit. "Just bathe in it." If it was strong enough to get rid of skunk scent would the thing be decent to eat? He seemed to think so but sometimes I suspected he was pulling a snipe hunt on me.

CHAPTER FOURTEEN

The tomatoes were actually pretty good and Bob was a valuable neighbor, even if his daughter was a pain. We found we could always count on him for tips that helped us along.

"There's a lot of aspen timber over near Ashton," Bob mentioned one day when haying was nearly finished and he'd stopped in to visit. "You oughta be getting out firewood purdy quick."

"I was going to ask you about that," Alma answered. "We should be ready to head for the timber in a couple of days."

"There's a bunch of neighbors goes up and works together. Some are already there. I'll go up with you when you're ready. We'll camp 'n' cut for a week or more before we start hauling. The wimmin do the cooking for everybody that's cutting. My boy an' girl can do your chores along with ours while we're gone."

"Sounds good to me," Alma made the decision for the two of us since I, because Emma-Jane was on the prowl, had disappeared. Alma knew about the hole I'd dug in the backside of one of our haystacks. It was where I hid if I was already outside when she came. For once he hadn't said anything.

"That should work out fine," he told Bob. "Thanks so much."

"Think nothing of it." Bob, with surprising agility considering his bulk, swung onto his fat bay stallion. "Come on, girl!" he bellowed at his daughter as he headed down the lane. "Let's git for home."

"You can come out, now." Alma chuckled once Bob and Emma-Jane were out of sight. I pushed my way out of the haystack and carefully covered my hole.

"That girl's got to be the most annoying creature God ever created!" I groused. "What's old Bob up to?"

"Came to invite us to a neighborhood wood-gathering in Ashton." Alma said. "We'll go up next week, share a tent with him, and...."

"Emma-Jane? Absolutely not! There's nothing on God's green earth that'll get me near that girl. You go. I'll stay and do chores."

"But Nephi, I'll bet she can cook up a storm. If you don't believe me, just look at old Bob's middle. And a warm armful like her on a cold winter's night would help liven things up for you. Just think. You could listen to that sweet voice every day, calling you whenever she couldn't find you, and...."

"Sure thing! That girl's spent so many days with her sheep, she smells like one. Her voice sounds like one too—always bleating. She's so dirty it's caked on and I don't think she's combed her hair in the last five years. If you're so desperate for a woman, *you* go after her! I'm not interested. I'll stay home and do the chores. You can go cuddle Miss Ewe."

"Actually," Alma laughed, "she and her brother are staying home and doing our chores as well as theirs. You can come in peace. We'll need you, for sure."

We went. We worked. And we heard whispers about it the rest of the time we lived on the Egin bench.

"Have you ever seen the likes of them Moulton boys? They're up a good hour before anyone else. They were cuttin' a-fore the rest of us was even out of bed."

"A body can't sleep with those Moultons around. It wasn't decent light, yet, and they was out dropping trees. Ever morning. And they was the last ones to quit at night, too. Made the rest of us tired just watching them."

Neither Alma nor I could see any reason to spend half of the day in bed. Eight a.m. on the job was for folks who didn't know how to peel the bed off their backs at five.

With the wood supply in, Bob helped us get spruce logs for the barn. Then the group of neighbors we'd helped with wood gathering came by for a 'barn-raising'. I was so nervous about having Emma-Jane around all day that I think I jumped every time I heard a female voice but, to my relief, the neighbor's wives kept her so busy helping prepare and serve food that she wasn't a bother.

By the time the last person left that night we'd doubled the size of our barn, put on a decent roof, partitioned off a granary, and turned a small corner into a chicken coop. Even the younger boys were roped into insulating the inside of the coop with a heavy daubing of mud mixed with grass.

Alma and I were shingling the cabin roof by the time the range pasture was gone and the sheep had to be returned to home pastures. With more time on her hands, Emma-Jane pestered us constantly. I sure got tired of hiding in the haystack while Alma fielded her never-ending invitations to Emma-cooked meals at Bob's house.

"I cook real good," she'd insist.

"I'm sure you do," Alma would reply, "and I thank you kindly but we're committed tonight." Tongue in cheek, Alma always faithfully relayed the information to me—as if I really wanted to know.

Finally, frustrated at my continual 'absence' in the daytime, Emma-Jane began rising extra early in the morning and appearing while I was cooking breakfast. She'd sneak across our porch so quietly I couldn't hear her.

"I was jest out fer a little walk," she explained the first morning she knocked on our door before dawn, her high-pitched, nasally voice whining. "It got cold. Could I get warm by yer stove?"

I was seething inside, but I couldn't very well turn her away. Within the week, her pre-dawn appearance on our doorstep was a regular occurrence and I started plotting revenge.

"I want the lambskin when we butcher," I told Alma.

"What for?"

"Never mind." I wasn't about to tell him.

Wherever I went during the next few days, my rifle and a pitchfork were never far away. In the evening hours, after it was too dark to work outside, I kept myself busy.

Alma watched with interest when I brought green willow shafts in and started to bend and weave them. Slowly a form took shape with a neck, legs and an open body. The evening we butchered the lamb, I took the lambskin and stretched it over my willow form, sewing the legs securely onto the frame.

"I didn't know you were so fond of sheep that you wanted to keep one inside," Alma commented, his lopsided smile quizzical. I didn't say a word. I had no intentions of letting him know, in advance, what I was planning.

With the 'lamb' finished, I started disappearing as soon as I'd fixed our supper, leaving Alma to eat alone, the expression on his face more puzzled every day. Finally I got what I wanted and appeared, one evening, smelling of skunk and grinning broadly.

"I need to borrow the lantern," I said as I picked up the 'lamb'.

"What are you up to now?" Alma demanded, following me out of the door. "Whew! That thing's ripe!"

"All the better. Now don't get down wind of this critter." I laid the 'lamb' on its side, picked up my pitchfork which cradled the skunk I'd just shot, and poked the carcass inside the cavity of the lamb's 'belly'. Making sure the cold evening breeze was blowing against my back, carrying the skunk scent away from me as much as possible, I quickly wrapped twine around and around the 'lamb' body to keep the dead skunk inside.

With the cavity tied closed, I picked up the 'lamb' with my pitchfork and carried it, at arm's length, out to the lane and down a little way toward Emma-Jane's home. There I propped it up and left it. Even with the lambskin coating, the smell was atrocious.

"If that doesn't take care of the problem of Miss Ewe, I don't know what will," I said as I walked around the house to the garden, Alma following at a cautious distance. I picked a hatful of ripe tomatoes, used them to scrub whatever skin was showing, rinsed off in water from the ditch that ran in front of the cabin, then shed my outer clothing on the porch outside the door and nonchalantly sauntered in for my supper.

Each morning, just before sunup, I removed the 'lamb' with my pitchfork and hid it at the far end of the pasture. Each evening it was returned to its spot by the roadside. To anyone walking down the lane in the dark, it smelled as if a live skunk was close-by.

Bob's daughter didn't disturb my breakfasts again all fall.

CHAPTER FIFTEEN

The pleasant days of bright blue skies, crisp sunshine and quiet breezes lulled Alma and me into thinking Indian summer would never end. We'd just begun building a derrick to transfer hay when our first Idaho winter whistled down the distant mountains, across the wastelands and over the little Snake River Valley farms along its path. Suddenly, shrieking like the very demons from hell, one blizzard after another tore at our farm, sending the stock crowding for shelter in the barn, our chickens huddled on their roosting pole, heads hidden beneath their wings, feathers fluffed for warmth, and me wishing I had their option.

The first storm began in the midnight hours of a late November day.

"Do you hear that?" The awe in Alma's voice reached through one of the most enjoyable dreams I'd ever had. Fishing pole in hand, I was standing on the bank of an unfamiliar, tree-lined channel of the Snake River where the fish-filled pool before me ran quiet and deep. Exposed tree roots curved out from the undercut bank then twisted back, casting their reflections in the water beneath. The contentment and sense of well-being I felt at the water's edge was something I'd never felt before—had never had time to feel.

"Mmmmm?" I was battled a wildly thrashing trout when Alma's voice reached me. Gradually the splashing of the fish on my hook changed to a howling noise.

"The wind," Alma said. "Listen to it!" The fish, the stream, the contentment and most of all the well-being were sucked away by reality as I opened my eyes.

"I hope that doesn't mean what I think it does. I'm going to look," Alma continued.

He sat up, lit the lantern on our bedside chair, and started for the door, lantern in hand. "Brrrr! There's even frost on the floor!" he exclaimed, lifting his feet high between steps. I laughed at his dancing in the cold.

An icy draft tore across the room when he cracked the door open, then slammed it shut. As he lifted the lantern higher, I could see a sifting of fine snow collecting on the window sill beside our bed and his footprints in the frost on the cabin floor.

"Hell's going to freeze over before morning," I said. "You'd better build up the fire." I laughed, again, as I watched him hurriedly stuff kindling wood into the stove, his red woolen underwear with the trapdoor seat brightened by the sudden flames. He didn't waste time getting back under our covers—where he promptly put his freezing feet on my warm ones.

"Hey!" I said. "Keep those ice blocks to yourself."

It was his turn to laugh.

Thinking the storm would blow itself out by morning, we drifted back to sleep, unworried. That was mistake number one.

Mistake number two came when Alma went out to begin chores, alone, at what we judged to be about daybreak. If anything, the storm was worse and he immediately became disoriented. By the time he stumbled back through the cabin door, his eyebrows and the beard he'd begun to grow were caked with snow, his entire body stiff with cold. His cheeks and nose were seriously white with frostbite. Exhausted and half-frozen, he slumped into a chair before the stove.

"Couldn't find the barn," he gasped. "Ended up face-first in that little ditch out front. If I hadn't fallen into it, I wouldn't have had any idea where I was and I probably wouldn't have found the cabin again."

I'd heard of people becoming disoriented in white-out blizzards and freezing to death just feet from their own doorsteps. The thought of it happening to Alma sent a shiver down my spine.

I scooped hands-full of snow off Alma's coat and cap and filled his hands.

"Hold this onto those cheeks so you can thaw yourself out slow," I ordered. "Your nose, too." Then, pulling my own heavy woolen pants and overcoat off their pegs on the wall, I began to dress for the out-of-doors.

"Where d'you think *you're* going?" Alma said.

"To do the chores."

"Are you crazy? You can't see anything out there. You'll get lost just like I did."

"Don't plan on it." I jammed on my cap, fastened it under my chin, then wrapped a long woolen scarf about my face, leaving only my eyes uncovered. We'd made enough mistakes. I wasn't going to make any more.

56

As I opened the door, I grabbed the heavy coil of hemp rope hanging from a peg on the wall—the rope Mother'd insisted we buy and I'd fought her about.

"You stay here and get warmed up," I said. "I'm going to establish a line between the cabin and the barn so this won't happen again. If I can't find the barn, at least I can get back home."

Next morning, I awoke to the pleasant smell and friendly crackle of bacon frying,

'Mother's up early,' I thought, groggily. 'Didn't call me to do chores, either. I wonder why?'

I wriggled deeper into the warmth of Alma's and my bed. But Alma wasn't there beside me.

Wait a minute. I shouldn't hear bacon splattering clear up in our attic bedroom. And if I'm in bed, where's Alma? My eyes flew open.

I wasn't in my home in Heber City. This was the cabin on the Egin bench.

The bed was by the cabin's stove and Alma was standing at the table, ingredients for hotcake batter spread out in front of him—eggs, flour, sugar, soda and our little crock of sour dough.

I frowned. "What's the bed doing here?" I asked.

"You don't remember?"

"Remember what?"

"Yesterday. The storm that's still going like there's no tomorrow. Me moving the bed over here when you came in so cold you couldn't even talk."

I thought for a moment.

"I went out and fed the stock. I was so cold I wasn't sure I'd make it back. And I couldn't open the door once I got to the porch. I don't remember anything after that."

"I heard you and let you in. You got the stock fed, then?" he asked as he cracked an egg into the bowl before him, then grunted as part of the shell fell in, too.

"Barely," I said.

"How'd you find the barn?" Alma shook his head. "How'd you make it back? A body couldn't see twelve inches through that storm let alone walk through it."

57

I watched as he awkwardly sprinkled two spoonfuls of sugar over his batter and started to measure the soda.

"Didn't try," I said as I slipped out of bed and began dressing. "I had the rope. I knew if I got lost all I had to do was follow it back home again. I tied one end around my waist and the other to the porch post. You didn't have a rope."

"No, but I couldn't stand up in this wind, either, and I didn't have the weight of the rope dragging me down." Alma walked over to the stove, smeared some bacon grease across the griddle he had heating, then poured four puddles of batter on top.

"Nobody could. I thought I was big enough no wind would ever take me down but I found out different. The minute I stepped off our porch it picked me up and slammed me into the closest snow drift."

"What'd you do?"

"Crawled."

"Wasn't easy crawling," Alma said. "Those drifts were already big before I went out."

"Floundering around was more like it," I said." All I could think was, '*Please don't change the direction of that wind.*' It was the only thing that kept me on course. You want to turn those hotcakes, now? They're ready."

I'd actually been praying but I wasn't going to tell my brother that. He probably figured it out for himself, anyway, but talking about deity was something I avoided. Just as I normally avoided talking *to* deity. It had to be a very special occasion .

"It's a miracle you made it," Alma tried to flip the hotcakes, landing one of them more on the stove than on the griddle.

'*I need to make him do more cooking,*' I thought but what I said was, "By the time I got to the corral I was thinking the same thing about you. You didn't have a rope."

"How'd you find the corral in the first place?" Alma scraped the hotcake batter off the stove, a look of pure disgust on his face.

"Calculated the direction the wind was coming from and made sure it kept hitting me from the same angle. I almost gave up," I admitted. "I only had a loop or two of the rope left and I was thinking of turning back when I bumped, head first, into one of the corral logs. I don't think I was ever so glad to find anything in my life. I knew we'd lose our animals if I didn't get them fed."

It was a morning I never wanted to repeat. Because the derrick wasn't finished, I'd carried the hay in armfuls from the stack-yard to the manger inside the barn—if I'd tried to pitch it over the fence into the corral it would have blown clean down to Utah. Our animals had no intentions of coming out into the corral to eat, anyway.

By the time I stumbled through the feeding I was so cold there was no feeling left in any part of my body. My steps were stiff and jerky like those of an old man and I knew what that meant. More than anything I wanted to stop but I didn't dare. I had to keep moving. Yet shuffling back towards the cabin was even harder than crawling out to the barn had been. My mitts were frozen so stiff I couldn't grasp the rope; all I could do was put my arm over it and follow it home. But was I ever grateful for that rope! It gave me the stability I needed to be able to stand in the storm. I don't think I would have made it if I'd been crawling.

More than anything I wanted to rest. To sleep. I was so tired. All I could think was, 'Keep moving, Nephi. Sleep means death.'

"I didn't think I'd see you again. I was really scared," Alma words startled me. I'd never heard my brother talk about being afraid, before. Not ever.

"After I got warmed up a little," he continued, "I put my snow clothes back on and went out to help but I couldn't see any sign of the rope. When I couldn't find it, I wasn't sure you'd managed to get it stretched out.

"I had no idea what direction to search in so I decided if you didn't make it through that storm, I wouldn't either. No purpose to be served in both of us freezing to death. I've never been long on prayer but I spent some serious time on my knees yesterday."

That was even more startling. I couldn't remember seeing Alma pray since we were little boys. Hadn't thought he even remembered how but I was grateful that he did.

"You don't think about what's happening or how close you are to death when you're in the middle of a storm like that," I said. "All I could think about, the whole time I was out there, was our animals and making sure they were cared for. That's what kept me going. I've never experienced such piercing cold."

"Too bad Emma-Jane wasn't there to warm you," Alma set a platter of hotcakes and fried eggs on the table I'd just finished setting.

"But since she wasn't, maybe you could have cuddled up to one of the sheep."

That winter brought sixty-four days of blizzard conditions—I kept track on a 'blizzard log' where I made a notch for each day it stormed. We got into the habit of eating and then drinking all the hot barley 'coffee' we could get down before going out into the weather. If there weren't screaming, ice-laden winds outside, it was paralyzingly cold. We were doing all we could, just to keep ourselves going.

After we ate and suited up for the storm that sixty-fifth day, I opened the cabin door expecting swirling snow. Instead, I was greeted by a soft, gentle warmth from a true southern chinook.

"Will you look at that!" I exclaimed.

"What?" Alma hurried to my side. As the wind hit his face he stepped back in shock then tore his face scarf and cap from his head. "Warm wind through my hair again. That's the most wonderful thing I've felt since I don't know when."

"Do you think it'll last?" I wondered.

It did.

The chinook stayed with us, melting the snow banks so quickly we could almost see them disappearing. The fields were soon covered with standing water that had no place to go because the ground was still frozen. The barnyard was a slushy mess, too, but we didn't care. Anything beat the winter we'd experienced.

Suddenly the chickens thawed out and began laying once more while Annie's cockerel-now-turned-rooster, crowed so much I seriously considered fricasseed chicken for Sunday dinner. Our milk cow, after a six-week vacation during the worst of the weather, dropped a healthy heifer calf and freshened again, producing enough milk for her calf and us, too.

"You know, barley coffee's alright in the worst of the cold," I said, smacking my lips over a cup of milk just from the cow—not even caring that it was still warm—"but nothing can beat fresh milk!" Alma was too busy drinking to answer me.

One by one, our ewes lambed—three of them dropping twins. Alma and I took turns staying up nights with the sheep until they were through lambing.

"Can you believe it?" Alma was jubilant the day the last ewe dropped her baby. "We didn't lose a one." I was relieved that we hadn't lost any but I hadn't changed my mind about sheep. They'd never be my reigning favorites.

I was a lot more enthusiastic about the cattle. All seven cows–the milk cow and last year's six yearling heifers–dropped heifer calves. I wanted to plate our young bull with gold. If he kept siring female calves, we'd have a decent-sized herd in no time. In my mind's eye I could see us buying some of the surrounding acreage just so we could raise the extra hay we'd need.

Alma, of course, looked at things a little differently.

"I'll soon be able to marry Maude," he said as we turned the last cow to calve out into the pasture with the rest of our little herd. I wasn't excited about the thought but I *was* proud of our accomplishments. We'd worked hard and it showed.

Life was looking really good. The first crop of hay was nearly ready to cut, and the grain and garden were making a fine showing when Father's letter came in early-mid June.

"Dear Sons;" it said.

I hope you are doing well and weathered the winter. Maude's uncle was down. Said it was a difficult one for your area.

It was a hard winter for your Aunt Mary's family, too. Franz was dragged by a wild horse in early March and hurt quite badly. It will be months before he'll be out of bed. Not long afterwards, Lyle fell on the ice. She's doing very poorly as well. The doctor isn't sure what her injuries are but it looks like her back might be broken. Your Aunt Mary needs a different home where she can care for Franz and Lyle more easily. I know it will be difficult for you to repay us but her needs are the most important right now and Mother and I will have to help her. Please send the money as soon as you can arrange for the sale of your farm.

As ever,
Your father
P.S. Did you hear Maude eloped the last end of January? Some traveling peddler from down south, we heard. I guess she's living in Cedar City now.

CHAPTER SIXTEEN
AUGUST 1905
DARBY, IDAHO

"Alma," I said as I lifted my pitchfork out of the parched, yellowish pile of alfalfa on our wagon and tossed a crackling forkful onto the small stack by our corral fence, "you know the leaves are falling off the stems of this hay. It's nearly worthless for feed."

"I know." Alma sighed as he bent to unhook Sleek and Sassy from our hay wagon. "Another year without enough water. If folks had built a reservoir and canals we'd be alright but spring runoff and summer rains aren't cutting it." He led our team to the tack shed where he started to unharness them. I continued pitching hay.

"What do you think we should do?" I asked.

"I don't know." Alma's voice sounded as discouraged as I felt. "I can't see us staying here. We need to move on."

"I'd agree with that," I said. "Where do you think we should go?"

"Not back to Utah."

"Definitely not." Go back to Utah with our tails between our legs? I'd starve first.

"I suppose we could look for a place near Ashton," Alma said.

Closer to the farm we lost? Didn't want the memories. But I wasn't going to say so. No sense stirring anything up.

"There's no irrigation system up there, either," I said.

"Maybe we should sell the cattle and take the horses out to Lewiston—use Sleek and Sassy to snake out logs in a lumber camp."

I stopped pitching hay and stared at my brother. No matter how discouraging these past two years had been, he'd never mentioned giving up. Until now. If he left, what would I do? Farming and raising stock were all I knew—all I wanted to know.

But if he wanted to quit, did I have the right to stop him?

"You can take the team and Darky if you want," I said, slowly. "I'll keep Star and hire out as a cowpuncher somewhere. I can't imagine doing anything else but working with stock."

"It was just an idea," Alma defended himself. "I don't want to do anything else, either, but I thought you might be ready for a change."

62

A change, yes. Where Salem produced several large stacks from a smaller amount of land, Darby yielded two miserly ones. Last year we'd sold off all our sheep—no huge loss there—because there wasn't enough hay and no money to buy any. We'd sold all our calves, too, so we could buy flour, sugar and such for ourselves, and seed for this summer. Even so we'd run out of feed in March. We'd had to hire ourselves out to Uncle George, who ran a feed lot of sorts, in return for him feeding our stock until spring.

"I'm tired of being hungry," I said.

But where could we go? Here it was, mid-August. Spring run-off had petered out weeks ago and there had been no summer rain. The hay was ruined. And we had no way to pay for the food Alma and I needed for the months ahead. If we could sell our Darby farm we'd have enough to buy winter staples—flour, sugar, baking powder, potatoes—but we'd still need a roof over our heads. I felt like I was staring into a black tunnel with no light at the end. If there was such a thing as light.

"Uncle Charles doesn't get away from his farm work all that often but maybe he'll have some ideas," Alma suggested. "We could ask him tonight."

The heavy weight of discouragement lifted slightly. I'd forgotten about Aunt Rhody inviting us for supper as soon as our hay was in. I could certainly do with her cooking after a day like today. Maybe there was a little glimmer of light.

I pitched the last forkful of hay over the fence.

"I'd forgotten we were invited," I said, standing my pitchfork in a corner of the tack shed. "I'm going to take a bath. We'll need to get there early enough for Aunt Rhody to throw some extra spuds in the pot."

"I'll be right behind you as soon as I bring Darky and Star in." Rope in one hand, a small pan of oats in the other, Alma strode out towards the lone spruce at the far end of the pasture where Darky and Star were huddled, nose to tail, busily switching each other for relief from the heat and flies. I thought of our horses, fondly, as I walked to the cabin.

Darky, a sleek black gelding, was Alma's. Star, a red chestnut mare with a large white star-shaped patch on her forehead and a white stocking on her right front leg, belonged to me.

Darky was a sedate, calm animal. He made a great hunting horse because a man could fire a rifle from his back and he wouldn't even flinch.

Star, on the other hand, was high-strung and spooked easily. Still fairly young and very strong, she had good endurance as a pack animal but a man needed to pay attention when he was riding her. Let a grasshopper click its wings as it flew by and she was just as likely to switch ends and head for Arab. How many times had she unloaded me when I'd started daydreaming? I quit counting long ago. She could be a royal pain but I still liked her. She was quick and her endurance was phenomenal. Star was definitely the horse for a long fast ride.

CHAPTER SEVENTEEN

By the time Alma caught our saddle horses, grained them and joined me, I'd hauled enough water from the well to fill the washtub, wedged it between our bed and the table, and was nearly finished scrubbing myself.

"You're as pink as a baby," Alma observed, seeing how hard I was scrubbing. "And you're going to have fun getting a comb through that mop of yours."

"Well, at least it's clean," I spluttered as I poured a bucket of cold well-water over my head. "Whew! Nothing like cold water to wake a fellow up."

Alma grimaced. "Even if it's hot outside, I still prefer a warm bath."

"I've heard a daily dip in a cold creek is good for the constitution. Maybe that's what yours needs." I stepped out onto the split-log floor and started drying myself.

"Maybe not, too. *You* can do it if you want but I'm not interested."

I chuckled until I tried to yank our comb through my hair. My dark waves had a definite mind of their own and weren't planning to lie flat any time soon.

"Better stick some bear grease on that tousle-top," Alma drawled as he stripped and stepped into the tub.

"Sure. And have Aunt Rhody run me out of the house? Nobody could stand to have me in the kitchen, let alone sit next to me at the table."

Alma laughed as he rubbed the bar of soap over his hair. "Seems you're awfully fussy about smelling good lately. You aren't setting your cap for Aunt Rhoda's hired girl, are you?" he asked.

I glanced at him. It was the first time since Maude that he'd mentioned anything about a girl. On the one hand, maybe he was coming out of the blue mood he'd been in for the better part of two years. On the other hand, maybe it meant he was thinking of looking, again, for himself. Better ignore that idea. Females weren't welcome on our spread. We had other things to think about.

"Not me. Just because I don't want to be run off before I get a taste of Aunt Rhody's good cooking doesn't mean anything except

65

that I'm tired of my own." I said as I finally managed to get the comb through my hair. "Stew got old six years ago."

"Six years ago we were still at home and hadn't even thought of leaving - *or* of eating stew every day," Alma poured a bucket of fresh water over his head. "We still had Mother's good cooking then."

"That's my point." I pulled on one of my high-topped work shoes and began tightening the laces. "I'm so sick of stew it seems like six years, but there isn't time to cook anything else. I don't know about you but I'm really looking forward to supper tonight."

"No more than me, my man. No more than me." Alma stood up and reached for the rough huck washcloth I'd left on the back of the chair that held his only change of clothing. "I'll tell you what, though," he continued, "I never *could* see how Uncle Charles could stay so scrawny with food like Aunt Rhoda's in the house. You'd think he'd be shaped a little more like her. Why she's a regular little five by five."

"Don't you know why there's such a difference?" Poker faced, I finished tying my other shoe and stood up to shake the legs of my pants down over my lace-up shoe tops.

Alma's glanced at me, paused, then sighed. "Ok, I'll bite," he said.

"It's simple. Aunt Rhody has to make sure her food's good enough to set on the table and by the time she's finished tasting everything down to the cream puffs there's nothing left for him."

"Nephi, that's not nice," Alma laughed.

"Prove it's not true," I challenged him. "Just look at her. Even with all those children to feed she still has to turn sideways to get through the door, while he's so skinny if you turned *him* sideways the only parts of him that would cast a shadow would be his hair, his nose and his mustache.

"You know as well as I do the minute grace is said, those kids attack everything in sight. You have to be quick or you come away hungry, and Uncle Charles isn't slow. But Aunt Rhody's so big it doesn't take much to figure she's doing a hefty amount of sampling before she ever sets it on. Probably knows that's the only way she'll get anything with that brood of hers."

"They sure don't eat like we did at Mother's," Alma shook his head, smiling.

I reached to take my coat down from a peg on the wall. Slinging it over one shoulder, I strode, jauntily, out of the door. "No, they don't," I agreed. "Well, I'm off to saddle the horses while you finish dandying up."

It was true. Aunt Rhoda's family didn't eat like we ate at home. I thought of it as I picked up the curry comb and brush from their shelf just inside the tack shed door. In fact, nothing in Aunt Rhoda's home was like the home I'd grown up in. I began currying Darky vigorously, following each stroke of the comb with one from the brush.

Mother's home was spotless. Her china shone. Her silver gleamed. Her dining table was polished daily and set, fresh, after each meal with a clean cloth—always damask—and glistening tableware. Then it was covered by another cloth so when it was time for the next meal, all Mother had to do was remove the top cloth and the table was ready.

With Darky brushed as shiny as my mother's table, I turned my attention to Star. Star was jumpy and the best I could hope for was a lick and a promise over her shaggy red coat. Star's hair was more like Aunt Rhody's table—lucky if it got wiped down once a week. That table had never seen a cloth, let alone a damask one. And Rhody's tableware was chipped and mis-matched.

No-one in Mother's home had ever been allowed to 'dig in'. We quietly asked for what we wanted. Napkins were used. Spills and sloppy eating were not tolerated and children were to be seen but not heard. Mealtime was for adult conversation.

By contrast, Aunt Rhody, with an indulgent smile on her round face and the latest baby bouncing on her ample knee, watched her youngsters swarm to the table like bees buzzing around a new honey tree. Her cardinal rule, if she even had one, was *"One foot on the floor at all times."* If that foot was actually a chair leg, so be it.

I liked the relaxed, easy-going atmosphere of Rhoda Moulton's home. Since it was unfinished—and probably always would be—the house, itself, was a far cry from being as shining prissy-clean as my mother's home. Aunt Rhody's tribe of energetic children frequently looked like they'd missed a scrubbing or two, as well. But what if a man had to look out for his own interests at her

67

table? The atmosphere was warm, easy and jovial—to tell the truth, down right noisy—and the food was just as excellent as Mother's.

Besides, to Aunt Rhody every child was a treasure to be doted upon—even if that child had long since left childhood behind. I wouldn't have admitted it to anyone but I didn't mind a little of her sympathetic concern once in a while. It had taken some of the sting from these last two years and I blessed her for it.

What a let-down the Darby years had been after that year on the Salem farm. I stopped trying to catch Star with the curry comb and leaned on the top pole of the corral fence, looking sadly at our puny hay stacks. By the time we'd finished haying in nineteen-two we'd had several large stacks put up and were ready to get our wood supply for the winter.

Thinking of the camaraderie I'd felt at that wood-gathering, I smiled as I ducked my head and stepped into the tiny tack shed to get Alma's saddle. Straightening up in the shed's cramped quarters, I struck my head a sharp, glancing blow on the center beam of the roof.

"Gosh darn it!" That shed would have made a better doll house. It sure wasn't built for a person with Alma's or my height. Now what we'd had in Salem.... One memory led to another until I found myself chuckling over how I'd resolved the Emma-Jane affair.

"What's so funny?" Alma asked as he came out of our tiny cabin. "I didn't miss any parts when I scrubbed, did I?" He removed his flat-brimmed hat and turned to display his neck and ears.

"You're fine," I answered. "I was just thinking."

"Share. I could stand something funny."

But I wasn't about to tell him. I didn't want to stir up his memories of the Salem farm and losing Maude.

He brought the subject up anyway.

"Doesn't look much like our place in Salem, does it?" He said as he mounted Darky, then gazed around our farmyard.'

"No, not much."

I could have said a lot more.

I could have compared our tiny cabin here with the cabin on the Egin bench. I'd thought that one was small until we moved to Darby. At least our Salem home had enough room to set the washtub in the middle of the floor when we wanted a bath.

I could have compared the healthy, deep green Egin fields with these sun-scorched yellow ones. I could have compared this farmyard to the one we'd left behind . . . but what was the use? There were no comparisons so I turned my horse away from the corral and started down the dry, dusty road toward Chapin.

CHAPTER EIGHTEEN

"I hear there's a homestead relinquishment over in the Jackson Hole country," Uncle Charles crossed his feet and tilted his chair back against the dining room wall, his hands behind his neck, fingers interlaced. "Couple fellows by the name of Crane came by here on their way out of the Hole the other day. Said they were giving up."

The light from the dying August sun, slanting through the bay window across the room, cast a soft rosy glow over the figures seated, still, around his large table. There was Uncle Charles, his short, spare frame almost overpowered by his mane of wiry brown hair, his large nose and his thick, flowing mustache. On either side of him were my cousins, T.A., Wally and John, while Alma and I sat across the table. The younger children had long since scampered outside.

"You can't be suggesting the boys go over to Jackson's Hole!" Aunt Rhoda cried, her normally cheerful, smiling face suddenly aghast. The stack of dirty plates in her plump hands made a clattering exclamation point as she set them abruptly on the table. "That's wild country over there, Charles, and you know it. It's full of horse thieves, murderers and cut-throats and it's no place for the boys to be going. Besides, it's nothing but desert–all those sage flats." Her little button nose wrinkled in contempt.

"If they couldn't make a go of it here for lack of water, how're they supposed to succeed in a dry, uncivilized place like that? The very thought of it!" She picked the plates up, once more, and stomped angrily off to her steaming dishpan, muttering something about men and their totally impractical ideas.

I was shocked. I'd never seen my easy-going aunt upset before.

"There's a canal for water so it isn't drought that's stopped the Cranes." Uncle Charles said. "They both got sick. Couldn't work enough to make a go of it and it *is* hard work, homesteading. Takes a strong body, a passel of grit and a lot of determination. I hate to see you boys saddle yourselves with a homestead, too, but if that's what you want it's there, is all I'm saying."

Alma and I exchanged glances and I leaned forward. "You *know* we've always wanted to homestead, Uncle Charles—" I said, "to have something we carved out ourselves, built from scratch."

70

"It's one thing to start a homestead," Uncle Charles cautioned. Sitting upright once more, he leaned his elbows on the table and rested his chin in his hands, gazing at us soberly. "It's another thing to prove up on it. I'm not saying it can't be done. It just takes everything you've got for a few years. You won't have a life other than work. The land will own you forty hours out of the day.

"You boys are workers, though, and if anybody could make a go of it, you could. But are you sure this is what you want to do? I know your place in Darby hasn't worked out the way you hoped but you might find something better here in the Basin. The winters are easier and the summers are longer than over in the Hole, that's for sure."

"We won't even realize what we spent on our place when we sell it." Alma sat back slowly, crossing his feet at the ankles and folding his arms tight across his chest. "The only way for us to have something of our own is to homestead and there's nothing left to choose from in this area. At least nothing that has water you can count on. Homesteading's a lot of work, yes, but we're not afraid to work."

"That's for sure!" our cousin, John, exclaimed. "I've never seen the likes of you two."

I squirmed. "I like to work. No use laying around. As long as there's something to do, a man needs to get busy and get it done."

"Well, one thing's certain. You boys have gave all there was to give to your place in Darby. We'll miss having you around." Uncle Charles' generous praise meant more than I could have said.

"Are you positive there isn't anything you'd like here in the Basin?" John's voice was wistful. Our mutual love of a good joke had become a strong bond between him and me. Move to Jackson Hole and we might get to see each other once a year if we were lucky.

Alma shook his head. "The water's too iffy in Darby and there's nothing better left in the Basin. We want to look somewhere else."

"I'd have to agree. I've thought of homesteading over in the Hole, myself." T.A. glanced at his mother's broad back—suddenly rigid in front of her dishpan—his eyes twinkling.

"Thomas Alma Moulton, you will not even **consider** such an idea!" Her voice was high pitched—bordering on sudden hysteria. "It's completely out of the question. Why, I'd no sooner see you go over there than you'd be strangled in your bed by one of those elk poaching cutthroats!"

"You mean Binkley and Isobel?" Wally asked, straight faced. "They don't strangle people, Ma, they shoot 'em. It's really an easy way to go. Those old boys can't afford to waste bullets so they've learned to shoot straight. You wouldn't have to worry about any of us suffering."

"Wallace!"

"Now, boys," Uncle Charles stepped in. "You leave your mother alone. If Alma and Nephi want to look at something in the Hole, let them, Rhody. They've been on their own long enough to know what they're doing." He turned back to us. "If we can help you boys, just let us know. We're more than happy to do it." He pushed his chair back from the table, signaling the evening's conversation had nearly ended.

"Go ahead and look around over there," he encouraged. "If you like it and you think you can handle it, more power to you. If not, there are other places to go. A lot of the west is still wide open and available. You need to get looking, though. If you take the Cranes' relinquishment you'll not want to move until spring because they didn't raise a crop this year. But if you're going somewhere's else, you'll probably need to get settled pretty soon so's you can be ready for winter.

"If things are in order at your place, you might want to spend the night here, tonight, and ride on over to the Hole tomorrow. We could spare you a couple days' worth of grub and it'd cut miles off your trip if you went up Fox Creek and through Death Canyon instead of over the Pass.

"That's the route the Cranes used coming out. Said the major road going north through Jackson Hole went right by their cabin. I'm sure if you follow that road you'll find folks who can tell you just where their homestead is."

"Did you see the look on Aunt Rhody's face when Wally started talking about Binkley and Isobel?" I couldn't help chuckling as Alma and I stretched out on the bedrolls Aunt Rhody provided. "I thought she was going to choke!"

"Not much chance we'd ever see them. The last time we were here Wally told me that Jackson Hole folks were fed up with the

72

slaughter. They were planning to run those men out of the Hole. Probably already have by now."

We'd heard gossip about elk poaching in the Hole but we'd been too busy to pay much attention. Besides, who in their right mind would kill an elk just to pull two teeth from its head and leave the rest of the carcass to rot? And why would the Elks Lodge want those teeth for talismans, anyway? If half what we'd heard was true I'd have been surprised.

Odd, though, that Uncle Charles' family seemed to believe every word. It wasn't like them to be so gullible. Oh well. I rolled over, closed my eyes, and counted elk running up a sparsely-wooded hillside until I fell asleep in the warm mid-August moonlight.

CHAPTER NINETEEN

Fox Creek Pass was a steep trail on a heavily wooded hillside, above a creek that was completely hidden by tall, thick willows. It wasn't my reining favorite place to be.

Needing meat and too broke to butcher one of our own animals, we'd hunted on Fox Creek the fall of '04. Alma was riding Darky that day and I'd borrowed Uncle Charles' lazy old horse, Dan. The pack saddle with all our gear was on Star, who we left tied to a tree at the bottom of the Pass.

I'd spotted a fat bull elk near the creek about halfway up the mountain and brought him down with my Winchester. Alma was quicker than me at skinning so I left him at it and went to fetch Star. Dan and Star were picking their way over the boulders and fallen logs littering the hillside between the trail and down where Alma was working, when suddenly all three horses became spooked. For Star, being jittery was a daily occurrence. For Darky, it was unusual. But for Dan to be snorting and dancing about was unheard of.

"Do you see anything?" Alma asked me, reaching for Darky's reins. I looked around but the timber on the south side of the creek was so dense I couldn't see a thing. Nothing on the north side, either. And no movement in the willows along the creek bed.

"Not a thing," I said. I had reached out to pat Star, trying to calm her, when a deep roar echoed up out of the creek bottoms. In a flash Star was gone. Alma dropped his knife and leaped onto Darky while Uncle Charles' old horse reared, nearly dumping me in the creek.

Both horses were instantly on a dead run, Alma and me pulling leather for all we were worth. Across the creek they flew, lunging over logs and rocky outcroppings as they struggled up the rugged hillside to the trail, then tore down it towards the Basin, bucking and jumping all the way. It was the most harrowing ride I ever took.

We were nearing the flat lands before we were able to slow our terrified horses. We'd seen camp gear from Star's packsaddle strewn all along the trail but the horse was nowhere in sight. Eventually we found her at home, breathing heavily, trembling, her packsaddle completely empty. I felt about as breathless and empty, myself.

Although we went back the next day, we never found all of our gear. What we lost probably rolled down the mountainside when it came off her saddle. The elk carcass was gone too—a clear trail showing where it had been dragged through the willows and up the hill on the south side of the creek. Alma's knife was missing as well—probably still in the elk.

It had to have been a huge grizzly to have dragged such a big carcass up that steep hillside. I wasn't inclined to follow his trail just to find out, though. Hopefully he swallowed the knife when he ate my elk.

Later in the fall Alma shot a moose closer to home. The flavor was much gamier than elk and the meat was unbelievably tough.

"My jaws are getting so strong from chewing on this moose meat I think I could beat that grizzly in a fair fight - so long as the grizz had it's paws tied behind its back!" I told Alma one night. It didn't matter how I tried to cook it, that moose came out as tough as the soles of my work boots. But it was food.

Now, as I rode up that too familiar pass I kept a watchful eye. Star was about as tense, frequently tossing her head and prancing sideways as we climbed the trail. If we hadn't been in the lead, I think she would have whirled and bolted back to Darby.

"Think I'll keep my gun out," I said, starting to ease my Winchester out of its scabbard as we neared the place where I'd shot the elk.

"You even cock that thing and Star'll unload you before you can pull the trigger. Better let me handle any shooting if it comes to that. You just be ready for a wild ride."

Did Alma think I couldn't take care of myself? I was a grown man, wasn't I? Even more irritating, though, I knew he was right. You couldn't shoot off of Star. But why did he have to remind me? You'd think I was a little kid again. His comment was down right uncalled-for.

I seethed all the way up the mountainside. By the time we got to the top of the pass I was so mad I would have left my brother and gone off by myself if there'd been anywhere to go. Unfortunately, the only choices were to ride straight ahead or go back to Darby and I wasn't going back to Darby.

But did I really want to go to the Hole? What if Aunt Rhoda was right? What if we couldn't make it here, either? Then where could we go?

I stewed about that all the way down through Death Canyon's steep alpine meadows, vibrant with paint brush, bluebells and columbine and framed by sheer purple-grey cliffs on either side. Even their dense color, as the thick carpet of flowers waved in the fresh mountain breeze, didn't penetrate my gloom.

Nor did the scene of the Hole that opened up when we rounded a bend in the canyon. Sure enough, Aunt Rhoda was right. Desert. Flat. Sage land. (The greenness of the little farms that dotted the sage like patches in one of Mother's patchwork quilts didn't even register.) Was I supposed to grub sage for the rest of my life? And where was that famous canal Uncle Charles talked about? On the bench that stretched south of the long butte before us? Was I supposed to believe that water flowed uphill?

Desert. I've had my fill of desert in Darby. Why are we wasting our time coming here? If Alma thinks he's dragging me into this God-forsaken country to grub sage and starve he'll find me kicking and screaming the whole way. Then I'll bail out and run.

I settled into a serious sulk as we rounded Phelps Lake and entered the forest beyond. Not even when Alma discovered a huckleberry patch along the trail—and huckleberries were almost my favorite fruit—did I climb out of my dungeon.

"Come on, Nephi," Alma coaxed as he dismounted Darky. "Let's have berries with our dinner." But I stayed on Star.

If Alma thinks a patch of huckleberries will make this desert hell-hole more hospitable, let him think it. I'm not that dumb.

CHAPTER TWENTY

It was evening by the time we reached the Snake River and nearly sundown before we'd located a crossing

"Which way should we go?" Alma asked when we finally found the wagon-track road in the forested river bottoms on the other side. "North or south?" Uncle Charles hadn't had any specific directions to give us.

I shrugged, looking first one way and then the other. There wasn't much to see—only cottonwood trees, a spruce or two and underbrush. Not a cabin in sight.

"Uncle Charles said something about the Cranes riding 'up' the road, across the river, and then through Death Canyon and over Fox Creek Pass," Alma continued. "Up generally means north, but where did they ford the river's the question. Shall we flip a coin? I think I have a penny in my pocket." If he did, he'd been holding out on me. I'd thought our cash was completely gone.

"Come on, Nephi. We're in this together and I'm asking for your thoughts," he went on when I remained silent.

"I don't have any. I don't know any more than you do," I said.

"Well, there's probably someone living along here somewhere. I say we go south and ask the first person we see."

We went south.

We didn't find a single cabin.

The sun went down.

Twilight deepened. Before long it would be dark and we'd be stranded out here in the middle of nowhere at the mercy of Aunt Rhoda's cutthroats and murderers. Would our parents even hear of our fate? Would Uncle Charles, John, Wally and T.A. come looking for us?

By the time we finally saw a horseman approaching, I was ready to wheel my horse and make a mad dash back to Idaho. Probably would have if he'd had a gun.

He was an older fellow, smaller than either my brother or me, mounted on a nice-looking black gelding and leading a large mule. The flat-brimmed felt hat perched over his head of thick dark hair, his well-worn work clothes and his deeply tanned skin all indicated an outdoorsman. But his dark eyes crinkled and I could see a genuine smile under his soup-strainer mustache when he reined in his mount and spoke a friendly hello.

"Good evening,' Alma replied. "Do you live around here?"

"Down the road a piece," he said, tipping his head in the direction he'd come. "Jack Grey." He offered his hand.

"Alma Moulton. And my brother, Nephi. We're looking for the Crane brothers' homestead. Would you happen to know where it is?"

"Yes, but you won't find them at home. They relinquished the place and left the valley a week or two ago," Jack told him.

"We heard about that. Thought we might be interested in taking over their relinquishment but we don't know where to find it."

"Ahhh." Jack smiled again. "Then I'd be your neighbor to the south. You'd be getting a good piece of property, probably the best in Zenith." He was a chatty fellow.

"That's the name of our community," he continued. "The Cranes had a field cleared up on the flats, a meadow down below the hill and good shelter from the winter storms here in the river bottoms.

"If you want to take it on you'll need to get settled as quick as possible, though. All the neighbors helped irrigate this summer since Jim and Fred were too sick to do much, themselves, but we haven't had time to cut their hay."

"There's hay?" Alma said. I wanted to ask if it was green or yellow but I didn't want to appear rude.

"Yes, It's not a big crop but it's decent. The alfalfa's probably two-and-a-half feet high."

Thirty inches. That beat what we'd had in Darby—our hay hadn't topped twenty inches anywhere in our field.

"How many acres ?" Alma wanted to know.

"Oh, I'd guess thirty or maybe thirty five," Jack said. "It's not a lot but it was a beginning for them." He squinted at the darkening sky above the tree tops, then changed conversational directions. "I'd better get goin'. I gotta deliver this mule up to Bill Menor and I want to get home sometime before midnight."

"Does Bill live far away?" Alma asked. So far, we hadn't seen any indication there was anyone living along this road.

"He's the fellow that ran the ferry you come across."

I blinked in surprise. "There's a ferry? That would have been handy."

"Don't tell me you rode across the river!" Jack exclaimed.

"Didn't know there was a ferry," Alma said. I could have added we wouldn't have had the money, anyway, but I didn't.

"Then you haven't met Bill yet." I could see we weren't going anywhere soon as Jack settled back in his saddle. "The ferry's about three more miles farther up," he said. "You'll want to take it across next time. You'll like Bill. He's got wit.

"Last time I was up there he was cartin' some eastern dude woman across the river, along with me and some other fellas. Guess she didn't think too much of all the sagebrush she'd seen. (I wondered if Aunt Rhody had been over here, posing as an easterner.) "Anyhow she asked old Bill what farmers raised in the valley an' he come back with 'Kids and hell and plenty of both!'" Jack chortled. "Sure shut her up in a hurry."

Alma laughed and I grinned. I wasn't too interested in raising kids but if I decided to stay in Jackson Hole I knew I could contribute something worthwhile to the hell-raising part.

"Well, it's late enough it's gonna be dead dark before you get to the Cranes' place," Jack said. "I better quit flapping my jaws and let you go. As it is, you'll have to use your ears to find the cabin."

I wondered what that had to do with anything but I didn't want to ask. Alma looked puzzled too.

"There's a pond just before you get there," Jack explained. "It's off to the left of the road, drains by a creek into another pond on the right. There's frogs all over the place and you'll hear them, easy, before you get so close they quit croaking.

"Once you cross that little creek you'll want to pay attention. Soon as you ride down into a small dip in the road, turn right and follow it. Cabin'll be on the right under a big spruce tree. It's the only spruce close so if you watch the tops of the trees against the stars you'll find it. Won't be too much moon tonight but the stars'll be bright."

"Frogs, creek, dip, turn right, spruce on the right." Alma repeated, motioning the turns with his hand as he committed Jack's directions to memory. I already had it memorized.

"Yeah. The frogs'll get you there–and if you get into a second creek you've gone one dip too far. You'll need to turn around and go back. The two creeks aren't very far apart," Jack said as he touched

79

his heels to his horse's flanks. "Come palaver with me when you're through lookin' around tomorrow. I'm just down the road a piece."

"Thanks again," Alma said. "We'll do that." I wondered why he wanted to palaver when we had other, more important business. Sometimes it didn't seem like my brother was long on serious thought.

CHAPTER TWENTY-ONE

We found the frogs—couldn't miss them—and eventually the cabin. As Jack Grey'd said, by then it was dead dark—August-warm with the dim shadow of a crescent moon and a million stars in the sky. Only a quiet breeze whispering through the trees and the occasional yip of a young coyote broke the general night stillness. That, and the frogs, and the constant murmur of the Snake River in the background.

"Where's that candle Aunt Rhoda sent with us?" Alma asked as we unsaddled our horses and tied each one's hackamore rope to a sapling.

"I have it here." I untied my bedroll, then fished around in my saddlebags until I found the candle and matches she'd thoughtfully provided. There seemed to be plenty of cobble rocks around. I picked up the next one I stubbed my toe on, struck the match against it, and lit the candle. I was closer to the cabin than I'd thought—almost hard against the door. I opened it and stepped inside.

The cabin walls were Engelmann spruce; dusty bark still on the logs. *Place needs scrubbing*, I thought as I looked around. But it was bigger than our cabin in Darby. Partially furnished, too.

"There's both a fireplace and a cookstove," Alma exclaimed as he followed me inside. "It'll be a lot easier to keep this one warm than either of our other homes." Sourly, I noted the positive ownership in his words.

"Have you already decided to take this relinquishment?" I asked as I fetched my bedroll into the cabin. "I thought we were in this together."

"I'd be a fool to make a decision in the dark of night but I like the size of this cabin is all I'm saying."

I agreed on the size. It sure beat the cramped one on our Darby farm. I looked a little closer.

To the left of the door was the cook stove. It had a large reservoir for heating water, a small warming oven above and a decent-sized wood box beyond. A simple table made of hand-hewn pine boards with pole legs stood against the wall on the other side, three pole chairs with rawhide caning for seats, pushed under it. I plopped my bedroll on top as I inspected the two hand-hewn planks resting on thick pegs driven into the wall above the table with smaller pegs poking out beneath. *Plenty of storage*, I thought.

The fireplace was opposite the door and cook stove. While I poked around in the stove, inspecting the firebox and the oven, Alma took some kindling from the wood box and lit a small, experimental fire in the fireplace. The chimney drew so well that his small fire soon flooded the cabin with light and heat.

"Whew! Open the windows and door!" I exclaimed. "We'll cook."

"Well, I guess we wouldn't have to worry about heat in the winter." Alma said as he reached to open the closest window. "Between this fireplace and that cook stove, we ought to be warm enough."

Again a drift towards ownership.

"I don't like those bunk beds," I said.

Opposite the table, close to the fireplace, were pole bunk beds, again with rawhide caning.

"Do you know," Alma said, slowly, "we've never spent a night in separate beds since you were out of the cradle? We've always been there to keep each other warm."

"Probably why the Crane brothers were sick," I said. "Too cold in the winter, sleeping alone, even with this fireplace."

"Maybe. I suppose if we get cold we can tear those beds out and make a single, wider bed."

Ignoring the fact he made our staying sound like a done deal, I picked my bedroll up off the table. "Which bunk do you want for the night?"

"You get the top," Alma said. "I'd probably roll out in my sleep."

I grinned as I spread my roll on the top bunk, unbuttoned my shirt, then started to unbuckle my spurs. As I bent down, I noticed the floor was made of rough-hewn planks. There were cracks between them. Ugly cracks.

"Bet this floor lets in some fearsome drafts," I said as I pulled my work shoes off and climbed up to my bed. The ride over the pass and through the canyon had been tiring and my tail end, gone soft from a summer of farming, was stiff and sore. No need to count elk tonight.

"That's what fur rugs are for," Alma rolled his bedroll out on the bunk below mine. "I know of a certain grizzly's hide that would look real nice stretched out in front of that fireplace."

CHAPTER TWENTY-TWO

Next morning I awoke at daybreak but the bunk below me was empty.

"Alma?"

No answer.

I peered through the dim light of dawn but my brother wasn't in the cabin. Darky and Star were still tied to their trees but Alma wasn't in sight. I looked around.

The cabin was situated on a gravelly river-rock strewn ridge. Short sticker-weeds, wild asters and honeysuckle grew sporadically, cobble rocks abundantly, but no grass. Great. Hungry horses, nothing to feed them and who knew where my brother had wandered off to?

Suddenly he breezed around the corner of the cabin.

"There you are," he said as if he'd been the one looking for someone. "About time you got up."

"What's the point of getting up when it's too dark to see?"

"Good way to get a head start on the day. Sunrises are always invigorating," Alma said, rubbing his hands together. I hadn't noticed. I'd always been busy working by sunrise—except when I'd been up a tree, trying to escape Emma-Jane.

"There's a decent-sized barn and a corral with a creek running through it and enough grass on the banks for the horses," Alma went on. "They can eat and drink while we look around."

"What's the point? You already have." Alma could have waked me when he got up. Or was he making all the decisions alone?

My brother smiled his lopsided smile.

"Let's get some breakfast, then" he said. "You'll feel better."

"Not hungry and I feel just fine."

"Then saddle Star and lead her down to feed and water. You may not be hungry but I'll bet she is."

"Why saddle her first?"

"Come on, Nephi," The look on Alma's face told me his patience was wearing thin. "You know she'll tank up on water and then your cinch'll be loose within the hour."

I knew it and I knew just how dangerous a loose cinch was but I didn't want him telling me what to do. I stood there like a bump on a log while he started saddling Darky. He ignored my bad humor.

84

"There's enough rock here," Alma commented as he pulled his saddle blanket out from under his saddle and placed it on Darky's back," that a fellow could build a mansion out of rock and never miss what he'd used."

"I'll pass," I said, finally unbending enough to begin saddling Star. With her blanket and saddle in place, I reached for her cinch, pulled the strap snug, knotted it loosely then tightened it again before finishing the knot. "If and when I ever get around to building a home of my own I'll want a stick-built house like the one we grew up in." I said.

If we stayed here, I wondered where I'd put a house if I ever built one. The cabin was at the north end of a clearing; the barn and corral on the southwest side. It would have to be somewhere in between.

"Those Crane brothers weren't stupid about how they laid their barnyard out. There's a spring and if it keeps running all winter we won't have to worry about water for our stock." Alma remarked. Again I noted the possessive.

Alma seemed determined to take on something we had no way of knowing we could handle. I didn't want to be pushed into something we might lose. I didn't want another disappointment.

"You wanted to look this place over before you made any decisions," I reminded him.

"Then let's go find the field."

I felt trapped.

"These bunks are comfortable," I said as I stretched out that night. "Sure beat those hard boards in our Darby house."

"Ummm."

I looked up through the darkness toward the invisible roof above me. I knew Alma had decided to take the relinquishment. A day of poking around, exploring the area and 'palavering' with Jack had me leaning a little more that way, too, but I wasn't ready to commit myself yet.

"So what do you want to do? Shall we go east up the

85

Gros Ventre* or north to Montana? I hear there's some really interesting things to see in the Yellowstone between here and the Missouri River country," I said. "And there might be a better place in Montana."

"Ummm."

"Hey!" I leaned over the side of my bunk but Alma was breathing de--eply. I considered wadding up my blanket and throwing it at his head, then decided not.

Let him sleep. We could talk in the morning. Besides, I still needed time to think.

I lay back on my bedroll.

I hadn't expected the Hole to be so much larger than the Basin. Nor had I expected such scenery. The mountains surrounding this valley were different from any I'd ever seen before. Vital. Vigorous. There was something about them that seemed to permeate everything before them. I had felt it.

And the Grand!

That! mountain, towering over every other peak, was like a magnet, continually drawing my gaze. From the moment I'd first seen it that morning, it had grabbed me, commanding my attention every second it was in sight.

All I could think, with its splendor before me, was that *here* was the throne of God.

As I pictured it in my mind, the discouragement of these past two years seemed to fall away. Was it the mountain's influence? If Alma and I took this homestead could we draw from its vigor? I was a farmer, a stockman. I could never be anything else. Could this valley, that mountain, give back the courage I seemed to have lost in the past two years?

I thought of the hours we'd spent with Jack, talking about the homestead and about living in the Hole, and analyzed what he'd said. Jack hadn't spared any details of the long, harsh winters—we hadn't dealt with that before?—the occasional snow in summer—that would be a new one—the ravening wolves—we had guns.

He'd warned us that elk ruined the homesteaders' fences and squirrels burrowed holes in the canal—poison grain and fence stretchers could solve that.

He'd even discussed the neighbors. They seemed like decent folks from his description. At least none of them had teenaged daughters.

I didn't see how this could be worse than Darby. Maybe as difficult in its own way, but not worse. And I was willing to bet we'd even have enough hay on these thirty acres to keep all of our animals fed all winter if we hurried and got it harvested.

The murmur of the frogs and river receded as I finally drifted off to sleep but in my dreams that night was the constant presence of the Grand Teton as I'd seen it that morning—towering, majestic, purple-grey against the vaulting, searingly-blue summer sky.

*Gros Ventre, the name given by French fur trappers, was generally spelled Grovont by the early English-speaking settlers of Nephi's time.

CHAPTER TWENTY-THREE

Next morning I awoke before Alma, once again with misgivings in my mind. I wanted this place. I wanted what I'd felt yesterday . . . but something held me back. I lay in the pre-dawn darkness, trying to understand.

It was a shock when I suddenly realized that this was plain and simple fear.

Fear!

Me?

What did I have to be afraid of? Alma and I were together. United, we could lick anything.

I slid off my bunk, stepped into my clothes, and slipped out of the cabin door. This was something I needed to confront and resolve and I needed to do it alone. Through the half-light of breaking dawn, I walked out toward the river.

Was I afraid of failure? ...Maybe. But farmers normally felt anxious until the crops were in.

This was different.

The undesirable residents Aunt Rhody talked about? ...No. As big as the valley was, I didn't see much chance of running across any of the poachers. We wouldn't have neighbors too close for comfort, either. A man could lose himself in these river bottoms and never see another living soul for days. I liked that.

I'd already been through the worst weather I thought I'd ever see. I hadn't enjoyed it but I'd survived. Things like that weren't something to fear. A fellow just had to do his best no matter what came along.

The only thing left was failure, itself. But of what? In a moment of clarity I realized that what I feared was making a thoughtless decision.

I'm afraid of making a fool of myself. I'm afraid of not measuring up. That was a shock. *Measuring up to whom?* As I searched my mind for an answer, I arrived at the edge of the river channel and sat down under a tree near the bank.

A small branch from some long-dead bush came floating along and, idly, I reached down and picked it up out of the stream. With the tip I made lazy circles, rippling the water, as I thought.

I'm not afraid of measuring up to Alma. I've worked by his side for years. There isn't much he can do that I can't do just as well. Besides, we'd be in this together.

I'm not afraid of measuring up to my neighbors, either. According to Jack none of them are as young as we are. Bet I could work circles around any one of them any day they wanted to name.

Who does that leave? My family? No. Well . . . not really my family. Suddenly I realized there was only one person whose scathing opinion I feared.

My father. I'm afraid of not measuring up to my father! I snorted at the thought. *Ridiculous. Why should I fear not measuring up to him? He's not that wonderful. If that's all that's holding me back....* I straightened up and, for the first time looked around me.

This river channel was deeper than the channels we'd crossed two days before and its waters ran slow and silent. One or two eddies swirled lazily, farther out toward the middle of the stream, but closer to me the water swung around in a gentle curve. I could see where it had undercut the bank a few feet away from me, leaving the roots of two trees hanging out over the water's edge, their gnarled, writhing shape reflected in the quiet depths of a pool beneath. At the bottom of those shadowy depths I saw fish. Big fish. Eight, nine, ten.... Trout, by the looks of them.

Wait a minute. Where had I seen this before?

Shocked, I looked up at the far bank. The trees . . . the channel . . . the pool . . . were so familiar. But I'd never been here before. How could I have seen them?

Then I knew. This was where I'd been in my dream the night of that first big storm on the Egin bench. This was the place where I'd felt such contentment and well-being.

For a moment I sat and stared. Then I smiled. I was ready to go back to the cabin and tell my brother we had found our home.

CHAPTER TWENTY-FOUR

We liked our new neighbors. Hard-working people, they were friendly when you met them but busy enough to mind their own affairs.

The Davenport brothers and the Lingenfelters, Henry, Jenny and their daughter, Mary, were Missourians. We didn't know the women so well but Henry Lingenfelter was a fellow who could take a practical joke as well as anyone I ever saw. I should know. I gave him a lot of opportunity to change his nature. Joe and Jim Davenport were easy to get along with, too.

Jack Grey, as he'd said, was our closest neighbor to the south. He was single—like most of the homesteaders—and a wealth of information on the people of the area. He was never too tired at the end of a long day to ride over and be neighborly and anything we wanted to know about the people in the valley, we could count on him to tell us. He offered highly entertaining opinions of why folks were doing what they were doing.

Up on the flats past our fields was a long string of homesteaders. Henry Cherry, first of the bunch, was an old man by the time we came—twisted and bent with 'the rheumatiz', as he called it. He was a little odd but he had a wealth of knowledge about the valley; its climate, its soils and its quirks. If we wanted to know something useful about running our spread, Henry was the man to visit.

There were several little farms past him. Of their owners, our favorites were Roy and Maggy McBride. Together with Frank, Roy's brother, and Charles DeVinney, Maggie's nephew, they were packed into one tiny little cabin like sardines in a tin but you never heard Maggie complain.

I often laughed at her though. Devoutly Mormon, she made sure Alma and I understood there was a congregation up on Mormon Row and we were welcome to attend services with her and Roy anytime we wanted. We didn't, and mostly ignored her little comments, but through the years that they lived on their little spread she never gave up trying. She was good natured about it, though, and didn't nag so I didn't mind.

Bill Newbold's wife, was a different breed of cat.

Bill lived farther up the flats towards Moose where Menor's ferry crossed the Snake River. There, his little farm hugged the base of the west side of Blacktail Butte. One spring he hired Alma and me to help him lengthen Tom and Rosa Brown's canal.

I'll never forget the day he showed up at our door. We'd just come in from helping a cow through a difficult birth and were washing up when we heard his carriage. I shook the water from my hands and grabbed a towel while Alma called, "Come in!" at his knock.

The door opened and standing in the doorframe was the fattest man I'd ever seen, barring none. The only light showing was from his shoulders up—on either side of his rather small head—and a little beside his shoes. I had to blink twice to make sure I was actually seeing right.

What does a fellow do when the fat man to trump all fat men shows up on his doorstep? I didn't have any idea who this person was but one thing for sure, if he wanted to hurt me, all he'd have had to do was sit on me and I'd be squashed. I decided I wanted to be polite.

"You the Moulton boys?" he asked as he eased his hulking body through the door, sideways. It was the only way he could get through.

"We are."

"Bill Newbold, here." he announced as he waddled across the room and literally fell onto one of our chairs, a big sigh escaping him as he sat, his bulk spilling over the edges of the seat—more of it off than on.

An immediate image of an overly inflated bladder, letting air out, came to mind as I held my breath, expecting the chair to splinter into a hundred pieces. Another image of Alma and me pulling splinters out of his more-than-ample backside followed immediately behind it. I tensed, but miraculously the chair held. It was our lucky day.

"I'm lookin' to lengthen Tom Brown's canal to my place," he said. "Frank Connell's helping me. Said he'd heard you have a strong team and a scraper. Like to hire you if you're available."

I looked at Alma, questioningly. Frank Connell, whoever he was, was correct. We had a scraper and Sleek and Sassy were always willing to work. We only had two more cows to calve out and it wasn't time, yet, to trail our herd to their summer range. Nor had the spring run-off begun in earnest so we didn't have irrigation water to worry about. And we could use the money. In fact, it would be very welcome. Silent communication passed between us—a quick nod from Alma answered by another from me—and Alma spoke.

"When do we start?"

"Tomorry. First thing."

Another look between us. Again, nods.

"That'll be fine," Alma spoke for us both.

"I have a tent you can sling yore bedrolls in. My wife Rhody'll do the cookin'. Wages're eight bits a day."

A dollar. Taken together that was two dollars a day. Good wages.

"How long do you think it'll take?" Alma asked.

"With Sundays off, prob'ly six weeks or so. Depends on how many boulders we find."

My ears perked up at that. "Finding big ones?" I asked.

"No," he said, slowly, "not too big—maybe ten, twelve inches long's the biggest but you never know with this soil. It's the rockiest I ever seed."

Our scraper could handle a twelve-inch rock. I was satisfied and I knew Alma was, too, as Bill hefted his bulk off our chair, one hand pushing against the wall for support while the other one shoved down on our tabletop.

With an, "I'll be seein' you boys tomorry, then," he lumbered to the door, pushed himself through and was gone. We heard the creak of a desperately overloaded carriage then a clip-clop and rattle as he drove away.

"Seventy-two dollars," Alma said. "That's going to come in handy."

"Yes, but he wants us first thing in the morning. We'd better get that scraper up there tonight."

"I'll take it up if you want to bring our gear. Why don't you ride over and tell Jack he can have our eggs if he'll feed the chickens and keep an eye on those two remaining cows?"

"I'll be with you in time for bed tonight," I promised and with that, we left the cabin—Alma to harness the work team and me to ride Star through the trees to Jack's cabin a mile away.

It was hard work, scraping down through the rocky soil, but I didn't mind the physical labor. The idea of having seventy-two dollars was such an incentive I scarcely noticed. We got along well with Frank Connell, who was a quiet but likeable fellow. Bill was amiable, too. The only fly in the ointment was his wife, Rhoda. I couldn't help comparing her to Maggie McBride.

Maggie was a slender, soft-spoken woman from Pennsylvania. She kept her mound of golden hair neatly braided and pinned in a halo around her head. Her home-made clothing was always spotless and fitted her well. And in all due respect to my mother, I believe her cooking was just as good if not a bit better. I never passed up an invitation to share a meal at Maggie's table. More important, she never pressured either of us about anything. She kept us informed in her quiet way, then let us make our own choices.

"There's a Christmas party over at the May's house," she might say as she passed a piece of her mincemeat pie. "Everyone from the Ward will be there. We'd be happy to have you come with us if you'd like." And that would be the last we heard of it. If we wanted to go, we could ask when this shindig was happening. If we didn't, she figured she'd said enough. We never went . . . not wanting to become all that close with other members of what we considered our 'parent's religion' . . . but we appreciated her willingness to keep us informed and then drop the subject.

Rhoda Newbold, on the other hand, with her seldom-combed hair flying every-which way, her sloppy Mother Hubbard dress that I swear she only washed once a year, if then, and her piercingly shrill English voice, kept up a steady harangue—generally aimed in Bill's direction but just as likely to find Frank, Alma or me as a target, instead.

"Now, Bill, you know it's going to be windy today." *Where do you get your information? It's a balmy spring everywhere but in your tent.* "You take your muffler and gloves with you. You boys, too. I don't want any of you getting sick on me. I have enough to do around here what with the cooking I do for the bunch of you, and all." *You call that greasy mess cooking? God is my witness I've fed better slop to hogs!*

"Bill, if I've told you once I've told you a thousand times...." *I highly doubt you've told him anything a thousand times—it's more like a million and counting.*

93

"Now, tomorrow's Sunday. I'll expect to see you boys in church. It starts at ten sharp so you best come a little early to make sure you get there on time. It's disrespectful to walk in late." *It's also disrespectful to talk all the time but the only time you stop talking is when you sleep—and you can't talk then—you're too busy snoring. We can hear you clear over in our tent.* "I'll save a space for you beside me," she'd continue, "and, Frank, you best be bringing Lucy and the girls—and your mother-in-law and Lucy's brother, Floyd, too. Those girls of yours need some religion in their lives. It's just not right the way you folks are raising them."

And on, and on, and on. Never-ending and nauseating. Frank shrugged her off. Alma smiled, politely. And I seethed.

After a couple-three weeks of Rhoda, I got to the point where there had to be some relief, somewhere, so I started plotting revenge.

Mother always taught me to be polite—particularly to women, although I sincerely doubt she foresaw anyone like Rhoda Newbold coming into my life. She never told me I couldn't harass them back in subtle ways, though. Forget the fact she would have if she'd thought of it, she had never told me so I wasn't weighed down with instructions I didn't want to follow. Still, I knew Alma wouldn't approve so I planned my revenge for a day when it was his turn to feed and harness our team in the morning.

Camping out there on the flats, as we were, didn't leave me a lot to work with. Once I made my plans, I had to find an excuse to go home. I know Alma was suspicious when I skipped supper one night and loped off on Star, but he didn't ask and I didn't volunteer.

It was dead dark when I arrived at our homestead cabin and it took a while to light a lantern and locate what I wanted—a small piece of tin, maybe eight or nine inches square. It was midnight before I got back to Bill's camp.

As far as Frank and Alma knew, I was fast asleep the next morning when they left at five-thirty to round up the teams. I wasn't, but both Bill and Rhoda were. Their snoring duet would have sent a grizzly bear on a wide detour around our camp.

I waited until I knew Frank and Alma were busy then slipped, barefoot, over to Bill and Rhoda's tent where I placed the little square of tin over Rhoda's stovepipe. Then I went back to bed to catch a few extra winks.

94

I don't know how long I slept—maybe another half hour—before the commotion started.

When I peeked out of our tent, smoke was pouring out of Bill and Rhoda's. Wearing nothing but his unwashed winter long johns, one button missing in the back so the trap door flapped half open, Bill was outside, desperately fanning smoke away from his face. Rhoda, hair flying and already in her dirty dress—or had she ever bothered to take it off the night before?—was bent over, coughing until I thought she was going to puke.

Bill lumbered back into their tent and presently I could hear him poking around in their cook stove, moving the lids, looking for the cause of the smoke. It wasn't there, of course. Soon he came back out, coughing and spluttering. Now it was Rhoda's turn—choking out her opinion of Bill's blindness and stupidity as she went back in, confident of finding the reason for the smoke. Bill wisely said nothing when she came out, coughing worse than ever, smoke still billowing about.

That went on for a while . . . Bill and Rhoda taking turns poking and peering, trying to figure out why their perfectly dry wood was smoking so . . . before Bill happened to look up and see the offending square of tin.

About that time Frank came in with his team of work mares and Rhoda lit into him, up one side and down the other.

"You did that, Frank!" she coughed, pointing her stubby, sausage-roll finger in Frank's face. "Of all the mean things to do. I would have thought you were a cut above such a trick!"

"Did what?" Frank was completely confused. He'd been busy enough with the horses that he hadn't seen what was going on or he probably would have come to help. "What are you talking about?"

"You did it and you know you did it. Don't you try appearing innocent. I'm really disappointed in you, Frank," she coughed out.

The look on Frank's face totally undid me. I dove for my bedroll and buried my face in the pillow to muffle my laughter. When Frank finally escaped Rhoda and sought refuge in our tent, I was still gasping for breath.

Frank wasn't anybody's dummy. One look at me and he recognized the real culprit. Good man that he was, however, he never told.

I suppose it was a rather underhanded thing to do to Bill, but one thing for sure, the raspy throat that smoke gave Rhoda had a wonderful result. Every time she tried to talk, she went into a fit of coughing. Except for the food, life around camp was quite pleasant for the rest of our stay.

CHAPTER TWENTY-FIVE
1908

Alma, pail full of milk in one hand, came out of the barn as I loped up to the corral early one morning.

"What's taken you so long?" he asked. In the three years since we'd moved to Jackson Hole I'd never come in so late for breakfast.

"Water's gone." I reined Star in, swung my leg over her rump, and dropped to the ground. "The canal's dry. Nothing but mud in the bottom. Another washout through a squirrel hole. I rode up to the headgate and turned the water off. How come you've just finished milking? It's past seven-thirty."

Alma sighed. "Elk have broken the pasture fence again. Bossie was up the river nearly to Davenport's. If we hadn't had a bell on her I'd have spent all day looking. Let's go fix breakfast."

I grunted as I flipped Star's reins around the top rail of the corral fence and followed Alma to the cabin.

"You know," he continued, "I'd hoped to clear fifteen or twenty more acres this spring. I don't think we've even managed an extra five since we came here."

"If we weren't spending all our time battling squirrels and elk...." I stoked the fire in the cook stove and grabbed a tin skillet from the shelf while Alma strained the milk.

"They're both more of a problem than I ever imagined," Alma agreed. "We've restrung every fence on the place at least once this spring because of elk. And those squirrels! Blasted things are everywhere."

They were, too. And right behind them came badgers looking for a squirrel lunch. Little squirrel holes became big badger holes. Badger holes meant broken legs for careless horses or cattle. Too bad it wasn't elk breaking their legs. I was beginning to think our valley shouldn't have banished Binkley and Isobel.

It was late afternoon before the canal bank was stable enough to hold water again. "I'd better go fix that pasture fence," Alma said, watching the muddy Gros Ventre river water surge through the headgate as I opened it. "Who knows where Bossie is by now."

"It'll be a good three hours before this water gets to the field," I said. "I'll start grubbing sage, then I'll set my dams just before sunset." I swung up onto Star. "I'll have a big patch grubbed before you even get Darky to the field."

"I'm not running my horse through this sage brush," Alma protested. "Can't see the badger holes."

I wanted to run Star but I knew he was right. I reined her in, frustrated. I wanted to be at the field this minute but I couldn't risk losing my horse.

Sage brush wasn't hard to grub, just tedious. With a few good twists I could jerk the top right up off its root system. It wasn't an enjoyable job, though, even if you liked the smell of sage leaves. The shrub was a breeding ground for ticks in the spring, particularly if there was a lot of rainy weather like we'd been having. Besides, my back got stiff from all the bending and jerking.

Despite the unpleasantness of the chore, once I got to the field and settled into a work rhythm I was so intent on getting as much done before dark as I could, that I didn't hear the approaching horseman with his pack mule until he spoke to me.

"Afternoon."

I started, straightened up, and peered, blinking, at the stranger who was sitting with the blaze of the late evening sun streaming over his shoulder.

"Afternoon, neighbor," I said. It was impossible to see the stranger's face under his wide-brimmed hat, given the brightness of the sun behind him. I squinted, putting up one hand to shield my eyes.

"Bin ridin' a long ways," the stranger drawled. "I'd like t' rest my horses 'n' clean up a mite. What's th' chance I could put up with you fer the night?"

"Welcome to." Western courtesy demanded that a householder shared what he had with every traveler—neighbor, friend or total stranger. Besides, folks living in isolated communities like ours were happy to have any company they could get. News was passed along that way from one community to another—sometimes from the outside world as well. If this stranger had traveled a long way, maybe he'd have interesting things to tell. I hoped so.

I dusted my hands off on my pants, picked up Star's reins and prepared to mount. "I'll have to reset my dams for the night but it won't take long," I said.

"I kin wait." The stranger seemed short on words. His voice, when he did speak—was high pitched and nasally—at odds with his massive body. He sat quietly in his saddle, watched while I changed the sets in the irrigation ditches, then whipped his horse to catch up after I had finished. His pack mule trailed wearily along behind.

I didn't know how to start a conversation with him so I rode in silence—wishing he would say something.

He didn't.

He was a curious fellow. I glanced at him occasionally, trying to identify what it was that made him different. He looked like someone who'd been long on the trail. His hair was ragged, matted and greasy. So was his beard—where there was an abundance of chaw and spittle.

The evening breeze changed direction and I suddenly discovered his buckskin clothing didn't smell so wonderful either. My nostrils fairly quivered in protest. *Bet the only bath he's had in a coon's age has been nothing more than a quick dash through a cold creek,* I thought. *No wonder he wants to clean up. He must have spent the winter running trap lines. That would explain why his buckskins are so crusted with dirt.*

Beneath his hat brim I could see thick brows and a long, hooked nose but the man's deeply hooded eyes were impossible to see, he squinted so. *Snow blindness, brought on by too much time outdoors in winter. He probably is a trapper although I wouldn't think that pack on his mule is big enough. Must not have had a very successful season.*

The horse he rode was a rawboned, rangy roan that looked almost as trail weary as the mule; the heads of both hung as they plodded along. Their hides were stretched tight over ribs that stood out and the mule had a limp, to boot. *Whole crew looks like they've had a hard ride and precious little grub along the way.*

Alma was milking when we rode up to the corral. He greeted the stranger but didn't get much reply as the man unsaddled his horse, unloaded his mule, hobbled them both and, after buckling a bell around the horse's neck, turned them loose to graze.

I'd already headed for the cabin. He would want hot water for a bath and I was anxious to get it heated as quickly as possible. I could think of plenty of things I wanted to do but sitting in a warm cabin eating supper with this smelly stranger wasn't on the list.

After he'd turned his animals out for the night, the fellow brought his scabbarded rifle and his bed roll to the cabin. I was busy peeling potatoes when he dumped his bedroll in the corner. Then, saying he'd be back 'purdy quick', he strode out the door and disappeared through the trees towards the river, gun in hand.

"Strange duck," Alma commented when he brought cold milk, a shank of ham and a fresh bucket of water in from the spring box down by the creek.

"Smelly too," I agreed. I set the potatoes, now boiling briskly, farther back on the stove and put our largest skillet in their place. "I thought maybe he'd mention his name but he didn't. Didn't say much of anything, really," I said as I sliced some ham into the skillet.

"I suppose we're better off not asking him," Alma remarked. "Jack says it's not wise. Tell you what, I'm not looking forward to eating with him here in the house. His odor's a mite strong!"

"I *hope* he'll clean up before supper," I exclaimed. "He said he wanted to."

"Good, I'll bring the tub in so he won't forget," Alma stepped over the doorsill to lift our washtub off it's peg on the cabin's outside wall.

There was definitely something unpleasant about our guest but maybe it was just his smell. Still, I wished he hadn't come along and I knew Alma felt the same. Too late now. Besides, it wasn't acceptable to turn a traveler away unless there was a good reason—and we didn't have one.

Supper was nearly cooked by the time the fellow returned. He set his rifle in the corner of the cabin behind the stove and began dipping water from the reservoir into the tub.

"You can have what's in the teakettle as well," I offered. I could heat more water for dishes while we were eating and I wanted to make sure he had enough hot water to soak some of that smell off.

After filling the tub, he lifted it by its handles and carried it to a stand of thick bushes outside of the cabin. Then he returned for the bucket of icy spring water Alma had brought, picking up a cake of soap and a huck towel I'd laid out on the table, before he walked out of the door again. I looked at Alma who was staring, with a contorted face, at the man's receding back. The smell in our stove-warmed cabin was overpowering. As the fellow disappeared we both breathed a quiet sigh of relief that this silent, smelly stranger wasn't undressing and bathing inside.

When he came back in, he was wearing much cleaner clothing. His hair, though still matted, was about ten shades lighter and perhaps a pound less greasy, and the chaw and spittle were gone from his beard. He smelled a whole lot better, too, I noted with relief.

"Food's ready," I motioned to the table. He silently pulled out a chair as we set the pan of potatoes, a plate of fried ham, a bowl of gravy and some biscuits before him. He waited until we had seated ourselves and passed him the ham before he spoke.

"Named my rifle Millie," he said. "We been a long ways together but I think I'm goin' to sell her. I don't guess I'll need her in civilizashun. Either of you fellers be int'rusted?"

"Maybe." Alma glanced at the still-scabbarded rifle in the corner. I knew what he was thinking—it might be a decent gun or it might not. "Care if we try it out after supper?"

"Go ahead." The stranger stuffed a large piece of potato into his mouth, following it with a quarter slice of ham. He chewed them quickly. "She shoots straight, I c'n tell you!"

Just then a knock came at the door and Jack Grey poked his head inside. "You fellows just eatin'?" he asked as he stepped into the cabin. He saw the stranger at the table and froze, momentarily. Recovering himself, he went on, "I'd have thought you'd be done and out galavanting around by now."

"Oh, you know us, Jack," I grinned. "We're always the last around here to do anything. By the way, where were you, today, when we were filling in the washout in the canal?"

"Sleeping in." Jack said. "So that's where you were. I dropped by before six this morning and the place was quiet as a tomb. You should've come got me. Say, you boys ever heard of a bed? Somebody needs to find you each a wife so's you can lead decent, civilized hours."

I thought of Maude and banished the thought just as quickly. To my knowledge Alma hadn't even looked at another woman in the five years since he'd found out she hadn't waited for him. He hadn't mentioned her either. And I sure wasn't going to.

"We don't need women around here. What can a woman do that I can't?" I demanded.

"We won't go into details." Jack grinned. "But for darned sure she'd fix your meals at a decent time so's you two could put on some weight!"

"You want us to look like Bill Newbold?"

"Well, you have to admit his wife can put on a spread," Jack shot back.

"If you want to call it that," I wasn't impressed. "Oh, there's plenty of it but even *I* can cook better than she can. Every time I look at Bill I think:

Old Bill Newbold,
Fed on slop,
Big in the middle
And little on top"

"Nephi!" Alma was embarrassed but Jack and the stranger laughed heartily.

"You know Bill?" I looked at the stranger.

"I've seen 'im a time or two."

Jack looked as if he were suffering from apoplexy, his face turned so purple. That was puzzling. I had the distinct feeling Jack knew who the stranger was but he wasn't saying anything and the fellow still hadn't offered his name. I sopped up the last of my gravy with a biscuit and stuffed it into my mouth, chewing thoughtfully.

Jack had once told me about the 4th of July, back in 1900, where some wise person hatched the idea that everybody in the valley should congregate at Jenny's Lake and have a good old-fashioned get-together. Nearly a hundred people showed up—most of the population of the valley at the time—and Bill Atherton, for whom Atherton Creek was named, had commented there were getting to be too many people in the valley for him; he would have to leave. And he did.

When I was shocked that a man would think a hundred people in a valley some thirty miles long and maybe ten miles wide was too many, Jack had chuckled at my innocence.

"Folks like Bill probably have a reason for not wanting too many people around who might recognize them from somewheres else," he'd said. "Sometimes, Nephi, it ain't healthy to ask too many questions. If a man doesn't offer information, you just don't ask." I decided this was one of those times when I shouldn't do any asking.

CHAPTER TWENTY-SIX

After supper we tried out the stranger's rifle.

The scabbard was rawhide—bull or buffalo I thought, but I wasn't sure. The rifle, itself, was a Model 94 .38-55 Winchester. With its big .38 caliber bullet, the Model 94 had enough power to drop a buffalo at over 400 yards. A popular gun, it was a favorite with hunters. While I studied the rifle, Alma grabbed an old flour sack for a target and asked where the stranger wanted it hung.

The fellow picked up his rifle, strode out our door, and set off through the trees towards the bench.

"C'm on!" he ordered as he went.

"Where are we going?"

My word but that man's legs were long. I had to trot to catch up. In fact, everything about him was long. And big. And yet he was quiet as he moved. I could hear Alma's footsteps and, of course, Jack's horse but I couldn't hear the stranger's steps. It was almost unnerving.

"Up top the bench," he replied, not slacking his speed.

Once we reached the hayfield I asked where he wanted the target. He grabbed the flour sack from Alma and held it up. Noting there were no holes in it, he tore off a piece, perhaps a foot square, and handed it to Jack.

"Go hang it on that tree up there," he commanded, motioning towards a tree along the canal some quarter-mile away.

"You can't expect to hit it that far!" Alma exclaimed.

"With Millie, here, you cin hit that far if'n yu're a decent shot," the man assured us, patting the stock of his rifle.

We waited as Jack loped his horse up to the tree. The piece of cloth was barely visible when it was hung—just a faint dot of white in the spring twilight. After Jack had ridden his horse a decent distance from the tree the stranger raised the gun to his shoulder, sighted down the barrel and squeezed the trigger, all in one fluid motion. The report echoed over our field.

Jack retrieved the cloth and hurried back to where we stood. As he handed the small square to the stranger I saw a clean bullet hole, dead center in the fabric.

"I can't believe it!" I fairly gasped.

104

"Try her yorself." the man replied. "If you think you'll want to buy her, you should at least shoot her once."

Jack returned the cloth to the tree and Alma and I each shot once. When Jack brought our target back the second time there were three distinct holes in it. Alma's and mine weren't as close to center as the stranger's but they were there.

"You're purty good," the stranger observed as we inspected the holes. "Few people c'n shoot like that... 'specially with a strange rifle."

"This gun's a beauty!" I exclaimed.

The stranger smiled.

"But why would you want to sell such a treasure?" I asked, running my hands over the stock. I'd forgotten Jack's warning to never ask questions.

The stranger ceased smiling. Quietly he took the rifle and, turning, headed down over the edge of the bench towards the river bottoms and the cabin.

"I think it's about time I get home," Jack announced. "You boys still have a set to make tonight, don't you? It's getting along towards dark."

"Water should be down by now," I said, puzzled. "I have my sets made for the night, though." I watched, thoughtfully, as Jack rode away with only a "See you later."

He's never been in a hurry to leave before. Why is he going home when the evening star is barely out?

As Jack and his horse disappeared through the trees, Alma and I hurried after the stranger. By the time we reached the cabin he had already rolled out his bedroll, pulled off his moccasins and crawled in. He neither spoke to nor looked at us. Silently, Alma and I went about clearing the table and washing the dishes. Then, just as silently, we removed our own work clothes and climbed into bed. I heard an elk snorting down towards the river before I went to sleep.

The next morning I had already changed my irrigation sets so it was probably 6:00 a.m., at least, before we sat down to breakfast. Again, the stranger had taken a walk through the woods before eating. He said nothing during the meal. Then, while I did dishes and Alma dried them, he rounded up his two animals. By the time we had

105

finished our kitchen chores, his horse was saddled and the pack was securely strapped onto the mule.

"Guess I'll keep m' rifle after all," he commented as he rode up to the cabin door. "Pree-shee-ate the bed an' grub. Could you show me the best fordin' place on the river?"

"Glad to," I had never been more serious in my life. I was plumb grateful to watch our guest ride his rangy roan out into the swirling waters of the Snake. "Goodby," I said, quietly enough only Alma could hear, "and good riddance."

"Amen to that," my brother added.

Jack was waiting for us at the cabin when we returned, relief written plainly on his face when he saw us ride up.

"Am I ever glad to see you!" he exclaimed.

"Why? Did you think he was going to murder us while we slept?" I asked. "I didn't care for him but he wasn't all *that* bad. Just a trifle odd." Jack sure could get carried away sometimes.

"Nephi," Jack looked at me pityingly. "You durned fools are lucky are alive. That man was Isobel."

CHAPTER TWENTY-SEVEN
1910

"You boys going to the Fourth of July rodeo next week?" Jack Grey poked his head through the open door of the cabin one evening. I looked at Alma.

"I suppose we could." Alma's voice was thoughtful as he motioned for Jack to pull up a chair. "We probably need to spend some time around other folks for a change."

I was pleased with his decision. I'd always looked forward to Fourth of July celebrations in Utah but we hadn't taken even one day off for pleasure since leaving home. I wondered what this celebration would be like. I'd never seen a rodeo.

"What's a rodeo?" I asked.

Jack laughed heartily. "Oh, there'll be roping and games, but I hear there's also going to be a relay race on horseback this year," he said. "It'll be a laugh a minit!" I looked at Alma. What was so funny about a horseback relay race?

"Funny?" Alma asked.

"Wild horse race is about what it'll amount to." Jack explained. "They're setting out a quarter-mile track to be run and each contestant has to ride it 10 times, using a fresh horse each time. I hear there's four men participating at this point and you know as well as I do there ain't forty broke horses in the whole valley." He laughed, again. "Leastways not forty that would be available. I got the idea there's gonna be all sorts of fun with that one."

A slow smile spread over my face. This sounded like something I wouldn't want to miss. Good weather or not, the work would to have to survive a day without us.

"Clear skies, today. Good day for the shindig." I observed the morning of the Fourth. I'd already hitched Sleek and Sassy to our utility wagon and had driven it to the door of the cabin while Alma was taking his turn at the household chores.

"You figure Jack's ready yet?" he asked as he stowed our simple picnic meal—a crock of water, a large hunk of baked ham, a wedge of cheese and some freshly baked, buttered biscuits—in a wooden box beneath the wagon seat before he climbed up.

"Well, if he isn't we can roll him out quick enough." I was anxious to be on the road as I slid over to make room for my brother to sit. With a "Tsst, Tsst!" we were off, heading toward our neighbor's little homestead cabin.

Jack not only wasn't ready, he was snoring loudly when we arrived. Alma jumped off the wagon seat and started toward the door, his fist poised, ready to knock.

"Pssssst! Alma!" I whispered him back. "He's still asleep."

"That's obvious."

"Let's sneak in. You grab his head, I'll get his feet and we'll throw him in the back of the wagon and take off."

"He'll get hurt." Alma looked at the hay-covered wagon bed, doubtfully.

"No he won't."

"What'll he do for dinner?" Alma was always practical.

"Come on!" I said, impatiently. "You packed enough for an army. We can share." I fairly danced in anticipation.

Alma couldn't help smiling. "He'll wake up when we open the door," he protested weakly, following me to Jack's cabin.

"Jack? Not a chance. He sleeps like a log." I slipped our neighbor's latch back slowly and inched the door ajar. The wider the opening, the louder the snores coming out. We stepped silently into the room and looked around in the early morning gloom. Tiptoeing to the foot of the bed, I grabbed Jack's pile of clothing and his work boots with one hand and reached around his legs—blanket and all—with the other just as Alma lifted our friend's upper body. With a whoop we headed for our wagon at a dead run.

By the time we were through the door, Jack was fully awake and roaring. "Here, put me down! What d'you crazy cayuses think you're doing? Put me down, dad-blast you all to smithereens, anyhow!"

I flung the clothing into the wagon box then reached for a better hold on his wildly-struggling legs. "Count of three." I yelled. "One." Alma and I swung Jack away from the wagon.

Jack bellowed. "You two are nothin' more'n the..."

"Two." We swung him again.

"south bound end of a north bound mule!" Jack roared.

108

"Three!" With a mighty heave, we sent him sailing up and over the wooden side of the wagon. Then, scrambling onto the seat, we sent our team careening off down the road.

". . . Of all the lilly-livered stunts...." Jack's cussing of the Moulton brothers must have continued for a good five minutes.

"You've got to admire Jack's cussing," I commented after we'd gone a considerable distance. "He hasn't used one single obscene word and at the same time I don't think he's used the same word twice, either."

Alma grinned as he eased the horses to a trot. "No, and half of those words I've never even heard before. Inventive fellow, isn't he?"

"Inventive, my eye!" Jack, now dressed, climbed up onto the wagon seat beside us as Alma reined the team in to a walk. "What did you idjits think you was doing anyhow?"

"Well, Jack," I explained in my sweetest voice, "it was getting late in the morning and you looked like you were mighty tired, still, so we thought we'd just let you sleep on the way to town."

Jack snorted. "Sure you did!" but he couldn't help grinning a little. "Late in the day is it?" He squinted at the sun. "I'll bet it isn't a minit past six-thirty in the morning. Don't you two *ever* go to sleep?"

"Of course we do." Alma said. "We got a good night's rest. In fact we overslept this morning. I think our straw ticks gave up getting shed of us."

Jack snorted again.

109

CHAPTER TWENTY-EIGHT

Other ranchers from as far away as Kelly to the east and Menor's Ferry to the north joined us until there was quite a group riding in front of, alongside or behind our wagon. A line of dudes from a ranch beyond Moose loped passed, waving energetically and calling noisy greetings.

"The dust them dudes leave behind is dry enough to gag a maggot," Bill Newbold commented.

"You kin always tell a passle of dudes by the way they ride," another man agreed. "Them folks always ride in a looooooong line, single file, and you kin hear 'em comin' long afore you kin ever see 'em 'cause they're always callin' out conversation from one end of the line to the other."

"Yeah, you don't see ranchers doing that." Jack agreed, waving the dust away from his face.

He was right. True westerners rode together in a compact clump, their conversations quiet. They left home early and traveled slowly enough to save their horses' energy for important things.

"Naw," the man replied, laughing. "Ranchers an' real cowboys are too polite to be yellin' to each other."

"We're of a quieter nature, anyhow," Rhoda Newbold declared, her shrill voice with its heavy English accent carrying almost as well as any dude's ever did.

"Oh, I don't know," I spoke up. "I heard Jack, here, yelling at his mule the other morning. I'll bet the folks clear into town could hear him, too."

"Who stuck the bee in *your* bonnet today?" Jack wanted to know. "You've been positively buzzing."

"Who, me? I'm just sitting here," I protested.

Alma looked sideways at me. I knew he figured there was going to be more mischief before the day was over and he was right. I'd been working too hard for too long. I was firmly resolved to find something to do to someone. I eyed Bill and Rhoda Newbold.

Alma knew me well enough he could see it coming.

"Don't you go spouting off your poetry about Bill, now," he ordered in an undertone.

"Hadn't even thought of it," I grinned.

110

"Yeah, well it's plain to see you're hatching something. Better keep a lid on it."

I shot him a disgusted glance and changed the subject.

"Jack, what did you say is happening today?" I asked.

"Well, there's a patriotic program at ten-thirty this morning," Jack began.

"Huh, and I hear Jane Callahan's going to do one of her readings again. You'll all need cotton for your ears. She thinks she's so good and she's soooo terrible!" Rhoda harrumphed in derision. I glared at her back. I didn't think much of a woman who cut others apart like Rhoda did. Poor Bill was shackled to a woman who was a lousy cook and had a two-edged sword in her mouth to boot.

"Then there's the picnic—" Jack began again.

"And I hear there'll be watermelon freighted in from Utah." Rosa Brown spoke up. She, her husband Tom, and her two sons had joined the group at the Gros Ventre River crossing. "It's been years since I tasted Utah watermelon." She laughed. "I used to raid the neighbor's melon patches when I was a little girl down in Ogden."

I looked at her in surprise. I'd thought she was from Rockland, Idaho.

Tom and Rosa interested me. Maggie'd said they were sweethearts when Rosa was in her early teens and Tom, ten years older, was a young buck. They had a lovers' spat. Rosa married someone else. Tom moped.

Although he left Rockland to homestead in the Hole, he didn't forget her. When her husband died unexpectedly, he returned to Rockland, offered her his hand and his heart, and returned to his home on the bench south of Black Tail Butte with Rosa and her young son by his side.

I liked both Tom and Rosa. Tom was a good fellow—quiet and a hard worker. As for Rosa, redheads were supposed to be hot-tempered and Maggie said that Rosa could get upset, occasionally, but I'd never seen her in much of a stew. I could take to Rosa long before I'd ever accept Rhoda Newbold.

"I hear the Mays is playin' for the dance after tonight's BBQ." Someone behind us remarked. I pulled my thoughts back to the group.

"Yes, and I expect every one of you fellows to be out there making the girls happy!" Rhoda ordered. "I've seen too many dances where the bachelors just stood around grinning and looking foolish and the girls had to sit everything out. Jack, Alma, Nephi, Floyd, did you hear me?"

"Ah, Rhody, let the fellers alone, now." Bill protested to his wife. "They've got to make up their own minds what they want to do."

"I'm too old for dancing," Jack objected. Alma didn't say anything; I seethed. Just let that bossy female start trying to drag *me* out on any dance floor. I'd...I'd...well, I didn't know what I'd do but she'd better not try. Maybe I could talk Alma into coming home early.

Still, I'd really enjoy some good music. They were sure to play my favorites. I hadn't heard 'Turkey in the Straw' or 'Old Dan Tucker' since leaving Utah. There had to be some place I could hide and listen where Rhoda couldn't find me.

"Anybody know if Willie Wolff'll be down?" Frank McBride asked. "He'll play his fiddle, too, if he is. Tell you what, that Frenchie can really strut his stuff."

"Yeah, and there's someone from Hog Island who plays spoons. I haven't heard good spoons in a long time," someone else added.

The conversation turned to valley dances—all night affairs in someone's living room with the rug rolled up, the kids bedded down in a back room, and whatever music happened to show up. I was content to listen, my anticipation growing by the mile.

CHAPTER TWENTY-NINE

The patriotic program was staged on a little grassy area near the base of the mountain a mile or so south of the Jackson town square. Someone had erected a temporary platform for the performers and the audience spread out around it—sitting on quilts, hunkered down on the grass, or listening from their buggies. Alma, Jack and I sat on the hay in the back of our wagon. From there we could see the program and watch the audience as well.

"Some of those folks look prosperous," Alma commented as we were waiting for the program to begin.

"They all live in town." Jack said.

"How do you figure that?" I was curious.

"Look at their clothes. Them ruffles and laces didn't come over the road *we* traveled today. They're clean. And they're light colored enough they'd show the dirt easy, while the country gals wear dark colored stuff that don't show the dust from the trail. And the fellers are the same. Just see the shine on them shoes." He motioned toward a young swell, perhaps my age, who was wearing a shiny white flat-brimmed straw hat, a starched and pressed white suit and shoes shined to where I thought I could have seen my reflection in them if I'd been close enough.

I looked at my own rough work pants. They hadn't felt the heat of an iron since we'd left Utah, my shoes were worn and scuffed, and my shirt.... Well, it had been clean when I left the cabin this morning. But it was so threadbare that I suddenly felt like a country cousin. I was glad when the program finally got underway.

The local cowboys, mostly bachelors, were noisily enthusiastic about the performances, the dudes were bored, the townspeople genteelly restrained. When a sextet of older teenaged girls harmonized on 'Columbia, the Gem of the Ocean', however, everyone joined in spirited applause.

Suddenly I noticed that the oldest one of the group, a tall dark-haired girl with a wide pale blue bow pinned to the back of her pompadour-do, had Alma sitting up and paying attention, his eyes following her back to her seat in the town crowd. Then, after the entire audience joined in singing, 'Hail, Columbia' and broke up for the picnic, my brother disappeared in her direction. I groaned. Didn't

113

look like we'd be getting home early. Good thing there was some hay in the bed of the wagon where I could stretch out and sleep while Alma did his sparking.

"Your brother been sneaking out of the lunch sack?" Jack raised his eyebrows, grinning. "Seems like he ain't too hungry all of a sudden—or maybe he's hungry for something else."

I grimaced. "Hungry to make a fool out of himself."

"I got a notion things might be changing out your way one of these days," Jack said.

"If you're hungry, there's plenty of food." I ignored his comment. "Water's in the crock."

Jack pursed his lips. "You're not much set on change, are you?"

"You want to eat or run your mouth?" This was a discussion I didn't plan to continue.

"No need to get upset." Jack had other ideas. He picked up a biscuit that I'd baked that morning and took a bite. "What's coming's coming, Nephi. You boys is young, healthy, and ambitious. You keep going like you've been and one of these days you're gonna find yourselves old broken-down men with nothing to show for it but some land you've gotten hunch-backed over and no one to pass it on to. You need to start thinking about that. It's time. How old are you anyhow?"

"Twenty-six. And I don't see any need to get in a stir. We haven't time to be messing with women, anyhow. Alma knows that."

"Nephi," Jack could be disgustingly persistently when he wanted, "you may not feel any great need for companionship other than your brother and them cows of yours but that don't mean Alma feels the same. You need to understand he's wanting something different from what you want.

"To you the land and your animals is all there is in life. For him it ain't that way. I've seen it coming for some time now. He's getting a little antsy, now and then. He's looking at the families he knows and he's thinking about what it would be like to come home to a ready-cooked meal and some female laughter. He's beginning to itch for the sound of little feet coming across the cabin floor. You can't fault him for wanting a posterity to pass his work on to."

114

"Wait a minute. How come you know so much about my brother? *You* never got married, yourself. How do you know how he feels or what he wants or what's best for us?"

"To begin with, he's told me." Jack said. "To end with, I know from my own experience. The only difference between you and me is that you're still young. I'm not. I've worked hard for what I have but I've always been too busy to worry about anything else. Now I'm getting on and I have no posterity. If you don't watch out, you're gonna wind up the same way I'm headed. Old, childless, and alone."

"Then let Alma get married. My portion can go to his family when I die. I don't care."

"If that's what you want, that's ok, too." Jack didn't seem very surprised. "Just don't stand in his way when he's looking. You don't have that right."

"If you're so worried about posterity, why don't you go looking for yourself?" I demanded.

"I just might do that." Jack grinned. Grabbing another biscuit and a slab of cheese he walked off, leaving me to stew over what he'd said.

Of all the ridiculous, cockeyed ideas. Ready-cooked meals, huh? If Alma wasn't satisfied with my cooking, maybe he needed to do a little more of it himself. And he wanted little feet pattering across the floor? And dirty diapers and being kept up all night by teething toddlers? The whole affair soured my mood to the point I even lost my desire for playing a good prank. Dad-blasted women!

CHAPTER THIRTY

I was still irritated by the time the rodeo began but the excitement was contagious enough I soon lost my bad humor.

When the Master of Ceremonies announced the first competition, Alma took his place among the other participants. It was a 'tree chopping' contest with the 'trees' being a row of posts, some ten inches in diameter, planted in the ground about eight feet apart.

"You hoping to catch the eye of a certain dark haired young lady?" Jack teased him and my brother actually blushed. Blushed! Like a schoolgirl. I couldn't believe it.

I took my place among the contestants, too. I didn't care about impressing the girl, I just wanted to best my brother—make him look foolish. Alma couldn't beat me in using an axe.

I could have saved myself the trouble. A burly lumberjack who was visiting friends in the valley walked off with the prize, leaving the rest of us eating his chips as they flew.

The lumberjack didn't do as well in the log-sawing contest that followed. Locals saw to it the only man who would pair up with him on his cross-cut saw was someone with no experience. I unbent enough to pair with Alma and we came in second.

By then the dark haired young lady had wandered off with her friends so Alma lost interest in the wild cow milking competition that followed. I didn't mind. It was hot, I was dusty from chopping and sawing, and I had no quarrel in letting someone else get kicked by a cow.

There were several cows locked in a pen at the side of a little corral—one cow per two-man team of contestants. Either man of the team could rope their allotted cow; then one would have to hold her still in whatever way he could while the other squeezed milk from one of her teats into a bottle. All they needed was one drop inside the glass lip.

I could see the handwriting on the wall. Even if they managed to rope their cow—and there was no guarantee they could—those teams would still have a fight on their hands to get any milk. I had a very healthy respect for the force of a fairly *tame* cow's kick. It didn't bear thinking what a wild cow, half-crazed with fear, would deliver. I crowded up close to the corral fence where I could watch.

Three sets of contestants lined up, ready to rope, hold and milk. The first set was obviously a couple of dudes from back east somewhere. Calls of "C'me on, now, you ain't come near to them horns with that lariat yet," and "Somebuddy slip grease on that lassoo of yours, there, pardner?" greeted their wildly swinging ropes. Both were in the corral hoping to catch a horn, a hoof, anything—but with no success. I was just thinking it was darned lucky the cow wasn't upset enough to start chasing one of them when she lost her sense of humor and sent them both scurrying over the high corral fence where jeering catcalls greeted them.

The second team was a little more exciting to watch. The cow they were given ran wildly back and forth across the corral, looking about her in frenzied fear. I didn't know either of the contestants but the man who dropped his lariat loop around her horns was about as neat a roper as I'd ever seen. He'd slipped cautiously into the corral when the cow's back was turned then stood, stump still, beside one of the fence posts.

A country cowboy, his clothing blended in with the fencing which still had weathered bark on the logs. The next time the cow ran near him he swung his lariat in a sideways arc and dropped it, neatly, over her horns. Jumping up onto the fence, he took a quick dally around the post and firmly pulled her in.

Catching her wasn't the hard part, though. His partner seemed at a loss on how to get her thrown. Even with her wide horns planted tight against the fence, her hind hooves still flew as she snorted, blowing foam from her mouth and nostrils, twisting and turning her body as much as her firmly tied head would allow.

"Git in there, Vern, an' twist her haid!"

"Naw, he'd better rope them hind feet n' stretch'er out."

"You fellers plumb loco? Vern ain't big enuff to hold that old heifer's heels. Takes a man to do the job."

"Come on there, Vern! Keep at it! You'll git her yet!"

And from Vern (whoever he was), a panting, "Gosh darn but that's the fightinist female I ever tried to hogtie!"

He kept trying to catch her feet in a snare but whenever he got in close enough to drop his loop on the ground the snorting cow would kick out at him viciously. More than once he wasn't quick enough and felt at least the tip of one of her sharp hooves. His partner, meanwhile, had tied his lariat tight and scrambled into the corral with a bottle in his hand.

"Here, you want me to ketch them heels for you?" He reached for Vern's rope just as Vern got the noose laid where he wanted it.

"Git outa my way, here, now!" Vern roared. He yanked up at the rope as the cow's left hind foot descended into the loop. "Got'er!" He backed up, quickly, wrapping the lariat in a U around the upper portion of his hips, stretching the wildly kicking cow's leg out behind her.

She fell on her right side, then tried to scramble up—her free hoof digging deep grooves in the dirt—as the first man stretched across her belly from her back side in an attempt to reach a teat without being kicked. One tiny stream of thin milk was all he got but when it hit the mouth of the glass bottle, he was up on his feet, again, like a flash—holding the jar aloft and yelling jubilantly.

Whistles, cheers and someone's lusty, "Gol dang but that's the best entertainment I've seed in my whole life!" greeted him.

The third cow was on the prod long before she charged into the arena. The crowd, already excited by the last display, was in fine humor, yelling and hooting at her as she repeatedly stormed the fence

"Ain't nobody gonna git any milk outta her!" someone shouted as the first roper cautiously climbed the corral fence, hard to the right side of a post.

Seeing him perched there on the top pole, the cow dashed for his side of the corral and literally started climbing up the fence with her forefeet. The cowboy dropped his lasso around her horns as she started up and jumped backwards off the fence, hauling on his rope as he went.

Running to the next post to the left, he took a quick dally around the top of it, stretching the cow tight against the right-side length of the post where he'd roped her.

Seeing his opportunity, the second contestant grabbed their bottle and, reaching through the corral poles to where her bag was stretched out, teats pointing towards him, grabbed one teat and pulled, squeezing tightly as he did.

Nothing.

"Dang it!" he exclaimed jerking his hand out just as a hind hoof tore bark off the pole his arm had been leaning against, "Her dad-blamed teats is smaller'n my little finger!"

The cow bawled, furiously, as he reached in again but she'd caught her hoof between the bottom and second poles of the fence and wasn't quite as active as she'd been before. The cowboy caught a teat again and, pinching it between his thumb and forefinger, stripped the milk from its tiny duct. It went just far enough for him to catch some in his jar and he leaped back, shouting. "I got it! I got it!"

CHAPTER THIRTY-ONE

The cowboy crowd was in high heat, now, more than primed for the horse relay to come. Each contestant in the race had two strings of horses, five to a string, with one string tethered at each end of a race course outlined by flag-draped stakes. The rules were that each contestant had to bridle and saddle the first horse of his number one string, mount it, ride it the quarter mile distance of the course, dismount, then transfer his saddle and bridle to the first horse on his number two string and begin the process all over again.

At least half the horses were green-broke at best and the local cowboys had been looking forward to this race ever since word of it first leaked out. Even the valley women, most of whom were still sitting in small groups where the picnic had been held, perked up and began to watch as the horses were led to their respective ends of the quarter mile stretch.

I'd never seen three of the competitors. Neither had Alma nor Jack Grey. One was a burly man of medium height who had obviously spent many hours on a horse. His legs were bowed, his shoulders hunched and his eyes had the hooded squint I'd come to associate with men who spent all their waking hours in the bright sunlight. I thought he just might win.

The second was tall and slender—late twenties perhaps. He had to be a dude. No cowboy would come to a rodeo dressed like as he was in a spotless grey suit and bowler hat. He wouldn't last more than a ride or two. I dismissed him without another thought.

The third was at least part Indian. His long black hair framed a swarthy face with black eyes, a hooked nose and high cheekbones. His graceful walk was silent, swift and sure. Most Indians knew horses. I expected him to give the burly fellow a hard run for his money.

The fourth was Frank McBride. Seeing him there beside the others, I shook my head. Whatever had possessed Frank to think he had any chance in a race like this? He'd spent his entire life farming. Probably never mounted an unbroke horse, let alone tried to ride one. All he rode was that lazy old team of Roy's—which were part of his second string.

"Frank must be desperate for some cash," Jack commented when he saw our friend line up with the other three contestants.

"How d'you figure?" I wanted to know.

"There's a healthy cash prize for the man who comes in first."

I raised my eyebrows. "And for the others?"

"Lesser prizes for the next two. A cream pie as booby prize for last place."

"Well, I guess we know who's going to get the cream pie," Alma laughed.

"I don't know," I argued. "Frank's no great shakes at riding but that dude doesn't look like he is either. Who are you betting on, Jack?"

"Hard to say. I don't—" a pistol shot signaled the beginning of the race and the excitement it generated in the horses, alone, was enough to put the audience on their toes.

The dude had his saddle and bridle on his first mount and was off down the course before anyone else had even gotten past the saddling stage. He must have picked the tamest on his string, I thought. The burly man and the Indian weren't too far behind him, though.

Frank's first horse, a wild cayuse, jumped away every time Frank tried to approach him with the saddle. He was still trying to get close to the animal when the skinny fellow came in on the second of his mounts.

That set the cayuse off. Rearing, he lashed out with one front hoof. Frank dodged, successfully, but the horse seemed to have it in for him, now. Whenever Frank tried to approach him, the horse reared and plunged, kicking wildly. Finally our neighbor gave up and moved to the last horse in his string—the one farthest from the devil he'd been trying to saddle.

This time he managed to get his saddle and bridle on. The horse even held fairly still while Frank mounted. Once in the saddle, however, the world exploded under the animal's feet. Squealing in rage it bucked, plunging wildly. Frank pulled leather for all he was worth. I winced at some of the spine-cracking jolts he was taking.

Suddenly the horse began to travel—sun-fishing as it went— right through the groups of women sitting, still, on their picnic quilts. The animal looked as if it were dancing on white-hot coals, the way it jumped around, head down, back arched and legs stiff.

121

The women scattered, shrieking in terror. The last I saw of Frank and his horse was when the nag landed in the remains of someone's fancy picnic lunch—one hoof in a bowl of potato salad, another in a still-uncut layer cake, frothy with swirled icing.

By then I was laughing so hard I didn't even see the horse plunge toward the willows along Flat Creek some distance away. I was still chuckling when the dude won the race.

It had been a good contest. While one horse would run flat out, putting his rider in the lead, the next one might object to even being approached with a bridle. There wasn't a contestant who didn't get at least a taste of Frank's ordeal.

I thought perhaps the slim fellow's height might have helped him get his tack on his horses but I couldn't account for the man's riding skills. He didn't look like he had any experience with broncs. It went to show a person couldn't judge by looks—especially since the Indian came in third.

Frank was back—horseless and dripping wet—in time for the awards ceremony. Heckling from the crowd greeted him as he walked slowly toward us.

"Hey, Frank, yore pony object to yore smell or somethin'? Cain't account for any other reason to give you a bath."

"Frank always takes bahths with his cloze on, he's so prim n' proper like."

"I wouldn't have thought the willers down by that creek would have given him enough privacy. He must really...."

"Hush! They's wimmin around. Frank, hows come yore walkin' so stiff?"

"I'll tell you what, boys," Frank shook his head, then grimaced in pain, "that's the hardest I worked for a pie in all my life."

As each cowboy contestant stepped forward to receive his award, Alma, Jack and I applauded along with the rest of the crowd. The Master of Ceremonies skillfully built anticipation before announcing the amount of each prize.

The entrants in the horse race received their awards last with the winner receiving $25.00, the second place prize being $15.00, and the Indian claiming $10.00. The booby-prize pie—kept for the very end—was housed in a box with a block of ice keeping the pie cold.

As Frank walked forward to receive his award the Master of Ceremonies opened the box and gasped.

There, nestled against the block of ice and cut into six even wedges, was a perfectly shaped . . . cowpie.*

The sky was beginning to glow pink above the Indian Head mountain on the east side of the valley when Alma slowed our team in front of Jack's cabin the next morning. Jack and I had bedded down on the hay in the wagon shortly after leaving the dance and Alma could have joined us, trusting Sleek and Sassy to get us home, but he chose to spend the hours of the homeward trip in solitary thought.

I didn't care.The music left me in a good humor and I'd slept soundly. As soon as Alma pulled the team to a standstill, however, I roused.

"Jack. Hey, Jack. You're home." I jostled our friend awake. After Jack stumbled sleepily out of the wagon and Alma started the team again, I stepped over the back of the wagon seat to sit beside my brother.

"Good music at the dance." I said, yawning and stretching slowly. "That Frenchy sure can play."

"It *was* good music. Good dance, too. You should have been there. Nothing like dancing to give a man good exercise." Satisfaction framed Alma's smile.

"I get enough exercise out here on the ranch. Besides, about time Rhoda Newbold tells me I *have* to do something you can bet it's the last thing I'm going to show up for. I noticed she dragged you out on the floor a time or two. There was no way I'd let her do it to me"

"Oh, she was looking for you, all right, but you're good enough at hiding I wasn't worried about her finding you."

"That's for sure." I yawned again, widely.

"You know, there's one thing about yesterday that's has me puzzled, though," Alma continued. "I could have sworn you were primed to pull another one of your practical jokes and I was sure she was going to be the butt of it. But the only prank I saw pulled was the one on Frank and I know you didn't do that one. You were with me all through the race. It must have been those teenaged boys that were running around." Alma yawned, too. "Well, whoever it was, I hope they enjoyed the pie. Speaking of food, is there anything left of yesterday's dinner? I'm hungry."

I stretched a second time then reached down under the seat of the wagon to pull out the box where I'd stowed the crock and the remains of our dinner. Setting it on the seat between us, I lifted the lid, reached inside and brought out a large, full-moon shaped pastry.

"You want a piece of cream pie?" I asked, grinning.

*Cowpie – polite cowboy term for bovine excrement

Alma Moulton circa 1910

CHAPTER THIRTY-TWO

That fourth of July rodeo marked a turning point in Alma. It was the oddest thing. He was still my quiet, good-natured older brother—but he wasn't.

He still worked hard on our little spread. He still irrigated carefully, and when we started to cut the hay in mid-July he swung that scythe like there was no tomorrow. But something was different. I can't say his heart wasn't in his work because he was as thorough as he'd always been, but something was missing and for the life of me I couldn't figure out what it was.

I started watching him, closely, but the more I watched and the more I turned the whole business over in my mind, the more puzzled I became. I could not put my finger on what was so different—or why.

At first I thought he was irritated about the pie incident, but that wasn't it. Alma seldom got upset, and even when he did, he was over it in a day or two. He couldn't stay angry with anyone for very long. Besides, his sense of humor was nearly as keen as mine.

Then I wondered if he was coming down with summer flu, or something equally unpleasant. But nothing came of that, either; he never got sick. And it wasn't as if he was hiding symptoms because I'd have known. Living in that little one-roomed cabin like we did made it impossible for him to hide anything from me.

So what *was* going on? The more I watched him the more uneasy I became. He'd sit down at the table morning and night, absolutely silent. Where he used to talk to me, now he never spoke unless I spoke first. His blue eyes that used to be so full of affectionate good humor, had a distant, faraway look.

I'd watch him work beside me each day and it was like watching my brother disintegrate before my eyes. I'd see him go to bed, then reach out and turn off the lamp. It was my brother's routine—but I wasn't seeing Alma. It was almost as if he was a shell rather than a man. A badger hole without the badger came to mind.

He's a stranger. He's not being moody like he was over Maude. He's just . . . well, vacant.

It didn't make much sense but I couldn't account for it in any other way. And the more I tried to figure out what was going on, the more it eluded me. Whatever was eating on him was so obscure I was completely stumped.

Then he started doing queer things. I remember the first one. It was a Saturday night and he stopped scything at six p.m..

"Let's quit for the night," he said. "We've worked long enough. Let's get cleaned up and go visiting."

You could have knocked me over with a puff of breeze. I *really* thought he was getting sick *that* night. But his face wasn't flushed and his eyes weren't red. I hadn't heard a cough out of him or a sniffle, either. What in the world was going on?

"The work's not done and there are still hours of daylight." I protested. "There's no one to visit, anyway. Jack'll still be working— Henry Cherry, Josh Coon, ..." I named off the neighbors who shared our canal with us. I knew they were all out trying to get as much done as possible in what daylight there was left—just like we should be doing.

126

"I want to visit Louis Joy's dude ranch. I met some of his wranglers at the Fourth of July dance and they said they have a little rodeo every Saturday night."

If he'd just dropped to earth from the moon I couldn't have been more astonished. I guess the look on my face must have said what I was thinking because he started trying to defend his position.

"We need to mix and mingle a little more than we've done, Nephi. That's as good a place to start as any."

"*I* don't have any particular need to mix—or mingle, either one. *My* vote keeps working." I turned back to the hay I'd been raking. There were at least two more hours of good daylight left and probably 45 minutes of serious twilight after that. A man could get a lot done in nearly three hours and that was exactly what I intended to do.

"Well, mine doesn't," Alma said, "I'll milk the cow but you can get your own supper when you get home," He started off across the field, heading for our cabin down in the river bottoms, leaving me gaping at him, my jaw hanging open so far a fly buzzed in and I didn't even notice until it lit on my tongue.

Ptooey!

Mix and mingle, huh? Mix with whom and mingle with what? So there are cowboys at the dude ranch. And his point is . . .? I should have seen it, then, but I didn't. I guess I'm a little dense at times. I tend to get focused on the job at hand and everything else goes flying by, unnoticed.

He came in late that night—really late. Late enough I'd faunched, and fumed, and rolled around in my bed until I'd finally fallen into exhausted slumber and didn't hear him slip through the door and ease himself onto his bedroll. Next morning he was up, as usual, before the grey half-light of dawn had even made a decent start across the sky. I wondered, when I followed him out the cabin door, if there would be a change in him . . . maybe the brother I knew would be back . . . but no. Whatever he'd hoped to gain from mixing and mingling with a bunch of cowpokes apparently hadn't come along.

Since he obviously hadn't found what he was looking for, I figured everything would have blown over by the next weekend and we'd carry on as usual. Wrong supposition.

Again he took off at six o'clock. Again I refused to go with him. Again he came home the same as he'd been when he left. Same scene the following week. And the week after that. By then I was beginning to get a little tense.

He's not talking. He's not doing anything but working himself to the bone all week, then gallivanting on Saturday night. And I haven't noticed it's doing him any good, either. He isn't any happier when he gets home than he was when he left—it's been the same for the past several weeks. In the mean time I'm putting in normal work hours. By myself, I might add. Whose ranch is this, anyhow? Mine alone?

About time I was starting to get a little more than tense, he came up with a new quirk. Sunday morning, after chores and breakfast were over and we were cleaning up the cabin, he mentioned he thought we ought to go to church.

"You know," he said, "we haven't been to church since we left Utah. The chapel over in Kelly has services at ten o'clock. Let's go."

"Since when did you get religion?" I demanded. Had somebody I didn't know suddenly invaded my brother's body? "Besides, if you really want to go to church," I pointed out, "the church on Mormon Row is as close as Kelly and at least you could see John and T.A. and Wally."

All three of our cousins had badgered Aunt Rhody into letting them come to the Hole a couple years before. I guess there was a fracas-and-a-half over that! Made me heartily glad I was already in the Hole, not back in Darby.

Aunt Rhody or no Aunt Rhody, the three of them were going out on their own—and doing it on the other side of the Tetons. Sons or no sons, Aunt Rhody was just as adamant that they were not—with multiple exclamation points afterwards. Finally everyone settled on a compromise—her sons could go to the Hole but they had to homestead on Mormon Row where they'd be surrounded by People of their Religious Persuasion.

It worked out alright. Sort of. T.A. went to church every Sunday; Wally did off and on. John, like Alma and me, decided he had other, more important, things to do.

Now Alma thinks he needs religion? That church in Kelly isn't even Mormon . . . it's Baptist.

Again, it was all right there in front of me but I couldn't see it. Nor could I see wasting a beautiful day by sitting in a building on a hard wooden bench, listening to some fellow drone on and on and on about hell and damnation—something I dealt with every day. . .hell from elk and squirrels and damnation from beaver in the river above our headgate.

But, again, Alma was adamant.

"I'm going to the church in Kelly. You coming or no?" he asked.

"Definitely 'or no'. I'm not going to waste my day with some fool thing like listening to that preacher rant and rave about how I'm going to toast my toes in hellfire." The very idea irritated me.

"It's not like that. You ought to come. You might like it." Again, Alma was defending his position.

"How would you know? Ever been to a Baptist church before?" I knew he hadn't.

"No, but you never know until you try."

"Try if you want. I'm not going. I have a ditch to clean out and the rest of the hay to load on the wagon."

"Suit yourself. I'll see you later." By then he was ready to go, leaving me staring and shaking my head in confused disbelief as he rode out of sight.

CHAPTER THIRTY-THREE

I didn't have time to think about Alma's quirks, though. As I loaded the last of the hay onto the wagon, Henry Cherry, our neighbor just to the east of our field, rode up. He was an abrupt old man—not given to much preliminary chit-chat before he got out what he had on his mind.

"I'm leaving the Hole," he said as he reined in his horse. I waited for him to continue but he didn't. He just sat there, his twisted back hunched in his bibbed overalls and faded-plaid cotton shirt. His bald head shone in the blazing August sun as he sadly looked across our field.

What did he want me to say? I searched my mind for something polite, then gave up and asked the obvious.

"How come?"

"Gettin' too old. Can't keep up with the long winters and short summers. Don't want to spend another winter here. My rheumatiz is bothering me already and it's only August."

I could believe that. Winters in the Hole were even more fierce than the winter we'd spent on the Egin bench, if that was possible. Alma and I hadn't had it as bad as our neighbors up on the flats, of course. We were protected from the wind by the river bottom's forest. Even so, it was rough.

It had to be ten times worse for those living where Henry did. And he was so stoged up, sometimes he walked all bent over. Is was a wonder how he got the work done that he did—particularly during blizzards—he was so gimpy.

"I'm sorry to hear that," I said, sincerely. Henry was a good neighbor, fair with his watering turn; always one you could count on to help out when squirrels dug holes in the canal banks, always the last one to leave with his little herd when it was time to separate cattle at roundup in the fall. We'd hate to lose him.

"Where are you going?" I asked.

"Depends on if I can sell my property," Henry said. "I was wondering if you boys was int'rested. Don't have a lot cleared but the water right is secure for the entire 160 acres."

My ears perked up at that piece of information. Alma and I had spent the last five years wishing we had more water rights so we'd have a longer irrigating turn. Longer turns meant better crops. Better crops meant maybe we could keep our cattle at home, winters, instead of trailing them out to Teton Basin for Uncle George to feed.

My initial prediction that there was enough feed on this place for over-wintering our stock had been so far off the mark I'd been totally embarrassed. To say nothing about frustrated. And we hadn't been able to spend the winter in Idaho, helping to feed our cattle, because there was a limit to how long we could be off our property if we were going to prove up on it.

So, for the last several winters, we'd kept our horses and bulls at home—we had enough feed for them—and trailed the cows and calves on a tedious trip across the Snake River, down to Wilson, up over Teton Pass and down through Victor to Uncle George's place on Chapin Creek. We each took a short turn staying with Uncle George, helping him feed cattle to cut the feed bill, but it was still costly and inconvenient.

Then we had to trail them home again in the spring just in time for them to go to the summer range. The young spring calves were totally exhausted by then, to say nothing of the nuisance of being gone at a time when we really needed to be irrigating with every ounce of water we could get instead of batching it out on a long trail ride. It would make sense to buy Henry's place but I sure hated the idea of being in debt.

"I don't know," I said. "What are you asking for it?"

Henry and I discussed prices and his needs for some time . . . me mostly listening. He was willing to take yearly payments after our calves were sold in the fall—which was the only way I was willing to buy—and he wanted me to know all about what he'd done and what he'd learned in the time he'd been living on his homestead.

I figured he had a lot of knowledge to shed my way if I just had the patience to keep my mouth shut. Sometimes it was hard because I didn't necessarily agree with his views but he'd been in the Hole longer than we had and he wasn't anybody's dunce. I tried to keep my attention focused.

"You got to plan on at least three deep cold snaps here a winter," he was saying. "I got a thermometer by my cabin door." I knew that. I'd been to Henry's cabin a number of times for one reason or another. "It'll get down around forty-five or fifty below zero during the snaps." That was information I didn't know because we didn't have a thermometer. I knew it got real cold but I hadn't realized it was *that* cold. Suddenly I understood why our animals had eaten so much more than we'd counted on.

"I remember one winter when it was sixty below ever day between Christmas and New Years," Henry continued, "and for several days past that. My little calves that I'd just weaned humped their little backs, huddled together, and survived. My biggest calf . . . the one I'd have thought would weather it the best . . . laid down and died.

"He was still alive when I found 'im. Got the McBrides and Josh Coon to come help me roll 'im onto a canvas and drag 'im to the cabin. I put 'im right in front of the fireplace, I did. Built a roaring fire, heated up milk and poured it down his throat, covered 'im with canvas and quilts, did everything I could think to do and it was like he had already departed even though he was still breathing. Simply lacked the will to live, he did." Henry shook his head at the memory. "He was just sort of vacant. . . kind of like a badger hole when the badger's done moved on. Finally he just quit breathing and he was gone."

That stopped me cold in my tracks! 'Vacant.' 'Already departed even though he was still breathin'.' Wasn't that what I'd been seeing in Alma recently? But what shocked me more was '...badger hole when the badger's done moved on.' It was all too eerily familiar.

And 'Simply lacked the will to live.' Was that how Alma felt? Suddenly I was frantic for Henry to leave so I could give this a good think.

Of course he wasn't in any hurry to ride off—I couldn't be that lucky. The sun was warming his old back, the breeze was fresh on his bald head, his hay was all in his stack yard and he was primed to chat. He really wanted to sell to us. He really wanted to gossip. And mostly, I think, he was just plain lonely.

Normally I enjoyed his infrequent visits but this time I had to struggle to be polite. I didn't want to antagonize him but I was unbearably restless by the time our neighbor was finally talked out and rode off towards his cabin.

CHAPTER THIRTY-FOUR

'Vacant'. I turned my team and wagon toward our barn in the river bottoms. *'Already departed even though he was still breathing.' That's Alma, alright.* But that Henry should have used the same way to describe his calf as I'd been mentally describing my brother made me shiver, hot sun or no hot sun.

'...like a badge hole when the badger's done moved on.' It almost made the hair on the back of my neck stand up. But the part that was most appalling was his observation that his calf had *'simply lacked the will to live'.*

Alma's working well enough so I don't think that fits. But, still,.... If my brother is lacking the will to live, I need to know why.

I thought about our lives—where we'd been and what we'd accomplished. It hadn't been easy, putting everything we'd had into the Egin place and then losing it. But I could feel satisfaction in knowing we'd left the farm better than it had been when we first came.

Although the Darby farm hadn't been satisfying, we'd given it everything we had, too. I couldn't feel bad about our performance there.

And the Jackson spread? It probably fell somewhere in between. We'd held our own despite elk and squirrels—and winter weather more than six months out of the year. We had recently proved up on it so the homestead was now ours.

I'm satisfied. And Alma should be, too. Granted, the work's hard. Granted, we've not realized our dreams . . . yet . . . but we're still young, for Pete's sake—Alma's only twenty-nine and I'm twenty-six. We aren't starving and we aren't falling behind. Truth be told, we have things better than our parents did at our age. What more could he want?

I'd never seen Alma this upset about anything, before, except Maude—and she was such ancient history I doubted he even remembered her name. So what could possibly be eating at him now?

Again, I should have understood because it was as plain as the blemishes on Emma-Jane's nose, but I didn't. I stewed about the situation, becoming more uneasy by the hour. I had to do something for my brother. That was plain. But the question was what?

133

Eventually I decided there was only one answer—buy Henry out. With more water and better crops, Alma couldn't help but be satisfied.

Then, again, maybe I wouldn't have to go that far. Maybe religion was all he needed and he'd come home, today, acting like his old self again.

I'd nearly talked myself into thinking everything would turn out alright without us making any changes when Alma came home. One look at his face and I could tell the church in Kelly hadn't given him what he was looking for. If anything he was even more remote than he'd been before he left. I didn't want to, but I knew I had to do something so I decided to jump in with both feet and hope for the best.

"Henry Cherry's selling his place," I blurted out.

"So I heard." His indifference, as he pulled his saddle off Darky and put it away in the barn, was heartbreaking.

"He's offered it to us—yearly payments—and we'd be getting his water rights along with it. That would give us half again as much water." He didn't say anything so I plunged on. "More water means we'd raise more hay. I hate being in debt to anyone but I think it's the only way, Alma."

"You're willing to go into debt?" Alma looked at me full on for the first time in I don't know how long.

"Yeees, I suppose so," I said, slowly. "I'd think we'd be safe enough if we were making yearly payments. We may need to find winter jobs to supplement but I've been thinking about it and I think we could make it work."

"Rilla Hedrick is selling out, too," Alma mentioned, casually. "She has twice as much land as Henry." He let that tidbit drop and said nothing more as he started currying Darky.

Rilla was selling out, too! I guess that shouldn't have surprised me so much. Since her husband's death, their double homestead was too much for her to keep up. She didn't have a lot of work—they'd broken up only as much as they'd had to—but they'd put in their five years and the required improvements . . . a small log cabin, ditches, and . . . ditches. . . .And water.

"Has she secured *her* water rights as well?" I asked.

"I suppose," Alma didn't seem to care.

134

"Alma, think what we could do if we had both Henry's and Rilla's spreads."

"We already have more than we can keep up with."

"No, *think man!* I'm not talking about clearing it all. What needs to be cleared, is cleared already. I'm talking about water rights. If we had water rights to another 480 acres we'd have all the water we'd need to make this place what we want it to be!" I could see it. Alfalfa-timothy chest high in our field and Henry's, and Rilla's land used mostly for pasture with its tall sage sheltering our newborn calves during spring weather. We could build Rilla's field up over time.

"Nephi, Rilla isn't willing to take yearly payments for her spread. She wants her full asking price, outright." At the sound of Alma's quiet voice, the golden image I was building disintegrated into a thousand tiny dark shards.

I looked at Alma.

The hollowness was still in his eyes—even more bleak than before because now there was hopelessness as well. Naked hopelessness. It frightened me so much that I turned away, making a business of examining my saddle. I didn't want him to see my fear.

Hopelessness means giving up. Henry's calf gave up. And died. Is my brother dying? I wanted to ask him what was going on inside. I wanted him to tell me what he was feeling and why—but I didn't know how to get him started. I groped, frantically, for something to say. Nothing came.

How far gone is he? Is it too late to change his thinking? What can I do? And then I knew. I knew what had to be done to bring Alma back. *We have to buy Henry's and Rilla's properties and we have to make changes, or I do, at least. Alma has to see progress—to see that his life isn't being wasted, that his dreams can come true. I'm the one who's kept it from happening. I'm going to have to bend and I'll have to hurry or he'll break. I'd sooner cut off my right hand than go into debt but this is my brother's life I'm dealing with. If debt's what it takes, then debt it'll have to be.*

Besides, when it gets right down to it, maybe he won't want to buy Rilla's spread. Maybe he'll say that Henry's place will be enough. Sure. That's probably what he'll say. After all, he's almost as frugal as I am. And maybe, if he sees I'm willing to give, he'll say we

135

don't have to buy anything. Maybe he'll snap out of this on his own and we won't have to go into debt at all.

But now what? How do I go about this? What do I say? Guess I'd better start with the basics.

"What's she asking for it? Do you know?" I asked.

He named a price. It was reasonable—roughly double what John was asking. I did some quick calculations in my head.

If he persisted in wanting this, and with decent weather so our crops could grow....

"Let's do it." I said.

"Do what?" Alma asked.

"Buy them both out."

Dead silence.

More dead silence.

Unendurable dead silence

My back was still turned to him and I was beginning to wonder if he'd fainted or something but he couldn't have. I'd have heard him fall. I wanted to turn around and look—and yet I didn't. I didn't want him to see how worried I was, to see the doubt, the hesitance, and, yes, the naked fear I was feeling. Fear for his wellbeing and fear for our financial stability, our freedom from debt.

Please, God, help him to snap out of this without wanting to buy anything! Please.

Finally he spoke. "I don't think I heard that, Nephi. What was it you said?" Very polite. *Very* quiet.

"You heard me. I think we need to buy them both out."

Silence, again. Then, finally, "That's a switch. What makes you figure?"

I turned to face him. "Alma, we're just barely scraping by. Fixing fences after those consarned elk break them down is about all we get done besides irrigating. And it wouldn't matter if we did clear more of our land—we wouldn't get any more water rights than we have right now, so clearing land doesn't make sense." I knew this wasn't news to Alma. He'd tried to talk to me about it before but I'd always refused to listen because I was so dead set against going into debt. I hoped, desperately, that I could make this sound believable, now. And that God was listening somewhere.

"We don't have enough water as it is because this soil's so gravelly the water sinks to China before the alfalfa even gets any," I continued. "We need more water rights—a longer irrigating turn—if we're going to do anything more than subsist." I was almost talking myself into the whole idea as I went along. Almost.

"I don't want to start over again somewhere else." *That* was the honest-to-gosh truth and I knew Alma felt the same. I gave him my final and best pitch. "We've proved up on this place. Let's do what it takes to build on it now." *Say we don't need to, Alma. Come on, say it!*

"I thought I'd never hear you say that." he said, softly, and I could have sworn I saw the glimmer of tears in his eyes. The emotions that crossed his face—wonder, hope, a beginning renewal— nearly broke my heart but as I stood there watching, Alma became, once again, the brother I'd been missing.

Forget the debt. Joy flooded over me so strong I almost wanted to hug him. My brother had finally come home.

CHAPTER THIRTY-FIVE

The change in Alma was astonishing. We hadn't even reached the cabin before he unleashed a tornado of ideas. He'd been withdrawing so steadily and for so long that when he started laying out his plans, it took me a while to realize this was something he'd been thinking about and wanting for a long time.

Not only that but he already had all his ducks lined up. Here I was, still in the agonizing, 'What can I do to help Alma?' mode, and he was cured, up, and running. He had all the alternatives, complete with their good and bad points, firmly fixed in his mind and before I quite knew what was happening, I was the possessor of knowledge I'd never wanted—mainly because this wasn't something I really wanted to do in the first place.

True, I'd suggested it—because I was desperate to give Alma something to cling to, something to think about. But I expected him to reject the idea of buying Rilla's place and just go for Henry's spread, if he even wanted that. It *was* a good idea to buy them both but the debt load was a lot stiffer than I really wanted to take on. Besides, I hadn't expected him to jump on it with such bewildering speed.

In no time I discovered he'd been asking around and decided he didn't want to work with anyone in the Hole—we were better off going to a banker in Idaho and he even knew the name of the best one to approach. - *I'd like to know where you came up with that information!*

The asking prices of both Henry's and Rilla's properties were reasonable and we were sure to get the loan we needed.

He'd looked over both properties - *Where in the world was I when you were doing this? Have I been that blind?* - and was familiar with their irrigation systems. Rilla's wasn't ditched well but Henry's was perfectly adequate. We could re-ditch Rilla's place this fall and have it ready for the spring. Grain would be a good crop for her acreage. And on . . . and on . . . and on, all through the time we fixed and ate our supper.

And then, as we were doing the dishes, the clincher came—the comment that showed me just how out of step I was with my brother.

"And I think we need to borrow just a little extra, buy ourselves some new clothes, and spend the winter in Utah."

"*Whaat?*" I nearly dropped the cup I was washing. "You've got to be joshing me!"

"Never been more serious," he assured me as he put our two plates, neatly dried, on the shelf beside the stove.

"And who's supposed to look after our cattle? If we buy Henry's and Rilla's spreads we'll finally have enough feed to keep our cows home for once. Actually, more than enough." I protested, a heat rising under my shirt that had nothing to do with my scalding dish water.

"You want to keep washing, there? I'm out of things to dry," Alma said. His voice was calm but even in the dim lamp light I could see an excited fire in his blue eyes. "We can split the hay with the McBrides in return for them feeding our animals along with theirs. Their crop was short this year. - *Excuse me? Where was I when you got all this information?*

"We haven't been back to visit the folks since we left Utah in oh-two," he continued. "John's been married these past six years and Malinda got hitched the year before last. Mother and Father are all alone, now, except for when Charlie wanders home. We need to go spend some time with them and we can if we plan it right."

Again, I should have realized what was going on but I didn't. I still can't believe I was so dense. But I wasn't looking for deeper meanings because he was right. Our clothes *were* worn—downright ragged, in fact. We hadn't been able to afford anything new since we'd left Heber City. And we hadn't been home since then, either— partly because we couldn't afford the trip, partly because the homestead laws had tied us to our land, and partly because of Alma's feelings about Maude. His sudden willingness to return meant, to me, that he'd finally and irrevocably put her memory behind him. That was a good sign . . . one I thoroughly approved of.

"If we go to Utah," I said slowly, thinking as I spoke, "we can get winter work from some stockman around Heber City—or maybe in one of the area mines. I'd think we could make a serious dent in our debt before the winter was over," I finished the last of the dishes and walked to the door to throw the dishwater outside. "I don't like the idea of borrowing extra money for store-bought clothes but I'm willing to buy a couple bolts of fabric. Mother's an expert seamstress. She'll make our clothes for us."

"I don't want to go to Heber City as threadbare as we are." Alma was adamant. "And, besides, Mother's likely to be busy. You know she mentioned in a letter, some time back, that she's being called on more and more as a midwife."

We argued back and forth for a while but I finally won out. We'd borrow for the train trip and the cloth, with the idea that if Mother saw how ratty we looked when we first came, she'd find some way to get clothes made for us—even if she had to ask for help from her friends. We'd wear the best we had to Heber City but change before she saw us.

Alma wasn't excited about our compromise but I was satisfied. I knew we needed new clothes and the idea of seeing Mother again was—well, it had been too long. We shook on our agreement and went to bed but I was too excited to sleep.

I'm going to see Mother again.

I wouldn't have come up with the idea on my own—I was always too focused on the job at hand to see other possibilities—but the more I thought of it, the more I wanted tomorrow to come so we could start putting our plans into motion.

I never guessed what this winter would mean to Alma and to our future—or how important our visit would be to our folks. If I'd had any idea, I'd have insisted on buying Henry's spread, only, on time payments and spending another bone-chilling winter in the Hole.

CHAPTER THIRTY-SIX

One of the most beautiful sounds I'd heard since I didn't know when, was the train whistle as we approached each junction in the Heber Valley. Each blast joyfully welcomed her valley boys home. I couldn't keep a grin off my face as I pressed my nose against the window, trying to see all the familiar landmarks that we passed.

"There's the draw where the trapper's cabin was. Do you think it's still standing?" I asked Alma. "I want to snowshoe up and take a look sometime this winter."

He didn't answer.

"Remember when we herded cows in that meadow?" I asked a few minutes later. "Lyman was supposed help us but he went off shooting doves up in the cliffs. Lazy bugger. I will say one thing for him, though, he sure can shoot." I hadn't thought about Lyman in a long time. "I wonder what he's doing these days? Probably still living off his mother. I don't think that'll ever change."

Alma still didn't answer but I didn't notice. In fact, he didn't say a word until we passed the Murdock home. By then it was deepening twilight and there must have been a dozen Aladdin lamps burning in each room of the red sandstone house as we passed. Light streamed through the windows and out across the early winter snow that blanketed the Murdock yard.

I compared the two or three inches of snow, here, with the foot or more there'd been in Jackson when we'd ridden our horses out of the valley to Teton Basin. Winter was coming on with a single-minded seriousness up there. Was that just yesterday? It seemed like we'd been on the train for a week.

"I wonder what happened to the Murdock girls?" Alma said in an offhand manner, as their house slid out of view.

"Probably married and gone." I couldn't have cared less. In fact, I'd forgotten the Murdocks even had girls although one sat in front of me in grammar school and I used a thumbtack to pin her braid to my desk one day. Got a whipping from the school master for doing it, too.

Ah, those were the good old days.

Suddenly I realized how much I'd missed Heber City's quiet, tree-lined streets, so different from the wild, untamed town of

Jackson. As the engine slowed I strained to see our grandparents' old house with its huge cottonwood trees, the Heber City Tabernacle just beyond. Then I jumped up to drag my grip off the rack overhead. I intended to be the first person off the train.

"Whoa, slow up!" Alma protested but I saw the smile in his eyes and knew he was as excited as I was to be coming home.

"You can poke along if you want to," I retorted. "I'm having one of Mother's home-cooked meals tonight. You take your time and there won't be anything left for you." By the time Alma caught up with me, I'd put on my ragged work coat and was already a block away from the depot, traveling fast.

We hadn't warned anyone that we were coming—we'd agreed to surprise Mother—and I was in such a hurry to get home and see her I nearly ran the entire eight blocks. Even Alma, with his long legs, was hard put to keep up with me. I could not wait to see the look on her face when we walked through her door.

I wasn't disappointed, either.

She was busy trimming the lamp on her dining room table—I'd nearly forgotten how stark-white her damask cloth was—when we slipped through her outside door, placed our grips in the hall, and tip-toed past the dining room and into the kitchen. I'd also forgotten how welcoming her warm kitchen stove could be on a cold wintry night—or how wonderful her cornbread with meat-and-onion gravy smelled.

And what was that simmering on the stove top? I lifted the lid and sniffed. Stewed prunes with dumplings. I thought I'd died and gone to heaven until mother walked back out to the kitchen and saw the backsides of two big, ragged men bending over her stove. The shriek she let out fairly curdled my blood.

Of course that brought Father on the run and things were a little exciting there, for a minute or two. I thought Mother might even faint. My mother, Lizzie Moulton, who was always so controlled and quiet, fluttered around, emitting high-pitched "ooohs", her eye twitching madly, while my habitually silent Father got pretty loud, as well.

But eventually the excitement died down and they got used to the idea that these ragged strangers were actually their two youngest sons come home for a visit. Father nearly wrung our hands off, he pumped them so hard, and Mother turned all pink and flustered and flew about setting more places on her table.

My, but it was good to be back home!

THIRTY-SEVEN

It didn't take me long to find a job with a dairy farmer just outside of town, milking cows morning and night, seven days a week, and feeding them between milkings. Sunday afternoons off.

Alma, on the other hand, wanted a job in town. He took a position as a clerk in the mercantile. I thought he was crazy but he said he wanted to be around people. I couldn't see the sense in that; I was as perfectly happy working with cattle as I'd ever been and wild horses couldn't have persuaded me to work in a store. But, whatever made his day....

And he seemed satisfied with his new job, what little I saw of him. The hours he kept were unbelievable, though. He didn't go to work before six a.m. like I did, of course, but he frequently wasn't home until midnight or later. I hoped he was being paid well for stocking the store all those late hours. I'd had no idea jobs in mercantile stores were so demanding.

We bought the cloth Mother chose and she set to work making a new suit for each of us. I didn't know what I needed a suit for—or Alma, either, for that matter—but I didn't say anything. After all, she was the one making the clothes. And even before the suits were finished, she'd whipped out a shirt and new pair of work pants for Alma. She said he needed to look good for his job. I guess she was right. It didn't matter what I looked like; the cows didn't care.

I'd see her in deep conversation with my brother, occasionally, on a Sunday afternoon when he was at home, but I had the feeling they changed their topic whenever I came near because all I ever heard was chatter about the clothes she was making us and I didn't recall ever hearing Mother discuss such a thing on the Sabbath. I figured they were probably talking about what all we'd been doing since we'd left home although I couldn't see why they didn't feel they could include me in the discussion.

It didn't bother me, though. I was too busy getting acquainted with my new nieces and nephews. There were so many of them it kept me pretty busy on my short Sunday afternoons. I knew Father wouldn't have approved but I took them tobogganing behind my brother, Joe's, horse every Sunday that I had the chance. Joe, Tom and Sarah didn't mind their kids playing on Sunday; I never bothered to ask John. I knew he *would* mind so his two little girls were never included.

Sarah's teenaged boys and her daughter, Deon, were as enthusiastic as all get out, though. So were Joe's Naomi, Nephi and Orville although they were much younger. Tom had mostly daughters but they were as wild as March hares and a lot of fun to haul around. We'd careen down the sleepy Sunday streets, sliding around corners, then gallop out into the countryside with the children shrieking in glee.

Sometimes I even took them clear to the foothills where we slid down the slopes, using the horse to pull the toboggan back to the top; the youngest children being allowed to ride. Those were good times. I invited Alma to join us but he never did. Sometimes Joe or Tom would, but never Alma.

Then I noticed, the Sunday after Christmas, a hint of the old hopelessness back in his eyes.

What's this new wrinkle? I wondered. *I went into debt to make him happy, didn't I? We bought the property he wanted, didn't we? We boarded our cows and came home like he wanted. Mother's making some right fine clothes for us—like he wanted. He has a good-paying job. What in the world's he moping about now?*

Before I got the chance to ask, he informed me he was going back to Jackson.

"I'm catching the morning train," he told me that night as we crawled into bed. "I want to check on our cattle and shovel the snow off the cabin."

"What for? Roy and Maggie are taking care of all that. They'd let us know if there was a problem."

"I just feel like I need to," he said. And there was no swaying him. He left while I was milking the next morning.

I fussed and fumed during the days that followed, wishing he'd hurry and get home. Nights were worse. I tossed and turned, feeling ill at ease without his presence in our old attic room.

Then came the telegram:

CATTLE OK STOP   WORKING FOR UNCLE GEORGE STOP SEE YOU APRIL 1 STOP   ALMA

CHAPTER THIRTY-EIGHT

"You know, Nephi, you can't expect Alma to plan his life around you."

I was moping around in the parlor, watching Mother while she sat in her rocking chair reading her Bible one Sunday afternoon when she decided it was Time to Give Nephi a Talking To.

I suppose she figured it was needed. I'd had absolutely no enthusiasm for going out with the nieces and nephews since Alma'd left. I ate, worked—frequently forgetting half my chores—, ate, stocked Mother's wood boxes in the kitchen and parlor—when I remembered them—, moped a while and slept. Then got up and did the same thing the next day.

"You've spent your life clinging to your brother and hiding in his shadow, son," she continued, taking off her spectacles and putting them, neatly, in her crocheted carrying case before setting them on the little tilt-top table beside her rocking chair. "You need this time apart from him as much as he needs to be apart from you."

I disagreed wholeheartedly and didn't hesitate to let her know it.

"I'd like to know why," I said. "We were getting along just fine. Why'd he go stay in Chapin, anyway? He was making more money working at the mercantile. The whole idea of this winter was for us to be able to pay off our debts faster." Alma had let me down—which was another reason for my moping.

"Nephi." My mother could be very firm when she wanted and right now she wanted. "His being in Chapin is much more important than getting out of debt immediately. Alma needs his space. He needs to be able to be his own man without having to worry about his younger brother. This winter will be good for both of you—help you become more independent."

"What's to be independent about?" I wanted to know. "Mother, Alma and I are partners. We've worked together all our lives and we've co-owned our spread these last eight years. Thick or thin, we've done everything together and we've pulled each other through the hard times. Why should he suddenly need space? It's not like being partners was all my idea. He's the one who wanted to take me along when we first left Heber City. If he's changed his mind, he needs to tell me."

146

"Oh, I don't think he's changed his mind about working with you, but I do think he wants to be his own person."

That didn't make sense. "Are you saying he wants his own cabin? That's a dumb idea. Why share everything else and live in separate quarters? It just makes for more housekeeping and cooking chores."

Mother sighed and closed her eyes for a moment before answering me. Her eyelid twitched enough times I knew she was agitated and I'd better pay attention.

"Nephi, it has nothing to do with you having a cabin of your own. There are things that are important to Alma that you don't care about. Hopefully some day you will, but you don't, now. He needs time and space to make his goals become reality."

"Whaaat?" I interrupted her, even more confused than before. "He hasn't any goals other than building up our ranch. It's what we both want. And him working for Uncle George is only going to postpone that because now we'll be in debt longer. Uncle George doesn't pay nearly as much as the Mercantile did."

"Nephi, he wants a family of his own just like his older brothers have."

There, she'd said it: the same thing Jack Grey was trying to tell me last July. Irritation flooded over me.

"Where did you get that idea?"

"We've talked about it," she said, calmly, as she rocked back and forth in her chair.

"You *what*?"

"Alma's talked to me about it," she repeated, her patience even more irritating than her words. "That's why he wanted to work in the Mercantile. That's why he was spending all of his evenings away from home. He was looking. But he didn't find anything that interested him here in Heber City so he left to look elsewhere."

I gaped at her for what seemed like an eternity, my brain reeling at the news. Here I'd thought his coming to Heber City meant he'd gotten women out of his system.

At first I wanted to panic, but then logic and common sense took over and I laughed.

"Well, I guess I don't have much to worry much about then," I said. "There's nothing to look at, up at Uncle George's, except cows." And with that I took myself off to visit my brother, Tom, leaving Mother to finish her scripture reading alone.

CHAPTER THIRTY-NINE

I wished Mother was as finished with her conversations as I was. It seemed almost every time she found me at home, alone, she had something to say about Alma and me and independence and dreams and families—which, correctly interpreted, meant marriage—and . . . and . . . and, until I was beginning to regret having come back to Utah in the first place.

"Nephi," she said one day as I began attacking a generous piece of dried-apple pie she'd just set before me, "why are you so against Alma pursuing his own personal goals? I don't have a problem with you not wanting to get married, yourself, but why do you get so upset over the idea of him finding his own brand of happiness?"

These days it seemed like she was *always* starting these conversations when I was eating. No better way to ruin a man's meal than to turn it sour with a discourse on marriage or dreams or something of that ilk.

"How would I know?" I mumbled between bites.

"If you truly don't know then you need to do some thinking about it," she said.

"It's just a stupid idea," I shrugged. "You know as well as I do marriage means unhappiness."

"Wherever did you get that idea?" She seemed genuinely shocked. I picked at my pie, not quite knowing what to say to her. She waited for a while, then demanded, "Now, Nephi, you answer me! I want to know where you came up with such a foolish notion."

"Look at *you*," I finally said. "You're not happy. Father's given you a bum deal ever since he brought Aunt Annie and Aunt Mary home."

It was a sore spot with her, and I knew it. I'd never have brought it up if she hadn't backed me into a corner, but she had and now I looked at her, seeing pain, mingled with astonishment, cross her face. I guess she never expected me to say something like that, and I felt miserable knowing my words hurt her.

But it was true. A lot of the valley residents admired my father and thought him a Very Fine Fellow, as Honest and Upright a Citizen as They Came, but I'd seen this pain, before, in my mother and I didn't agree with them. To me he was cold, distant, and dictatorial.

His world was one of community and church service with precious little attention and even less financial support going to his families.

Mother, being Lizzy Moulton, had managed fairly well these past twenty years or so. When the United States outlawed polygamy she, as the first (and with the new law, the only legal) wife had taken charge of the family finances. She held title to everything he owned—his farm, his animals, even their home. I thought it was Father's just dues that he didn't dare have anything in his own name for fear it might be confiscated.

Not being a dunce, either—except, maybe, when she married Father—Mother'd been determined that her children would no longer go without because of Annie's and Mary's demands. Sarah, Joe and Tom had been big enough, by that time, to hire themselves out and bring in money, too. Through her frugality, she was soon able to purchase the home she now lived in—a comfortable house with two gabled upstairs bedrooms; a kitchen, dining room, and ample parlor, as well as a bedroom for herself and Father, downstairs.

There were no dust kittens in her house and no weeds in her garden. And she was as perfect as everything she owned. The only mistake she'd ever made was to marry Father. But she'd been young, then. One could chalk her single lapse of good judgment up to innocence and the desire I knew she had to live the life of a Godly woman who fulfilled her Place in the World.

I guess she saw I was off on a different planet about then for she said, with more firmness than I'd ever heard from her before, "Nephi, if there's one thing I want you to understand it's this: I married your father because I respected, admired and loved him deeply. I've been married to him for over forty years, now, and my respect, love and admiration for him have grown, not diminished. He's an honest, hard-working pillar in this community, who's done a great deal to build up the valley and to make life easier and safer for everyone in it. He's served whenever and wherever he's been asked, and he's done it well with no complaint at the inconvenience to himself."

"Has he ever thought of the inconvenience to you?" I asked.

"Son, a man can do good work only when the woman beside him is also behind him. If he doesn't have her support, his contributions will be nothing more than mediocre at best. Your father shines in what he does, and I'd like to think it's because I've given him the freedom to do so. To my way of thinking, what he's accomplished in this town and in this valley is my accomplishment as well. Of course I'm not on the town council or the Sunday School board, but if I was a nagging, complaining wife he wouldn't be, either. I'm very proud of who he is and what he's accomplished.

"If he has any real fault it's that he cares, perhaps too deeply, about everyone around him. He didn't *love* Annie and Mary like he did me—he never has, and he never will—but he's tried to give them the very best he could. He's tried to be a good husband to them, even if it hasn't worked out so well."

"If he loved you, but didn't love them, why'd he marry them?"

"He married them because he was gentleman enough to try to rescue them from an impossible situation with their stepfather. Maybe it didn't work out the way he'd hoped or wanted, but you can't fault him for trying."

I thought *I* could but it was just like my mother to try to shield him.

"You may not understand your father," she continued, "but he's always loved every one of his children with all of his heart."

I doubted that. I couldn't think of any time when it had been apparent, and the snort I gave in answer to her ridiculous statement told her so.

"Nephi," she said sharply, "you need to learn a lesson or two about life!"

I wondered what she thought she could tell me that I didn't already know. Life hadn't been all that easy for Alma and me. I figured she was going to give me a lecture about marriage or parenting or something of that nature but she surprised me. When she resumed talking, after a significant pause in which she sat quietly with her eyes closed, her hands pressed together and her fingertips under her chin as if she were praying, she didn't even mention either one.

"You like cherry pie, Nephi," she said.

I was startled. She sure knew how to get my attention by changing conversational directions.

"But even cherries have pits," she continued. "If you're not careful you can break a tooth on a cherry pit you aren't expecting." I'd almost broken a tooth on a cherry pit, once, and she knew it, so she had my attention this far.

"Life's like that, Nephi," she said. "There's the good part that we all like—the sweet cherry pie—but there's also the part we can break ourselves on if we get careless—the pit. It's our choice. We can whine about the pits, and develop a 'woe is me' attitude, making ourselves totally miserable, or we can use the difficult times to help us become more cautious and to make the blue skies and sunshine that follow the storms seem more brilliant and warm by contrast.

"There have been rocky spots in my life, yes. I've stubbed my toes a few times when it really wasn't necessary. Sometimes I've been nearly consumed with resentment and anger. But Son, I've learned to take the pits and use them to help me appreciate the sweet fruits of my marriage.

"Your father is a good man and I'm a lucky woman to be his wife. I know he loves me. I know in reality I'm his first and only love. Everything else is duty and he's spent his life doing what he understood to be his duty. Whenever he's been called upon, he's answered the call. What more could I want?"

What more could she want? How about a husband who belonged only to her? What about a man who was home with her at night instead of galavanting off to the church or city hall or some other such place—another wife's house, for instance? I could think of a whole bushel load of things she might want, but I could see they really didn't matter to her. I didn't agree with her line of thinking but I had to admire her loyalty and commitment.

"Son," she said, gently, "life is changing for you now, and it will continue to change. It will never be the same again. And it shouldn't be. You need to learn and grow and so does Alma. You can mope around, stubbing your toes on resentful feelings, being torn by bitterness and breaking your teeth on unwillingness to accept things as they are if that's what you choose to do but, if you do, you'll end up the one who's bruised, bleeding and miserable. A smart person accepts change, looks for the good in it and moves on with life. *That's* the way to true inner peace and happiness."

At the time I thought she was talking about Alma and me being separated for the winter. I should have known better. Mother handed me the letter one night in mid-March just as I was coming in from work. It was dated February 25, 1911.

Dear Father and Mother; (it read)

Uncle George and Aunt Ada send their regards. Uncle George is working in a local sawmill. I'm doing all his feed lot chores by myself. Aunt Ada spent several weeks getting ready for Lenora's and my wedding on January 20. We will stay with Uncle George until April when we'll meet Nephi at the ranch in Jackson. Please tell him to cable us when to expect him. Nora and I send our regards.

Respectfully your son,
Alma

CHAPTER FORTY

After I read the letter, I just stood there. I couldn't think of anything to say. I couldn't think of anything to do. I couldn't even *think* straight. Here I was planning to go back to our little cabin with him—just him and me—in another couple of weeks and he'd already been married for the last six.

He's not said a word. Not one word. And my cousin, Lenora, of all people!

I tried to remember what she even looked like. I hadn't paid much attention to the girl. She was one of the oldest in a whole brood of noisy, ill-mannered children—most of whom were quite a bit younger than Alma and me and had the nasty habit of dying like flies at an early age, anyway. I couldn't think how old she was—middle or late twenties, maybe?

By the time we'd bought our farm in Darby, she was working away from home and we never saw her at Uncle George's. I didn't think I'd laid eyes on her since we were kids. I couldn't have told if she was tall or short, fat or thin.

She's dark-complected, I remember that, and she has to be ugly or she wouldn't be single, still, at her age. That or she's saddled with a sour disposition. Or both.

What in the world has my brother been thinking? Why was he so desperate he had to settle on Nora, our own cousin, when he's good looking enough and good natured enough he could have had anyone he wanted?

What does he want a woman for, anyway?

"Mother, what in the world is he thinking?" I stormed at my Mother who sat in her rocking chair, calmly knitting little soakers for an expected grandbaby. Her eye twitched a time or two but other than that, she looked peaceful.

"The same thing I've been trying to tell you he was thinking, Nephi," she said. "He wants a family. He wants someone to love."

"He had me. I'm family, aren't I?"

"Family, yes, someone to love, no," she said, putting her knitting down and folding her arms tightly across her chest for emphasis. I knew the action. It held hands with her, 'There will be no arguments about this!' voice.

"You aren't a woman and, even if you were, sometimes I think you'd be a rather difficult person for any spouse to put up with, let alone cherish," she continued. "You go off on rages too much and you bury your head in the sand and refuse to face reality."

I gasped. I couldn't believe my mother said that.

Bury my head in the sand? Refuse to face reality? Where was she when Alma was going through his doldrums over Maude? Does she know how well my brother and I work together—how compatible we are—and the tremendous effort I've made to keep it that way? If living with him is burying my head in the sand or not facing reality, I want to know what reality is. I've not only faced it, I've overcome it. I've pulled him through, supported him, kept him going. And we have a nice, tidy little ranch to prove it.

And I go off on rages, do I? I most certainly do not! I never rage. Well . . . not hardly ever. No, I don't get angry. I might get disgusted occasionally—I'll admit to that. But I don't rage about. I just get even—wear off my energy with a practical joke or something. The very thought of me going off on rages! I was really spluttering over that. *I've never known my mother to be so wrong in judgment.*

Well, I can see I won't get anywhere talking to her about this. Of all the people I'd have thought could see the trap Alma's gotten himself into, my mother should have been the first—after all she's put up with from my father all these years—but no. Here she is, peacefully knitting little things, again, and humming softly to herself, with a look on her face that clearly says, 'All's well in Zion,' while my world's crumbling about my ears.

I stomped out of the house and down the street, completely forgetting the supper still sitting on the table in Mother's dining room.

I walked blindly for a while, not knowing where I was or even caring.

Alma's married! I screamed inside, pushing the very thought away from me. *The two words don't even sound right together. Not like Alma's a rancher, or Alma's a cattleman. Alma and married, just don't fit.*

It can't be. Alma with a woman by his side; a woman calling him, wanting his time and attention. A woman expecting him . . . whatever it is women expect of their men.

Their men. I turned a corner, not even knowing where I was headed.

Her man.

Alma belongs to someone else now. The brother I've always counted on to be there with me isn't there anymore. Our partnership's become a threesome and threesomes mean trouble. Look at my father's three wives if you want an example. That wasn't a match made in heaven. More like hell if you ask me, what with Mary indulging in her continual bitter gouging, Annie in quiet whimpering, and Mother keeping a brave silence.

Alma and I have been best friends all our lives but I can't see that *continuing for long. Any time a couple of close friends invite a third person to join in, suddenly pouf!* I threw my hands into the air, *Every point in the relationship explodes like gunpowder near a match.*

And if that isn't bad enough, what does my brother expect me to do about sleeping arrangements? Lay on the top bunk while he and his sweetie-pie chase each other around the cabin? I could see it now. *Is he thinking ahead at all? Does he expect me to turn my eyes to the wall at night and pretend I don't know she's undressing? Plug my ears while.... I don't think so!*

Add to that, where does he expect me to be when the queen of the house decides it's bath time? Outside, waiting in the...ohmigosh! –My mind reeled. *What's my brother trying to do to me?* The horror of it made me want to hunch over with my hands in front of my crotch and my back turned to the world as I literally shrank inside my coat, wanting to become invisible.

I don't know how much later it was that I found myself coming around the corner of my brother, Tom's, house. I thought of knocking on his door—maybe he'd have some answers for me or at least sympathize with me while I vented—but just then I saw him hurrying up the dimly-lit street with Mother close behind. They were only a house or two away when I heard a piercing shriek from my sister-in-law, Aurora, inside the house; Tom and Mother doubled their speed. So much for Tom's ear tonight. The baby Mother was knitting for was making its entrance into the world.

Towards the end of March I bought a ticket for Victor, Idaho, packed my bags and took leave of my parents. We hadn't talked much since the night Tom's baby was born. To give her credit, Mother'd tried on the few occasions when we were both home together but

155

most of the time she was at Tom's house caring for the older children. Besides, I wasn't in the mood for chit-chat. I had some serious decisions to make and listening to her platitudes about how every man needed a wife and one day I would, too, only took needed think time.

As far as Father was concerned, he seemed about as pleased as Mother was. But then, he would be. After all, he was the fellow who had brought two extra wives home, unannounced, with no thought of my mother's feelings, needs or anything else. No question about his views on the subject.

Don't tell me Alma's beginning to be like our father—not caring about anyone but himself! That thought occurred to me as I sat in the cold, swaying rail car and watched Utah fade away behind me. I gave it careful consideration but eventually rejected the idea.

Father knew what he did was against Church policy—that a man wasn't supposed to take on extra wives unless Church authorities asked him to, and then only if his financial situation was such that he could afford to care for them, AND his first wife gave her permission. But Father did it anyway.

I knew enough about Mary and Annie's background to know they'd been immigrant teenagers, unable to speak the language and regularly beaten by their step-father. So I supposed, grudgingly, that Father might have been thinking of being chivalrous when Jens Jensen offered him the two girls as brides in exchange for the note Father held on Jens' home. He probably wasn't, though. More likely my father was just leering at two pretty girls and lost his head.

Is that what happened to Alma? Nora isn't a pretty little teenager by any stretch of the imagination—I'm sure she's nearly thirty—but did she exert some sort of wiles on my brother and snare him into her net? Most likely. I hated to think ill of Alma but he sure must be gullible.

I fretted and stewed about it all the way to Victor.

CHAPTER FORTY-ONE

I'd wired Uncle George of my coming, but not Alma. I wanted to get the lay of the land, so to speak, first.

I really hadn't decided what I was going to do, but I had no intentions of living in the same cabin with my brother and his bride. I considered taking my bedroll and a tarp, and bunking in the barn loft. It might be itchy, but I would probably be warm enough if I wrapped the tarp around my bedroll and pulled hay over the top. It was the best idea I'd thought of so far.

The bath situation was another story. I might like a cold bath, but chipping out ice for a quick dip in the Snake River in the wintertime wasn't all that appealing. There had to be some other alternative. I figured I'd be wise to get whatever information I could get from Uncle George and his family before I made any final decisions.

Rodney, their fifteen-year-old, met me at the station in Victor, leading Star behind his horse. I was surprised that he was alone. Normally wherever you saw Rodney, you also saw Bacil, his younger brother.

Neither of them were exactly my favorites, but then I'd never been all that fond of any of Uncle George's kids. Still, Rodney had been there all winter and he knew what was going on, so I asked.

"I hear your sister is now my sister-in-law," I started out. He sniggered.

"How was the wedding?" I asked.

"About like any other wedding, I suppose," he said. "They're boring as hell. There was a houseful of people—Uncle Charles and all of his family that still live around here, our Bishop and his family, some neighbors, and the family from Driggs that Nora's been working for. Our house was bulging so that Bacil and I were betting it would burst."

"But what about the wedding, itself?" I tried to steer him back to the topic of interest. I really didn't care who was there or how full the house was. I wasn't sure exactly what information I *did* want but it wasn't this.

"Oh, I don't know," Rodney said. "Bacil and I spent our time tweaking the carrot-top braids of the Bishop's daughter while Nora was saying her "I dos". I counted every freckle on the back of her neck—just because Bacil said I couldn't. He counted, too. She was so mad at us."

I could see he couldn't tell me any information of practicality—he wasn't the possessor of any—so I quit listening to his banal chatter.

Then suddenly I heard, "They spent the next week holed up in her old room upstairs. I don't think they even came up for air."

Where had that come from? I was puzzling over this new piece of random information, wondering what had brought it up, when he offered more.

"Basil and I sneaked up the stairs, just after they went up to her old room, and laid on the floor out in the hall. There's enough of a crack under the door we sure had an interesting view." He sniggered, again. I was scandalized, and not just a little incensed that they'd invaded my brother's privacy like that.

"We couldn't see anything *intimate*, of course," he continued, "but it *was* interesting. Must have been a lot of smooching going on 'cause she was sitting on his lap, in the chair across the room, for the longest time. Then we started seeing clothes drop.

"There was enough people, still, downstairs that we couldn't hear what they was saying, even though we tried. But first something of Alma's would drop and we'd hear some giggling. Then there'd be a shriek and something of Nora's would fall. They had to have gotten buck naked right there before they even went to bed, from all the clothes they dropped! We even seen them take off each other's stockings; his hand sliding down her leg, hers down his—tickling his toes."

That made me almost sick and my opinion of Rodney, which had never been the highest, plummeted to way below zero. I was a stockman, of course, so I knew enough about the mating habits of animals and I'd always figured, when I'd bothered to think about it, that humans engaged in something similar, but I didn't want a graphic image in front of me.

"That was almost the last we saw of them even though we peeked, occasionally, when Ma wasn't around," he went on. "Alma'd come out when the chamber pot needed emptying, or they wanted something to eat. But they ate in their room and didn't talk to us at all. We didn't even see Nora the whole time."

I tried to digest that piece of information, too, but the more I thought of it the less I liked it. Alma emptied the chamber pot. Alma got the food. And fed his ladybird in bed, no doubt. Sounded to me like Miss Nora had a ring in his nose and he was either blind enough or stupid enough to allow himself to be led around like a bull panting after a heifer in heat. For darned sure I wasn't going to be caught living in a cabin with *her* in it. If my name hadn't been on the deed to that ranch I'd have lit out for Victor, again, in hopes of catching the milk train back to Utah.

CHAPTER FORTY-TWO

I tried to be cordial to Uncle George—and Aunt Ada, too, who wanted to share all the details of a wedding I no longer wanted to hear about—but the thought of sleeping in the bed Alma and Nora had lived in for a week, nearly did me in. If Uncle George and Aunt Ada hadn't expected me to spend the night, I'd have gone to Uncle Charles' home. But they did expect me and I had no handy excuse.

After I said my goodnights I paced the floor of her old room, then sat in the chair by her window until way past midnight. By then I was so bone tired I knew I had to stretch out on something, so I pulled the bedding onto the floor and curled up. It was cold and I didn't get to sleep for a long time, but as I laid there, shivering in the dark, I made some decisions.

Aunt Ada had breakfast ready before light the next morning so I saddled Star as soon as I'd eaten. I had a long ride ahead of me—if I even got to the Hole that day—because I was going back to Victor and up over Teton Pass instead of taking the shorter route over Fox Creek Pass and through Death Canyon.

I knew it would be a harrowing day—the Pass was a difficult road, even in summer—but I had no idea just how harrowing it would be.

I left Victor behind a freight sleigh, so the first five miles went more or less smoothly. Then we started to climb.

The Teton range had received snow early the day before—about a foot of it along with a stiff enough wind to cause serious drifting—and nothing had been over the Pass since. Even though the freight sleigh, a covered affair that wasn't loaded very heavily, had a six horse hitch, it was still a struggle for the horses to break through the crusted snow.

Star was doing alright when we were following behind on the already-broken track, but once we started up the incline the freight sleigh had to stop to rest the horses so I passed them with the idea that Star and I could help break trail for a while.

The going was rugged. Farther up the mountainside, Star came to wide drifts that were belly-high on her, and she had to rear and plunge to get through them. In no time, she was breathing nearly as heavily as the six-horse span behind us.

I rested her for a while—let her stand as I tried the snow out, myself. As soon as I swung off my saddle, I sank to my hips in snow that seemed to suck me down. I thrashed about, trying to pull myself out, and managed to lose a boot in the bargain.

From there on out the day wasn't very pretty. I had one boot that was wet from the outside in, and one that was wet from the inside out—once I dug it out of the snow. My horse was skittish, particularly when I was flailing around beside her, and I wasn't in a placid mood, myself. But there could be no stopping; we had to make the top of the Pass by nightfall.

Eventually another sleigh caught up with us—a four-horse span—and the second teamster took turns breaking trail with the freight sleigh whenever we hit a spot wide enough for one to pass the other. That gave Star and me a chance to rest a bit. Still, it was rough going and it didn't get any better.

About a mile from the top of the Pass was the beginning of a stretch called Windy Gulch. Snowdrifts spanned from way up the mountainside to far down the steep canyon below us in an unbroken sweep, making it impossible to know where the cut edge of the road actually was.

One of the freighters gave me a pole and tied Star behind his sleigh. For the rest of the way to the top, I flailed my way through snow that was frequently clear up to my armpits, as I thrust the pole down, over and over, marking the road edge for the teamsters. I was breathing so heavily that icicles formed on my eyelashes and eyebrows. But at least I had a pole, rather than a heaving, skittish horse, to help me leverage myself out of that sucking snow.

My feet were freezing, the rest of me drenched with sweat from the struggle. There was no question of stopping, though. Before it turned dark we had to reach the top of the mountain where a cabin and barn stood, outfitted for travelers. I doubt it got warmer than ten degrees above zero all day and once the sun went down the temperature would plummet. We had no choice but to keep going.

We managed it—barely. The sun was down and the long mountain twilight nearly over before we unhitched the teams, unsaddled Star, and turned all our horses into the barn and feed at the top of the mountain. Even at that, we'd left one of the sleighs a good

161

half-mile down the mountainside and hooked all ten draft horses to the lead sleigh just to get it to the top. The two teamsters would go back for the remaining sleigh in the morning while Star and I broke a track down the Hole side of the mountain.

After a simple supper of bread and cheese, I spread my bedroll out on one of the cabin's bunks and was asleep before I was completely stretched out.

CHAPTER FORTY-THREE

The next day dawned bright and clear—one of those cloudless, blazingly blue-sky days you see in late winter. The warm sun transformed the fresh crusty snow into thousands of tiny, flashing shards of light. I could hardly keep my eyes open, it was so bright. Not only that, but the sun's warmth that morning made going down the mountainside extremely treacherous by the time we rode past the Glory Bowl.

I knew conditions were ripe for snow slides. Good thing Star wasn't given much to neighing. I didn't want a loud noise setting off the snow in the Bowl. But quiet as we tried to be, it slid anyway just after we'd passed it.

I'll never forget that sight—a good quarter mile of deep snow mingled with boulders and big spruce trees that had snapped like matchsticks, all billowing and tumbling down the mountainside together, tossing over and under to a rumbling roar such as nothing I'd ever heard before.

And I'd been in its path not three minutes past.

I didn't have time to watch it, though. Star, terrified at the rumble that made the very ground under us shake, started squealing—bucking and plunging in terror. If it hadn't been for the depth of the snow she'd have unloaded me and headed for Arab, but finally I got her calmed enough we could go on—very cautiously, I might add. Later, I saw other, smaller, slides run but fortunately none of them were close to the road.

It was late afternoon before I reached Wilson at the bottom of the Pass. I decided to room at Nick Wilson's, known to everyone in the valley as Uncle Nick, rather than try to push on towards Jackson that night. Star was exhausted and I didn't feel much better.

Besides, I liked Uncle Nick. I'd met him before, a time or two, and always enjoyed his marvelous yarns—stories of his days as the adopted son of Chief Washakie's mother or of his experiences as a pony express rider. I listened, once again that night, to the tale of how he'd gotten the horrid scar on his scalp from a Piute arrow during an Indian raid. It was the arrow that caused him to rethink his priorities and change his occupation.

I wondered if my brother's marriage would be my Piute arrow.

Next day it was nearly noon before I managed to cross the Snake River and push on into Jackson. I'd come that way because I wanted to purchase provisions at Pap Deloney's Mercantile. I had no intention of living with Alma and Nora, so I needed food I could easily fix on my own.

I hadn't wanted to buy anything in Idaho because I knew the trip through the mountains was going to be difficult—although I'll have to admit it was a lot worse than I'd expected—so I'd come over the Pass where I had a more or less straight shot into town without having to ride past our cabin.

As soon as I bought what I needed and got it packed behind my saddle, I swung up onto Star and started north out of town. My goal was to reach Henry Cherry's cabin by twilight. I almost managed. It was just becoming dark by the time I stopped at Roy and Maggie McBride's. I intended to stay just long enough to beg the use of a lantern and enough dry firewood to see me through until tomorrow, but Maggie refused.

"You're not going to a cold cabin with no food, no fuel and nothing to feed Star at this time of the night," she said. "You just undo your bedroll and I'll put some of Frank's bearskins down on the floor in front of the fireplace. We're having elk steak and Roy can whack off one for you, too. I'll fry it up with some spuds and we'll just have a right good get-together tonight. You can tell us all about your winter in Utah."

I'd never heard Maggie order anyone around before, and I didn't counter her. I fed my horse in their barn, brought my provisions into the cabin, and spent a pleasant evening in front of their fireplace.

"Now, what are your plans, Nephi?" Maggie finally asked me as the evening began to wind down.

"Henry's cabin is empty," I said, "and we own it. I'll settle down there."

"It won't be the most convenient situation," Roy said. "Alma has the cows down on the river where they'll have tree shelter for calving. Besides, we're sure to have some nasty spring storms, still."

"I know that," I replied. "But I'm going to do it anyway. I absolutely will not live in the same house with Alma and Nora." And I had no intention of telling them why.

164

Frank, who'd been quiet all evening, spoke up. "She's a very pretty woman. Alma's got himself a real looker there. I can see why he's smitten with her."

That was unexpected. Frank never commented on women. Besides, I'd decided Nora must be highly deficient in the looks department. Well, then, it had to be her temperament that kept her single so long.

"I wouldn't know," I said. "I haven't seen her since we were kids."

"Oh, no doubt about it," Maggie informed me. "She's a real beauty. Cooks good, too." I looked at her in surprise.

"They invited us in for dinner the day we trailed your cattle to the river," she said. "She puts on an excellent spread."

That was something to think about, but it didn't make me change my mind about spending time in their cabin. She could cook all she wanted to. I still knew how to throw together a nourishing stew, and a pot full of that would last me several days.

"What will you do for firewood?" Roy asked. I think he was trying to discourage me but I paid no attention.

"There's plenty of downed wood in the Gros Ventre river bottoms," I said. "I'll find a log and hitch Star to it. She's good at dragging things. I'll get to it first thing tomorrow."

"Charlie can help you cut it up with our cross-cut saw and after we feed our cattle, Frank and I will come over with the sleigh. We'll haul your wood for you. A sleigh-load should last you until summer."

It was settled, then. Roy hadn't used all of Henry's hay so there was enough feed for Star. By this time tomorrow night I'd have wood to warm myself with. I was back in the Hole and, except for one certain female fly in my ointment, all was well with my world.

165

CHAPTER FORTY-FOUR

I was there a day or two before I saw Alma. Someone apparently told him I'd arrived and where I was staying because one day he came riding across the fields and knocked on my door.

It seemed funny to have my own brother, with whom I'd lived for nearly thirty years, *knocking* on my door. But it wasn't my doing. He was the one who'd gone off and gotten married. I opened the door, not quite knowing what to expect.

I don't think he did, either. He smiled, a little nervously.

"I see you've come back," he said. "Did you have a good trip?" He didn't say a word about the fact I hadn't wired him like he'd wanted me to.

"It was fair."

"May I come in?" he asked, since I hadn't invited.

"If you wish." I stood aside.

He stepped into the little cabin and looked around. There was my bedroll on Henry's bunk, a rough table with one chair under the lone window, some pegs on the wall, and a shelf near the fireplace. The shelf held the provisions I'd bought in town. Nothing fancy, but I didn't need fancy so it suited my purposes.

A tin plate, knife, fork and spoon were on the table. I kept them there. A kettle of water was hung on an iron crane over the fire in the fireplace, and my dishpan was filled with half-dirty water. I'd been scrubbing the cabin walls.

I motioned him to my one chair and resumed my scrubbing.

"You don't have to live here," Alma said.

"Yes, I do."

"Nephi, you are always welcome in my home. You should know that."

"No thank you, Mister Moulton." I could tell the formality hit him hard.

"Nephi, be reasonable. You've always been a part of my life. Just because I'm married and going to be a father doesn't mean I've deserted you, or that we're no longer partners."

I stared at him.

"You're what?"

"I'm married. You know that. Otherwise you wouldn't be here in Henry's house," he said, patiently.

"I know you're married. What else did you say?"

He flushed and smiled, a shyly proud smile. "Oh, the father business? Nora's in the family way. About a month gone, we think." He was trying to be casual but his eyes shown and there was a glow about his face I'd never seen before.

"Congratulations," I said dryly and did some quick mental math. "You didn't waste any time."

"No need to. I'm not getting any younger. I want to enjoy my children."

I pondered that. It sure was a far cry from my father. I didn't remember *him* ever being around long enough to enjoy me. This whole business was so strange, I wanted to be left alone to think.

"I guess you need to be going back to your missus," I said, moving towards the cabin door and opening it.

I saw a fleeting look of hurt and uncertainty cross my brother's face. Then he stood, saying easily, "You're right. It's getting late and I need to feed the yearlings. I actually came to invite you to dinner tonight."

"No thank you," I said for the second time that afternoon. "I can cook well enough. Someone else's cooking would upset my stomach." I knew he understood what I was saying but I didn't care. I would stay in my own home.

"If you change your mind, we'll be eating at six. Nora's frying elk steak and baking some potatoes and she has fresh-made butter and bread," was all he said as he walked out of my door.

CHAPTER FORTY-FIVE

I had potato soup for supper that night—rather watery and not terribly filling but it was my own cooking. What I really needed was a fresh elk carcass hanging out in Henry's barn where I could cut a chunk off whenever I wanted. Too bad it wasn't hunting season. There were a few fence-breakers I wouldn't mind putting in my stew pot. I let that thought flit around the edges of my thinking while I scrubbed my cabin walls and took some time over the Alma situation.

A father in the works, was he? The prospect of having nephews like Rodney and Bacil did not appeal. Then I thought of Alma saying, "I want to enjoy my children," and wondered if he would be a better father than ours had been.

Of course that led to thinking about Father and his three wives and twenty-three kids. Mother said he'd married Annie and Mary out of chivalry. I hadn't bought her excuse but maybe I was missing something. What did I know about Annie's and Mary's relationship with their step-father? I searched my memory as I emptied the dirty water out of my dishpan and filled it with fresh hot water from my teakettle.

My earliest memories of Annie and Mary began the winter the U.S. Marshalls started raiding the valley, looking for polygamists. Father went into hiding. My half-siblings never knew, when they went to bed at night, if they'd wake up at home or in someone else's house across the valley. It was a tense time for everyone.

With Father gone, my older brothers had all of Father's work besides their own to do. Uncle Heber came over to help as often as he could but he had a large family of his own.

Then, to add a little interest, Annie, weak from baby Heber's recent birth, became delusional, believing herself to be a grand lady in Denmark, her native land. I guess it helped her cope with the rough-hewn granary walls, the mice that crept between her slivery floorboards and the Marshalls who burst through her door at all hours, upending beds and poking through her belongings, looking for Father.

Finally, one night when things were quiet in the valley, Father borrowed a fast horse and a cutter, slipped down to Heber City, and took Annie to the hospital in Provo. Her four children were split up between Mary and Mother.

Hoping to coax Annie back to reality, Father asked Mother to purchase a home for each of his other wives. With Uncle Heber's help, she found a house for Mary. I went along when they presented her with the deed.

Even as a young child, I recognized the fear that filled Mary's eyes when she opened her door to find Uncle Heber and Mother standing on her doorstep. I didn't understand it at the time but I'm sure she thought something terrible had happened with Annie or, even worse, the U.S. Marshalls had captured Father.

"We have good news, Mary," Uncle Heber's rich baritone voice filled the half of the granary that was hers. "Joseph wanted Lizzie to buy you and Annie each a piece of property and we've found one with a house on it for you." He handed her the deed.

Mary looked, first at him then at Mother with a blank, uncomprehending stare. Then she opened the document he'd handed her and read it . . . slowly. By the time she got to the end, she was sobbing and laughing at the same time.

"Iss diss true?" she cried, looking from Uncle Heber to Mother, then back again. Aunt Mary always reverted to heavily accented English whenever she was excited or upset. "Iss real?"

"It's true, Mary," Mother said. "It's real. It's not a granary or even a log cabin; it's stick built and you can move into it as soon as you're ready and we get some wood hauled for you. Heber says he will help."

"I cannot belief it!" Mary pressed the document to her breast. "A home uff my own. A home I can make preety, vere I can haff flowers and my own garden and efferyfink!" Her voice caught in a sob, then rose, almost to a hiccuppy wail. "Oh, sank you, sank you!" She threw her arms around first my mother and then Uncle Heber. She and Annie had always been so much more demonstrative than my reserved English parents. I saw Mother stiffen, slightly, but Uncle Heber just laughed and hugged her back.

It was while Mary was living in that house that I saw Jens Jensen, her step-father, for the first and only time. I'd been over at Mary's, playing marbles in the street with Chase and Franz, my half-brothers who were just younger than me, when he rode up to her door.

The first thing we heard from him was a growly, "Here, you lazy scalawags, get out of the way! Get in the yard, now!" Then he

169

deliberately rode his horse through our ring of marbles, dismounted and kicked what marbles were under his feet—including my prized taw—into the gutter. He could have tied his horse anywhere on Mary's fence instead of breaking up our game.

Not daring to follow him into the house, Chase, Franz, and I crouched under Mary's living room window where we could listen to the conversation.

"Your children are dirty ragamuffins, Mary. How do you expect them to ever amount to anything when you're so shiftless and lazy, yourself?" was his initial, bellowed greeting as he burst, unannounced, through her door. I looked at the window above me, then back at my half-brothers in astonishment. Mary always kept her children so clean I sometimes wondered if she rubbed them up and down her washboard along with their clothes. The woman made more trips to her well for scrub water than any other woman in town except, maybe, my mother.

True, their clothing was worn. But so was mine. We all had older siblings and hand-me-downs never looked brand new. What was Jens Jensen talking about?

As I listened, the abuse continued. Mary said nothing, which was unusual for her, and I wondered at her silence.

Then suddenly Jens' tack changed.

"Why doesn't Joseph provide better for you?" he demanded. We could hear him stomping around the room, bumping into furniture, pushing first one thing, then another, aside. "You call this a house? It's a hovel! Any man who loves his wives provides better for them than this! All you and Annie are is slaves. Slaves! Just so his precious first wife can have an easy life. You know it's true. You know Lizzie gets it all. And here you are, working in your husband's fields, milking his cows, working yourselves to the bone for what? This pigsty? You and Annie are nothing but sows." There came a word from Mary, then a sharp slapping sound followed by a scream and a thud.

Suddenly I heard Mary's voice, high and tight, pouring out a stream of Danish I couldn't understand. I glanced at Franz and Chase. They were rooted to the spot, eyes fearful. At that point I didn't care what Jens Jensen said, I ran for Uncle Heber.

I wasn't allowed to follow him back to Aunt Mary's so I didn't know, exactly, what happened but I was sure there was a scuffle. I'd never seen my uncle become upset enough to raise his hand against anyone. He just wasn't that sort. But when I saw him later that night, his face was a little scraped up. I asked Franz and Chase the next day, but they wouldn't answer me . . . just looked away and didn't say a word.

To my knowledge, Jens Jensen never came back to Heber City.

If Father hoped having Mary live farther away from Mother's home would relieve the problems with the Marshals, it didn't. They wouldn't leave either Mary or Mother alone. Determined to find Father, they usually came in the night, rousing us all, plowing through Mother's and Mary's homes like bulls on a rampage. Mary was furious, Mother was frustrated and Father was alone, living in the hills in an abandoned mining shack.

Finally he slipped down to Uncle George's house in Keetley where he wrote a note to Mother. I was still up, playing behind Mother's parlor drapes, the night she read it to Uncle Heber.

My dearest Lizzie;

My heart hurts when I think of you and Mary, my beloved wives, facing all the troubles you have had to face, alone. I have thought about this long and hard. I do not believe the United States will repeal the anti-polygamy law and if we stay in Utah, we shall be hounded the rest of our lives. I want to take my families to a place where we can live, together, in peace.

I think it best that you and Mary sell your homes and we go to Mexico where my sister, Lottie, and her husband live. Please do all you can to arrange a speedy departure. As soon as you have sold the houses, send me word through George and Ada. I will come and we will leave immediately.

Give my love to my children and please share this letter with Mary. I love you both.

As ever, your affectionate husband,

Joseph

Mother's home didn't sell; Mary's did. She had lived in it less than six months.

171

Lizzie's family prior to leaving for Mexico
L to R back – Nephi, John, Tom, Joe, Charlie, Alma
L to R front – Malinda, Lizzie with Annie's Heber, Sarah,
Annie's Lillian

CHAPTER FORTY-SIX

Annie was still in the hospital when we left Utah but her children were with us. One hot summer day, as we were traveling between Demming, New Mexico and Colonia Dublan, Annie's baby, Heber, became ill.

"Joseph," Mother said when we stopped for supper that night, "I don't like the way Heber sounds."

"What do you think it is?" Father asked, taking his youngest son from Mother's arms.

172

"At first I thought it was a summer cold. Then it sounded like croup, but listen to him now," Mother said. "Watch how he coughs until he retches. I'm afraid it's whooping cough."

"No!" Mary came running from the back of her wagon where she was putting Annie's little girl, Violet, to bed. "No, you must be wrong, Lizzie! Not Annie's baby!" Just then little Heber went into a dry hacking that didn't want to quit. Finally he began retching and his face turned purple as he gasped for air.

"Do somesink!" Mary cried. "Lizzie, Yosef, do somesink!" but there was nothing they could do. Eventually the spasm was over and little Heber lay in Father's arms, a limp rag doll of a toddler.

We stayed in camp the next day. And the next. During that night, Heber died. We buried him as deep as we could there in the hot Mexican sand, then one by one our wagons rolled away leaving Annie's baby forever alone in a searing wasteland of cactus, rattlesnakes, coyotes and sand.

We rolled into Colonia Dublan during the worst drought in Mexican memory.

"Joseph," I heard Mother say one night shortly after our arrival—I was frequently awake, miserable in the sweaty heat—"What can our boys do here?"

"I don't know, Lizzie." I heard tiredness and discouragement in my father's voice. "I just don't know."

"I can't see any future for them in Mexico," Mother continued. "There's no way to farm because there's no water and there's no other work, either. There are no good girls for them to marry and they couldn't provide for their families if there were. They'll become as shiftless and lazy as the Mexican natives outside of town." Laziness was something Mother abhorred.

"I don't want that any more than you," Father said. "Maybe there's work in Casas Grandes."

But there was none. Father even went to Bacadehuachi where there was a little lake, but there was no work there, either.

Then, one evening, Mother came storming into the house, Sarah behind her.

"Joseph," she said, "those Mexicans were making passes at Sarah and me, making obscene gestures. We can't even go out in the streets, now, and feel safe. I still have my home in Utah. I'm taking my family back to Heber City."

I had never seen my mother so upset. And there was no arguing with her.

Father begged Mary to come, too, but she refused.

"Mary, you are my wife," he said as he, Mary and Mother sat around our kitchen table the night Mother announced her intentions. "Let's all go back to Utah."

"No, Joseph," Mary said, tears streaming down her face. "Here I am your wife. There I am considered a prostitute even though I married you legally. Here you can come to my home and no-one cares. There you will have to be in hiding again."

Father and Mother sat, silent. It was true. According to the Edmunds-Tucker act, passed eleven years after Mary and Father were married, Mother was the only legal wife. Why, when Mary and Father's marriage had been legal for eleven years, was it suddenly illegal? It made no sense to me. But that was the way it was. Mary could never live with Father in Utah.

"Besides, I'm in the family way again," Mary added.

Mother gasped. Father was still, as immobile as a block of granite, for long minutes. I wondered when he was going to speak and what he would say.

"When will the baby come?" Mother finally broke the silence.

"Late May, I suppose," Mary said.

"It's not been long. Are you sure?"

"I know the day after. It's the same every time." I didn't know what that meant but, counting the baby that had died before I was born, this was Mary's eighth child. I guessed she probably knew.

"You should know," Mother said, finally. "Well, what do we do now, Joseph?"

Again, Father sat without saying a word. Maybe Mother and Mary were accustomed to his silences but I was getting edgy and I could see my siblings begin to fidget, too.

"I'll take you back to Utah, Lizzie," he finally said in a heavy voice. "I'll build a house for you and Annie, Mary, and I'll make sure I'm back in time to help with the baby's birth."

"You're leaving me here, alone, all winter with all these children?"

"What else am I to do?" Father asked. "Lizzie won't stay here and I can't blame her. There's nothing for Sarah and the boys. Besides, Lottie and Willard are here. They'll help you. You won't be alone."

"And what of my Josie and my Sarah Amelia? What about Bill and Chase and Franz?" Mary asked, quietly. "You have not even mentioned my children. Everything is always for Lizzie."

"Josie is only fourteen, Mary," my mother said. "My Sarah is twenty-two already; a grown woman. Joe is twenty and Tom almost nineteen. Things would be different if your children were as old as mine but they aren't. Right now my responsibility is to the children who are old enough to start their own lives."

"Besides, your home sold. I need to build a new one for you and Annie." Father said.

We left within the week.

I looked for little Heber's grave on the trip back but all I saw was vultures perched on animal carcasses. Owls, coyotes and wolves cried at night. Besides the grief that hung over us, the endless days of searing heat and no water took its toll. It seemed we would never reach Deming and the railroad.

Once on the train, though, the rest of the journey flew by. How wonderful the Wasatch valley looked with its mountains glowing in autumn colors. How wonderful to see our grandparents again, and Uncle Heber. How grateful we were that Mother's property had not sold.

Father slaved all winter to build a home for Annie and Mary to live in. His health wasn't good—the winter in hiding, then the trip to and from Mexico, had worn him down—but he wouldn't rest even when Mother begged him to.

"Joseph, you're sick. Listen to that cough," Mother would say, a worried frown wrinkling her forehead. "Please stay home tonight. Don't go back out to work."

"No, Lizzie," he'd answer. "I have to have a home for Mary— and Annie, too, when she's well enough to come home again. The boys can help me." I had to give him credit for never quitting no matter how tired and ill he was.

I remembered how cold it had been in those evenings after chores. Our fingers grew numb and our feet lost their feeling as we helped him hold and nail studs and joists and rafters into place. Remembering brought the sudden realization of how much he *had* invested in his families.

Annie—to her credit—pulled herself out of her delusional state and was discharged from the hospital, another reason why Father insisted on working although he was so ill he could barely drag himself around. She wasn't strong enough, yet, to live on her own but he wanted a home ready for her when she was.

In the meantime, Jens Jensen was determined to play with her thinking. One night my father confided in Uncle Heber when he came to spend an hour or two helping us with the house.

"Heber," my father said, "I just don't know what to do. Jens is lying to Annie and she's still fragile enough she doesn't know what to believe. I've written to her but he takes my letters and twists everything I say.

"I want to visit her—to assure her that I love her and want her to come back to Heber City—but I don't dare go. Jens would have a Marshall breathing down my neck before I even got the chance to say 'hello'. He'd like nothing better than to see me in jail."

"It's a tough situation," Uncle Heber said, slowly. "If you want, I'll go see her. But how will I tell her about little Heber?"

"Please do go," Father begged. "Tell her I love her but don't tell her about the baby. She doesn't need to know that right now. Just tell her he's with Mary, if she asks. In a way, he is—and, besides, she may not think to ask. I don't know if she even remembers she gave birth to him."

It was a grim Uncle Heber who came back from Salem.

"Jens told Annie you killed the baby and abandoned Mary," he told my mother and father. "Poor Annie doesn't know what to believe. She's not strong enough for lies like that and she's distraught over the baby's death."

Father was nearly beside himself. Again Mother urged him to not push himself so hard.

"You're going to have a breakdown, Joseph," she told him. "And then where will we be? It won't hurt you to take a few days off. You'll make up for lost time when you go back to work, a well man."

176

But Father wouldn't listen to her and we went out to work right along beside him.

As I remembered those frigid winter nights, I realized I'd never understood the pressures my father was under.

Still, he should never have married Annie or Mary in the first place, Jens or no Jens. They weren't his responsibility. Part of me argued that, difficult as they were, his problems *were* his own making. Another voice inside my head reasoned that he did care for his Danish wives and couldn't have known that polygamy would become illegal when he married them. A poor choice, yes, but he couldn't have foreseen the outcome.

I stared at the log walls in front of me realizing, suddenly, that I was in Henry Cherry's cabin in Jackson Hole, not Heber City where I'd been raised. I couldn't even remember when I'd finished scrubbing, I'd been so busy remembering. Not that I could see it had done me much good. I'd spent hours with long-forgotten memories, and although I felt I better understood my families' sacrifices and feelings, I still couldn't see why Alma was so desperate for a wife and children that he'd married our cousin, Nora. Look at all the trouble Father had because he was hot to trot to the alter. I was convinced Alma's marriage was even more doomed for disaster.

I had no idea how terribly right I was.

CHAPTER FORTY-SEVEN

With the cabin all cleaned, there was nothing pressing for me to do; time to start helping Alma.

It was now early April and calving season. He needed my help with feeding and checking the cows, so after a couple-three hours of sleep I rode Star down to the barn and had Sleek and Sassy grained and harnessed by the time Alma tore himself away from his new bride and opened his door. I raised my eyebrows when he came out—he'd always been as early a riser as I was. I could see *that* was changing along with everything else.

He stopped short when he saw me leading the team out of their stall.

"Hello!" he said, "I didn't know you were here."

"Someone has to get things started in the morning," I grinned. "Seems you're having a hard time peeling that bed off your back."

"Very funny."

"I thought so, too." I positioned Sleek and Sassy on either side of the sleigh tongue and he stepped up to hook them to the doubletrees. It was good to be working with him again. I hadn't realized how much I'd missed the comfortable rhythm we'd developed over the years. Suddenly the loneliness of this past winter was erased. I was working with Alma once more.

I maintained my distance from his cabin and wife, though. Nora would stand in the doorway, occasionally, and glare at me.

I'd turn my back.

Alma politely invited me to dine with them.

I politely declined. Their home was my home no longer. Only the fields and forest-lands were mine. That and the work.

"Alma, since you're living here in the river bottoms where the herd is, if you'll take the night shift, I'll walk through them after I grain the horses in the morning and again after we've fed the calves in the afternoon," I suggested that first morning.

Alma hesitated for only a moment before agreeing. "Let's hope I don't need help in the night," he said. "I still wish you were closer. You ought to think of being down here—at least until calving season is over."

"Don't think so. Besides, you have Nora to help you."

178

"Women have no business seeing a cow give birth and you know it." Father had always forbidden his wives and daughters to watch an animal birthing so I could accept that opinion. But it was his next sentence that caught my attention.

"Besides," he said, "Nora's too likely to be sick."

"Sick?"

"She generally loses her breakfast, and frequently some of what she eats in between. The sight of a cow with a backwards calf would make her so queasy she'd be of no use to me."

"That's ridiculous! She's milking you for attention!"

"No, Nephi, women get like that when they're in the family way." Alma was plainly in his 'let's be patient with Nephi' mode.

"Says who? I don't remember Sarah or Nettie or Aurora or Susan throwing up." I cited our older sister and sisters-in-law for proof. I had no idea how things were with Malinda because she'd moved away from Heber City but I was sure she was no different.

"We weren't ever around them in the first months, either," he answered.

"Cows don't puke. If they did, we'd do nothing but tend sick cows. She's just trying to get sympathy. She wanted to be a rancher's wife; make her buck up and be one."

"She still doesn't belong around a birthing." He was determined to change the subject and I knew it.

"Then put her on Darky and send her up for me. If you don't mollycoddle her, she'll get over the puking business."

She did, too, eventually. It took her a while to get it through her head that neither of us was going to cater to her but she did learn.

In the meantime, I discovered a marvelous way to torment her.

It happened one day when we'd had a particularly difficult birth to deal with. The mother was a heifer—two years old so this was her first calf; a huge one with one of its front legs laid back against its body.

We found her struggling, off by herself, when we were feeding. Alma jumped off the sleigh and began to haze her toward the corral while I finished pitching the rest of the hay to the cows. By the time I got there, he had her in the barn, her head locked in a stanchion, and was clear up past his elbow trying to find the leg to pull it into place beside the other one.

We must have struggled with her for over an hour before we finally got that hefty bull calf out. I was heartily wishing one of us was a smaller man before we were through because having your arm inside a cow that's trying to birth a large calf isn't the most comfortable thing to do. But, then, I suppose it probably wouldn't have mattered if we'd had arms like matchsticks. Her bruiser calf was so large there wasn't room for a baby's arm, let alone a grown man's.

Then, wouldn't you know, she prolapsed—her womb followed the afterbirth out.

"Alma, we've got problems!" I exclaimed as I frantically tried to catch it. He looked up from where he was vigorously rubbing the lethargic calf with a gunny sack.

"Oh, boy!" he straightened, quickly. "Can you get that back inside her while I get a needle from Nora's sewing box?"

It was a struggle. I got it back in and held her birthing channel shut as best I could, but she was still straining. Her body didn't seem to know it had finally rid itself of the calf. When Alma returned he had a small darning needle threaded with a long hair from the tail of one of the Percherons.

I wished I could have poured a bottle of whisky down the throat of that poor heifer. Stitching her up with nothing to dull the pain only added insult to injury. She bawled and danced around until I finally shouldered her up against the side of the stall and wedged her there. That made sewing her up a real trick but we finally managed to finish the job. It didn't look like any vet had done it but it held and eventually we let her out of the stanchion to be with her calf.

By then, of course, we were both covered with blood to our shoulders and all down the fronts of our shirts. I was looking for a clean patch of snow to wash myself with when Alma suggested the obvious.

"Come into the house, Nephi, and get washed up with hot water. Snow isn't going to clean that mess off your hands."

He was right and I knew it. I hesitated but finally decided I may as well. It wasn't going to kill me to scrub up in Nora's home. Besides, this could be a good thing. She probably wouldn't enjoy the sight of all my gore.

I smiled in anticipation as I followed Alma across the barnyard to his home.

Still, it felt awkward, going back into the cabin that was no longer mine. I tried not to be obvious as I looked at the new interior.

She'd done the woman thing. Snow-white muslin curtains, all fussied up with blue gingham ruffles, covered the windows. We'd never cared if anyone riding by looked in but she obviously did.

Apparently she didn't like having her clothing in view, either. There was a white drape hanging over the pegs where we'd always hung our clothes. The ruffle on the bottom matched those on the curtains. Weren't we getting fancy?

Alma's bunk, I saw, had been replaced with a wider log bed and I noted she had blue gingham ruffles on both the top sheet and the pillowcases, a blue patchwork quilt for a spread. I turned towards the kitchen stove and the wash stand that Alma had built years ago. The bleached huck towel she had hanging on a new peg above it had a band of blue gingham on it, too. My word but the woman had a fixation on blue! It was everywhere. I felt like a bull in a china shop— afraid to touch anything for fear I'd soil it. We'd always kept the place clean but it had never seen this kind of fancy before.

Resentment welled up into every corner of my being. If she wanted fancy, she should have married a city boy, not a country stockman. What was she doing, here, anyway? What we'd had was good enough for us. It should have been for her, too.

I looked at the table. It was set with a white cloth with blue gingham edging. The plates on the table were blue enamelware and so was the teakettle on the stove. I glanced up and saw a new shelf on the wall where more blue plates, standing on edge, were displayed. A fellow couldn't turn around without being confronted by blue.

Don't misunderstand me; I like the color. There's nothing prettier than the deep blue of a summer sky. But in the house? And all frills and furbelows? I wanted to run—to get away from the fanciness and fussiness.

"You'll eat with us, won't you, Nephi?" Alma asked.

I couldn't quarrel with the smells coming from her kitchen stove. My nose told me she'd been cooking steak and potatoes although I couldn't see them. Apparently she had Alma's dinner in the warming oven. Did I really want to run?

I wanted to run.

But dinner smelled so good . . . better than anything I'd had since I'd left Utah and Mother.

Besides, we still had the calves and bulls to feed.

If I went home, I'd be eating cold cracked-wheat cereal left over from breakfast.

I guessed it would be more convenient—less time wasted—if I stayed.

"Thank you," I said, as politely as I could manage. "As late as it is I suppose I should." Alma smiled and indicated a chair. I didn't look in Nora's direction.

I'll say one thing for Nora, her cooking tasted as good as it smelled. Steak, smothered in seasoned flour and fried in hot butter, boiled potatoes with milk gravy, homemade bread, and fresh-churned butter. She even had a jar of huckleberry jelly. It was almost as good as anything Mother could turn out . . . that or I was hungrier than I thought. As I ate, I decided I could stand the fussiness for one meal a day if Alma invited me.

The most awkward part came when we were finished and getting ready to go back out to our chores. I honestly didn't know what to say to Nora. I didn't really want to say anything but I knew I should; after all, she'd cooked the dinner and it *was* a good one. She hadn't spoken to me since I'd come in and I hadn't to her, either. Alma had been the go-between who'd carried on a conversation with us both. That made it even more difficult. What was expected? I hadn't the foggiest idea.

For the life of me, I don't know what prompted it but, for want of something to say as I walked out the door, I ran my hand up her back and said, "Purr like a pussycat". Don't ask me where it came from . . . I really don't know . . . but the result was electrifying, to say the least. Nora, who had started washing the dishes from the table, whirled and threw the plate she had in her hand at me. If I hadn't been so quick on my feet, it would have hit my head.

"Don't you ever do that again!" she screamed.

I beat a hasty, very astonished, retreat to the corral. As I picked up the reins and started the team and sleigh out towards the field and the closest haystack, I thought about what had happened. Glancing at the cabin, I saw Nora outside, busily throwing up on a patch of snow.

Attention-getter!

182

Well, obviously Alma wasn't doing anything to encourage her to stop. So I might as well. The reaction I'd gotten from an innocent statement definitely had possibilities.

CHAPTER FORTY-EIGHT

I learned to time things perfectly so I could escape without being hit by whatever she threw in my direction. And she'd throw anything—spoons, plates, cups—good thing those dishes weren't china. She even snatched an iron skillet, hanging on one of the pegs under her plate shelf, and sent it flying after me. I think Alma spoke to her about that one. I was a little more careful afterwards but she only threw it at me once.

I was smart enough not to harass her every day so she never knew when I was going to rub her back and tell her to purr. I wondered, occasionally, if she ever purred for Alma. She sure didn't for me. She sounded more like a tomcat yowling on a picket fence at midnight.

I guess she must have complained quite a bit to Alma. He spoke to me about it every time her royal highness got disturbed, begging me to get along with her. I didn't pay him any heed. Or give any thought to what it was like for him when Nora was riled up. I was having too much fun planning my next assault on her majesty's dignity. And I'll have to admit, even with her swelling body, she proved to be a valiant foe. We detested each other equally.

The awkwardness of my living arrangements, being so far away from Alma's cabin and the barn and corrals, combined with Nora's and my thriving enmity, appeared to weigh heavily on Alma's mind as the summer passed. He was patient with me—and I'm sure he was with Nora, too —but I knew the tension he was living with occasionally bogged him down. I couldn't feel particularly sorry for him, though. His problems were of his own making. After all, *I* wasn't the one who married the woman.

And so life went on. I harassed Nora whenever I could and worked to the point of exhaustion the rest of the time. The only real cloud on my horizon, besides Nora, was when Jack Grey sold his spread to some fellow from Illinois by the name of Seelemire. How I missed Jack's cheerful evening visits! Alma probably didn't notice. He was too wrapped up in his lady-love.

At harvest time we traditionally hauled the last half-dozen wagon loads of hay down to the barn loft for feeding the horses and milk cow during the winter. We were pitching off the very last load, late one golden September afternoon, when Uncle George drove up in a light buggy, his mongrel dog sitting on the seat beside him. He had brought fruit for Nora to can.

Of course it was so late in the day he couldn't go home that night. Besides, Nora was overjoyed to see him. Instead of starting on the addition we were planning for the corral, I went to my cabin as soon as the hay was unloaded. I knew Alma wanted to spend time with his father-in-law, too, and George would have to return home early the next morning. We could start digging post holes after he left.

When I came down to help Alma the next day, I found him and Uncle George hitching our team to the hay wagon. Nora must have been complaining because they were going to Timbered Island for house logs.

I was a little surprised and a bit disgusted at her whining, but the new cabin made sense. With them in a home of their own, I could live in the original cabin. That would be so much easier all the way around. I had to admit I hadn't looked forward to spending the winter at Henry's place up on the flats.

I set about digging postholes by myself as they drove away, Uncle George's dog on the wagon beside them, his light carriage standing by our barn, and his horse, complete with a bell, wandering around in the house pasture with Darky and Star. I didn't see Nora and I didn't eat in Alma's cabin that day.

Around noon the next day, I heard an awful racket coming through the woods—the pounding of horses' hooves, someone yelling, a dog barking, a horse bell gone wild. I dropped the crow bar I was using to pry a boulder the size of Utah out of the posthole I was digging, and ran toward the road.

Almost immediately I saw our Percherons streaking through the trees and seconds later I heard Uncle George yelling for me to open the gate of the corral. Again I ran.

I'd barely swung the pole gate open when George's dog chased Darky, Star and George's horse through it. I swung the gate shut just as my uncle pulled our heavily-lathered team to a snorting halt outside the cabin. I had a fleeting glimpse of my brother, curled up on a bed of pine boughs, his face contorted, blood everywhere.

"Nephi," Uncle George roared as he jumped to the ground, "Get my horse harnessed and hitched to the buggy, quick! Nora! Nora, come here! Bring rags – a sheet – anything!"

I latched the gate and ran.

CHAPTER FORTY-NINE

I can hardly bear to remember what happened next. Alma's axe had slipped, burying itself to the bone in his ankle, severing an artery. He'd held it all the way from Timbered Island—miles away—trying to staunch the bleeding. But whenever he moved his hand—and with all the jouncing and jolting of the wagon on the rough, uneven road he couldn't keep constant pressure on the cut—blood spurted all over the wagon. The pine boughs beneath him were stained bright red and the dirt on the wagon bed had become red mud.

Uncle George ripped one of Nora's fancy blue-ruffled sheets into strips and, with her help, made as tight a bandage as he could with a tourniquet above it while I harnessed his horse and hitched it to the buggy. Then George and I lifted Alma onto the seat.

"I'm coming, too," Nora said, trying to pull her front-heavy body up onto the buggy seat by her husband.

"I don't need you having that baby while we're on the road," Uncle George's voice was raspy as he took his seat beside Alma. "Stay home and pray like you've never prayed before!" He reached for his whip as he slapped the reins on his horse's rump. Although he was traveling fast, I had caught Star, saddled her and was beside him before he'd reached Jack Grey's empty cabin.

I stayed beside him for a few miles but once we reached the top of Botcher's Hill I spurred Star into a dead run. I knew she could outrun Uncle George's horse with her eyes closed and I wanted the doctor ready by the time my brother arrived.

There was a 'Doc Reese' in Jackson but when I pounded on his door, some woman answered and said he wasn't at home. She suggested a couple of places to look and I finally found him in Rube Tuttle's saloon, nine sheets to the wind, and not exactly willing—or in shape—to come help my brother.

"Whash y' shayin'?" he mumbled after I'd repeated my need several times. His bleary eyes were bloodshot and his hand, around his whisky glass, trembled.

"My brother's bad hurt." I practically shouted in his ear. "He's cut, deep. Come stitch him up." I wanted to lift him by the lapels of his dirty dogstooth-check coat and drag him out the door.

"Catsh me later," he mumbled. "Cansh y' shee I'm buzhy."

I asked Rube for a glass of water and dashed it in the doctor's face. He jerked, then looked up at me.

"Why'd y' do tha'?" he asked in a querulous voice. "I washn't doin' y' any harm."

"No, but if you don't get out of that chair and come help my brother, I'm going to do *you* some harm." Rube handed me another glass of water and I splashed Doc Reese again. That time he got mad but at least he was a little more sober.

"Calm down, John," the bartender said. "Buck up, now. This fellow needs help."

"Needzh help?" Doc looked around. "I need help?"

"Not you, *me!*" I pulled him to his feet. By then he'd forgotten it was me who had doused him.

"Why didn't y' shay show?" He staggered, righted himself, then started with an unsteady gait, towards the door.

"John, you'd better have some coffee before you go. You're gonna need steadier nerves than you have right now," Rube thrust a large mug of hot coffee into the doctor's hands. "Drink up, now."

"Thanksh," Doc Reese mumbled. I put my hand under his arm to steady him as he tipped the mug toward his lips.

When every drop of the coffee was in him, I handed the mug back to the bartender with a quick word of thanks, then hurried Doctor John Reese out the door and down the street towards his home and my brother. I was beginning to wonder if I was wasting my time. Uncle George and I may not have had his education and experience but we both had steadier hands.

By the time Doc and I arrived, Alma had been there for a while, deeply in pain, his bandage, despite the tourniquet, soaked with blood. Uncle George and I lifted him out of the buggy and carried him into Doc's office where we laid him on the stained oak surgery table in the middle of the room.

The doctor's hands still trembled as he dug around for the ends of the artery, finding them, losing them, and swearing under his breath each time he did so.

Alma groaned in agony until I wanted to shake the doctor, I was so angry.

"Can't you give him something for pain?" I finally asked. I was almost ready to take over and do the job myself.

"Don' b'lieve in it. A man'sh gotta deal with what a man'sh gotta deal with."

And he'd been dealing with *what* in the saloon? I wanted to ask what right a man of his profession had to be so drunk he couldn't perform his job. Didn't he have a responsibility? But I kept my mouth shut and my clenched hands in my pockets. My brother didn't need me to take John Reese's attention away from his work.

Eventually the artery's ends were reattached, the bleeding stopped, and the wound sewed shut. Alma gritted his teeth with every stab of the needle but he never uttered a sound. I wondered if I could have been so quiet.

"I'll get a room at the hotel so you can keep an eye on him," I told Doc Reese.

"No, no need. He'll be alright." His speech wasn't quite so slurry and he seemed a little more aware. "Jush' take him home and have him shtay off that foot for a week or show."

"Are you sure?" I was dubious.

"Of courshe. He'sh good azh new, aren' you, boy?" Doc Reese patted Alma on the shoulder. "Keep 'im off water, now. He'll pro'bly beg but don' give him more'n a teashpoonful at a time."

I'd never heard of such a thing but what did I know about medical issues like this?

Uncle George and I carried Alma out to the buggy but as we were trying to get him in, he cried out in pain and blood seeped from his wound again. I ran back into the Doc Reese's office.

"What do we do now?" I shouted. "The bleeding's started again!"

He looked at me through still-bleary eyes and mumbled, "I've done all I c'n do. Don' give him water even if he azhksh for it—only a teashpoon at a time, now—an' make him azh comfer'ble azh y' can." Then he slumped down on his chair and immediately started snoring.

I gave up. With no other doctor available, Uncle George, Nora and I would just have to do the best we could.

Before I left town, I stopped by Daisy Steele's drugstore where I bought a bottle of laudanum. I didn't care if Doc Reese didn't believe in pain relief, my brother was in agony and I intended to relieve it.

Daisy knew the doctor and his opinions. She didn't even ask if I had a prescription. With a sympathetic look on her face, she took a bottle off her shelf and handed it to me.

"Come get more if you need it," she said, softly. "I hope your brother feels better soon,"

I've always thought Daisy could probably have done a better job than Doc Reese. At least she would have been more sympathetic and careful.

We took Alma home, elevated his foot, and took turns watching him that night. The tourniquet helped staunch the bleeding, of course, but by morning Alma was in serious agony. His face was flushed, his body burning with fever, and there were red streaks leading from the wound up his shin.

He was so thirsty, alternating deep groans with piteous begging for water, that I finally threw Doc Reese's instructions out the window and started giving him as much as he could drink. It was plain, though, that he was fading. The laudanum didn't seem to be helping or, if it was, I would have hated to see him without—and we hadn't the faintest idea what to do for him.

"Father, what now?" Nora sobbed when she saw the streaks on his shin. Alma groaned, moving restlessly. "Hold still, Alma, don't move your leg." She tried to hold his leg steady but he was stronger than she. Blood, tinged with pus, seeped from the wound.

"Nephi, we need another doctor," Uncle George said. "Is Star rested enough to make the trip to Idaho? There's Doc Crisler in Driggs."

"She'll make it." I snatched my coat and ran to the door, grateful to be doing something that might help.

I thanked my lucky stars for Star that day. I needed every ounce of her speed and stamina as I rode out of the valley to fetch Doctor Crisler. And thank God he was home, sober, and willing to come when I arrived!

But even though my horse was fast and I took the shorter route through Death Canyon, it wasn't enough. When the doctor and I arrived back at the cabin, my uncle had cut down a spruce tree and was preparing to saw planks. Except for a low sobbing from Nora, the cabin was silent.

My beloved brother was dead.

190

We dressed Alma in the suit Mother had made for him and laid him in the casket George and I built. Then we placed it in the utility wagon. I helped Uncle George load his fruit back into the trunk at the back of his buggy before roping Nora's small hope chest, stuffed with her belongings, on top. Then I drove our team, with its sorry load, to the cemetery in town. Uncle George followed behind—his daughter by his side. I was grateful that the clip-clop of Sleek and Sassy's hooves, as well as the creaking of the wagon, drowned out most of Nora's sobbing.

There was no funeral—just a brief graveside service on a dark, drizzly day. We buried Alma in the Aspen Cemetery on the mountain south of Jackson where he could see the Grand Teton. I guess I could have buried him out on the ranch but the thought of my brother's grave being so close was more than I could bear. Besides, Nora wanted it where she could come visit, once in a while, and she had no intentions of ever again setting foot on a ranch where I was living. We'd never gotten along and, of course, she blamed me for his death. As soon as the casket was covered she went with her father back home to Chapin.

Those of our neighbors who had heard the news, came to be with us and lingered after my uncle drove off but I could not talk to them. When Uncle George wheeled his buggy around and drove down the hill, I turned and stumbled through the trees above the cemetery, putting distance between myself and the little group gathered around the grave. Eventually they, too, drifted off.

With the last one finally out of sight, I made my way back to Alma's grave.

My brother . . . my hero . . . my best friend . . . lay beneath that dirt and I would never see him again.

Suddenly the black clouds above me broke and rain hurtled down, nearly cutting my skin with its sharpness. It matched my mood. Lifting my face to the leaden skies, I screamed, "NOOOOOOOOOOOOOOOOOO!"

CHAPTER FIFTY

Silence. Eternal silence. Henry's cabin was silent and empty when I finally returned late that night, soaking wet, hungry and alone. There was no food on the stove . . . no lamp in the window . . . nothing but the dismal beat of rain on the roof and the drip, drip, drip of raindrops falling down the chimney and striking the hearth.

I didn't want to stay in that cold cabin but I didn't want to be where my brother had died, either. Someday I would have to go back, but not tonight. I sat in the lone chair, watching water sheeting down the windowpanes of the small window above the table, numb and not wanting to think but knowing I could not sleep, either.

Finally, exhausted, I laid down on the bed but I tossed and turned all night. In the darkness I could see Alma on the wagon, smiling and waving to Nora and me as he and George drove away thorough the trees.

I saw Alma laying on his pine-bough bed, his face pale and contorted, trying to hold the wound shut while blood spurted through his fingers as the wagon bounced over the rough track that served as a major road.

I saw Alma grit his teeth—his face pasty white—as Doc Reese, hands trembling from too much whisky, tried to stitch him up. The whisky should have been in my brother as an anesthetic instead of in that quack of a doctor!

I saw Alma laying on Nora's snow-white sheets—now stained bright red with his life's blood—burning with fever, groaning in an agony I'd never witnessed before, ugly red streaks slowly inching their way up his leg.

I saw Alma, cold and stiff in his coffin, his hands folded across his chest and his eyes closed in eternal sleep as I helped George position the lid and nail it down.

Over and over the scenes played in my head until I thought I would go mad. I wanted to weep but tears would not come. I groaned with pain much as Alma had groaned. His had been a physical pain brought on by injury and fever; mine may as well have been. I thought my insides were being torn out of me, it hurt so bad. And there was no escaping it. Pain, paralyzing pain, wracked me all through that endless night.

The dawning of day brought no relief. Light meant work, which should have helped, but work meant solitude. The ranch that Alma and I had built together now oozed solitude, dripped solitude, reeked with solitude . . . and everywhere I went was unbroken, damnable, eternal silence. Not even the birds sang for me now—or if they did, I couldn't hear.

Unable to bear Henry's cabin, I moved back into the cabin Alma and I had shared, but the river's soothing murmur had ceased. Magpies and ravens pecked at the clots of blood stuck to the boards of the wagon and I ran at them, screaming, but I heard neither their pecking nor my own screams. I scrubbed the boards with lye soap until I could no longer see the stains. The birds stayed away.

I tore out the bed Alma had built for Nora, keeping only my bunk. I eradicated every trace of my cousin that I could find but, still, I could sense her presence. Why could I feel hers but not my brother's?

I lit fires in the stove and the fireplace, trying to tame the increasing autumn chill, but there was no companionable crackling of the pine wood as it burned and, although sweat rolled off my face and down my back and chest, it was an icy sweat and I remained caught in merciless chill.

I was as cold as my brother lying beneath the rocks and soil of that desolate, gradually freezing mountainside.

And the silence—that horrible silence—was deafening. I finished digging the postholes for the corral but there was no sound as I struck rocks and pried them out with the crow bar. I nailed the rails to my newly-set posts but there was no sound of the hammer striking steel.

I saw Darky silently nicker to Star as the two stood, heads drooping sadly, near the cabin door. I saw horsemen and, occasionally, a buggy or wagon, pass by on the road but, rocky as it was, there was no creaking, no clip-clop. Nothing.

Only solitude.

And silence.

And nightmares.

Alma lying on the rocks of the riverbed, the water washing over him—over his pleading blue eyes, his uplifted arms, while his life's blood oozed out, spreading in an ever-widening, ever-deepening stain. And in my dream it was the only water I had to drink.

193

Nightmares.

Alma, blood spurting from his ankle, reaching for a baby wrapped in a blue blanket but as he reached, he slowly faded away and disappeared and all that was left was the baby, its blanket now stained with his blood, its tiny arms reaching towards where he had been.

Nightmares.

Alma, his eyes closed in death, moldering, disintegrating as rocks and gravel settled over him until there was nothing left that had been my brother.

I worked like a madman every day, hoping for relief at night, but night brought no peace. I arose each morning, more exhausted than I had been when I went to bed the night before.

I butchered the prolapsed cow and hung her in the tool shed to cure. Cold weather came, the meat froze, and I was so exhausted at the end of each day that it was a struggle to cut a chunk of meat from her carcass, cook it and eat.

Washing my dishes at the end of my supper meal took all the strength I had.

I don't know how I survived that fall and winter. I don't know how I chopped my wood and hauled it to the cabin or how I managed to feed my cattle. Just harnessing the team and hitching them to the sleigh was a monumental task.

Banking the fire in the fireplace at night took more strength than I had. But somehow I managed. Somehow I survived.

194

One late November day my cousin, John, stopped by after a trip to visit his parents and left a note that Nora had a baby boy. I wasn't home when he came.

By spring of the next year, I was beginning to regain my hearing. And that brought fresh torment. The mourning doves I'd loved to listen to now reminded me of my loneliness and why I *was* alone. Alma was gone. I wanted to shoot every dove I heard.

Geese, loudly mating on the riverbanks, and ducks, quacking companionably in the ponds, reminded me that, while they were enjoying the association of each other, I had nobody. Alma was gone.

Sparrows in flocks, hopping around on the ground, searching for seeds, reminded me that the days of socials and get-togethers were past. Never again would Alma ease the way for me, say the right word, make the proper gesture.

Never.

He was gone.

I struggled through irrigating, hating my loneliness and solitude. Frequently a week or more would go by and if I saw anyone at all, it was a distant horseman maybe a mile or more away. Someone dropped my mail off at the cabin, occasionally—putting it on my table since I was seldom home—but I never opened it. I could not. It was all letters from my parents and siblings, all of whom were married. I didn't want the reminder of my solitude. When their letters arrived, I stuffed them into a small chest and shoved it far under my bed.

That's probably why my father and mother came, without advanced warning. They'd written. And written. And when I did not respond, became alarmed enough to leave the farm in Heber to check on me.

Mother was horrified at the dirt in my cabin. She spent several days cooking and cleaning while Father walked the fields with me. He didn't say much more than he'd ever said but he was there. I wasn't any more at ease around him and yet, somehow, I appreciated his presence.

The night before they left, Father finally started a conversation.

"Maybe you need to come back to Heber City, Son," he said as we were polishing off a rhubarb pie Mother had served. I looked at him, startled.

"Why?" I asked.

"You've taken your brother's death pretty hard," he said. "You've lost a lot of weight and you aren't looking well at all. I think you need a rest but you won't get it here. You have a fine ranch with beautiful scenery but it's wearing you into the ground."

"I can't leave Alma, Father," I said. "He's here. I'm staying here, too."

"Your brother is dead, Son," Mother said, gently. "There's no bringing him back. Besides, he's with God now. He wouldn't even know or care." This talk of Alma being with God made me very uncomfortable. I didn't want my parents' religion and, besides, my brother was turning to dust on a mountainside ten or eleven miles away, not somewhere in the sky with an invisible God.

And it was my fault.

Somehow my father must have understood what I was thinking because he totally changed the direction of our conversation.

"Nephi, you are not responsible for your brother's death. It was an accident. Alma wouldn't want you pining away here. He'd want you to go on."

Finally I voiced the feelings I'd not even allowed myself to examine since my brother's burial.

"I can't leave him. I killed him, you know."

Mother gasped and my father dropped the bite of pie he was lifting to his mouth. Both sat, silent, for the longest time. Finally my mother asked, "Whatever do you mean, Nephi? You weren't there when his axe slipped. You weren't even here when he died. You did everything you could to save him."

"If I hadn't listened to that quack of a doctor!" I said, hitting the table with my fist so hard that the dishes bounced. My mother frowned and I explained.

"He said to bring Alma home and not give him any water. I listened. Maybe if I hadn't, my brother wouldn't have gotten blood poisoning. Maybe he'd still be here, today, instead of rotting under six feet of rocks and weeds."

"It might have helped him be more comfortable, to begin with, if he could have had water but I don't think it would have prevented the poison. I've seen this sort of thing before," my mother said. "From what I've heard I don't think that doctor was very careful about cleanliness. Besides, you can't expect to be exceptionally clean when you have to travel over miles and miles of dusty, rocky roads."

"Maybe if I'd gone for the Driggs doctor sooner...." I wanted to cry.

"You went as soon as you saw the poison start up his leg," my father spoke up. "George told us that."

So they had been talking to Uncle George. I could just imagine what he'd had to say.

"He told us you nearly ruined Star trying to get a doctor here. It wasn't your fault the doctor in town was a drunk who didn't know what he was doing." So Uncle George thought I'd about ruined my horse. Well, I supposed it was true. Had Star been any other horse, the pace I'd kept her at *would* have killed her.

"He told us how hard you tried to save your brother, Nephi," my father said in a tone I didn't remember ever hearing before.

I hesitated, "What else did he say? Did he tell you why they were getting house logs?"

"To build another cabin?"

"Yes, but did he tell you why they were building another cabin?"

My parents looked lost.

"It was because I was harassing Nora so much." There. It was out. My brother died simply because I had refused to listen when he begged me to stop.

"Nephi," my mother said, gently, "George had planned to come over and help Alma get logs ever since Alma and Nora got married. Nora wanted her own home. Alma was willing to have you stay with them for a while but Nora never wanted to share this cabin with anyone but her husband.

"You need to understand something about Nora. She hasn't always been the easiest person to live with. That's probably why she didn't get married at a younger age.

"Knowing you, I'm sure you added your share of fuel to the fire Alma was living with, but the accident truly wasn't your fault. He wasn't harvesting logs because of you. This decision was made while you were still in Heber City."

I sat there with my head in my hands, thinking about what my mother had just said, and suddenly the tears I'd not been able to shed started to flow.

I thought they would never stop.

CHAPTER FIFTY-ONE

Life was easier after that. Not necessarily more enjoyable but easier. My parents insisted if I was staying in the Hole I needed to hire someone to help with harvest in the summer and feeding and calving in the winter and spring. They were right. I knew I couldn't take care of all of it by myself, the place was too big now. Alma and I had had all we could do to finish the harvest with the two of us working from sunup to sundown and I simply could not go through another winter like the one I'd just spent.

I hired Frank Connell's brother-in-law, Floyd Wilson. He moved into the cabin with me for the rest of the summer and I was grateful. I wasn't alone any more. Floyd snored like nothing I'd ever heard before, and was forever spitting tobacco juice around the room, but he was company and he stayed with me until the harvest was over.

It was that following autumn that I went hunting alone for the first time in my life. It was the last time, too.

I started out on a beautiful fall day—one of those incredible blue-sky days when the leaves are all golden, the air is still, and the sun holds the promise of an Indian summer that will last forever.

I was out of meat and none of our—my—cattle needed to be culled so I didn't see beefsteak on my table any time soon. Since nothing else was pressing, I saddled Darky, loaded Star's pack saddle with a tent, some grub and my bedroll, grabbed my coat, some ammunition, and Alma's 30.06 and headed for the hills.

It took several hours to reach Antelope Springs on the flats past my cousin John's place. (I actually stopped by to ask if he wanted to come with me but he and T.A. were busy helping Wally with some fencing so I rode on.) At the springs I turned eastward and started up the mountainside.

It was rough country up there. I spent the rest of the day riding up one mountainside then down the other until, along towards evening, I finally camped by a swale up on the Mount Leidy saddle.

There was a beautiful sunset that evening. I set up camp, started a fire and sat in the opening of my tent while I ate supper and watched the flame in the western sky as it was mirrored in the water, first pink, deepening to rose, progressing to a flaming red then fading to purple just before the grey of approaching night took over. I slept more peacefully that night than I had in nearly two years.

Next morning I left the horses picketed at the edge of the swale and struck out on foot to see what I could find, my rifle under one arm, a coil of rope for hanging a carcass in a tree, over my other shoulder. The weather was still warm enough I knew the elk would be up in the high country so I climbed up one of the gullies leading to the top of Leidy.

I didn't see any sign of game, whatsoever—no tracks, no droppings, nothing. So I started on down the other side. It was a steep descent; difficult going.

A little alpine lake lay nestled between the north-eastern base of Leidy and the steep wooded slopes of adjoining mountains, its edges thick with waving grasses, its waters clear and clean. *Good watering hole*, I thought. I skirted it, looking for the game trail I was sure would be there.

It was. From the tracks and droppings I could see evidence of deer and elk and probably moose as well. The trail they traveled wound through the trees up a mountainside whose slopes made Leidy look like child's play.

After a short rest and a biscuit, I climbed as quietly as I could, looking and listening for game as I went. I had scrabbled my way nearly to the top, grasping low-hanging branches, shrubs, even tree roots at places, to pull myself up the steepest parts of the trail, still not seeing or hearing any animals, when suddenly a cold wind swept up the mountainside from the north.

I shivered. Where I'd been sweating only moments before, now I was unexpectedly chilled. I looked at the sky as I hastily slipped into the coat I'd tied around my waist. An angry black cloud, heavy with moisture, roiled over the mountains to the north, bearing down on me with astonishing speed. As I looked to the southwest, I realized the sun was a lot closer to setting than I'd thought.

Here I was on a remote mountaintop, nearing night, with what felt like a vicious winter storm beginning to unleash its fury. I turned back down the trail.

One can go down much faster than up. The game trail became a slick, slimy mess as the snow started to stick and I was soon sliding, grasping at the branches and bushes I'd used to help me climb, trying to slow my descent. Battered, bruised and definitely more than a little damp from sliding down the track, I finally arrived at the lake, barely managing to stop before tumbling into the water.

Panting, I looked toward the western side of the lake. I couldn't even see Leidy, the snow was falling so thick.

I couldn't have found my way back to my camp through that mess even if I'd felt like trying. But I didn't feel like tackling Leidy; I was too tired. I had to make camp for the night.

Try to start a fire in a blizzard.

I looked around for a good place to build a fire.

There wasn't one.

With the wind coming from the north, my best bet was the north side of the lake where a mountain stood between me and the worst of the storm.

Try to find something dry enough to catch fire in a wet snowstorm. I had to have enough twigs and dry branches handy to keep my fire going—and going well—once it started. That meant dry evergreen needles and dead branches and twigs that I could strip from the trunks of live trees. I could manage that.

But I also had to have some way to block the wind— something wider than I was so I could start the fire once I got it laid. A firepit would help but I had nothing to dig with. I looked around.

There was plenty of downed timber in the area, some of it blackened, half-rotted stuff left from an ancient forest fire. I dragged a few lighter logs over, made a small three-quarters crib directly south of the largest fir tree I could find, covered the outsides and top of the crib with branches torn from the trees around me then started stockpiling dry wood inside my shelter, arranging it in such a way that it would provide me with additional shelter from the wind. Then I made a ring of large stones at the opening, with the driest pine needles I could find in the center, a small teepee of twigs over the top.

Finally, I was ready to light my fire.

Try to start a fire in a snowstorm with only one, broken-stick match.

I searched my pockets again.

Then, frantically, one more time—the wind, all the while, swirling my little pile of twigs and red pine needles.

All I was carrying was my pocket knife, my watch and that one lousy match. The odds that I could get a fire going in such a wind with only one broken match were what? A million to one? And if I didn't get it going? As cold as the day had become—and as *I* had become—I stood as good a chance of freezing as I did of lighting a fire. Already I was starting to shiver and my fingers were stiff with chill.

Bone weary, late in the day, wet snowstorm, biting wind that was steadily getting worse, not better, and me with only one half-a-stick match.

Stupid, Stupid, **Stupid!**

I scrabbled, feverishly, for more fuel. I'd be lucky to get a fire started in the first place but if I did, by the time I struck that match I was going to have plenty of material close-by to keep it burning. On top of that, I couldn't afford to have my one short match go out without igniting my carefully re-arranged pile of needles and twigs. And I wouldn't have much time before it burned down, burned my fingers, and fizzled out.

I knelt again, hunched over the fire ring, and with trembling, ice-cold fingers fetched the match out of my coat pocket. Cupping my hand over it, I struck my match on a small dry stone, then gently pushed it just under the pile of dead pine needles.

It flared—and immediately went out. I stared at my carefully-laid teepee of needles and twigs, wondering what I was going to do. My match was gone, I didn't have a fire, and, although the wind wasn't quite as fierce as it had been at first, those little flakes of white were still coming down hard.

Visions of a skeleton in my clothing, lying on its side in that makeshift shelter, floated before my eyes. Would I ever be found? Would anyone even know who it was if they did find me? And what of Darky and Star back on Leidy? Would wolves find them before they starved?

Worse thought, would the wolves find me? I wasn't too worried about a wolf attack while the storm raged but would I still be alive when it was over? Alive, but not alert enough to defend myself?

I could almost see grey fur rising in front of me.

Then I realized there was a thin curl of smoke coming from under the pile of needles and twigs. My match had done its job.

CHAPTER FIFTY-TWO

Although I was exhausted, I didn't get much sleep. I was too worried about the fire going out. I couldn't let that happen but I didn't want to set the logs and branches of my makeshift shelter ablaze, either. That meant I had to tend it frequently. Besides, it was snowing and blowing, still—and I had to keep warm. Daybreak found me slipping and sliding, scrabbling back up and around Leidy towards my camp on the other side.

I did a lot of thinking during the long hours of that cold, wet night. I couldn't believe how stupid I'd been to leave camp so unprepared. It would never happen again

But I also thought about the fact that nobody knew where I was. Nobody would have missed me. Even John, T.A. and Wally would have thought I'd gone home without stopping by. Had my fire not caught, it could have been weeks before anyone even knew I was missing and then they wouldn't have known where to look.

There was no-one to know.

No-one to care.

I felt an aloneness I'd never felt before—even after Alma's death—as I realized, for the first time, that I was completely isolated from the rest of humanity and there was nobody—now or ever—that would be concerned. If Floyd had still been working for me, he would have become worried after I'd been gone a few days. But he wouldn't have known where to look for me. I'd never really thought, before, about the reasons Alma and I had gone out together. It was just what we did—simply because we did *everything* together. For the first time in my life, I felt a deep need to have someone by my side. Not a brother who would get married and move on, but someone who would stay.

Another thought that occupied those lonely hours was my own mortality. I was young, strong, and healthy. I'd always assumed I'd live to a ripe old age, able to do my own work, able to take care of myself. That night showed me how wrong I was—how precarious life could be.

Alma's death was an accident. Mine would have been, too. But accident or no, I would have been just as dead as my brother. The only difference was that he had left a wife to mourn his passing, to visit his gravesite, and a child to carry on his name. No one would have even known where I was; nobody except for the wolves, coyotes and carrion birds.

It was a very unsettling thought.

Sometime that winter when Floyd was back living in my cabin and we were sitting around the fireside one night, I told him about the incident.

"You were lucky," he said.

I knew that.

"Good reason to take someone with," he added.

"I don't plan on a repeat," I said. I was whittling a chain from a block of cedar as I spoke. He nodded, leaned forward, spat at the fire, then settled back in his chair. After staring into the fire and working his chaw around for a while, he spoke again. "Why you never married like your brother did?"

I stiffened.

"I don't need a woman!" I jumped up, brushing wood shavings from my pants.

"No need to get your hackles up," he said, mildly. "I was just wonderin'. Come set back down."

"*You* should know. I have enough to keep me busy—no need to have a woman making life miserable on top of it." I didn't add that I thought the main reason he'd cheerfully left the Connell place to work for me whenever I asked was to escape, not only his sister, Frank's wife, but his mother as well. Both were absolute terrors, keeping life continually stirred up in their home. I knew Frank was miserable in his marriage and his three children were cowed, pathetic little girls who hung in the shadows, afraid to move for fear of being screamed at or beaten. I shook my head, amazed at Floyd's question.

"Not all women are like the ones in my family," Floyd said as I sat back down to my whittling. "What are they like in yours?"

"My mother's a gem," I said. "So are my sisters. They put up with a lot more than any of them should. If I could have ever found a woman like my mother maybe I would have thought about marriage."

Where had that come from? The very thought startled me. I'd never ever even *considered* marriage before—at least not in relation to me. Floyd smiled.

204

"So if you could find someone like them you'd consider gettin' hitched?"

"I don't know that I would," I said, suddenly confused. "I've never really thought about it." Besides, even if I had I didn't want to discuss it with some old bachelor who didn't know a decent woman from a fence post. ...Not because he wasn't smart enough but because the other type was all he'd known.

Again he surprised me.

"I was married onct," he said, quietly. *That* made me sit up and pay attention. I'd known him for several years and never had any inkling he'd ever been anything more than a dried up old prune of a single man. "She was the sun, moon and stars to me," he continued.

Floyd talking poetic was the absolute last thing I'd expected. If he was trying to get my attention, he was certainly succeeding.

"What happened?"

"She died in childbirth. The baby lived for a few hours. Little girl," he said, his voice wistful. "She looked like her mother—lots of dark, curly hair, cute little mouth, long slender fingers." His eyes were sad as he watched sparks explode off the pine log in the fireplace and fly up the chimney.

Presently he added, almost as an afterthought, "I would have made a good father." Then, a while later, "And my Sarah Ann was so lookin' forward to bein' a mother. We had the world in each other and our little farm out in Califoroy. It was producing well. We were happy with it. We were happy bein' together. Then, in an instant, she was gone. And our baby went, too. I lost everything that really mattered to me in one single day. There was nothin' worth stayin' on the farm for after that."

I was skeptical about the happiness he'd said he had. "If everything was so perfect, why didn't you remarry?"

Floyd smiled, wryly. "Perfection only comes once, Nephi," he said. "I couldn't have ever found another woman who did for me what my Sarah Ann did—and havin' had it once, I wasn't willin' to settle for anything less."

I thought about that for a while. Why had Floyd found someone so wonderful while his brother-in-law, Frank, who was a truly fine fellow in my opinion, had gotten saddled with such a shrew? Since Frank's wife was Floyd's sister, I didn't think I should voice my opinion, though. It wouldn't be polite.

But I'm sure Floyd guessed what I was thinking, because he brought it up without my asking.

"Frank could've found a good woman, too," he said, "if he'd been more careful. He was seein' my wife's cousin. She was a fine girl; a lot like my Sarah Ann. Then Lucy decided she wanted him. He wasn't cautious enough to keep his pants buttoned up like he should have been."

I squirmed at that information. It wasn't my business why Frank had married Lucy although maybe that explained a few things.

"Nephi," Floyd went on. I could see he wouldn't give up on whatever it was he wanted to tell me so I resigned myself to his preaching, "you need companionship. Something other than me and your cows bein' around occasionally."

Wait a minute. That sounds familiar. I searched my memory for when I'd heard it before. Then it came back to me—Jack, at the Fourth of July picnic when I'd stolen the cream pie, had expressed pretty much the same thing.

What exactly was it he said? 'You may not feel any great need for companionship other than your brother and them cows of yours but that don't mean Alma feels the same.'

That was it. He was right, too, only I had blinders on and wasn't willing to see and accept the fact my brother had desires I didn't share.

Would things have been different if I'd paid more attention, encouraged Alma in his searching? Would he still have married Nora? Or would he have taken the time to find a woman more like Floyd's Sarah Ann?

Floyd didn't give me time to think about it before he went on. "To you right now," he said, "your land and your animals is all there is in life. You eat, breathe, and live this ranch."

"What's wrong with that?" I demanded.

"You need to find a balance." Floyd spit into the fire again. "Me, I found it once. I won't be findin' it again but that's ok for me. I'm contented with the memories because I know she's there, somewhere. She's never really left me.

"But you, you ain't found it yet. You need a woman to make comin' home to this cabin worth while . . . someone who can appreciate your sense of humor, your capacity to work yourself to the bone and back . . . someone who will give you kids to pass this land on to when you die. As you stand, now, where's it going to go? If you'd died up on that mountain what would have happened to everything you've give your life for?"

It was a good question; one I didn't like thinking about because I didn't have an answer. Apparently Floyd figured he'd said enough because he got up, went outside to do the necessary, then came in and went to bed. Soon he was snoring peacefully, leaving me alone with my thoughts beside a slowly dying fire.

CHAPTER FIFTY-THREE

After Floyd stirred me up, I thought about what he'd said all winter and spring. As I fed my cows, I wondered who would get them if anything happened to me. My parents? My brothers and sisters? They weren't interested in my ranch. This land and the herd I'd worked so hard to build up would just be sold. That wasn't a comfortable idea.

The problem was what to do about it.

Alma'd solved it by getting married and starting a family as soon as he could—and I'd had to buy his wife out since she didn't want to stay on the ranch with me. (Thank God and the grey Goosewing Hills for *that*!) But getting married just so I'd have someone to inherit my property wasn't on my to-do list, either.

Unfortunately my list didn't include anything to take the place of Alma's choice. It was all about building my place up while I was alive.

It never occurred to me that Alma's choice had nothing to do with passing on the land; that he'd married for a companionship I couldn't give him. He'd tried to tell me. Jack had tried to tell me. My mother had tried to tell me. And Floyd was trying to tell me. But their words were falling on deaf ears and so I kept brooding over the question of what I should do.

It didn't seem to make any difference what angle I thought from, I couldn't come up with a plan to keep my ranch going in the event of my death. I didn't want to will it to any of the other ranchers around. They had more than they could manage without adding my spread. None of my family thought the Teton scenery so wonderful they were willing to live in the cold, inhospitable Hole. I didn't want to see it go back to wilderness: I'd put too much of myself into it. What was left except posterity? And how did one get posterity? Through a woman. I felt like I was running in circles with one shoe nailed to the floor.

I kept on running, too—kept brooding about it for months. Meanwhile, calving season came and went. At the request of our new Forest Ranger, Jim Imeson, Floyd and I took my herd to a new summer range way up the Gros Ventre. Then we took turns irrigating and fixing fence until, before I knew it, it was time for another Fourth of July shindig in Jackson. By then, we were both more than ready to enjoy it.

We did, too. Well, I did anyway. I'm not so sure about Floyd. Just after our picnic dinner, we walked over to the corrals, arriving just in time to hear Jim Imeson's brother, Tom—our local blacksmith—jokingly bet that his saddle horse could unload anyone in the crowd.

"Where'd you get that old nag, Tom?" one of the cowboys asked. "Payment for a shoeing job?"

"Nag!" Tom laughed. "My horse can unseat anyone that tries to ride him." He practically pushed his horse into the corral, then pulled it around the perimeter so everyone could inspect it. Sway backed, dull of coat and sleepy eyed, the animal stumbled along behind Tom. I thought it might keel over dead before it even made one lap around the small arena.

Neither Floyd nor I had seen the horse before that morning when Tom joined our group as we rode through Jackson on the way to the shindig, but it hadn't seemed overly ambitious then, either.

"Floyd, what do you think about that horse?" I asked, quietly. To me it looked like nothing more than a placid old plug on its last legs.

"Unload anyone? That's not likely," Floyd said, only he didn't bother to keep his voice down. I squirmed.

It wouldn't have been so bad if he'd stopped there but he didn't. "That nag couldn't unload anyone if he tried," Floyd continued, his voice clear. "He's too old and stoged up. I've seen plugs like him before. Wouldn't even call him a horse."

The crowd laughed and I could have happily crawled under a rock. Tom just looked at Floyd and smiled, angelically.

"Care to back that up with a little wager?" he asked.

"Find a rider and I will," Floyd said. "I don't see anyone that's even interested."

A murmur rippled through the crowd of cowboys gathered around the corral.

"You ride 'im, Sam."

"Not me. I'd git myself hurt just sittin' there while that hoss fell asleep under me. I'm savin' my energy for the real stuff this afternoon. Why don't you try 'im?"

"Naw. If I'm gonna ride a hoss I want a real hoss under me. This one's just a carousel plug."

"Maybe Boots, here, could stay on him."

Snort from Boots, "If I wanted to try."

"You could fall asleep together—you an' that hoss."

And so it went. Drawn by the commotion, more and more men joined us around the arena. Finally, some fellow from Green River stepped up to the plate.

"All right. If none of you fellas has the courage to try, I'll ride him," he said. "If he'll wake up." He walked through the gate, carefully closing it behind him. "Don't want that hoss to buck his way through the gate and leave me behind." He winked at Floyd then made a big show of removing his vest, folding it and laying it in a neat little pile by the gate. Then he laid his hat on top, rubbed his hands together and shouted, "Powder River, let'r buck".

"Now wait a minute," Tom said. "Talk softly. You're going to spook my horse." The crowd hooted. The horse looked like it was fast asleep.

Floyd's comment of, "Not much chance anyone's going to wake that nag," was met with laughter.

"Maybe not," Tom said, "but we haven't taken bets yet. You said you wanted to bet, Floyd. Anyone else care to join in?"

Plenty did.

"Hold your money out, then," Tom said. "You think I'm going to pay up on something I can't see?"

I saw bank notes and coins displayed all around the corral. Floyd held up a five dollar gold piece. Between the local yokels and the rich eastern dudes there was suddenly a lot of money flashing around.

"A fool and his money are easily parted," I hissed in Floyd's ear, quoting one of my mother's maxims. "You better put that gold piece back in your pocket before you lose it."

Floyd laughed. "Don't worry, Nephi. In a few minutes I'm going to double it," he said.

"Use your head, Floyd. Where's Tom going to come up with enough money to pay off all these bets? Is business at the smithy that good?"

I was seeing more and more money displayed and the higher the gambling excitement got, the more doubtful I was about that cow pony being anywhere near as complacent as it appeared. Floyd began having second thoughts, too, but it was too late to take back his bet. Tom had already seen and noted his gold piece.

"Like I said, fools and their money…." I repeated.

"Well, maybe that horse is as lazy as he looks," Floyd was hopeful.

"You know darned well if that horse was so easy going Tom wouldn't have been offering bets," I said. "Someone's going to get unloaded here real quick."

I seemed to be the only person who thought so, though.

Gambling fever was running at fever pitch by the time Tom pushed his horse into the chute and the rider mounted it. Tom opened the chute gate again but the horse just stood there.

"Haze him out of the chute!" one of the Eastern dudes yelled.

I saw Tom snicker as one of the cowboys started waving his hat and hollering. Suddenly that sleepy cow pony came unglued. It lunged out of the gate and started whirling so close to the corral fence I expected a collision. Around and around and around it went with its rider grabbing leather for all he was worth.

At first the fellow was fairly well seated. I thought he might manage to ride it out until the horse either tired or got so dizzy it fell over. Floyd seemed to think so, too.

"Go to it, boy!" he shouted. "You're doin' 'er. Your mount's tiring. Hang in there!" I was both surprised and amused. I wouldn't have expected so much racket from Floyd.

I turned and was about to say something to him when he groaned. Glancing back, I saw the first sign of serious trouble. The rider, starting to lose his balance, had let go of the reins as he grabbed the saddle horn with both hands, clinging for dear life.

"Keep goin'!" Floyd shouted. "Don't give up!" His voice was lost in the general din of the crowd. Hoots and whistles mixed with desperate instructions like Floyd's filled the hot, dusty summer-afternoon air.

The fellow managed to stay on for a couple more rounds but it was all over when one of his feet slipped out of its stirrup. Still he tried, valiantly, to cling to Tom's horse with his knee and heel but it was plain to see he was too dizzy. Finally his balance shifted and the next moment he sailed out of the saddle, landing with a bone-jarring thud in the thick dust of the arena.

The cow pony immediately stopped whirling and, after standing still and shaking its head for a minute or two, stumbled back to the chute. Before long it ambled back out with Tom actually *standing* on the saddle on its back.

"This is the kind of horse those Green River fellows can't ride!" Tom hollered as he rode his plug around the arena, a huge grin on his face.

"Very funny," Floyd said in disgust.

The crowd went wild.

CHAPTER FIFTY-FOUR

The rest of the day was uneventful. Floyd wasn't in the mood to try any of the contests; he was moping too much over the loss of his gold piece. We watched, but everything paled after Tom's stunt.

I was getting a little antsy by the time the rodeo wound down, anyway. Mose Giltner, one of the valley ranchers who was ranging up on the Gros Ventre with me, had donated a beef and I could smell it barbecuing. It had been so long since I'd had a really good meal I couldn't wait for the rodeo to finish and supper to start. I wasn't disappointed, either. That food sure tasted good after my home cooking.

We stayed for the dance that night, too, although it was just to listen to the music. We both managed to dodge Rhoda Newbold until she finally gave up trying to find us.

The supper and the music mellowed Floyd—soothed his wounds from losing the bet enough that, with the dark to hide behind, I dared ask some questions on the way home.

"Floyd," I began, "what was it like being married?"

Dead silence.

I was beginning to wonder if he'd gone to sleep or died or something. Finally he spoke.

"What do you mean?" he asked.

"Oh, I was just wondering what it was like to come home to a woman in the house. I never have figured out why Alma was so keen to get his wings cut."

"With the right woman," he said, slowly, "there's a happiness—a deep satisfaction, I guess—that you can't find any other way." He was quiet for a while and I was trying to think of how to ask what I wanted to know when he went on.

"Nephi, the right woman can make you feel complete in a way you aren't without her."

I thought about that for a time. I hadn't noticed I wasn't complete. I was pretty happy with my life the way it was. Whenever I looked at my ranch and my cows, I felt a deep satisfaction. The only lack I felt was when I thought of my dying and what would happen to my place when I did. I didn't understand what he was talking about.

Then he spoke again, "You look at everything you own and you're pleased with it. But that's all. It's pleasure, not real happiness. *Things* can't give you happiness, Nephi. Happiness comes from something else. It's knowing your own worth, feeling your value in the world. Part of that comes from the kind of life you live but the other part comes from the esteem others have for you, particularly the people you care most about."

"I'm happy," I said. "I like what I'm doing and I'm good at it. My folks care about me. What else is there?"

"Yes, you are good at what you do. And yes, you probably are happy. But *happiness*, itself, is more. There's a joy in a good marriage that you won't find feeding cows, or branding calves—or anywheres else, for that matter. It's satisfaction and contentment and ecstasy and ...."

"Enough," I said. "I see the picture." I didn't but I'd listened to all I wanted about wedded bliss. And I still hadn't learned what I wanted to know. I thought a while then tried again.

"But what was it like to have someone there in the house when you came home? Didn't you feel like you were pressured or kind of put in a squeeze chute?"

"No," he said, his voice thoughtful, "it wasn't that way at all with Sarah Ann. She was loving and supportive of whatever I was doin' or wanted to do. She made me want to be around her because she believed in me and she was always so glad to see me when I came in from work. It made coming home a joy. But, then, she was loving and kind to everyone. Now if she'd been like my sister, Lucy, I'd have probably run for the hills by the time the honeymoon was over."

I thought I would have, too. More likely, I wouldn't have even lasted out the honeymoon. Probably wouldn't have lasted the day of the wedding.

"You talk about how wonderful Sarah Ann was," I said. "How did you manage to find her?"

Floyd snorted.

"Mostly dumb luck," he said. "But part of it was because I was looking for someone as different from my sister as I could find. I thought of every bad quality Lucy had and then made a list of the opposites and started looking for girls that fit my list."

I wouldn't have expected such thinking from Floyd, especially not after he'd suckered so thoroughly for Tom Imeson's stunt. But what he said he'd done sounded like a smart plan to me. At least a fellow would have something to go on as he looked.

"How she treated other people, especially her home folks, was real important to me," he continued. "I met some girls I thought was pretty nice until I visited them at home. Any woman who speaks disrespectful to her family members is going to talk the same way to her husband once the honeymoon is over, and maybe even before."

I could see where that had come from. Lucy, was such a shrew. I knew henpecked husbands—Bill Newbold came to mind—but Frank was beyond henpecked. Around Lucy he was as cowed as his little girls.

"There was a lot of things that was important to me," Floyd continued. "I wanted a woman who cared enough about herself to keep herself looking good. The tones of voice she used, the way she dressed, her intelligence—it was all important to me." It was odd, hearing this from Floyd, who had never seemed to me to be all that thoughtful . . . or interested in anyone else's intelligence or appearance.

"And, since I was a farmer, I wanted a woman willing to participate in farming activities," he went on. "If she wasn't suited to bein' a farmer's wife she wasn't going to be of any use to me. A woman needs to be easy with a man's life work."

I agreed wholeheartedly, remembering how I'd felt about Nora's frills and furbelows. That was quite a list he'd put together, though. I wondered how any woman, including his Sarah Ann, could have had all those virtues.

"Did Sarah Ann fit all that?" I asked in disbelief.

"Actually, yes," he said, "she was all that and more. She was kind. She was gentle. She was soft-spoken. She was smart. She was talented. Perfect in every way."

"Sounds more like an angel than a human." I muttered.

"Maybe that's why she didn't stay," he said. Through the darkness, I sensed his sadness and longing. "She was too good for this world."

"I don't think I'd want a perfect woman," I said, "What's the point of having her and then losing her? Besides, I'd want a little fun once in a while."

"It's better to have loved and lost than never to have loved at all," Floyd's voice was solemn. I wasn't so sure I agreed. If I was going to take the trouble to have a woman around I wouldn't want one so perfect I either couldn't enjoy her, or I'd lose her first thing—but I didn't see any point in arguing.

I'd gotten the general picture. Floyd was one of those rare birds who'd been so utterly contented with his marriage that he'd never been interested in looking for another woman to take Sarah Ann's place after she was gone. I wondered if I'd ever met another man who felt the same way. I also wondered if such a woman as his Sarah Ann had really existed in the first place. Much as I thought of my mother, I didn't think even she could fit that mold. Close, maybe. But it was only a maybe.

"Have you ever met any man who felt the way you do?" I asked. "For sure Frank doesn't."

"No, he doesn't, poor fellow," Floyd agreed. "If you ever decide to start lookin', Nephi, make sure you keep your suspenders up and your fly buttoned."

I decided to ignore his remark. I didn't want to travel down that route.

"I don't think Bill Newbold's all that happy either," I said. "I don't see how he could be. Rhoda can't cook. She won't keep house. She doesn't do anything but carp all day."

Floyd chuckled. He knew all about Rhoda.

"Roy McBride might feel that way," I hazarded. "Maggie's pretty nice. Tom Brown probably isn't—at least not if the rumors I've heard about Rosa's temper are correct. I really don't know about that, though. I've never seen her when she wasn't the most pleasant of women. I really like her."

"She's about Rhoda's opposite, all right," Floyd said. "Not only in temperament but Rosa's one woman who can put on a spread! She keeps herself lookin' nice, too."

I agreed.

That pretty much covered the couples I knew up on the flats. Down below, in the river bottoms, there were the Lingenfelters. I couldn't see wedded bliss written on their lintel even though I liked them both. Henry was noted for being a crusty old codger when he wanted to be. I hadn't been round Jenny enough to know how she handled him.

"What about the Lingenfelters?" I asked. "What do you think of their marriage?"

"Oh, I think they've lived together so long they're pretty used to each other by now," was all Floyd would say. Did he mean they were compatible or did he mean they'd grown tolerant? I wasn't sure.

"Have you met the Seelemires?" I asked. "They're the folks that bought Jack Grey's place two years ago." It was the summer Alma died but I didn't say so. My brother's death was still too painful even though I'd come to terms with it. Sort of.

How I'd missed Jack after Alma was gone! His absence from the neighborhood had left a gaping hole just when I needed him most.

"Haven't met them," Floyd said.

"I have. They seem pleasant whenever I'm around."

After that we lapsed into silence. We'd gone through the list of married neighbors that lived close by and there wasn't anything more to say. I sat and thought as the miles passed.

What is it, I wondered, *that makes one woman a saint and the next one a shrew? Actually, it's probably the next ten thousand that are shrews. Saints are hard to come by.*

Mother fits the category but I still don't think she's all that happy with my father, regardless of what she says. It isn't her fault, though. It was the polygamy issue that undermined her marriage.

My sisters are sweet women, too. Sarah's forbearing but Lindy's a polished gem. Suddenly it occurred to me that the only shrews in my family were Mary and Annie. *And that's more their choice than anything else. Mary's spoiled and Annie's sullen.*

Suddenly something I'd never considered before crossed my mind. Were Annie and Mary the trial to Father that Lucy was to Frank? I'd felt somewhat better about my father after he and Mother came up, but I still wasn't what I'd call 'easy' with the man. Maybe I needed to re-examine what I knew of him.

CHAPTER FIFTY-FIVE

I didn't spend much time thinking about him, though. I wrote my half-brother, Bill, and asked what his views were. I thought he might have seen another side of things from what I remembered. Then I went back to my farming.

I could have written to Lyman, too, but I didn't bother. And when Bill didn't answer immediately, I put all thoughts of family and home on the back burner. There was too much work to do for me to worry about anything else.

Nephi's hay fields

Late August had a definite chill that summer. Floyd and I were so busy trying to get my hay cut and stacked before it started snowing in the high country that we were worn to a frazzle.

`"We're almost home," Floyd said, the evening of September ninth. "I'd say maybe another two days and we'll have the hay all off the ground. Looks like a storm brewin', though."

It felt like it, too. There were clouds moving in from the northwest and the wind was nippy.

"If the snow would just hold off for another two or three days ...." I guided Sleek and Sassy to a stop in front of the barn loft door.

"Wouldn't hurt my feelings if we didn't get snow for another month but I don't think we're gonna to be so lucky," Floyd said.

"No," I agreed. In fact, I was sure it wouldn't happen.

It didn't snow in the valley that night. Didn't even rain, so I figured the mountains would be bare but I wasn't that lucky. There was a heavy dusting of white on both the Grand and the Indian when we drove the team and wagon up to the field the next morning. How that moisture had missed my ranch was beyond me. I'd have thought it would have rained in the valley if it was going to snow in the mountains, but it hadn't.

"Well, you know what that means," Floyd said as he looked from one mountain to the other. "Right about now your cows is headin' for lower elevations where their feed isn't under a foot of snow." I knew he was right. "Can't say as I blame them," he went on, scratching his head. "Don't expect I'd like having my mush served with snow over it, either."

I laughed. I'd never heard of dried grasses being referred to as mush. Floyd could be quite entertaining, when he chose.

"I guess I can put the cows in the river bottoms until we get this hay up," I said as I turned my team around and guided them back down the dugway Alma and I had carved out the first fall we'd been in the Hole. "You get the saddle horses and your mule in. I'll round up enough grub to last us a couple of weeks."

If my cattle had summered on the Kinky Creek watershed before that year, they would have known their way home. Since this was their first year, however, I knew they could end up in Lander or Green River or Pinedale or Dubois or anywhere else but the Hole. With fresh snow on their feed, they wouldn't care what direction they went so long as it was toward a lower elevation.

219

Floyd and I tied our bedrolls, a tent, and grub for a couple of weeks onto his mule and headed east

Past Brown's hill and Black Tail Butte, the ride along the Gros Ventre river was pleasant enough. It got real pretty once we started up into the mountains above Kelly. Aspens, shimmering gold in the autumn sun, made a bold contrast against the fresh white snow on the mountainsides above. As we passed Guil Huff's place at the northern base of the Indian, the red soil, where the snow had melted, added another stark color. How I enjoyed Wyoming's scenery. It didn't matter where I went, there was always something new and different to see.

As we rode along, saying little, I looked around me. The Gros Ventre was so different from the Hole. Its bluffs—high, rounding and red—had backward-sloping almost purple cliffs above. The space between the two was broken by evergreens and sage.

Past Slate Creek, however, the reds of the lower Gros Ventre changed to layer upon layer of cold grey near-vertical cliffs. Imposing. Forbidding. Softened only by the pines above and below.

We didn't follow the riverbed; there were too many willows. Instead, we rode up and over the low-lying, sage covered hills on the south side of the river. Cottonwoods, along the riverbed, were a subdued yellow-brown but the aspen up on the hillsides glowed gold. With the bright sunshine, the brilliant blue of the sky, and the golds, reds, greens and greys beside us, I felt as if I was in an ever-changing painting.

"Do you ever feel like this scenery is unreal?" I asked Floyd.

Not in a talkative mood, he only spat at a sagebrush, nodded, and rode on.

It was late in the day by the time we got to Lightning Creek and found several of the other ranchers from our area already camped and cooking their supper: Peter Hansen and Lee Lucas from Spring Gulch, Mose Giltner, the Barber brothers, and Joe Deyo from along the Gros Ventre. I knew the Barbers pretty well, disliked Joe intensely, and was acquainted with the rest. That night Floyd and I set up camp beside theirs and I could only hope the wolves I heard in the midnight hours weren't headed the same direction we were. I wondered how my herd had fared this past summer.

By late afternoon the next day, we came to the Darwin Ranch around the bend of the Gros Ventre river. Sometime after we'd trailed our herds past his spread the previous spring, Mr. Darwin had built a buck-rail fence clean across that narrow valley, fencing in not only his own place but a large strip of Forest Service land as well. I guess he thought he owned the Forest Service's part, too. That or he didn't want us around.

We had already taken poles down, led our horses through, repositioned the poles and were mounting our horses on the south side of his property when he saw us, came out with a rifle, and started in our general direction, shooting into the air and screaming threats at the top of his lungs . . . something to the effect that if we ever came back....

Had he been aiming in our direction I'd have worried. But he was obviously just making a show. It didn't help, though, that Joe hung around, trading insults with the fellow from a distance.

"I don't believe Darwin likes folks coming to visit," Floyd commented as we loped down the trail leading to our range farther into the Kinky Creek drainage.

"I think you're right," I said. "I wonder what bee got in his bonnet? He knows we have our cattle up here."

"I dunno," Floyd said. "Sometimes livin' so far away from civilization addles a man's brains."

CHAPTER FIFTY-SIX

When Charlie Lemmon, our herder, rode into camp later on that night, we were all sitting around the fire, just finishing our supper and discussing Darwin's unexpected behavior.

"What have you been doing to upset Darwin so much," Joe demanded before Charlie had even dismounted.

"Minding my own business—or trying to," Charlie said as he swung off his horse and started to unbuckle the cinch. "But I'll tell you what, he's made it awful tough. He's been continually trying to herd any of our cows he can find back through that fence of his. Only thing I can figure is he either doesn't like cows or he doesn't want people around."

"He didn't seem to take too kindly to us being there," Buzz Barber said. "He acts like he's plumb mad."

"Maybe he's been chawin' loco weed," his brother, Sam, suggested.

"I heard he was a remittance fellow," Pete Hansen said. I'd never heard the term before.

"What's that?" I asked.

"Someone from a wealthy family that pays the person a remittance to stay away," Pete told me. "There have been several in the valley."

"Why would your family pay you to stay away?"

"At least in some cases—and probably in Darwin's, too, from the looks of things—it's because they're crazy."

I wondered if Darwin really was. Cows go where the pasture is good. I could understand him not wanting someone else's cows in his pasture. I wouldn't want his cows in mine, either. But to fence off the entire valley, including government land, was not only ridiculous, it was illegal. And then to start shooting around people who weren't doing any harm …. Maybe Pete was right.

"He's not loco," Joe blustered. "He just thinks he's above the law. Did you tell him what he was doin' was illegal? If I'd been here I'd have tore those buggered fences down as fast as he built them. And I'd have told him a thing or two while I was about it!"

Sometimes it didn't take much of Joe's brag and bluster to make a fellow just plumb tired.

"I'm sure you would have," Charlie said, "and I'm equally sure you got close enough to him, this afternoon, to talk quiet-like and tell him what you thought, didn't you?" Charlie voice, as he turned his horse loose in the camp's makeshift corral, dripped disgust. He knew even better than us what had gone on today because he'd been dealing with it all summer, but sometimes Joe acted like he was a couple-three aces short of a full deck and Charlie's patience was obviously wearing thin. "I tried to talk it out but if I'd got close to him I'd have got shot and then you wouldn't have had *any* cows to come get, now would you?" he asked as he joined the group around the fire.

Joe shut his trap and gave us some peace for a while.

"What do you fellows propose we do about it?" Pete asked, looking around the circle. No one spoke. "Mose?" Mose shook his head and spat into the fire. I'd heard Mose was part of the posse at the Cunningham cabin massacre and it turned him pacific. That was all I knew except that a rancher normally didn't go out into the hills where wolves, bobcats and grizzlies prowled without a gun but, of all of the ranchers in the group, Mose was the only one who hadn't brought a rifle. I'd never seen him with a gun of any sort and I'd never seen any sign of one in his cabin, the time or two that I'd visited him.

"I ain't goin' after no one," he said. "I'd give up my cows and ranching rather than get in a fight."

Joe looked like he wanted to counter Mose but he'd been put in his place neatly enough he wasn't quite ready to slip out yet. The rest of us at least partially understood Mose's unwillingness to use a gun and we respected him enough that we didn't argue.

"Sam, John, Buzz—you fellows got any ideas?" Pete asked the Barber brothers.

John had a branch he was using to draw circles in the dirt at his feet. He shook his head without even looking up. Buzz had a smaller stick that he was breaking into pieces, throwing them into the fire. He, too, had no comment. Sam sat on his haunches, staring into the flames, working his huge wad of chaw around and around in his mouth.

Finally he spat and said, "I don't got no wonderful idees. Looks like we either take our cows up through the highlands or down here through the Darwin fence. I don't see any other way to go."

"You can take your cows up through those mountains if you want," Charlie said, "but I ain't helping you. It's one thing to trail a single cow, or maybe even a small bunch, through that timber but if you try taking a whole herd of 'em up there you're asking to lose half of 'em."

None of us had an answer for that.

I looked around the ring of faces, seeing the firelight playing with the features of the men. Except for Floyd these were all rugged fellows who had put in the required time to prove up on their homesteads but Floyd looked just as rugged as the rest. We were all tanned and tough.

But tanned and tough wouldn't stop a bullet.

Finally Lee Lucas broke the silence. "Charlie, you've spent the entire summer trying to deal with this problem. Besides that, you know the area, here, much better than any of the rest of us because you've ridden it. What do you think?"

We looked at Charlie. Charlie squatted down on his heels, his back against the log that some of us were sitting on, and looked at the fire. He took his wide-brimmed hat off and carefully put it on the log, then scratched his dusty blond head. He shifted his weight from one booted heel to the other. Finally he stood back up, thrust his hands deep into his back pockets, and spoke.

"You fellows put your cattle up here at the Forest Service's summons so they could keep the Green River cattlemen from taking over this range, right?" he asked. We all nodded. If it hadn't been for the Ranger, Jim Imeson's, request none of us would have even considered trailing our cattle so far from home. "Then why don't we let the Forest Service take care of the problem?" Charlie suggested. "They need to come see what's happening, anyway. It's their land he's fenced off along with his own."

I don't know why the rest of us hadn't thought of it. It was a brilliant idea and everybody seemed to think so—except maybe Joe, who was pouting in his corner.

"Then who should go?" Lee asked.

"It better be someone with some fire in his blood," Joe finally crawled out of his pout enough to speak. "And with a gun. Don't want old man Darwin gettin' the upper hand when it comes time to ride back through his spread."

There were times when I really disliked Joe.

"I don't know," Floyd said. "It's up to you fellows how you handle this but I don't see how bein' trigger-happy is going to solve

224

anything. Nephi and I brought our rifles in case we needed them against wild animals. I've never figured on havin' to use mine on humans, though, and I don't intend to start now. How about you, Nephi?"

"I'm not shooting anyone," I said. To a man, the rest of the group agreed.

"So who *is* going to ride down?" Lee asked again.

"I'll go if the rest of you is too lily-livered to face a fight." Joe puffed up his chest and squared his shoulders. "I'm not afraid."

"Maybe you *should* be the one to ride, then," Charlie agreed, "since you're not afraid to go through that fence again. I know *I* wouldn't want to. But I think we need Imeson up here as soon as possible. In fact, the sooner, the better and it's two days' travel each way. Whoever goes ought to leave now and ride as far as he can. Do you think you're up to another ride tonight, Joe?"

"I don't know if any of us is up to that," Pete said. "We've had a pretty hard ride today as it is, Charlie. I'm sure Joe is as tired as the rest of us."

"Oh, no," Joe said. "I'm just as fresh as I was this mornin'. But I wouldn't want to steal nobody's thunder. Maybe there's someone else who wants to go get Jim." He wasn't so anxious to leave now that his bluff had been called.

"I don't, pertikerly. I'm plumb wore out," John Barber said, yawning widely.

"Me, too," Sam said.

"I'm ready for bed, myself," I fought to keep a straight face. I knew what Charlie was doing. We all did. "What about you, Floyd? Think you'd be up to a midnight ride?"

"Not me," Floyd shook his head. "I was just about to turn in."

"So was I," Lee stood up and stretched his arms high above his head. "My saddle got awful hard today."

Joe looked like he'd been caught with his hand in the cookie jar. "I'd be happy to go," he said, "but my hoss is just as tired as any of yours."

"Oh, I have horses that are fresh," Charlie assured him. "You take your pick from my string and we'll get you going while the night's still young. I'd guess you could probably get a quarter of the way back to Kelly before you have to stop."

"I could probably get all the way to Kelly," Joe boasted but it was more show than conviction. He'd been maneuvered out of harm's way and he knew it.

Nobody cried when he rode back up the trail toward the Darwin ranch. Mr. Darwin wouldn't see him in the dark and by the time morning came he'd be long gone. For the next few days he had only himself, Charlie's horse and Jim Imeson to irritate.

CHAPTER FIFTY-SEVEN

While Joe was gone, we combed the hills for many miles around. By the time he finally showed up with our Forest Ranger, a good week-and-a-half later, we'd given up on finding any more of our cattle. I was still missing three cow/calf pairs and a bull; Mose, who owned the largest cattle herd in the valley, was shy over a dozen head and Lee, Pete, and the Barber brothers were missing some, too. Who knew how many Joe might be missing, since he hadn't been around to count for himself?

There was a lot of beautiful country up Kinky Creek but a lot of wild country, too. One of the meadows I rode had one of the prettiest waterfalls at one end that I'd seen since I was a child in Utah; its cliffs jutted out above tall, narrow pines. Mountain sheep stood at the top, watching us comb the area, but there were none of our animals in the meadow and none in the forest near the falls. It didn't matter where we searched, we couldn't find more cattle.

It was time to go home.

We were all of the general opinion that Joe had taken his sweet time in getting to town just to get revenge, but the night Joe and Jim rode into camp, Jim explained why he'd been so long in coming.

We were sitting around the campfire, eating supper, when Sam Barber asked Joe, "Say, Joe, what took you so long getting' to town an' back? I thought you wuz goin' to make extry good time."

"I did," Joe said, "but Jim, here, wasn't in the valley." I looked at Jim. He smiled, wryly.

"I was on a manhunt," he said. I could feel sudden tension in the group as Jim went on, "Fred White, the J.P., had to go to Kemmerer on legal business so the Game and Fish sent all the money they'd collected this past year—hunting and fishing license sales, you know—for him to turn over at the district office. He never got there and he never came back. I was called out to help hunt for him."

"Did you find him?" Floyd asked when nobody else in the group spoke.

"No," Jim said. "Didn't find any sign of him. We thought he went down the Hoback and up through Bondurant but none of the ranchers up there had seen him—we checked with every one of them. We went clear to Pinedale but he hadn't been there, either."

"And he never made it to Kemmerer?" Lee asked.

"Nope. Nobody knows what happened to him."

"His horse could have slipped and fallen into the Hoback river," Pete said.

"It's very possible. If that's where he ended up, they'll never find him unless he washes ashore out in Idaho somewhere."

"I've heard the Snake flows clean to the ocean," John said. "If that's where he is, he'll probably be fish et before too long."

Lee half smiled. "Well, I guess it wouldn't matter to him. He'd never know." Then, turning back to Jim, he asked, "Is this the first time you've had to do this sort of thing, Jim?"

"Yes, it's a little out of my normal line of duty," Jim said. "I've never been on a manhunt before. I've never even known anyone who has. It was a . . . different experience, I guess you could say. I suppose it's probably about like being on a posse. I don't know. Any of you men been on a posse before?"

Except for Joe, the group went suddenly quiet. Seeing that no-one else was going to speak, Joe opened his mouth and, in his typically insensitive way, inserted both feet.

"Mose has," he said. "He was part of the posse at Cunningham cabin back in '92 or '93, weren't you, Mose?"

I could feel instant tension, like a red-hot steel band, descend on the group circling the fire. I'd heard of the incident, of course. Everybody knew of it. But it had happened more than ten years before Alma and I came to the valley and I had yet to meet anyone who would actually talk about it. I'd wondered plenty but, with what Jack said so long ago, 'Sometimes, Nephi, it ain't healthy to ask too many questions. If a man don't offer information, you just don't ask,' still ringing in my ears, I'd decided this was one of those things I shouldn't ask about.

I can't say I wasn't curious, because I was. With the exception of Jim and, maybe, Floyd, I was probably the least-knowing of the group. All I'd heard was that Mose would ride miles out of his way to avoid coming within sight of where it had happened rather than relive the day when the posse he'd been deputized into had, in cold blood, gunned down George Spenser and Mike Burnett as alleged horse thieves. There had been no trial, no reprieve, and no chance for either

228

George or Mike to admit their guilt or defend their innocence—or even to survive. And Mose, like every other member of that posse, didn't care to talk about it.

Even most of the local ranchers who hadn't been involved—and who'd gossip all day and half the night about any other subject you cared to name—were reluctant to discuss the shootout. It took someone as inconsiderate and insensitive as Joe Deyo to push the issue.

His voice quiet, his face somber, Mose finally spoke. "I was part of the posse that went after those supposed horse thieves up at Pierce Cunningham's place in '93, yes," he said.

And that was all he said.

"*Supposed!*" Joe exclaimed. "They *were* horse thieves."

"Supposed," Mose said, again, in a firm voice.

I looked at him closely. He wasn't looking at any of us—or at anything else in particular. His eyes, in the flickering light and shadows of our campfire, were far away. Sad. I could see pain, too.

"Everyone knows they were but you act like you don't believe it. Are you ashamed to have done your civic duty?" Joe exclaimed. "Why I'd have been proud to have been on that posse and I would have been there, too, if I'd been living in the Hole when it happened. A person has a civic responsibility to get rid of such people." Joe sure liked the word, civic.

"It wasn't anything to brag about," Mose said.

Again, I was surprised. I wouldn't have expected him to brag but something in his voice—I couldn't quite put my finger on what it was—sounded a little off.

Floyd, who was squatting on his heels beside me, seemed to sense it, too. I saw his body tense ever-so-slightly. He cocked his head to the side and looked intently at Mose.

Joe spat in the dust. "*I'd* be proud of doin' in hoss thieves," he said.

I wasn't sure I would have been *proud,* but horse thieves were a real threat to us all. Our horses were our livelihood. They plowed our land, hauled our hay, summer and winter, and carried us wherever we needed to go in between times. The loss of our horses meant certain economic ruin, and for those who lived many miles from civilization, possible death. That was why horse theft was punishable by hanging. But these horse thieves hadn't been hung. They hadn't even been given the right to a fair trial.

"You wouldn't be proud of doin' it the way we did," Mose said, his voice so quiet we strained to hear. "There'd been some problems with horse thieves south of the Hole an' clear down into Utah; more problems up in Montana. An' then these boys suddenly appeared from nowhere with a whole herd of horses.

"I don't know who started the rumor, that winter, that they was the horse thieves we'd been hearin' about but we all knew what the loss of horses meant so everbody was anxious to git them horses back to their rightful owners as quick as possible." He stirred the fire with a stick then, standing, bent to add more wood.

"That fellow, Anderson, who President Roosevelt named head of the Yellowstone Forest Preserve, stopped by my place late in the evenin'. He wanted to deputize me. Said he was clearin' the area of horse thieves an' wanted my help. I didn't take the time to stop an' wonder what he was doin' down at our end of the valley. I believed everything he said an' followed along."

"What he said was correct," Joe declared. "Those government men know what they're talking about." The look Mose gave him was pity mixed with disgust.

"That's what I thought back then, too," he said. "Anderson said there was horse thieves wintering at Pierce Cunningham's cabin—had a whole herd of stolen horses there—and we needed to go git 'em back." Mose shook his head. "I trusted him—what with his important title an' all—and I was as anxious as the next man to put a stop to thieving so I didn't hesitate. I saddled up my pony, grabbed my gun and ammunition, and followed along.

"We rode all night; come down Cunningham's hill just before dawn. The boys spread out and circled the cabin, several of us in the shed and the others spread around, hidin', while those men was still asleep inside. And we waited. I thought with our numbers they'd give up easy and we'd take 'em in for a trial but that wasn't what Anderson had in mind.

"When the first one—Spenser, I think it was—stepped out of the cabin to go tend his horses that mornin' I called to him to 'throw 'em up' but he didn't. Instead he drew his pistol an' fired at the shed. Probably thought we was thieves, ourselves.

"Anderson should have identified who we were. I should have. Somebody should have. We could have. We could have tried to talk to him. But we didn't.

"Anderson opened fire. Didn't say nothin'. Didn't warn him or try to talk to him or nothin'. He just opened fire. Spenser tried to pertect hisself but he'd been hit and' when we saw blood we all went crazy. Spenser was down immediately.

"Burnett stayed in the cabin for a while but when he come out with a rifle, it was all over for him, too. One shot and he was dead. He never even raised his gun.

"It was done in what seemed like seconds. Before I knew what was happenin' both of 'em was dead.

"Everbody was jumpin' around and yellin' and congratulatin' each other. Then they buried them boys in a shallow grave right there by the corner of Pierce's corral and we all went home."

"I'd have been congratulating everyone, too," Joe said. "What's your problem with it, Mose? Weak stomach?"

Mose looked at Joe, not even trying to hide the distaste in his eyes. "We live in a country that gives us freedoms to life, liberty an' the persoot of happiness," he said.

Again, I was surprised. I had thought Mose was just a rough, homespun cowboy but he obviously had some education past what I'd acquired. He was talking more like a lawyer.

"That's why we get rid of rustlers and horse thieves," Jim Imeson commented, "so honest men can be free to pursue what they will."

"Yes, but we believe in due process of law," Mose answered. "Them boys didn't get that."

"They shouldn't have been out breaking the law in the first place," Joe's scowl was dark.

"They weren't." There was a conviction in Mose's voice that made me pay close attention. "We was just a bunch of young hot heads out followin' a man who wanted to shove his weight around and make a name for hisself."

"What makes you so certain?" Joe demanded.

A look of extreme sadness crossed Mose's face. "We got word, later, they was legitimate horse traders who was tryin' to support families back home—they'd needed a place to winter the horses they'd bought and made arrangements with Pierce to winter at

231

his cabin. We weren't sustainin' the law. We didn't even give 'em any options. What we did was cold-blooded murder."

I had nightmares that night . . . nightmares in which the men at Pierce Cunningham's cabin were Alma and my father, and I was the posse. I awoke to congratulatory yells that were, in reality, the hair-raising howls of wolves circling our herd.

CHAPTER FIFTY-EIGHT

After a long night of little sleep, it seemed totally possible that wolves were responsible for a substantial amount of our cattle losses. There wasn't any reason to stay in the area and give them the opportunity to take more so we started home.

As we neared the Darwin place, however, Lee asked Jim the question that was on all of our minds.

"Jim, what are you going to do about Darwin?"

"Oh, I don't know," Jim said, carelessly. "I'll talk to him. I'm sure I can work something out."

"Ten spot says you can't," Floyd muttered under his breath but I noticed he didn't say it loud enough for anyone to hear but me. I grinned.

"I don't think you said that loud enough for anyone to hear," I told him. "Fellows Floyd, here, wants to bet...." But that was as far as I got.

"Never mind what Nephi says," Floyd exclaimed. "He's just blowin' hot air."

Darwin, of course, heard us coming and was waiting on our side of his fence, rifle in hand.

"You gentlemen aren't coming across my land!" he cried as soon as we got close enough to hear. "This is my property and you aren't crossing it.... You can't take my fence down, I won't let you.... Don't come any closer, now, you hear me?"

It's one thing to tell a horseman he can't come closer. He'll probably listen and stop where he is.

We did.

It's another matter to order a cow to stop when she's bent on going home.

Jim motioned for us to wait—and we followed his lead—but those cows kept right on going until they were crowding around Darwin. He backed up against his fence, waving his gun in the air, a terrified look on his face.

Jim pushed through the herd until he was close enough to Darwin to talk to him quietly. None of us could hear what he said; we were at the other end of a milling herd of cattle that wanted to move.

Whatever he said, though, was effective. Mr. Darwin put his rifle down and helped Jim remove enough poles that the herd could get through. None of us said a word as we drove our cattle down the National Forest side of the valley but Mr. Darwin seemed extremely pleased when Floyd and I tipped our hats to him as we rode through his fence.

When we were well out of earshot Joe's curiosity overcame him and he called across the herd to Jim, "What did you say to Darwin back there? I thought at least one of us was going to be laid out deader'n a doornail but you had him eatin' out of your hand!"

"Oh, nothing much, Joe. He just wants to be treated like a decent human being," was all Jim would say.

The rest of the trail drive home was uneventful—except for the constant threat from wolves. We didn't see them during the day but nighttime was another matter. Actually, we didn't see them at night, either. We heard them—and sometimes I thought hearing them was worse. A man with a gun could deal with a predator he could see. Had we spotted them in the daytime, one of us would have had a house full of wolf-skin rugs.

As it was, they skirted the herd all night long every night, first this way and then that. The cattle could smell them as well as hear them, and were restless. So were the horses. We kept perimeter bonfires burning and rode night herd in shifts, circling the uneasy cattle, rifles ready.

Still they prowled.

I would have thought there was enough game in the hills but apparently they thought beef was better.

"I heard those wolves up close the night I went for Jim," Joe told us the morning after we'd gone through Darwin's ranch. It was the first any of us had heard about him having a run-in with wolves on his way home, so I don't think anyone paid much attention. "I didn't think it was to my advantage to stop and camp so I just kept on ridin'," he added.

"That's good," Pete said, poker faced. "We needed you to keep going so you could get to town and find Jim real quick." Joe had let slip to Lee that he'd spent two nights at home with his wife before he'd even gone to town. He'd excused himself by saying it hadn't mattered, Jim hadn't been around, anyway.

234

"And I did, too," Joe said. "I found him as soon as he got back into town."

"How much time did you spend at home in the meantime?" Sam wanted to know.

"Well, I had to do *something*," Joe excused himself. "I couldn't just sit around town waitin' for him."

Arguing with him wouldn't have accomplished anything. It wasn't worth it.

"We need to keep a perimeter watch goin' at night, now," Joe brought the subject back to the wolf situation. "Got to make sure them wolves don't get any more of our cattle. They're probably the reason we've lost so many already." I wondered where he'd gotten the idea he was range boss all of a sudden.

"Joe sure gets delusions of grandeur, doesn't he?" Lee chuckled, quietly, to me. "Guess he's self-proclaimed range boss, now."

"That's a good idea, Joe," Pete said. "There are nine of us. We can divide it up equally."

"That would be hard to do," Joe said. "Two men to a shift will leave one man out. I'll be the odd man and fix breakfast every day."

"No, Joe," Jim said. Young as he was, his voice held authority. "There are ten of us. I'll stand watch with the rest of you. We'll divide into five watches of two men each, starting at eight at night. Before that, everyone needs to help pile sage for perimeter fires and fix supper. We'll all get up at six and we can all help with whatever needs to be done for breakfast and breaking camp."

Joe wasn't pleased. He didn't want to ride perimeter with wolves howling just outside the circle of light from our fires, and he didn't want to be working with the rest of us on anything, either.

"I catch one of them wolves eatin' one of my calves and I'll have a wolf-skin rug in front of my fire!" he exclaimed when the howling and prowling started the second night.

"Aw, Joe," Lee stretched out on his bed roll, preparing to sleep as long as he could before his shift started at two in the morning. "You know you couldn't hit the broadside of a barn if you were standing right beside it. Better leave the shooting to Pete."

"I can too!" Joe spluttered. "I'm a crack shot."

"Yeah, and when he puts a rifle to 'is shoulder, everbody else had better run for cover," Sam said. I noticed he waited until Joe was out of earshot before he said it, though.

"Is he really dangerous?" I asked Sam.

"Well," Sam drawled, "you've seen how he is with everthing else. A blowhard and a braggart. He ain't no different with a gun in his hands."

"It's the ghosts of Lobo and Blanca seeking vengeance," Joe said at breakfast the next morning. None of us had slept well the night before; the howling would have been enough to straighten Emma-Jane's frizzy hair if she'd been there.

I heard Joe and laughed.

"Lobo and Blanca's ghosts?" I said. "What's the matter with you, Joe? You superstitious or something?" I could understand a little superstition—the howl of a wolf didn't exactly thrill me, either—but ghost wolves? That was stretching things a little far.

"I'm serious," Joe bristled at my laughter. "Did you see the tracks out on that sand bar this morning? They don't make wolves that big!"

"Well then, Joe, I guess you needn't worry when you're riding perimeter tonight. Ghost wolves can't do you any harm."

Joe stomped off, highly offended at our laughter. I didn't care. He *was* a braggart and a blowhard. But I can't say I was sorry when we finally left the mountains and the wolves stopped following us, either.

CHAPTER FIFTY-NINE

We'd finished separating our cows on the flats southwest of Brown's hill when I noticed Star had thrown a shoe. Since I didn't have a smithy of my own, that meant a trip to town and Tom Imeson's blacksmith shop. Jim told me he'd help Floyd take my cattle home, so I forded the Gros Ventre and rode south, hoping Tom wouldn't be busy when I got to Jackson. I wanted to be home, hauling in the last of my hay.

It was late in the afternoon when I reached Jackson but, good-natured fellow that he was, Tom stoked up his forge and tended to Star immediately. Thinking it was a good time to buy supplies, I strolled over to Pap's Merchantile. We were getting low on potatoes and baking powder, I knew, and a slab of bacon wouldn't hurt Floyd's feelings. Mine, either.

I was signing a credit receipt for my purchases when Jim Francis, our local sheriff, hurried through the door.

"Nephi," he said, before the door was even closed, "I saw your horse at Tom's and he told me you were here." That didn't sound good. I wondered what I'd done wrong. Jim Francis was a distant neighbor of Joe Deyo's. Had my ribbing of Joe upset him enough to sick the sheriff on me? I decided I'd better be quiet and let Sheriff Francis put his cards on the table.

"Did you hear about Fred White?" he asked.

I nodded, "Jim Imeson told me."

"A prospector found his body down Snake River Canyon. He took that route, not the Hoback, and he got jumped. He was shot through the head."

"Robbery?" I asked.

"I'm sure the money's gone."

I wondered what it had to do with me. Surely he didn't want Star to pack the body home. Freshly butchered game was one thing but a putrid human body? She'd object to that.

"The prospector thinks he saw the murderer," Sheriff Francis continued. "We're putting together a posse. I want to deputize you and have you with us. You're a crack shot and your horse is one of the best in the valley."

"Wait a minute! You want me to come help you kill a man?" Cunningham cabin style? Don't think so!

"No, I'm not out to kill him. That's why I want you there. You're a good enough shot to lay bullets all around this fellow without touching him."

I wondered where he'd gotten his information. I'd never shot at a man before. I'd never even pointed my gun in another person's direction. Yes, I was accurate but that didn't include shooting at *people*, for Pete's sake.

"I don't know who told you that," I said, "but I've never shot at a man and I'm not much for the idea of starting now."

"We may need some rifle persuasion with this fellow. Something to put the fear of God in him. I don't want him dead; I want to bring him in. That's why I want you."

"I'm not interested in shooting *at* a man *or* around him," I said. "Sorry, Sheriff. You'll have to get someone else. Ask Tom, maybe."

"I've already deputized Tom," Sheriff Francis said. "He's finishing up your mare and checking the other posse members' horses. It's rough territory down in that canyon. We don't need any of our horses throwing shoes."

"No, you don't," I agreed, politely. "Well, that'll give you time to find someone else who shoots well." Time for me to get on Star and disappear back to my ranch was what I meant, but I wasn't saying so.

"Nephi," he said (I could see why he'd been made sheriff... he didn't give up easy), "there is a federal law called Posse Comitatus that gives me the authority to require your compliance."

My, my. Sheriff Francis was sounding like a lawyer, too. I didn't have the foggiest idea what he'd just said.

"Sheriff, I only had a seventh grade education and that's way beyond me."

"Basically, that means I have the authority to force you to join my posse. I'd rather you came on your own, though, so why don't you just raise your right hand and I'll swear you in. Then you can stow those groceries somewhere at Tom's place and get ready to ride."

Put that way, what else was there to do? I raised my hand, became a temporary deputy, and rode out of town with a group of men who were bent on bringing in a person they thought was a killer.

I was less than enthusiastic.

My enthusiasm dropped even lower after we'd ridden a few miles together. I had no idea where Sheriff Francis came up with some of those fellows but they weren't exactly what I would have described as the cream of the crop—mentally or in any other way. As I rode at the back of the group—deliberately, I might add—I listened with growing alarm to their boasting about what they were going to do to this murderer and exactly how they were going to capture him and bring him in, dead or alive—preferably dead.

Regardless of Sam's opinion of Joe Deyo, I thought I probably would have been safer in his company.

Tom apparently shared my thoughts. After listening to his fellow posse members for an hour or so, he dropped back to ride with me.

"I think we're in trouble with this bunch," he commented in a low voice.

"Lot of hot air, there," I agreed. "Trouble is, wind coming out of the mouth means nothing solid between the ears."

Tom grinned, then sobered. "I'm afraid you're right," he said. "Folks need to have a cool head if they're going to be in a posse. Some of these boys may be alright but there are some of them that are lacking in common sense."

I nodded.

What I'd heard Mose Giltner say—and even more important was what he hadn't said—about his being a member of the Cunningham cabin posse left me very uneasy about this bunch.

I knew Sheriff Francis by sight. He had a small spread just south of the Gros Ventre in Spring Gulch. But I'd never really spent time with him; gotten to know him. He'd told me he wanted to bring this supposed murderer in, alive and unharmed, but if that was the case why had he chosen this crew? Our leader might be as dangerous as the posse he led.

"Do you know Mose Giltner?" I asked Tom. Regardless of how close-mouthed other valley residents were about the Cunningham incident, I wanted to talk about it.

"I've met him," Tom said. "Wasn't he up the Gros Ventre with you recently?"

"Yes, his was the biggest herd in our bunch."

"What about him?" Tom asked.

"He was with the Cunningham posse."

"Really."

We rode along in silence for a while before I got out what I wanted to say.

"That Anderson fellow who led that posse didn't want to bring those men in," I said. "At least Mose didn't think he did. He said the posse members were a group of hotheads and what they did was murder." I knew Tom had heard me but, again, he didn't speak.

"I've thought about that all the way down the Gros Ventre," I said. "How difficult would it be to live with the knowledge that you were a murderer?" I didn't add that I knew from personal experience just how much hell it was. I'd lived with that thought for months before my mother knocked the notion out of my head. While it had been with me for less than a year, Mose had lived with it for over twenty. I couldn't imagine how he'd stood it.

"He said those fellows they killed were legitimate businessmen with families back home that they were trying to support. I'm sure what happened to those families has been eating on him. Did they starve? Did they survive? Were they broken up—the children farmed out to relatives or even strangers? Maybe never saw each other again?

"They say Mose was so affected by it that he won't even go any place where he'd have to see Pierce's cabin. I don't want to have to live with something like that.

"I don't like this posse business at all. I don't know Jim Francis well enough to know if he can control his men and after listening to this bunch, I'm not sure anyone could, no matter how good of a sheriff he was."

"He's a good man," Tom assured me. "I've seen him operate around town and I trust him. I'm not so sure about some of these fellows, though. There are several I don't think I'd want behind me if things got difficult. They might get a little trigger-happy."

240

CHAPTER SIXTY

I thought Jim Francis was going along with the sentiments of the crowd but when we stopped to camp for the night, he gathered us all around and laid the groundwork for as safe a manhunt as we could have.

"I've been listening to you fellows this evening," he started. "I know some of you are a little nervous. Some of you are pretty excited. I don't know that any of you have ever been on a manhunt before."

Nephi, the manhunter? I'd been thinking of myself as Nephi, member of the posse. But Nephi, the manhunter? Nephi, the rancher, sounded a whole lot better to me.

"I've heard you talking about what you're going to do when we find this alleged killer," Sheriff Francis continued. "and I'm here to tell you right now it isn't going to happen. You are, none of you, going off half-cocked, because I want absolutely nothing to do with a Cunningham cabin shoot-out.

"We're going to trail this fellow and we're going to do our level best to talk him into surrendering peacefully because my job is to bring our man to trial so a jury of his peers can determine whether he's guilty of a crime or whether he isn't." He looked around the circle, taking the time to look each of us straight in the eyes. "Men who get out of control cause more problems than they solve. I want you to know this right now, get an itchy trigger finger and you'll walk back to Jackson without your horse and without supplies and I won't care if you make it or not."

That sobered a few faces. It was autumn, it was chilly and the place we were going was many rugged miles from town.

"You will do exactly what I tell you to do and when I tell you to do it. I brought Nephi, here," he pointed at me, "because he's about the best shot in the valley. Unless I tell any of the rest of you that I want you to open fire, you will keep your fingers off your triggers. Is that understood?"

"If Nephi's the only one who's doing the shootin', why'd you bring us?" one of the mouthiest of the bunch asked.

"When you go after a killer you want a man who's in control of himself," Sheriff Francis said. "I've watched Nephi when he didn't even know I was around. I've seen him hunt. I've seen him work. I've heard what others have said about him. I'm confident he'll keep his head and he'll do what I tell him to do. That's the kind of a man I want behind me when I'm in a tight situation."

I think my eyebrows must have raised a foot. I couldn't think of a single time I'd been hunting when the sheriff had been anywhere around, but either he was putting on a good show or he knew more about me than I knew about myself.

"I brought Tom because he's pretty much the same way," Jim Francis continued. "I've never seen him out of control. He's big and he's strong. I don't know about his shooting; I've never seen it. But he knows his way around animals and he's big enough if we have to manhandle this fellow he can probably do it all by himself. I like knowing I have strength on my side."

I looked at Tom and grinned. He *was* a big fellow. Several inches taller than me, his red hair capped a good-humored face that was neither thin nor round. His broad shoulders and heavily muscled arms were typical of a blacksmith. While I had always held my own in wrestling matches, I figured Tom could probably pin me with one hand tied behind his back, he had that kind of strength.

"Why'd you bring us along, Sheriff," the mouthy man asked, again. "It doesn't look to me like you need us."

"There's a place for each person on a team," The sheriff matched Alma in patience and tact. "You each have your role to play. For some of you it will be to take care of the horses—to have them ready for anything that might happen—if we have to go on foot in order to get to the killer. You'll have to be alert, to be able to listen and hear even if you can't see what's happening.

"The rest of you will have to do whatever it is I feel needs to be done once we find him. If we find him.

"Will he be fishing in the river? Will he be out in the mountains or deep in a draw? Who knows? You don't know. I don't know. You'll just have to wait and I'll make the calls when I see which way things are progressing."

It was a much more sober, quiet group of men who rolled out their bed-rolls and went to bed that night. I don't know about Tom— how he felt about what the sheriff had said—but I had mixed feelings. It was nice to be counted upon; to be looked to for support. On the other hand, I still had no stomach for shooting at a man.

The smell of rotting flesh led us to Fred White's body the next day, shortly after noon. He'd set up a camp down on the river's edge, beside a clear mountain stream near the end of the canyon. It was a pretty spot he'd chosen, thick with shrubs and undergrowth, occasional cottonwoods and plenty of evergreens—pines, fir and a smattering of cedar. It looked like he'd probably been cooking something; the charcoal remains of his fire were in front of him, with a blackened tin skillet on top.

He'd been shot between the eyes by a large caliber bullet that had left a hole in the front but had exploded the back of his skull. There wasn't a lot left of the rest of him, either —just what the ravens and magpies couldn't get at through his clothes.

I felt a cold fury as I proceeded to disgorge my dinner right there on the spot. Most of the others lost theirs, too, and even those who didn't turned a puke shade of green. The smell of what was left of Mr. White, along with the sight of his cleanly-picked bones, was something I wish, heartily, that I could forget. I was a rancher. I'd seen what ravens and magpies and time did to dead animals, but it's one thing to see a decaying animal; it's a totally different story when it's a man.

His horse was gone, and along with it the saddlebags carrying the Game and Fish money, but his bedroll was still there, laid out as he'd left it. Sheriff Francis took one of the blankets from Mr. White's bedroll and put it over him. Then, motioning to some of the other posse members to help, they slipped one edge under his body, flipped it over until the body was lying on top of the blanket, and folded the sides over poor Fred's remains. Taking a large canvas meat sack off the sheriff's saddle, they slipped the body into it.

"What are you going to do with him?" Tom asked.

"Leave him here, ready to transport when we go back," the sheriff said. "Gerald, you stay with Fred's body and guard it. I don't expect you'll have any trouble. Everything the killer wanted, he took in the beginning. But you can stay out of sight if you're concerned. Ride your horse across the river, whatever you want to do. I just want you where you can keep an eye on this sack." Gerald was the loudest blowhard of the bunch.

One out of the way.

I was impressed with the way our leader had taken care that we wouldn't have this Gerald fellow getting trigger-happy later on.

We remounted our horses and proceeded down along the bluff above the river.

It wasn't long before we smelled smoke from a campfire.

"This is where we leave the horses," the sheriff told us. "I don't know where that fire is but as I understand it, the fellow we're looking for has two horses (presumably his and Fred's) and a pack mule. I don't want our animals nickering and announcing us." Then he detailed three more who were inclined to be obnoxious to stand guard over our mounts. I studied the river, trying to keep a straight face.

"You hear any shooting, you bring those horses. But be careful. You don't want to get shot, yourselves," he instructed them. "You'll have to pay attention so you'll know where the shots are coming from—whether they're farther down the river or whether they're up in one of these draws. I hope there won't be any shooting at all but I can't guarantee anything."

We set off, once again, down the river but this time we were afoot.

"Keep it quiet, boys," the sheriff hissed when one of the men stepped on a fallen branch that snapped, loudly, under his weight. "Watch where you put your feet, now. Sound can carry a long ways."

We went over a ridge and down into another draw but there we stopped. We could smell the faintest breath of someone's cook fire but there was nothing but cliffs before us—some of the most rugged ones I'd ever seen. They dropped clean to the water's edge and the river, there, wasn't shallow. To get on the other side, we either had to do some serious climbing or take a swim.

Sheriff Francis stopped, fished a pair of binoculars out of the pocket of his coat, and studied what we could see of the mountains above us for the longest time. Finally he spoke. Quietly.

"I don't know where that smoke is coming from," he said. "But I don't see any sign of it here on this side of the cliffs. We'll climb that ridge we just came over, go up the other side where it's wooded. You all stay under cover until we can locate that fire."

So we backtracked and climbed. It was steep and it was strenuous, a rugged hike through smaller ravines and over ridges, but it wasn't as bad as either Mount Leidy or the mountain beyond it so it didn't bother me too much. Some of the fellows were puffing before we even got halfway up to the spine of the ridge, though. They were really hurting by the time we finally reached the top where we had a clear view of the gullies on both sides.

The smoke wasn't coming from anywhere on our side.

Cautiously, we crept along the razorback ridge behind the cliffs until the sheriff stopped us with his raised hand. We were nearly on top of the cliffs, now.

Again he took out his binoculars—this time to search a tree-lined gully far below us. Slowly he swept its entire length, from high up in the mountains where a stream started, down through the trees that lined the brook and on to the river below. He paused . . . went on . . . came back to something . . . studied it a while . . . then handed the binoculars to me, pointing to an area near the creek's end.

"In the trees, there," he whispered. "What do you see?"

I looked, adjusting the binoculars to my own eyes. There, in a little copse by the stream, I could see the shapes of two—no, three—horses. A small fire was nearby and a man was sitting on a large flat rock by the fire. I passed the binoculars to Tom. Eventually they went around the group and back to the sheriff who was busy studying the terrain.

"Boys," he said, quietly, when the last man had located and studied the campsite below. "The way I see it, we can go down this gully right below us, but it's pretty steep—especially at the bottom. We can go down that rib, but it's steep, too. Either way we're likely to slip and make a lot of noise – maybe even cause a rock slide. He'll be gone the minute he hears us.

"The only other alternative is to go back and work our way down to the creek he's camped on then follow it. It won't be so steep and the noise of the water will mask any noise we make if we're careful. We can split up with half of us on either side of the creek so if he chooses to make a run for it, it won't matter which way he goes, someone can cut him off. That makes the most sense."

While he spoke, I was watching the campsite we'd found. Suddenly the man stood up, walked into the copse, and came out, leading one of the horses. Something about the way he moved seemed very familiar. I touched the Sheriff's arm.

"Give me those binoculars again," I breathed.

I trained them on the figure below.

He was a tall, well-built fellow with unusually long arms and the horse he had lead to the creek was a rangy roan. When I'd first met him, years before, I hadn't known who he was—but I did now.

Our man was Isobel.

CHAPTER SIXTY-ONE

We inched our way, stepping carefully, down along the banks of the creek until I was close enough I could clearly see him, sitting on the rock once more. I saw him set a pistol down at his side, then take Millie out of her scabbard and rub her barrel with something— probably whale oil he'd picked up at some mercantile store.

Suddenly one of our illustrious posse members slipped on a rock, lost his balance, and crashed into the creek. Instantly, Isobel snatched the pistol off the rock beside him and was gone. I never saw a man run so fast in all my life. I hardly knew what was happening before he disappeared through the trees with Sheriff Francis in hot pursuit, calling for him to stop in the name of the law. I jumped the creek and pounded along behind.

Up Isobel went. Up the steep side of the ridge to the west of his camp. Zig-zagging through the evergreens. Dodging from tree to tree. Never giving us time to catch him in our sights, even if we'd stopped to do so. The fellow who'd fallen in the creek was cussing up a storm. Two or three of the others were, too.

Up over the crest of the ridge we scrambled. Slipping on rock. Grabbing shrubs to steady ourselves. Then over and down through the shallow ravine on the other side.

At the bottom we came to a dead stop.

We were out of the trees and Isobel was nowhere in sight.

Sheriff Francis stood with a frown on his face as he looked, first up, then down the ravine. A few small, isolated shrubs grew on the other side but a man couldn't hide behind them. The only other living thing on the hillside before us was a clump of cedars so dense they were growing together as if one tree. And unless Isobel was in the cedars….

"Get down," Sheriff Francis hissed as the men straggled up behind us. "Nephi, stay where you have a clear view of this ravine."

Tom dove under a heavy fir to my left. The other men disappeared as well. I was too busy trying to figure out where Isobel had gone to pay any attention—or to think of finding refuge for myself.

He had to be in the cedar clump. But it was so dense.

I searched for a movement, a shadow, anything to indicate his presence. Then suddenly I saw it—the barest tip of Millie's barrel up near the top of the trees.

It was pointed at an invisible spot right between my eyes.

I stared, horrified.

Cold sweat trickled.

My hands numbed.

My legs were jelly.

A hundred thoughts whirled through my head. Not one of them had anything to do with hiding. I was so mesmerized by that one little glint of cold, merciless steel that for the life of me I couldn't have moved even if I *had* thought of it.

Slowly, ever so slowly, Millie's barrel moved just a little away from me, then back as if Isobel was trying to get my attention. It swung, again, and stopped, pointing at Tom's hiding place. Then, one by one, Isobel showed me that he knew exactly where each of the other men were hiding, as well. I hadn't known where they were. But he knew. From his vantage point, he could see every one of them.

"Sheriff," I breathed to the man beside me, "in the cedars. See his rifle barrel? Up towards the top."

"Where? Oh."

"You know this man?"

"Heard of him is all," the sheriff answered.

"He stayed at our house one night, years ago. I've seen him shoot."

"Good?"

"Better. Used that gun. Shot at a square of cloth nearly a quarter mile away. So fast I don't think he aimed. Just raised his rifle and shot. Hit the target dead center."

Sheriff Francis swore, softly. "One of those," he said.

He stood for long moments, wordless. Meanwhile Millie showed us both, once again, that Isobel knew where each member of the posse was hiding.

He had the advantage, being high on the side of that ravine. He could cover pretty much the whole thing.

I could have shot him. …Maybe . …No, I couldn't have. By the time I started to raise my rifle I'd have been a dead man. And no-one else in the group stood much of a chance, either.

They didn't know where he was.

And he was too quick.

Isobel, the poacher, the killer, had every one of us at his mercy and he knew it.

And he made sure the sheriff and I knew it, too.

But what was he waiting for? He could have killed any one of us. Or all of us. Why hadn't he?

Somehow I felt like he was trying to tell me—or maybe the sheriff and me—something. But I had no idea what it was.

Suddenly the sheriff did something that flabbergasted me at the time and still has me shaking my head in wonder. He stepped out and walked, quietly and calmly, up the side of the ravine right to the cedar trees where Isobel was hiding.

He knew Isobel was a killer. He knew Isobel could shoot him any time he chose. But he did it anyway.

He wasn't looking up at Millie's barrel as he walked. He wasn't holding his rifle anywhere close to being at the ready. Instead, he was looking, closely, at the ground as if he were searching for something. As if he were tracking something—which, of course, he wasn't because tracks didn't show in that gravel-shale soil.

I couldn't figure out what he was doing. I was so engrossed in watching him I forgot to watch Millie, I was that astonished at his bravery—or stupidity—whichever it was.

When he reached the cedars, I glanced back at Millie and saw her pointed down at Sheriff Francis. Then the sheriff spoke, softly, for a while. I couldn't hear what he was saying, I could only hear the sound of his voice. When he finished I heard Isobel's high pitched tones. Again, Jim Francis spoke—quietly. I looked, again, at Millie. She was pointed, once more, directly at my head.

There was a pause.

Time stood still.

A cloud's shadow come slowly down the ravine.

Passed over me.

Disappeared.

The river roared, low.

An eagle screamed overhead.

249

Will I live to walk out of this ravine?

Will I lay here for that eagle to pick at until I look like poor Fred?

What will become of my ranch?

Has the Sheriff turned to stone in front of that tree?

Finally he spoke again—loudly. "Well, boys," he said, turning towards us, "Looks to me like this is the end of the trail and our man has got away. Let's go back home."

"He said *what?*" Floyd asked in disbelief when I was telling him about it later. "He couldn't have. He's the sheriff. It's his job to bring 'em in, not let 'em go."

"I know that," I said. "He knew it, too. He also knew it wasn't going to happen. Isobel had us right where he wanted us and the sheriff knew it. He could either let him go, and save his men, or he could have insisted we try to take Isobel out and probably every one of us would have died.

"I've seen the kind of man Sheriff Francis is. He's rational. He's calm. And he's about as determined to do his job as any sheriff I've ever heard of. But he also cares about his men. Our safety was as much a part of his responsibility as trying to bring Isobel to justice.

"By the time we got to the far end of the canyon he had his posse sized up pretty well. He gave us clear instructions. He put the ones who might cause the most harm out of harm's way. He chose the safest route for us to follow. And, in the end, he put our safety over everything else.

"You know, I wouldn't have wanted to be in his shoes. Seems to me it was one of those situations where he was damned if he did and damned if he didn't. I think the way he saw it, he could bring all of his men home in one piece without the man he'd gone to get, or he could sacrifice the lives of all of his men and still not bring the killer in. He chose to save his men."

What I didn't tell Floyd, and what no other man on the posse knew except me, was that the sheriff had bargained for my life. That was the price Isobel offered—his freedom and his promise to leave Wyoming forever, or my life, first, the sheriff, second, and everyone else as they came.

I don't know if Sheriff Francis had seen Isobel snatch up his pistol. I don't know if he realized he didn't stand a chance of taking

Isobel out before getting shot, himself. I don't know if he thought he might be able to get his man. All I know is that he wanted to bring Isobel in, but he made the decision to protect me, and the rest of his men, at the risk of losing his own personal reputation. How opposite Anderson's attitude at the Cunningham massacre.

I wondered what decision I would have made had I been in his shoes.

CHAPTER SIXTY-TWO

It was late October – about a month after the manhunt – when Pete Hansen stopped by, one afternoon, with my mail and a piece of news.

"The valley cattlemen are meeting at the church in Kelly this coming Saturday to discuss the wolf problem," he said. "We're raising money for a bounty hunter. You'll want to attend."

He was right. After that trail drive home from Kinky Creek, I was as anxious as the next rancher to be rid of the threat to my livelihood.

That following Saturday, ranchers from all over the valley swarmed into Kelly. The church was packed and, one after another, the cattlemen had stories to share. It began with a rancher from the south end of the valley showing the hide of one of his young steers. A wolf had torn what looked like a ten pound chunk of flesh – hide and all - from the animal's rump. The rancher had had to put the animal down. I felt sick and every other stockman in the building looked a little green around the gills, too.

Other ranchers shared their stories of the difficulties they were encountering. As the afternoon progressed, it became clear there were too many wolves and there was too much devastation. But it was some fellow from Moran whose encounter showed us what we were up against.

"I was hunting east of Leidy," he said. "Found a huge bull moose down at the edge of the lake and shot him. He was too big for my two pack mules."

I'd seen moose that big, but not very often.

"The head was gigantic," he continued. "I held it up on one of the horn tips and the span came clean up past my head." The man wasn't quite as tall as I was—I judged him to be, hmmm, probably close to five foot ten or maybe eleven. That was a darned big rack of horns. The head that had carried them had to have been huge.

"I wanted to get the head stuffed," the fellow continued, "and hang it in my cabin but I knew neither of my mules could carry the head and the meat, too, so I decided to leave it with the hide and hooves for the next day.

"When I came back the next morning, the hide was there, and the hooves were there, but the head was gone."

"What makes you think a wolf took it?" Pete Hansen spoke up. "Maybe it was a man—someone who thought your trophy head would look good in his own cabin."

"There were huge wolf tracks in the snow all around," the fellow answered. "I read that Lobo's prints were well over five inches, nearly six. These were almost that big. I put my hand over them and they came clean to here." He showed us his hand, palm out, and measured from the heel to a spot on his middle finger where the animal's paws had fit. I would have said it was a good five-and-a-half inches.

He went on, "And the trail was plain. He dragged that head straight up the side of Leidy. I followed to the top of the saddle and saw where he'd tried to get it to roll down one of the gullies.

"About then it occurred to me I was dealing with an animal that was probably a lot bigger than myself, and if he wanted the moose head that bad, it might be a good idea to let him have it." Appreciative laughter rippled across the room.

"What I'm saying is, we're dealing with at least one wolf that's huge. Maybe more than one. If we don't stop them now, the wolf population is going to grow to the point our animals aren't, any of them, going to be safe. We won't be either."

Cries of "Here, here," filled the room. By unanimous vote we hired an up-and-coming young bounty hunter by the name of Jim McInelly as our wolfer and I antied up for the bounty along with everyone else in the room.

Jim proved a good choice, as fearless as he was diligent. He could track and trap about as well as anyone I ever heard of—including E. T. Seton, the man who'd finally brought Lobo down back in the '90s. By late March, Jim had taken care of all he'd found except for one pack of five or six that was holed up in the Gros Ventre mountains.

He followed that pack relentlessly until finally, one day, he found them on the west slope of the Indian.

"It was getting close enough to spring," he told our cattlemen's group when he reported his activities to us and collected his bounty, "that there was just enough crust for me to travel fast on my webs. Those wolves were heavy enough, though, they were falling through.

"I followed them north across the Gros Ventre River near Turpin Creek and on to Antelope Springs. The day was getting warm and the snow was softening up. Had they stayed in the hills I might have lost them but they decided to cut across the flats toward the Snake River. When they made their turn, I knew I had them.

"The snow was too soft," he continued. "They broke through every sage brush they crossed but my webs kept me on top. Before long I was close enough to shoot every one of them." He showed us a photo of himself with the wolf skins. He also had brought the pelt from the largest wolf—a huge animal, undoubtedly the one that had taken the moose head. We were more than happy to pay Jim's well-earned commission.

None of our herders reported hearing wolves that following summer. Nor did we have the losses we'd had in the past several years.

CHAPTER SIXTY-THREE

With all the excitement over the wolf problem, I didn't give much thought to my family; at least not until Bill's letter came in late March. I'd gone down to Joe Deyo's place early one afternoon when the weather was nice and I didn't have anything pressing to do. Joe's wife, Margaret, was the Zenith postmistress at the time and she kept the post office in a corner of her parlor.

I don't know how long Bill's letter had been there. I guess she'd had it for a while because she remarked it had been there so long it was collecting dust. Nobody had taken the time to go pick up mail since shortly after Christmas.

"What other mail do you have?" I asked. It was expected that anyone in an isolated community such as ours would get and distribute the mail for everyone who lived along the line.

Between my ranch and Deyo's were the Bikes, the Price family, and Will and Camilla Seelemire with their little girl. Past us were Joe and Mary Davenport (Joe had recently tied the knot with Henry and Jenny Lingenfelter's daughter, Mary), the Lingenfelters, themselves, then Pete McCabe and, finally, his sister, Lizzie. All our other neighbors lived up on the flats. We didn't collect mail for them, of course; just for those along the road in the river bottoms.

"Let's see," Margaret looked at the slots in her mail wall. "There's a letter, here, for Amy Bike, a Montgomery Ward's catalog for Seelemires, one for you and two different catalogs for Jenny Lingenfelter. Jenny and Henry have several letters from Missouri and a large package. Think you can manage all that?"

I loaded it all in my saddlebags, except for Henry's package which I tied on behind my cantle, then I set out for home. Henry was coming to visit that evening and I didn't want to miss him.

I dropped Amy's letter off, left the catalog at Seelemire's, then hurried the last mile to my cabin. Probably hurried too much because by the time I arrived, the paper around Henry's parcel was torn. The smell from inside the package was rank; home-grown tobacco from one of his friends in Missouri. Now, what was I going to do with that? When Henry collected his mail he would still have nearly three miles to carry it on his horse.

Floyd and I looked around.

I had no boxes to put loose-leaf tobacco in and the only paper I had was an old newspaper. I knew that wouldn't hold up, particularly not if it started to snow.

Finally we rounded up every tea tin we had in the house—Floyd was a heavy tea drinker and I kept the rectangular tea tins to store beans where mice couldn't get them. By the time Floyd had come to work for me, I'd started drinking real coffee and I had several large empty coffee cans, as well. We emptied the beans into my coffee cans, then filled the tea tins with tobacco. There were over half a dozen. I knew Henry would be hard put to find space on his saddle for all those tins but it was the best I could do for him. Besides, the round coffee cans would have been much harder to tie on.

As I looked at the tins piled neatly beside his stack of mail, I had an irresistible idea. I took one of the coffee cans, now filled with beans, went out to the tool shed where I had a half-pig hanging, cut the tail off, and stuffed it in the can. Back in the house, I carefully wrapped the can in newspaper, tied it securely with a web of twine, and addressed it to Henry. Then, in large black grease-pen letters I labeled it *Pork and Beans*. Floyd watched, snickering, as I carefully set it with Henry's other mail. Then we waited for Henry to arrive.

When he saw the stack of tobacco-filled tins, my elderly neighbor was almost beside himself. He'd been out of tobacco for a while and his need had nearly driven him to distraction.—It occurred to me it had probably driven Jenny to distraction, too, since she had to live with him.— He was anxious to get the tins tied on his saddle before it got dark so he set to the job immediately. Floyd and I watched from the window as he carefully tied them on, happily chewing a large wad of tobacco as he did.

He got the catalogues and letters into his saddlebags without too much trouble and managed to stuff one tin in each bag as well. He carefully tied the other tins with the leather saddle strings then started looking for a place to tie the can of 'pork and beans'.

Back and forth he walked around his horse, trying to find a place to tie that can. There were no unused strings. His lariat was too stiff and long. He kept searching.

Finally he came back into the cabin.

"You fellers happen t' have some string a feller could borry?" he asked. "There's jist no place on m' hoss t' tie this here can. I figure th' only way I'm gonna git it home is t' tie it on m' back."

"String," Floyd said when I hesitated, afraid I'd laugh. "Nephi, we got any string?"

I held my breath for a moment to control my voice.

"I think so," I said. "Where's that ball of string I've kept from our flour sacks? There isn't a lot but you're welcome to whatever you need. You don't want to put it on right now, though. May as well wait until you're through visiting."

"I'd better git fer home," Henry said. "I don't know how them tins is gonna ride and I wouldn't want to lose any of m' baccy in the dark."

"I guess that's so," I said, poker faced. "It's too bad your package broke open, Henry. We were looking forward to a visit but I guess we'll have to visit another time. Floyd, will you help me harness this can?"

Neither Floyd nor I dared look at each other as we made a harness to go over Henry's shoulders and tied the can securely to it. How we managed to keep straight faces as Henry set out for home I'll never know, but once he was gone we both collapsed, howling, on Floyd's bed. I hadn't played such a good joke since I'd stuck the tin over Rhoda Newbold's stovepipe.

Rhoda Newbold's stovepipe....

Frank and Alma were with me then....

Alma....

That's when I remembered the letter I'd received from Bill. It was still in my coat pocket but I decided I'd wait until Floyd had gone to bed before I brought it out.

As I sat by the fire that night, I wondered why I was so reluctant to read it? After all, understanding my father had been important enough last summer that I had written to Bill with questions. Somehow, though, I was feeling hesitant about revisiting painful family issues. I thought about that all evening as Floyd and I sat in front of the fire, oiling Sleek and Sassy's harnesses.

Was I afraid of finding out something that might change the ideas I'd held about my father? Or was it no longer important enough for me to care about his choices?

257

I'd blamed him, bitterly, for spending so much time in civic pursuits but my experience on the posse had changed my thinking on that score. One did what one had to do for the good of the community. I hadn't wanted to go on that manhunt; I'd wanted to be at home, harvesting the rest of my hay. But I'd done what I had to do.

Afterwards I realized my father had done what he'd had to do, too. He may not have been deputized, as I was, but whenever he'd seen a need, he'd filled it without hesitation.

I thought of that old tintype Mother still kept on her dining room wall and remembered her telling me how he'd served his community as a scout during the Blackhawk Indian war. He'd been the youngest man in the militia—a mere teenaged boy.

I wondered if he'd ever had to fire at an enemy. Had he seen the sights of an Indian's gun pointed at him? Had he known jelly-legged fear? If he had, he'd never talked about it. I'd seen my father ill, exhausted and discouraged but I'd never seen him bowed in either defeat or fear. Always, he'd stood as straight and tall as when that photograph was taken.

I thought of his work in planning and overseeing construction of the irrigation system for the Wasatch valley. His efforts kept a lot of people from suffering the setbacks Alma and I experienced in Darby. Had he complained about the time it took him from home? I never heard of it.

He'd had no formal education, yet he was an avid reader. We had books at home—classics, Mother called them. I'd never cracked a one, but Father knew them intimately. His vocabulary far exceeded that of other men in the community. He'd even helped start the Young Men's Literary Society in Heber City. I wondered when I'd last read a book. Not since I'd quit school in the seventh grade, probably. I didn't even own any books.

Of course he'd always worked in his church, serving in numerous positions. I didn't want to go there. Religion still wasn't the priority for me that it had always been for him. But I had to respect his willingness to pitch in without hesitation whenever he was called upon.

How many times had I done that? Neighbors helped neighbors, of course. It was a way of life that everyone lived. But I wondered if I'd ever gone out of my way to actually look for something I could do. I didn't think so.

Truth be known, holding myself up to the example of my father didn't leave me standing in a very good light. I'd been rebellious, resentful and, frequently, down-right mean. Although I'd attended school my education, not his, was practically that of an illiterate. I'd never gone out of my way to do anything for anyone else, either. And the only time I'd served in my community was when I'd been forced to do so. It was with that self-realization that I finally opened Bill's letter.

Dear Nephi; it read

I hope you will never think of our father as a bad man. For he never was, and you need to remember that your mother was his first love, and we who have never been married in polygamy know little of what we would do if placed in their places. Perhaps many of us would do much worse than Father has ever done. There are many in our church who do not believe in polygamy, but father still does. He has a right to his belief, and you to yours. I also wish to say that while some of our members in high standing do things that they should not do, yet they are only human, and not perfect. And show me a church, or a people, who are perfect and never make mistakes or do anything wrong. So let us not be too hasty to say what we could do, or to judge others.

With love from your brother,
Bill

He has a right to his belief, and you to yours. Bill knew I'd drifted away from the religion of my youth but he wasn't judging me. What he was saying was that I, myself, should not judge others— particularly our father.

I thought about how harshly I *had* judged my father and, yet, when I looked at myself beside him—beside the man he'd made of himself despite the obstacles of his origins—I could see my own inadequacy.

In all honesty, I couldn't say that I was half the man my father was. I worked as hard, yes, but my father expanded his horizons to serve beyond the circle of his own little world. I did not.

Suddenly I both felt and heard a snap inside my head, as if a thin steel band had broken, and the old feelings of resentment and prejudice were no longer important. For the first time in my life, the habits and intolerances that had held me bound were as if they had

259

never existed, and solutions to the issues that I had struggled with for the last several years began to emerge.

CHAPTER SIXTY-FOUR

It wasn't that my basic nature changed. It didn't. Relaxation through discretely personalized persecution had always been my stock in trade and my imagination had lost none of its fertility . . . or its need to be employed.

I remember the night I heard that Joe Deyo was leaving early in the morning to visit his mother in Iowa. I'd been down to pick up my mail, again, and overheard him talking to Margaret. Or, more accurately, Maggie was talking to him.

"I don't see how I'm supposed to get my sleep, Joe," she said, "when you insist on leaving so early in the morning. You'd have plenty of time to get to Victor before the train comes if you waited until seven in the morning instead of leaving at five. It's inconsiderate, that's what it is!"

"I'll put everything together, Maggie, so all I have to do is pick it up and ease my way out the door. You won't hear me, I promise."

That was an interesting view of the Deyo's domestic arrangements. Joe Deyo, the blusterer on the cattle range, was Joe Deyo, the cowed, at home. I thanked Maggie for my mail and went back to my ranch.

But I didn't stay there.

Late that night, after Floyd was asleep, I collected a couple of cow bells, muffled their clappers, tied them to a length of rope, saddled Star, and rode the three miles to Joe's house. When I left, the . . .gently unmuffled . . . cowbells were hung on his porch in such a way that, when Joe . . . oh, so quietly . . . opened his door the next morning, the rope they were tied to was also tied to his doorknob....

I always did think folks ought to rise *early*.

I heard through the grapevine that Joe was seriously questioning whether he should come back home after his visit to his mother or if, maybe, he ought to just keep on going.

Although I still indulged in my favorite entertainment at every opportunity, I also gave a great deal of thought to the direction my life was heading. It was one thing to see solutions to my issues; figuring out how to bring them about wasn't quite so easy.

261

How could I measure up to the man I now recognized my father to be? Was I man enough to make the impact for good on my community that he had done on his? It would require some serious life changes.

I had spent my entire adult life concentrating on my own self-interests. In order to make a positive impact on my community, I needed to expand my horizons, to identify issues that needed my energy. I started looking around—visiting with and listening to my neighbors. Those who had children seemed to be more interested in the school situation than anything else.

I was up at Tom and Rosa Brown's home one day, dickering with Tom about the sale of a bull he wanted to buy from me, when Rosa gave me an ear-full about the local schools. I'd asked her where their son, Harold, was that day.

"We sent him away to school," she said.

"Oh, is he boarding in town?" I asked. I knew the parents in the outlying areas boarded their kids in town, during the week, so they could go to high school but this was a Saturday. "Who's he staying with?"

"He's not in Jackson," she said. 'He's going to school in Salt Lake City."

"Salt Lake!" Why send him all the way to Salt Lake City where he could only get home once in the school year—if he was lucky—when there was a high school in the valley?

"The school here in town is so violent we didn't think it was safe for him to attend," she continued.

"Are you serious?" I asked. I couldn't believe the local school board was so lax they allowed violence in the school. Jackson could be a little wild and wooly, at times—in the bars and a few other places—but a saloon had, or should have had, a different atmosphere than a school. "What's been happening?"

"Last fall Maybelle Smith's daughter was walking past a group of boys in the hall between classes when a fight broke out. Nobody was watching who they punched and she was beaten so badly Maybelle had to take her out of school," she told me. "Here a month ago one of the students was knifed. In class. The teacher didn't even turn the boy with the knife in. And those are just a few examples of what's happening. I *will not* send Harold to something like that."

"No, I wouldn't either." If we'd acted like that when I was in school we'd have been expelled so fast we wouldn't have known what happened. And the whipping we'd have caught from our parents when we got home would have made hell look welcoming. I thought about that all the way back to my ranch. By the time I got to my cabin, I knew I had found my civic cause.

Now I needed to start attending school meetings so I could learn the issues, become acquainted with the personalities, and determine how I could make a difference.

I broke the news to Floyd gently.

"Floyd, I was over at Tom and Rosa's and found out they're wintering their son clear down in Salt Lake City to go to school," I said that night as I was eating supper. Floyd had already finished and gone to sit by the fire.

"So Frank was tellin' me."

"Did he tell you why?" I asked. "That our local high school isn't safe?"

"Yes, he's not plannin' to send his girls here either."

That was news to me. I thought the girls would probably be better off going somewhere else; getting away from Lucy was by far the best thing that could happen to them, but it wasn't right that the local school conditions should be the reason.

"I'm going to the next school meeting," I said as I broke open another baking powder biscuit and started to butter it.

Floyd stared at me in amazement. "What you doin' that for?" he said. "You're an old batch. You plannin' to go back to school, yourself?"

"Pretty figure I'd cut in a classroom, now, isn't it?" I laughed at the idea.

"Probably be kept in the corner with a dunce cap on," Floyd agreed. "So why you goin'? School meetins is for parents, not batches."

"I'm not sure I agree," I said. "It isn't right that parents should have to send their children away for an education just because the local school is unsafe. This is a community issue, not a private one. This is America, Floyd. Those children have the right to an education and they have the right to have it in their own community. Parents ought to be able to keep their children at home when there's a school available. It's just plain wrong for Tom and Rosa to have to send Harold away for his safety."

Floyd sat, quietly, for a few minutes. "What difference do you think you can make?" he finally asked.

"I don't know, yet," I said, "but I intend to find out."

I knew Floyd would spread the word that I was concerned about Tom and Rosa's boy attending school so far away. It would keep the neighborhood busybodies from suspecting other reasons for my choices—reasons that I didn't want to discuss.

CHAPTER SIXTY-FIVE

My new sense of purpose led me, naturally, to the second change I determined to make in my life. If I was going to speak for the children, I had better at least be as educated as they were. My father was a self-educated man who knew good literature. I hadn't read a book since leaving grammar school in the seventh grade. I started ordering books through the catalog.

Floyd was astounded the first time he picked up a heavy package of books for me at Margaret's post office. "What you got in this thing?" he demanded when he set it down on our table. I opened it eagerly. There was a book on business practices that I'd been wanting, two or three on history, Milton's *Pilgrim's Progress* and Sir Walter Scott's *Ivanhoe*.

"What's that for?" Floyd said. "You goin' high-brow on me?"

"No, but I told you I intend to make a difference in the school system. I need to be familiar with what the children are studying." I didn't tell him I wanted to acquire the knowledge and vocabulary my father possessed.

Tied up with my interest in the school issues and my own self-education was my third goal. I needed someone to pass my ranch on to when I died. I wanted a posterity. The patter of little feet on the floor in the mornings. And, since the patter of little feet meant a woman to produce them, I needed a wife.

She couldn't be just any woman. I made a mental list of what I wanted. Before I did, however, I took the time to identify some of the qualities I didn't want, just like Floyd had done.

I didn't want a shrew like Frank's wife, Lucy. I didn't want a lazy woman like Joe's wife, Margaret. I didn't want a carp like Rhoda Newbold who couldn't cook, keep a clean house, or keep a civil tongue in her mouth.

I wanted a woman who had a sense of humor; someone who wouldn't be scandalized at my own. That was important. My wife needed to be able to laugh.

I wanted a woman who could cook. Forget the Rhoda Newbold type that couldn't produce anything fit to eat if a French chef had cooked it for her first. My wife needed to be able to cook as well as Rosa Brown or Maggie McBride, at least.

I wanted a woman who wasn't afraid to help out on the ranch. She needed to be just as at home in the field as she was in the kitchen. I didn't want her to do heavy work. That wasn't important. What I wanted was a woman who could lend a hand if I needed it—drive the team while I pitched hay to the cows or take care of the chickens and pigs while I was irrigating.

It wouldn't hurt if she was independent enough in her thinking to bring water out on a hot day or maybe even lemonade, if we were able to buy some lemons. I definitely wanted her to be able to plan and produce such things by herself.

I wanted a woman who liked children, of course. Actually, that went without saying. What was the point of hearing the patter of little feet if their mother, like Lucy, was resentful of their existence?

I hoped the woman I found was musical. I wanted someone who shared my love of music. It wasn't a priority but it sure would be nice, on a cold winter's night, if my wife could play some instrument while I oiled harnesses.

And one other thing—it was imperative to have a woman who would keep a clean house. I didn't want fuss and frills like Nora had brought in, but I did want clean.

Those were the qualities I wanted in the mother of my children.

Mother of my children . . . that sounded good to me. Comfortable. I had visions of a cheerful woman rocking my infant son, singing a lullaby like my mother did.

Infant son. Infants became toddlers. I could hear that pattering of little feet. I could hear the joy of children's laughter. Children. School. And there I was, at the school issue once more. My goals all seemed to go hand in hand. By the time my children were ready to attend high school I intended to make sure that school in Jackson was safe.

As I visited neighbors and attended meetings, I found a voice I hadn't known I possessed. I truly *was* concerned about the local school situation, although not for the reasons everyone thought. To the other concerned citizens, I was being very selfless; a bachelor speaking for the safety of their children. No-one guessed I was there

266

because I wanted a safe school environment for the children *I* intended to have one day. Had anyone even suggested such an idea, everyone else would have scoffed. *Nephi Moulton is a died-in-the-wool bachelor and that's something the entire county can count on never changing.* So I was free to further my own purposes without any comments other than approval for my unselfish efforts.

School meetings brought me more benefits than my children's future. I was involved in preparations for their educational success, yes, but I was also observing women. Single women.

Unlike most of the valley's bachelors, single women frequently came to school meetings with their married friends or relatives. It was a social outlet. And it gave me the opportunity to watch them without anyone knowing that I was. If a single woman spoke up, I paid close attention without anyone suspecting I had anything on my mind other than the issues we were discussing.

Single women also helped furnish refreshments, which didn't hurt my feelings either. I learned to be casual as I asked who had made the delicious.... I sure found out who could bake and who could not.

The frosting on the school meeting cake, however, came in the form of the opportunity to visit with T.A. once in a while. T.A., married for the past several years to Lucille Blanchard from Driggs, now had two little children. So he was as interested in the school system as I was. We campaigned, together, for reforms we thought were necessary. Then I took our ideas to my home community, Zenith, to discuss with my neighbors who didn't attend the meetings.

School issues weren't the only thing T.A. and I discussed, though. I remember one meeting, in particular. It was being held in the little church building on Mormon Row, close to T.A.'s home, and I was late arriving. Fortunately T.A. was sitting at the back so I slipped into a seat beside him.

"Did you hear the news?" he whispered to me as soon as I was settled. "Wally got married last week. He and his bride are coming home tomorrow."

That was real news to me. I hadn't known Wally was even looking.

"Who did he marry?" I asked.

"A girl he met out in Idaho when he was visiting Mother and Dad," T.A. said. "Her name's Elizabeth Chandler." He corrected himself. "Or was."

"Well, tell him I said 'Congratulations'," I said, and we turned our attention back to the meeting. At least T.A. did. I found my mind wandering.

So Wall's finally tied the knot. I wonder how John feels about that? Maybe I need to pay him a visit on the way home. I won't be around for a shivaree, if they have one, but I'll bet he'll be glad to help me put out a little surprise for Wally to find when he comes home. We can have all sorts of fun at Wally's expense. I almost rubbed my hands together in satisfaction. This was one school meeting that was lasting far too long.

Then it occurred to me that visiting John after the meeting would present a problem. He lived about a half-mile past T.A.'s home. Marriage had settled T.A. to the point I doubted he'd approve of John and me decorating Wally's cabin—which was precisely what I had in mind—and, since I'd have to travel with him if I was to visit John after the meeting....

Suddenly I turned to my cousin, "I need to excuse myself," I said. "Not feeling too well. I better go home."

T.A.'s face showed instant concern.

"Coming down with a cold or the flu?" he asked.

"No, probably something I ate at dinner," I said. "I *have* to go!" I stood up as inconspicuously as I could and slipped out of the room. School issues could do without me for just this one night.

John's little cabin was dark and quiet when I arrived. That was disappointing. *We could've had so much fun decorating Wally's house. But if John's asleep, already, he's either really tired or he's sick.* I decided not to bother him.

The only problem was, I didn't have any decorating supplies with me. Hmmm.

But John does . . . and if I use something of John's, Wally will recognize it and blame his brother . . . this holds promise. I needed to search John's barn.

I hadn't been there often enough to know my way around in the dark but I knew he kept a candle and some matches on the frame above the door. I found them, then made sure the door was shut before I lit the candle. I didn't want John to wake up and see a strange light coming from his open barn door.

As I looked around, I saw the usual—saddle, bridle, horse blanket. A large bin that held oats . . . and scurrying mice.

I stepped out into the middle of the barn and held the candle high. Light glinted from metal above my head. Bells. Hanging from the joists of the loft. Horse bells. Cow bells. Even some smaller bells that he probably used for sheep or something. And John's brand was engraved on each one. I wondered what I could do with them.

Don't want to hang them on Wally's porch. Already did that to Joe so it would be a dead give-away. What else can I do with them?

As I considered the possibilities, I looked for something to carry them in and something to hang them with. John's large ball of twine that he used to sew his grain sacks shut would work for the hanging part. And I found an empty grain sack for carrying. Soon I was on my way.

Wally's cabin was cold and dark, of course, but I knew where he kept *his* candles, too, and his house was far enough away from John's and T.A.'s homes that I wasn't worried about them seeing a light in the window. I lit a candle and looked around.

I considered hanging John's bells from the rafters but that was too tame.

I might have done it if I could have run a cord from each bell to the door so they would all ring when he carried his Elizabeth over the threshold but the door opened in, not out, so that wouldn't work, either. What to do?

Then I saw the perfect spot. Half an hour later I blew out the candle, closed Wally's door, and was on my way home.

I understand John caught all sorts of hell for tying his cowbells to the springs under Wally's short-sheeted bed.

When John tied the knot the next winter, he made sure I didn't find out until several weeks later.

CHAPTER SIXTY-SIX

I was feeding my cows one morning, shortly after Wally's marriage, when a new problem occurred to me. Here I was, planning to bring a wife home, and I had no suitable place to put her. There wasn't a decent woman on the face of the earth who would want to share my cabin with Floyd in residence. The very reasons I'd moved into Henry Cherry's cabin when Alma married Nora came flooding back. Lack of space was part of it but the major problem was lack of privacy. What would my bride do when she wanted to bathe? And I had no burning desire to sleep in a conjugal bunk above or below Floyd, either. Besides, he snored like no other.

I couldn't get rid of Floyd. I needed his help.

I refused to give up my goal of marriage and a family. That was just as important.

What to do now?

I was on my way to another school meeting when the answer came.

I'd ridden up over Brown's hill and joined Tom and Rosa on their way to the meeting. As we rode down Mormon Row, we passed Henry May's home—a fine, relatively new, frame house with a wide porch, high, narrow windows and a small verandah on the upstairs. As I looked at it, realizing Henry had built it so he would have room for his rapidly expanding family, it occurred to me that I needed a frame house of my own. It took all my concentration to keep my mind on the meeting that night.

After I'd said 'Goodnight' to Tom and Rosa and was on my way back across the flats to my own place, I was finally free to think about the house I needed to build.

I'd need a kitchen and parlor, of course, and two bedrooms— one for us and one for Floyd. I wanted a large pantry where I could store flour and sugar and other staples without them being in the way like they were in the cabin. And I wanted a well with a hand pump in the kitchen. My future wife would appreciate not having to haul water all the way from the spring.

I didn't need a finished upstairs like Henry had, so I decided I'd have a hip roof—maybe with a dormer window or two in case I wanted to make bedrooms up there at a later date. Bedrooms for children.

I liked Henry's windows but I wanted plenty of them. I was tired of the darkness in my cabin.

And I wanted a large covered porch. One that extended the entire south side of the house so there would be shade in the kitchen and parlor in the summer.

The house would be clapboard, of course. With shingles on the roof.

By the time I arrived home, I was more than ready to sit down and draw up plans.

Floyd sat, open-mouthed, when I eventually showed him the plans I'd drawn. Then he looked at me, suspiciously.

"Why you wantin' to go to the expense of buildin' a stick house?" he asked. "This cabin's plenty big enough for the two of us. You plannin' to add permanent company?"

I knew what he was referring to but I pretended I didn't.

"More mice?" I asked. "Don't think so. The only permanent company I'm thinking about is a cat. Look at this, Floyd," I spread the large sheet of paper out for him to see. "I'm going to have a pantry here and I'm going to have big metal canisters that I can store my flour in so mice can't get into it. I'm going to have a well dug before I even start the house and there will be a hand pump, here, so we don't have to haul water from the spring. And I'm going to buy a separator so we can have cream and sugar on bread without having to skim the cream off the milk pitcher."

"Whoa," Floyd said. "All that fancy stuff you're talkin' about costs money. Where do you aim to come up with it?"

"I'll get a loan," I said. "I'm going out to Driggs tomorrow to talk to a banker. You'll need to feed the cows alone." Good thing spring had come and there wasn't so much feeding to do. I'd have felt guilty leaving everything to Floyd, otherwise.

But I would have done it anyway. It was late April and I needed to arrange my loan and find a builder. I wanted my new home finished by fall.

As I rode Star through the mountains to Driggs the next day, I thought about how I'd changed in the five years since Alma's death.

271

I'd been dependent on him, then; afraid to open my mouth in the presence of women and even shy about talking to men I didn't know. Now I campaigned for school reform without giving public speaking a second thought.

I remembered how I'd been so reluctant to go into debt in order to buy Henry's and Rilla's spreads. Now I planned on borrowing money to build a house for a wife and family I didn't even have.

While Alma was still alive, I had hated women—convinced I would never marry. I'd had no desire for children of my own, then, either. Now it seemed every waking thought was of the wife and family I was determined to have.

I fed my cattle and saw my sons pitching hay at my side. I milked my cow and visualized my children with white mustaches from the foam of fresh, warm milk. I fixed my meals and, as I put the food on the table for Floyd and myself, I saw a cheerfully smiling woman sitting in the third chair, filling our plates and passing them to us. A gracious hostess.

Floyd and I moved into my new home five months later and by then I was even more involved in school issues.

Nephi's home

CHAPTER SIXTY-SEVEN

I campaigned all the next winter for total reform in the school board. Elections were coming in April and the closer they came, the more time I took to publish my views. I still had my cattle to tend; I didn't neglect them. But I hurried through my chores every day so I could spend time talking with neighbors—even those quite a distance away—urging them to vote.

It was exhausting. I was up long before dawn and it was often nearly midnight before I got back home. Floyd did a lot of cooking that winter and he complained about it, bitterly.

"I ain't no cook, Nephi," he said one day. I had to agree with him—only Rhoda Newbold's cooking was worse—but I couldn't stay home to cook and go out and campaign at the same time.

"Once the election is over I'll be back home to relieve you," I assured him. "It's just one more week." Floyd wasn't appeased.

"I don't see why you have to spend so much time campaignin' for something you aren't even goin' to see the good of," he said. "You don't have kids. You've never *had* kids and you ain't never *goin'* to have kids. You're an old batch. You need to stay home and let those that's got kids do the footwork. You've gone all out of balance, campaignin' to the exclusion of ever'thing else."

That wasn't true but I didn't want to get cranky with him although I felt like it. He was a good help and he'd been loyal to me through the years since Alma's death. Still, I didn't like his complaints.

It wasn't as if he had all that much extra work to do—just the cooking of his evening meal. And if he'd tried, he probably could have made those meals a whole lot better. But he didn't try. He wanted things the way they'd always been with me doing the cooking. His complaints were getting on my nerves to the point that, between his grousing at home and the resistance I sometimes met in my campaigning, I was beginning to feel like a too-tightly wound spring. I realized I was in serious need of some relaxation.

So I started plotting my revenge.

Floyd knew me well enough he'd learned to tell when I was hatching a scheme. I was cooking breakfast one morning and he was straining the milk, getting ready to carry it out to the spring box, when he looked at me and asked, "Who you planin' to upset this time?"

"What do you mean?" I pretended ignorance.

"You know full well what I mean." Floyd said. "You're plannin' one of your schemes again. I can tell. Who's your victim goin' to be?"

"Don't know what you're talking about."

"Sure you don't!"

He started watching me, suspicious of what I might do. I waited. I'd already decided on the perfect prank. I just had to bide my time.

That was Sunday. During the rest of the week, I carefully worked on the gag I intended to pull on him.

I couldn't do anything when he was around and the only time we weren't together was when he milked the cow, took the milk to the spring box after he'd strained it, or went to the outhouse to do the necessary. I gathered my supplies and every time he was gone, hammered a few more nails into the ceiling of my kitchen.

I didn't hammer them all the way in . . . just most of the way and then I bent each one over. Eventually I had a line of them reaching from a spot above the shelf between my table and the stove, up across the ceiling, and down to the door leading into my living room. I strung two lengths of sturdy sisal twine from the door, through the line of bent nails, to that shelf on the wall where I kept my spare bucket for drinking water. All I had left to do was figure out how to get the bucket to tip without the whole thing sliding off the shelf—and I was running out of time.

Saturday night wasn't a good evening for campaigning. It was bath night all over the valley. I stayed home and made a nice meal of fried potatoes to go with an elk roast I'd kept in the oven all afternoon, and Floyd and I ate until I thought we both were going to burst. It was so nice to stretch my legs out and rest without feeling I needed to be somewhere, talking to someone.

As was our normal routine, I took my bath in the washtub between the stove and my table and had fresh water heating for Floyd by the time he came in from milking. When he took the milk to the springbox, I pounded a small nail into the base of my spare bucket and bent it toward the bottom. Then I filled it with fresh, coooold well water and put it on the shelf.

274

I slid one sturdy twine through the handle and tied the end, securely, to the nail at the base. I tied the other heavy piece of twine directly to the nail. After bending the nail over even farther, I turned the bucket so my work was against the wall, then slipped into my chair beside the stove and started unlacing my shoes. It wasn't two minutes before Floyd was back through the door.

I stretched, yawned and stood up. "Think I'll turn in," I said as I pulled first one shoe and then the other one off and put them neatly by the stove. "It sure feels good to be home for a change and be able to get to bed at a decent hour. Campaigning makes an old man out of you."

"About time you figured that out," Floyd said as he hung his coat on its peg on the wall and proceeded to unlace his own shoes. "Soon as I have my bath I'll be right behind you."

I made a show of putting a large chunk of wood in the cook stove and opening the oven door so Floyd would have a warm room for his bath. Floyd started unbuttoning his shirt.

"Good night," I said as I put the lid back on the stove. "See you in the morning."

"Night" Floyd wasn't paying any attention as he unbuttoned his red woolen underwear and pealed them off. I walked through the door into the parlor, almost closing it behind me.

Peeking through the crack, I could see his reflection in the window as he dipped water out of the reservoir on the stove and poured it into the tub under the water bucket. He had just stepped in and sat down when I pulled the twines.

I doubt Jackson Hole has heard yells like that since the Indian war in '95.

"You know, Nephi," Floyd said when he'd calmed down enough to speak instead of splutter, "there's a lot of folks gettin' rather tired of your pranks."

"Really?" I pretended interest. I didn't care if they were; I was having too much fun.

"Really," Floyd said, firmly. "When I went down to pick up the mail the other day some of your neighbors was there talkin' about you. They've decided it's time your wings got cut so they can have some peace. You might want to think about what you're doin' before you manage to alienate ever'one around."

275

I couldn't help chuckling as I turned the covers down on my bed. Little did they realize I had the same goal they did. The right woman would come along; I was sure of it. I didn't know when or where but when she did, I'd know her. I was sure of that, too. She wasn't, however, going to clip my wings, even after I married her.

CHAPTER SIXTY-EIGHT
April 1917

The day of the election dawned clear and cold. So much for spring coming. It was April and I'd been looking forward to permanent warmer weather. Oh well. As Roy McBride always said, "If you don't like the weather in Jackson Hole, just wait five minutes. It'll change."

And it did. By the time we finished feeding the cattle, Floyd and I had to hang our coats on the rail of the hay rack, and the team was straining to pull the sleigh through the slushy snow.

"Today's the election," I said as Floyd and I unhooked the team from the sleigh that afternoon. "You're coming with me, aren't you?"

"No, I'm stayin' with Frank and Lucy's girls so they can go. They need to vote, not me."

That meant I'd ride to Kelly alone unless one of my neighbors hadn't left yet. I looked at the sun. It was mid-afternoon already and we hadn't even eaten. I needed to hurry.

"I'd better skip dinner," I said, "and just grab a biscuit or something. I don't want to be late. I need to stop by Will and Camilla's and see if they're going. I'll ride with them if they are."

I'd talked long and hard to the Seelemires about needed school reforms. After all, their girl was nearly high school age. But they'd been wishy-washy about getting involved. I suspected they didn't care because they'd already decided to send their daughter out of the valley. Some folks were like that. So long as their child was cared for it didn't matter what happened to someone else's child.

I did stop at the Seelemire house. They weren't going. I rode on.

Their place nearly matched mine in size and their east gate was up on the flats about a half mile from the Gros Ventre River. As I approached their east fence, I saw three horsemen coming from the direction of the Bike cabin. By the time I got off Star and opened Will's gate, they were close enough that I could tell they were women, not men.

I waited by the open gate.

"Nephi, hello!" one of them called when they were near enough to see who I was. The warm April sun behind them cast a halo around their heads, obscuring their faces. I squinted. One was Pete Hansen's wife, Sylvia, the second was Amy Bike, but the third was a stranger.

She was a small woman who rode sidesaddle, her dark skirt flowing down the side of her mount, a stylishly short woolen coat slung, easily, over her shoulders. The shirtwaist beneath had tucks down the front and lace at the collar. Then I saw her face under her wide-brimmed hat. It was cheerful with a clear complexion, a slightly crooked nose and wide grey eyes.

"Mrs. Hansen," I said, taking my hat off, politely. "And Mrs. Bike. You ladies going to the election?" I continued to hold the wire gate for them to ride through.

"Yes," Amy Bike said. Then she did the oddest thing. She nodded to Sylvia, just the slightest inclination of her head, and the next thing I knew both were whipping their horses, leaving the stranger still coming through the gate I was holding.

The strange woman gasped as she stopped her horse on the Kelly side of the fence.

I stood there gaping.

Sylvia and Amy disappeared around a bend in the road ahead.

I still stood, thunderstruck, until the stranger said, gently, "Well, I guess you're stuck with my company, sir. I hope you don't mind?" Her voice was soft and musical but strong enough to bring me out of my trance.

I fumbled with the gate, embarrassed and at a loss for something to say. Then I laughed as I swung up on my horse.

"I suppose they're getting even with me for some of the pranks I've pulled on their husbands," I said. "But it doesn't seem fair to you—leaving you to ride with a stranger."

She smiled. Then she tilted her head, almost bird-like. "Then I think we need to do something about that. I'm Mathilde Stuve, teacher's replacement for the Zenith school." She reached over her horse and offered me a small, gloved hand. *That's* why I hadn't seen her before. I'd heard there was a replacement for our ailing teacher but I hadn't known it was a young woman.

"Nephi Moulton," I said. Her grip was firm—not the dead-fish handshake most women gave. It said she was confident; independent. I held her hand perhaps a moment too long and was embarrassed, again, as she laughingly withdrew it.

"So you're Nephi," she said. "I've heard how you've campaigned for school reform even though you have no children of your own."

Given who she'd been riding with and what they'd done to leave her with me, I wondered what else she might have heard. The reasons why my neighbors thought my wings needed to be clipped came to mind. But if she'd heard about that, she was merciful and didn't say so.

"Being a school teacher," she continued, "makes me appreciate the efforts you've made, Mr. Moulton." I think I glowed. I know I turned red but I sure was pleased, too. I should have said 'thank you' or something but my old shyness overcame me and I couldn't think of a thing to say. Fortunately, she carried the conversation long enough for me to gather myself together again.

"I think it will be an interesting meeting, tonight," she said. "Mrs. Hansen told me these election nights get pretty heated. I guess I'll get to know a lot of folks in ways I haven't known them before. Politics has a way of bringing out the true natures of individuals, don't you think?"

By then I'd found my tongue and I pulled it out of my throat enough to ask. "Have you attended many elections before?" It was more of a croak than a question.

"One or two out in Oregon," she said. So she'd come from Oregon. I filed that away for future reference.

"You grew up in Oregon?" I managed to get out.

"Oh no," she laughed. Was she laughing at the fact I was tongue-tied and it was obvious, or was she laughing because of a joyous personality? "I came from a little farming community in Wisconsin. I used to milk cows and slop hogs and work in the fields with my father," she continued. "Then my aunt, who lived in Idaho, was paralyzed for a while after she gave birth to a set of twins and my uncle asked if I could come help. When she was able to get around again, I went to the academy in Weiser and earned my teacher's certificate. I taught in Oregon before I came here."

She knew how to farm. Check mark.

She was independent. Check mark.

She seemed to be cheerful. And she was certainly charming and easy to be with. Although I hadn't thought of them before, I added those to my mental check list then checked them off, too.

"Do you enjoy teaching?" I asked. It was getting easier to talk to her.

"Oh, yes," she said, again laughing. "The children are so enjoyable. That's why I chose to be a teacher. They say the funniest things."

Check off another must.

"But tell me about yourself, Mr. Moulton." She changed the subject. "How long have you been in the valley?"

She was interested in people other than herself. Another check mark although I hadn't thought to put that quality on my list either.

I told her about Alma and me coming to the Hole, about how much I'd liked it here even though the weather was often difficult. She said she'd felt at home in the Hole because the weather was a lot like Wisconsin, where she'd been born.

She asked about my family and I told her about Alma's death. I'd never really talked about it before—not about how I'd felt or how difficult it had been—but she was so sympathetic and easy to talk to I found myself rattling on and on. She didn't seem to mind. She related it to the loss of a baby sister she'd really loved. While she didn't think her loss was anything compared to mine, still I could sense that she understood and was sympathetic.

Then we got into a discussion about our respective families—hers, immigrant Norwegian, and mine, immigrant English. It lasted until we arrived at the school house in Kelly where I ignored the cunning smiles on Sylvia Hansen's and Amy Bike's faces as I held Miss Stuve's horse and helped her dismount.

CHAPTER SIXTY-NINE

It *was* an interesting meeting—just as Miss Stuve had predicted. Heated. Almost rabid. Each current school board member gave his campaign speech as did each man running against him.

She sat at the front with the teachers, the administrators and the current and-hopefully-future school board members. I sat more to the back.

As a member of the education system, she spoke of her experiences in other schools—what she'd seen in children who'd had little or no discipline. She was observant, intelligent and articulate. She was also obviously popular with the parents who knew her.

When the meeting was opened for opinions from the general public I spoke, at length, on home and family values and how important I felt it was that teenaged children be kept close to home if at all possible. I also talked about how I felt all parents deserved to be able to feel confident that their children were safe at school.

I ended with, "Jackson has a reputation for being a rough place—wild, wooly and full of fleas—but that reputation needs to end at the doorstep of our schools. Parents don't send their children to school to be beaten, knifed or bullied. We need a school board and an administration that will ensure an atmosphere in the schools where the children in their care are free to learn, to grow and to develop." I sat down to cheers and cries of "Here! Here!" and flushed as I saw Miss Stuve looking at me with interest and approval.

With the voting over—a landslide victory for a totally new administration—general socializing began. I wanted to ask Miss Stuve if she wanted company on her ride home but I couldn't think of how to approach her. She was surrounded by people who obviously knew her and enjoyed her wit because they were laughing at everything she said.

I wanted to join the group—to enjoy what she was saying, too—but I couldn't just go barge in on their conversation. I tried to think of something I could say but nothing came to mind. Had I been Alma it would have been no problem but I wasn't and Alma wasn't here to open a way for me, either. I started talking to Tom and Rosa just so I wouldn't look like a fool.

Suddenly a jubilant T.A. tapped me on the shoulder.

"We did it!" he exclaimed, pumping first my hand, then Tom's. "We pulled it off."

"Yes, we did," Rosa said, happily. "Now Tom and I can think of bringing our son back home." I could just imagine her joy.

Then T.A. made a comment that caught me totally off guard. "Nephi," he said, "did you hear? John got married two weeks ago. Married Lucille's younger sister, Bartha."

I think my mouth must have dropped a foot.

"He didn't want anyone to know," T.A. said. "He didn't want any cow bells tied under his short-sheeted bed." He winked in my direction and I knew my cousins had figured out who'd visited Wally's home the night before he'd carried his bride across his threshold.

When I turned to look at Miss Stuve's side of the room, again, hoping the crowd around her had thinned a little, she was gone. Sylvia and Amy were still there but Miss Stuve was conspicuously absent. The gathering suddenly lost its luster. I excused myself to Tom, Rosa, and T.A. and left.

Her horse was no longer tied beside Star at the hitching rack but, although it was a clear, bright, moonlit night, I couldn't see her anywhere.

It felt like the bottom had dropped out of my entire world. Had she gone home with a friend? Was she spending the weekend with someone there in Kelly? Was someone else seeing her home? Considering the crowd around her, she probably had a number of men interested. And why not? She might not have possessed a classic beauty but she had such an intelligent, animated, pleasant face, she seemed truly beautiful, and her wit was captivating. Those around her obviously thought her the life of the party. I could understand that, too.

What did I have to offer a woman like her—a woman as traveled and as educated and as experienced as she was? I'd never gotten past seventh grade in grammar school. I'd never been to the coast. I'd never traveled half-way across the continent or taught school or cared for ill relatives. My world had consisted of farming and ranching in the Wasatch valley in Utah, the Upper Snake River and Teton valleys in Idaho, and Jackson Hole with its surrounds. It was restricted by comparison.

As I rode away from Kelly I felt about as discouraged as I'd ever felt in my life. I was certain that what I wanted in a woman was embodied in a certain tiny schoolteacher, but would such a woman be interested in me? Would she overlook my glaring inadequacies?

I was probably halfways to Brown's hill before something I'd been hearing finally registered. Music. Singing, to be specific. A clear, soprano voice that carried over the moonlit expanse of sage and snow in a siren song. It wasn't the first time I was very grateful for Star's fast gait.

She heard me approach as her horse was nearing the Butte and she reined her mount to wait for me. Had she known it was me, I wondered, or was she waiting for someone else?

"Miss Stuve," I said as I slowed Star from her mile-eating trot to a walk. I tipped my hat at her and she smiled at me in the moonlight.

"Hello, Mr. Moulton," her voice was clear.

What could I say, next?

As if she realized I was, once again, tongue-tied, she spoke. "Are you pleased with the results of the election?" She touched her horse with her heel. I spurred Star and we started on.

"Would you like to see a pretty sight on the way home?" I asked. "And, yes, I'm very pleased with the results. I think we have some good men who will make a difference."

"I agree. And I think a pretty sight would be a nice cap on an excellent evening," she said, so I guided her up and across the flat expanse of Brown's hill rather than the way we'd come that afternoon.

We chatted about various things until we neared the edge of the bench. It was shortly after we'd passed Tom and Rosa's home that I reined Star in. We had been so deep in conversation that she hadn't noticed the scenery ahead of us but as we came to the edge of the bench and I stopped Star, she looked about her for the first time. I, of course, had seen this scene many times when I'd come home from late school meetings, but this was her first. Her gasp as she surveyed the snow-covered mountains before her was well worth the effort of taking her there.

"Oh, my!" was all she said as she looked at the mountains straight ahead, then turned to see those farther to the north. When she came to the Grand, in all its snow-covered, moonlit glory, she stopped. "Oh," she breathed, again, "how incredibly beautiful!"

I couldn't have said a word if my life depended on it but I totally agreed with her. The Grand, seen in daylight with a blue sky behind, was spectacular. The snow-covered Grand, in winter's moonlight with a black sky behind it, was unforgettable.

"I've never seen it from here at night," she said, softly. "I had no idea anything could be so majestic."

I remembered being awed by its majesty the first time I'd seen it, too—and just about every time I'd looked at it since.

Then she spoke, again. "You know, you might think this silly of me but have you ever looked at the outline of the Grand?" She traced it with her gloved finger. "See where it juts out there and where it's more flat on the top? Then you have the outcropping on this side with a dip in the middle. The first time I saw that mountain it seemed to me that I was seeing the throne of God."

Miss Stuve, school teacher

CHAPTER SEVENTY

It was easy to visit Miss Stuve without anyone knowing. It was calving season and I had to walk through the cows after supper every evening, anyway. If nothing needed my attention, I kept on walking—down through the forested river bottoms to her cabin. By the time I arrived, she was usually finished grading papers but sometimes, if she wasn't, I helped her.

The teacherage where she was living was a small cabin but she'd made it pleasant. She had photographs of some of her family members displayed, along with her collection of books, on the shelves of her writing desk. The shelves were dust-free, I noticed, as she introduced me to each photograph.

Check mark for good housekeeping.

Her photos were of pretty girls, most of them. And most of them were her sisters. Her brothers, she said, were older and she didn't have photos of them. Or of her parents. Anyway, her mother didn't like having her photograph taken.

She spoke of her family with warmth and humor, telling me a variety of funny stories about their antics, her favorite being the time she and her next younger sister had decided they wanted to see what it was like to wear boys' pants.

"We dressed up in Carl's and Hans' pants," she told me, "and were down by the creek, pretending to be cowboys, when we heard our folks' team and buggy coming home." Her laughter pealed.

"You should have seen us run." she said, wiping her eyes. "Those pants were much too big for us. We were scrambling to get out of the willows but we couldn't keep our pants up and we were forever tripping because the pant-legs were too long. By the time we reached the house we were laughing so hysterically, we had tears streaming down our faces."

"Did your parents catch you?" I asked, chuckling at the mental picture of two little girls slipping in the mud, clutching at pants three sizes too big.

"No," she said. "In fact, it wasn't even their team and buggy. But it was a close call and we never tried it again." She giggled. "Father probably would have seen the humor of it, but Mother was always afraid her girls would go bad. I don't think she would have thought it quite so funny."

In turn, I told her about the time John and I had been left home from church the summer I was six. "We'd both been sick with the summer flu," I said, "and John was still not quite on top of the world. All he wanted to do was sleep but I wanted to play. I was really disgusted with him." She nodded, appreciative of my six-year-old feelings.

"I wandered out to the barnyard to try to find something to occupy my time but every animal we had seemed to be of the same opinion as John," I continued, "that Sunday was for sleeping.

"I kept wandering around until I finally found a small pool filled with tadpoles."

She giggled. "I can just imagine what you did with those," she said. I grinned.

"You should have seen John come alive when I dumped a double-handful of wriggly tadpoles on his face. He came boiling up off his bed like there was going to be no tomorrow and, for a few minutes, I was convinced there wouldn't be one for me. I lit off down the street as if my life depended on it—and, who knows, maybe it did."

"Did you get away?" she asked.

I chuckled. "Yes. But only because I was six and little enough I could scoot under the fences, while my twelve year old brother had to stop and climb over." I paused. "Maybe that's why he's always disapproved of me."

She smiled. "If he still holds that against you, I feel sorry for him," she said. "It's things like that that make children so endearing."

Another check mark. She certainly had a keen sense of humor and if she hadn't gotten the picture of who I was—and always had been—it wasn't because I hadn't warned her.

She could cook, too, I found out. The first Saturday I was able to get away to visit her, she was in the middle of doing laundry and baking. She had fresh, hot bread on her table and sugar cookies in her oven and I thought I'd died and gone to heaven.

There was only one more thing on my check list—a woman who was musical. I knew she sang. I'd heard her clear, beautiful soprano the night I met her. I wondered if, miracle of miracles, she might be able to play an instrument, too.

286

"Do you play any instruments?" I asked, hopefully, looking around but not seeing anything remotely musical.

"Oh, yes," she said. I smiled, broadly. The final check mark appeared on my mental list.

"Which one?" I asked. Visions of her playing a piano or maybe a violin while I read by the fireside kept me from seeing the mischief in her eyes.

"The radio," she said, smiling sweetly.

"You *dunce!*" I gasped.

The radio. She'd got me with the radio. I couldn't believe I'd been so busy wondering if she'd accept the prankster in me that I hadn't seen this coming. It was plain I'd have to keep my wits about me whenever I was with Miss Mathilde Stuve or I'd come out the loser.

But I couldn't help smiling. Life just might become very interesting in the future.

CHAPTER SEVENTY-ONE

Although I'd known the night I met her that she was the woman I wanted, now it was a crystal-hard decision. The only problem was I didn't know how she felt about me.

She acted like she liked me. She smiled when she opened her door at my knock. She listened to what I had to say. She laughed, heartily, at my stories of my childhood antics, and yet, when we got into deep discussions, she seemed to consider my ideas intelligent and important, worthy of her attention.

Still, I was unsure. My experience with women was so limited I didn't know what to expect or even to look for as I tried to determine her feelings.

I didn't want to ask Floyd for guidance. I knew he was wondering what was keeping me occupied away from home in the evenings, but whenever he asked I avoided the question because I didn't want it to get noised around that I was 'seeing the schoolmarm'. No one knew, yet, that I was even considering marriage, let alone had found the woman I wanted.

Finally her teacher's contract was ended—school was out—and I decided the next step I needed to take was to bring her to the ranch and let her look around.

That took planning.

I wanted it to be a nice day but I didn't want Floyd to be there. I watched the weather, religiously, and I fussed, in my spare time, over making sure everything was relatively clean.

"Seems to me you're getting' to be nothin' more than a fussy old batch," Floyd complained, one day. "All you do is go around pickin' up things and puttin' them somewhere's else. What's got into you, Nephi? You expectin' company or somethin'?"

"Well, I wrote my parents about my new house," I made the first excuse I could think of, "and I think they're planning to come see it. Trouble is, I don't know when to expect them. You know how mothers are. I don't want mine to be scandalized at our bachelor quarters."

He seemed mollified. Which was a good thing because it was a fine spring day and I wanted to get Miss Stuve's visit over with. I was to the point where my nerves couldn't take much more. I *had* to know where I stood with her.

"Floyd," I said presently, "I'm going to stick close to home, today, because I'm concerned about that brindle cow. I didn't think she looked quite right this morning. I need you to ride up to the head of the canal and see if there's any beaver work we'll have to pull out before we start irrigating." It was a more-or-less legitimate request. Beaver dams shutting off water to our headgate were a constant problem, and it was almost time to turn water into the canal.

Floyd knew, however, that what wasn't there today could well be there tomorrow. It didn't make a lot of sense to have him go look when we weren't ready to fill the canal yet. He gave me a funny look but he didn't say anything; he just saddled his mule and rode off.

As soon as he was out of sight, I made a beeline for Miss Stuve's cabin. I had a good three hours before Floyd would be back home and I wanted to make the most of it.

"Miss Stuve," I said when her face lit up in a smile as she opened her door to me. "I know where there's a large patch of buttercups blooming. Would you like to go for a walk and see them?" I didn't tell her they were blooming right behind my home.

She got her coat and we set out.

It was the first time I had touched her except when I'd helped her off her horse the night I'd met her. Now I offered my arm and she took it, her little hand just fitting in the crook of my elbow. I liked the feeling. Almost too well. It was suddenly difficult to breathe and I had to concentrate just to keep my head. Was this what a woman did to a man? Was this the way Floyd had felt about his Sarah Ann?

We walked through the forest, over the path I'd been wearing to her door. I helped her over logs, my hands on either side of her slim waist, and that felt good, too. Too good. Dizzying. I didn't want to let her go. But I didn't dare not.

"Where are these buttercups, Mr. Moulton?" she finally asked after we'd been walking for some twenty minutes.

"Close," I said.

"Are you sure?" she asked.

"They're just up ahead." By then we were beside the creek between my house and where Jack Grey had lived. She hesitated.

"Where to now?" she asked. "You don't expect me to wade this creek, do you?"

"I could carry you across," I said, grinning.

"I don't think so." Her voice was firm.

"Why not?"

"Because it isn't proper," she said.

I wasn't surprised. She'd never given any indication she was anything but proper. I could have added prim, too, but her sense of humor belied that.

"Well, you don't have to worry," I said. "There's a log across the creek up the stream a ways. You'll be able to walk across."

"Good."

So there wasn't going to be any play.

I still had no idea how she felt.

As we neared my farmyard I kept her attention on the forest floor—pointing out a shrub here, a tree root there, an interesting leaf a little further on. Finally we reached the edge of the clearing and I paused.

She stopped, too, and looked up. Her eyes grew wide, her mouth made a delicious little 0 as she looked, first at my steeply-roofed log barn, then my pole corrals, on to my shed and, finally, at my house.

I followed her gaze. It was a fine house, I thought proudly. The clapboard siding was still the mellow golden-brown of new lumber, the windows shone in the spring sunshine, the porch looked inviting. It was a fairly large house, thirty by thirty—with the porch extra.

She looked up at me, then cocked her head to one side, quizzically. I said nothing, waiting for her to speak. Finally she broke the silence.

"This is yours, Mr. Moulton?"

I smiled acknowledgement. "Would you like to look around?" I asked. "The buttercups are right behind the house."

"Show me," was all she said. So I did.

I showed her the buttercups first. My mother loved flowers. I thought Miss Stuve might be more inclined to think well of my home if she saw there were flowers, already.

Then I took her inside.

She oh-ed and aw-ed over the large pantry, the indoor pump and the separator. She approved of the kitchen and the parlor, liked their spaciousness. But she refused to set foot in my bedroom. She looked from the doorway, but that was as far as she would go. It was probably just as well. For the first time in my life I understood how Frank had ended up married to Lucy.... Did I ever understand...!

Had Miss Stuve been a little less proper....

We were out on the porch—I had brought two kitchen chairs out and we were sitting, chatting, in the late afternoon sun—when I finally managed to choke out the words I'd been wanting to say ever since the night I'd met her.

"Miss Stuve..." I hesitated. She looked at me; turned the full power of those wide, grey eyes on me. And I was speechless.

"Yes, Mr. Moulton?" That endearing, frustrating, bird-like little habit she had of tipping her head to one side as she looked at me—especially when I was struggling to find words to say—never made organizing my thoughts, *or* expressing them, any easier. She did it now as she waited for me to speak. As usual, my tongue hid—probably down in my stomach somewhere. It certainly wasn't in my mouth.

I wondered if this was really such a good idea. What if she laughed at me? She hadn't seemed to be insensitive but....

What if there was someone else she was interested in? I hadn't seen any sign of anyone else coming to call but....

What if she was just using my visits to relieve the boredom of living alone—isolated in a forest with no close neighbors?

Her eyes twinkled as if she knew full well my dilemma and was vastly amused by it. "You wanted to say something?" she asked.

That didn't help, either.

She started to laugh. "Why are you so afraid of me, Nephi?"

Nephi! She'd called me Nephi. I would have lapped water from a mud puddle at her feet if she'd asked it. My name—which I'd never liked all that much—was music on her lips.

"Say that again," I managed to choke out. She looked taken aback.

"Say what?"

"My name."

"Ask me what you were wanting to ask me and maybe I will," she teased, looking sidewise at me from under her dark lashes.

The minx! I had almost talked myself into thinking this wasn't such a good idea, after all, and now she was holding my desire over my head. I was sure she knew, full well, what was on my mind. How could she not?

I cleared my throat.... And sat.... The words would not come.

She laughed, her laughter pealing out, merrily. I could have cheerfully choked her. She cleared her throat, too, smiling mischievously. "Well, we got that much out," she said.

"Will you stop?" I exclaimed.

"Why? You're being funny. Besides, why are you so afraid of me?"

"I'm not!"

"You are, too. You didn't bring me here just for a sunny Sunday walk. You have something on your mind. You know it. I know it. So let's get it out and then you'll feel a whole bunch better. We'll both enjoy the afternoon a lot more if you're happy."

I wondered if I'd be so happy once *she* found out exactly what I wanted to ask her and *I* found out what her answer was. Finally I took a deep breath and blurted it out. "Miss Stuve, would you like to share this with me?" I gestured to my home, my farmyard, my ranch beyond.

She smiled, again, mischief tugging at the corners of her mouth. "I might consider it," she said. "Maybe."

I could have wrung her pretty little lace-collared neck.

"What do you mean, maybe? I'd think either you want to or you don't."

She laughed. "Nephi, what, exactly, are you asking of me?"

My name, again. If she had any idea what that did to me.... But somehow, I thought, she was totally aware of what she was doing.

"Be my wife."

"Well, now, that wasn't so hard, was it? You've been wanting to ask me for weeks but it sure took a lot to get it out." She laughed, again.

"Yes, it *was* that hard. What's your answer?"

Again the mischief. "Well," she drawled, "I might consider it."

"*What*? Consider it! And when do you plan to give me the answer *you* decided on weeks ago?"

"What makes you think I've come up with an answer?"

She sure could be a demure little miss when she wanted to be. But I'd had enough of her brand of play. Without warning, I reached across the space between us, scooped her up and deposited her in my lap. Before she could do more than gasp, I was kissing her.

Thoroughly.

I'd never kissed a woman before, but I found out it wasn't all that difficult. I guess it comes naturally.

"Mr. Moulton!" Her eyes were flashing when I came up for air, and she slapped me roundly. The woman could pack a punch when she wanted. "I am *not* a loose woman!"

"No, ma'am, you aren't." I caught her by the wrist and pushed her hand down behind her back where I grasped it, firmly, in my other hand. "And I'm not exactly a patient man. Now I asked you like you wanted and you're going to sit here until you answer me. And I don't really care how long it takes because I rather like having you right where you are. So, are you going to marry me or not?"

It was my turn to make her squirm. She'd been doing it to me and I didn't figure this was going to hurt her any. It wasn't as if her reputation was at stake. There was no-one to see and spread rumors, and I wasn't planning to tarnish her virtue, anyway.

She glared at me, her body rigid. I smiled. I was suddenly enjoying myself, tremendously. She really was attractive when she was angry.

"You know, you're quite pretty when you're angry," I told her. I cupped my palm on her cheek then slid my hand on around until my fingers were entangled in her soft brown hair. "I think I'm going to kiss you some more while you make up your mind." I pulled her head, slowly, toward me. "Mmmmm."

Suddenly she relaxed, then began to giggle. "Oh, all right," she said. "I guess I'll marry you if you really want me to."

Excuse me? It was that much of a sacrifice? I had no intentions of tying myself a woman who felt it was her duty…. Then I realized what she was doing; she'd neatly tipped the scales again. The weight, even though I still held her in an embrace she couldn't wriggle out of, was once more on her side.

I laughed.

I could see being married to Miss Mathilde Stuve, schoolmarm, wasn't going to be boring.

I checked the final requirement off on my list.

I just might have met my match.

If I wasn't careful, my wings would be clipped beyond my power to mend them. And I wasn't even sure I'd mind. In fact, she may have already done the job without me being aware.

Oh well.

I kissed her again. Just for good measure. A nice, long, drawn-out kiss that *really* made me understand Frank's predicament. But I managed to keep control. To begin with, her virtue was my responsibility. Besides, I did want to marry her and I wasn't stupid enough to think she couldn't change her mind. This woman was too much her own woman to let anyone decide her future.

When I was finished, I gently sat her back on her chair.

"All right, Miss Stuve," I said. "Let's make some plans."

That was in late May. On Saturday night, June ninth, I told Floyd if he would irrigate for me the next day I would give him a long-overdue week's vacation.

"What you doin' that for?" he demanded. "You sure are getting' queer, Nephi. I don't get a vacation 'till the fall."

"Well, I'm giving you one now. We're caught up on the fencing until the next herd of elk comes through, and I can handle the irrigating for a week. You be back next Saturday night and I'll take care of things until then."

"Where you goin' tomorrow?" Floyd was still suspicious.

"I'm going up to visit John," I said. "I haven't seen him for a while . . . not since he got hitched. I think it's about time I give him a little something to think about."

"You would," Floyd said. But I knew he had no idea of the real surprise that I planned for my cousin.

CHAPTER SEVENTY-TWO

Next morning, after I'd finished my chores and we'd eaten breakfast, I rode Star north, through the trees. Floyd thought I was riding up to Moose and then over to John's. I wasn't.

I stopped at Joe and Mary Davenport's house and knocked on their door. When Joe finally answered, it was obvious I'd waked him up. His hair was all tousled, his eyes only half-open, and the pants that he'd hurriedly slipped over his long johns were held up by just one suspender.

"Nephi," he said, "What you doing here this time of day? Don't you ever sleep?" It occurred to me that I'd heard that before. I never could figure out why people spent the best part of the day in bed.

"Oh, are you sleepy, Joe?" I asked in my most soothing voice—like a mother would use to calm a fretting child. Suddenly Joe gave me a suspicious look.

"You didn't go stuff another burlap bag in my chimney, did you?" he asked. I laughed. I'd almost forgotten having left my calling card some months back.

"Joe, I even told you it was there," I protested. "It's not my fault you didn't believe me. I gave you fair warning. And, no, I haven't done anything to anybody for a while, including you. I wanted to know if I could borrow your buggy for the day."

"I suppose so," Joe wasn't awake enough, yet, to be very cordial. Besides, maybe he wasn't feeling cordial after the burlap sack incident. Oh well. That was his problem. I'd put it in his chimney, true, but when I'd met him on the road later on, I'd felt guilty and told him it was there. If he'd believed me and looked, he wouldn't have gotten smoked out, now would he? I couldn't find it in me to feel too sorry for him.

"Thanks, " I said. "I'll bring your buggy back this evening." I led Star toward his tack shed where I knew he kept his harness. Joe closed his door.

He was back out, fully dressed, by the time I finished unsaddling, harnessing, then hooking Star up to the buggy. As I climbed into the seat and slapped the rains on her rump—guiding her down the road towards my house—he called out, "What you wanting to use my buggy for, anyway?"

"I'm getting married." I said. I knew he'd find out sooner or later, anyhow. I also knew he wouldn't believe me now.

"Like fun you are!" he said, just like I'd known he would.

Mary told me, later, that after I was out of sight, Joe scratched his head and muttered, half to her, half to himself, "I wonder if the old fool really *is* getting married?" He found out, soon enough

Miss Stuve was ready and waiting for me when I arrived at her cabin. I thought she'd never looked lovelier. Her hair was fluffed out in a pompadour with tendrils curling at her ears. Her cheeks were pink; her eyes glistening.

She was wearing a dress of some soft sort of white fabric with plenty of lace at the neck. Tiny tucks from each shoulder met in a V in the front. The sleeves were long and full and decorated with lace at the wrists, too. There was a tight cumberbund around her waist, then the skirt swept away in graceful folds that hugged her body when she walked while still flowing out behind her. I knew I'd better get her trunk fastened on the back of the buggy and her person out of that cabin before I lost my head.

She pinned her wide-brimmed hat on while I secured her trunk. Then, taking my outstretched hand, my bride stepped out of the cabin home where she'd lived for the past few months, closed the door, and walked with me to the buggy and her future.

It was a beautiful day. Birds were singing, the sky was a clear blue, the sun warm and bright. She was so light, as I swung her up into the buggy, that I felt like the strongest man in the world. When I tucked a lap robe around her dress then climbed up beside her, I didn't think any man had ever been more proud and happy. I had a beautiful woman beside me—one that would soon be my wife. I had a new home, a good ranch. All was right in my world.

Kelly's minister had just finished his sermon and bid the last of his parishioners goodbye when we arrived.

"Hello, Miss Stuve," he said as we drove up. "Mr. Moulton."

"Reverend Baxter," my bride said, "Mr. Moulton and I are getting married today. We would like you to perform the marriage, if you would."

I'd agreed to the Baptist preacher. She was Lutheran, but she'd been attending his church whenever she could and she liked him. I didn't really care. As long as we were legally married when I took her to my home that night, it didn't matter to me who performed the ceremony. If Reverend Baxter would make her happy, then Reverend Baxter was who she'd have, as far as I was concerned. Besides, we'd done a little negotiating. She got her minister; I got my cousin as a witness.

"Miss Stuve!" he was all smiles. "Congratulations! Just wait until I tell my Sophie. Now, you do have your license, don't you Mr. Moulton?" I fished the document out of my pocket. He glanced at it, then hurried to get his wife. Presently, with his horse hitched to his buggy and his wife seated by his side, Reverend Baxter followed us across the sage flats to John's house at the very north end of Mormon Row.

John's new wife, Bartha, answered the door. She was as little a woman as my bride, with dark hair and a full figure.

"I'm Nephi," I said when she looked inquiringly at, first me then the two buggies behind me. "John's cousin," I added.

"Oh," she said. "The one who borrowed John's bells to decorate Wally's place?" Obviously my still intact reputation had preceded me.

"One and the same." I grinned. "Where's John?"

"Well, I hope you aren't planning to do something of the sort here," she said tartly.

I could see she didn't have anything near the sense of humor that her husband possessed. Poor John.

"I'm not," I assured her. "I actually came to ask him to witness my marriage." Her eyes widened. She looked past me once more to my bride sitting in her white dress in Joe's buggy, the Reverend Baxter and his wife beyond.

"Oh," she said, again. I wondered if she had anything else she normally said. A single word vocabulary, maybe? "John's out in the field pulling trash out of his headgate."

She did know something else.

"If it's alright with you, maybe my bride could wait in your home while I go find your husband," I said. It was a question as much as a statement. She flushed.

297

"Of course," she said. "Your friends, too." Then, "Come on in," she called.

I lifted my bride down and left her in Bartha's care while I walked out into John's field to find him. I knew I'd get razzed when he found out what I wanted, but today I didn't care. John could razz all he liked.

A half hour later, we stood in John's yard, the bright June sun shining warmly on us, as my bride and I said our vows.

"I, Mathilde, take thee, Nephi...." Her voice was soft but unafraid. No more Miss Stuve to me; now she was my Mathilde.

. . . My Mathilde.

This tiny bird-like woman, putting her trust in me to protect and care for her no matter what happened in our future, was now mine. I had never felt so powerful. So much like a giant. So awed.

When it came my turn, I looked up at the Grand directly west of John's home. There was the mountain that bound me to this valley, to my ranch and, ultimately, to my Mathilde. Winter's snow was still on it's cliffs and glaciers but the outline was clear. In my mind I pictured God sitting on his throne, smiling benevolently down on me, as I began my vows. "I, Nephi...."

THE END

Nephi and Mathilde circa 1917

AUTHOR'S NOTES

In writing "I, NEPHI", I have tried to sort out the tangled threads of the relationships in Joseph Moulton's polygamous family. Much of the material in this book has been taken from letters and memoirs written by Nephi's father, Joseph; his uncle, Heber; Joseph's two Danish wives, Annie and Mary; and Nephi's half-brothers, Bill and Lyman.

I have gleaned information concerning Joseph's community involvement from the book, *How Beautiful Upon the Mountains,* a history of the Wasatch valley in Utah compiled by the Daughters of the Utah Pioneers. Many of the stories about early Jackson Hole happenings came from the unpublished memoirs of Nephi's oldest son, Willard. Some of the historical information about early Jackson Hole was obtained from the Grand Teton National Park Service's web site; some from Marion Allen's now-out-of-print book, *Early Jackson Hole*.

I want to make the following clear: while Nephi maintained that his older brother, Lyman, was extremely lazy as a youth and this was the reason Lizzie sent Nephi with Alma, he also said that, as an older adult, Lyman became "a working fool". That's saying something because when I asked John Moulton about Nephi the first thing he said was, "Well, he got up an hour before any other rancher in the valley."

Other attitudes that I've portrayed in this novel toward Jackson Hole settlers and events are as close as I could discern Nephi's real attitudes to be. Still, as with any novel, the reader needs to keep in mind that this is a work of fiction even though it is based, heavily, on fact.

Nephi and Alma did host Isobel as it is told in this book. Fred White's demise and the manhunt were not connected. Although both happened, I don't think the identity of Fred's murderer was ever discovered and I'm not certain which sheriff conducted the manhunt I described. Isobel probably was not the subject of the posse's search, either. I only know the manhunt occurred and what its outcome was; not who was involved.

Also, I don't know that Nephi actually heard, first hand, Mose Giltner's comments on the Cunningham massacre; that information came from John Moulton, who did. Nephi's opinion of the incident was in keeping with that of other valley residents and, since Mose was his neighbor, it's certainly possible he heard Mose's declaration that the posse members were nothing more than hot-headed murderers.

The stories concerning early depredation by wolves, and their extermination by wolfer, Jim McInelly, are true.

Nephi was such a committed prankster his neighbors were nearly beside themselves by the time Sylvia Hansen and Amy Bike conspired to leave him in the company of Miss Stuve, replacement schoolteacher for the Zenith school. I suspect they only planned to make him squirm. I doubt they ever envisioned the ultimate result of their plan for revenge.

In his own way, Nephi left a definite mark on the valley. He served, for several years, on the school board and was responsible for District #2 keeping the old Kelly schoolhouse and grounds when the children from that area were transferred to the Grovont School next to the little Mormon Church on Mormon Row. The present Kelly schoolhouse is situated on the piece of property Nephi fought to retain.

He also served for several years as a County Commissioner. His was the tenacious voice behind the purchase of the first road grader to enter the valley. One doesn't have to wonder why he wanted better roads.

In his later years, long after the deaths of his parents, Nephi returned to the religion of his youth. He died, December 2, 1966, at the age of 84 years. At the death of his daughter in 2000, his ranch was passed to The Nature Conservancy. It is no longer farmed but has been sub-divided and most, if not all, sold – the very situation both of them wanted to avoid.

Wally and Elizabeth eventually sold their ranch and moved to Winton, California. John (who lived to be 103) and T.A., sold their ranches to the Grand Teton National Park where their internationally famous barns are preserved on the National Historic Register. Nephi, John and T.A. are buried with their wives in the Victor Cemetery, Victor, Idaho. Alma is buried in the Aspen Hill Cemetery, Jackson, Wyoming, as are Jim McInelly and Mose Giltner.

Nobody knows what happened to Isobel.

CPSIA information can be obtained at www.ICGtesting.com
Printed in the USA
LVOW042022201211

260341LV00001B/269/P